PARTS UNKNOWN

KEVIN BRENNAN

wm WILLIAM MORROW

An Imprint of HarperCollins*Publishers*

PARTS UNKNOWN

A Novel

HarperCollins books may be purchased for educational, business, or sales promotional use. For information please write: Special Markets Department, HarperCollins Publishers Inc., 10 East 53rd Street, New York, NY 10022.

FIRST EDITION

Designed by Judith Stagnitto Abbate

Printed on acid-free paper

Library of Congress Cataloging-in-Publication Data
Brennan, Kevin.
Parts unknown : a novel / Kevin Brennan.—1st ed.
p. cm.
ISBN 0-06-001276-5 (acid-free paper)
1. Landscape photography—Fiction. 2. Remarried people—Fiction. 3. Divorced fathers—Fiction. 4. Photographers—Fiction. 5. California—Fiction. 6. Deserts—Fiction.
I. Title.
PS3602.R45 P37 2003
813'.6—dc21
2002069606

03 04 05 06 07 RRD/WB 10 9 8 7 6 5 4 3 2 1

For my wife, Susan—

"Merrily, merrily, merrily, merrily . . ."

ACKNOWLEDGMENTS

I'd like to thank Michelle Tessler and Claire Wachtel for their confidence in this book. Gratitude is also due my good friend Jonathan Stark for twenty-five years of camaraderie, encouragement, and inspired madness.

SOUR INSIDE

Nora

My husband, Bill Argus, always said that he took pictures just to catch the struggle between light and dark that was always in play, but it was obvious to me that he wanted to freeze moments in time. It was his big weakness. He couldn't hang on to his moments, or didn't want to, which was one reason he fled to the desert when he was still a young man and gave himself over to a life of photography and routine and extreme conditions.

At least until I came along. I softened things up for him quite a bit. Moved into his old hacienda outside Oasis, California, and married him a little while after that. Wedded bliss way out there with the rattlers and jackrabbits.

Most people hang on to their key moments by staying close to the people who helped make them, but Bill wasn't able to do that. He had left all those people behind. He still had some things in his head concerning them, but as the years went on—forty of them by the time he was ready to go back—those things had become confused or merged or fogged with the constant reinterpretations he'd indulged in. It was hard to tell what was true and what was imaginary anymore, and there were no pictures from home he could consult to help verify the record one way or the other. He often had to wonder, Did I dream that? Was she that beautiful? Was my old man as cold as I want to say he was?

Naturally, I was no help to him there. I had to take his word for it when he told me stories of growing up in Pianto, a little cow town in Northern California, the life of a cowman's son. His father had a cow ranch, never bigger than a hundred head, a wife, two boys, Bill and Cameron.

This was so long ago that I wasn't even born yet, and I'm looking at forty.

It was around the time of our ninth anniversary that Bill told me he had a new project in mind. He had turned sixty-three not long before, and his chest had been getting these aches that were finally proved to be nothing but acid reflux disorder. Bill didn't know what they were at first, these pains, thought his mortality was starting to claw at him from the inside, but in the throes of one of these attacks he got the idea to go back to Pianto and take some pictures. For a new book.

If you're a fan of Bill's, you know he hadn't put out a book of his black-and-whites since '82 or so, and that one didn't sell. He'd been a perennial calendar man after that, like a cut-rate Ansel Adams of the desert, but his pictures tended to depress people and even the calendars didn't move all that well. Bill liked the desert because it offered a lot of variations of the light and dark Slug-A-Thon that he was so fond of, and because he believed that the whole world would likely be a desert one day anyway.

But seriously, the idea of Bill Argus putting out a new book at the age of sixty-three was nothing less than pie in the sky. I knew immediately that if I agreed to go with him, I'd be indulging a late midlife crisis and possibly setting him back a few notches when things up there in Pianto proved not to match up to his mental pictures. On top of which, there could be problems.

For instance, he still had a kid up there.

A kid. The kid would be a little older than me by now.

Well, here is where I should say that Bill and I have a strange kind of simpatico, because my father left me when I was three years old, and Bill ran from his boy too. And Bill, like my daddy (I'm looking at forty and I still call him "daddy"!), never looked back, never contacted the boy or the ex-wife—except to bring the divorce to fruition—never mentioned them in his interviews in *Aperture* or the little bios that accompanied gallery shows. In fact, like my daddy, Bill had no reliable idea that they were even still alive, just as they didn't know, now that he wasn't famous anymore, whether he was alive or dead.

He didn't know whether they cared either.

+

THERE WAS ONE moment that Bill *could* pinpoint when he made the significant choice to remain invisible. That was in 1977, when he got word from his younger brother, Cameron, that both parents had died in a car accident and maybe it was time for Bill to come back home. This was during the height of Bill's fame, such as it was, and he was torn. He didn't think he could face his son and wife, yet he felt like he ought to be there to acknowledge his parents, even though his old man had always been a colossal bastard. Mom was an innocent, though. He felt like he owed her something. And Cameron too.

He kept Cam's letter taped to his darkroom wall. Imagine, a blunt letter to bring news like that! Had Cameron lost his mind? In tight little handwriting, red ink, it said, among other particulars, "Mom and Dad were hit by a train. You missed the funeral but the reading of the will ought to be worth the trip."

It reeked of cynical intent. Scared the shit out of Bill.

Both parents dead in one bloody miscalculation, and he couldn't decide what to do. Cam needed him, it sounded like, yet it could also be a trap. How can you trust a brother you haven't seen in more than fifteen years? Maybe the will was going to be a "blast Bill to Hades" fest. Or maybe Annie, the ex-wife, and the kid would show up with clubs to beat the bejesus out of him, having ordered a third grave while the diggers were at it with the other two.

This is the way the exiled mind works.

In the end, after a long hike up into the local mountains, he decided not to return at that time. The heat he suffered during that walk made his mind shrivel and shake, and his body went rubbery, feverish, almost like a toxic was working on him. He let himself imagine the scene when he rolled into town, those people all changed and aging, his son unrecognizable because the last time Bill had laid eyes on him he was a toddler with a gaping grimace of a wet mouth and a head too big for his body. Grappling hands, a zombie waddle.

It wasn't that Bill didn't like kids, or his kid in particular. It was a combination of many things. Of course I pestered the hell out of him early in our alliance for his life story, and he told me about it as best he could, for a man who has trouble hanging on to his moments. He said he ran impulsively, for reasons that had less to do with who he was married to and who his little kid was and more to do with what was wrong in his own head. Full of an uncontainable anger, moved to act in treacherous ways. He couldn't trust himself. The impulse to run then brought about the need to stay away, out of shame, I imagine. He was gone. Wouldn't be all that missed. That was how he saw it then, and how he had seen it all these years, until here lately.

I had told him, one night early in our conspiracy of two but after he confessed some of these things, that I forgave him. "I do it out of love," I said, "because you won't forgive yourself."

"It's not your place to grant me a pardon for that." He sounded defensively firm, like he hadn't let himself consider what being forgiven could mean to him. "That would have to come from up there, and I'm not going up there. But I love you for not judging me over it."

I thought he was going to cry there for a minute. We were in bed, under thin sheets for the Oasis summer, and he buried his face in my neck and consumed me in arms and legs. "I can't be too hard on you. You're not that different from Daddy, are you."

He didn't want to confront a Freudian kettle of fish, but he did say, in coarse whisper, "You let me be what I became instead of what I was, and that's generous."

"My pleasure."

"I don't deserve it."

"But you'll take it." I was smiling at him in the dark. One of his fingers went to my lips and touched teeth.

"I will take it." The crackle in the throat of a choked-up man. "I'll live on it if you let me."

When he got home from that canyon walk, after Cam's letter, he decided to play dead, and he justified it in the way I imagined all men like Bill and Daddy justify this. He told himself, They are better off without me.

It's just that he didn't know how literally true that was, and how long ago they had decided it for themselves.

—|—

CALENDAR PAGES FLY by, and Bill milked his fame until it evaporated like the water in a desert salt flat. (Metaphors for decay are all over the place out here.) He was secretly flattered when little hippie girls would appear at his door from places like Ohio, saying that his pictures had spoken to them spiritually and they had to come and meet the man who had made them. And he wasn't too proud to avoid taking advantage of these girls either. It was the only social life he had. Beggars can't, indeed, be choosers, especially when they've dropped out of society and snipped their tethers. He would be very sweet with these girls and treat them the way they hoped a man with his spiritual imagination would, meaning that he'd fuck their brains out and make them see that there are more important things in life than taking pictures. And then he'd send them on their way with an autographed calendar and some bus money.

Everyone was happy.

Actually, I was in more or less the same category. It was about ten years ago, and I had fallen off my own high horse and got myself into a little trouble. I'd been arrested in La Jolla for what was technically prostitution, but all it was was going down on men for dollars in the beach parking lot. I never went all the way, couldn't bring myself to, even though I'd have made more money at it. But this was the line of work I picked after my first marriage failed (my own fault), and my ex-husband, Dennis, refused to cut me any slack and provide emergency funding. I'd lost my waitressing job, which was really, let's face it, transitional. I couldn't type or file or take crap from anybody. I was disoriented and, although the word is overused, desperate. Besides, at fifty bucks a pop, it wasn't too shabby a way to accumulate a little nest egg, with professional expenses limited to mouthwash and scrunchies to keep my hair back out of the way.

I wasn't terribly happy. Even less when my nest egg got cracked and scrambled by the legal system.

One day after the arrest, I was walking down Pearl in downtown La Jolla while I tried to figure out how to earn some money without falling back on my God-given skills, and I saw these black-and-white pictures in a gallery window. Desert shots, dramatic and powerful, and I went in and asked who the photographer was. The lady said he used to be quite well known but had faded into obscurity, Bill Argus. A recluse, we hear. Hard to reach. And anyway his work isn't really in demand these days, though it sure is awfully beautiful.

I used a Visa card and bought myself one of his framed prints for seven hundred dollars, then sold nearly everything else I owned. I had no intention of paying that Visa bill. I wasn't entirely reformed. After that, I left La Jolla and drove out past the mountains and into the desert in search of the man who had made that picture.

Why? Because it spoke to me in a way that nothing ever had before. I was at rock bottom; I read things into things so I'd feel better. What Bill was saying in this picture (to me) was that everything has a soul, from sharp white stones to clawing thorn-bushes, from the shit a coyote leaves behind to the bones of the jackrabbit he ate. And if everything like that has a soul, then so must I.

I don't know what consolation this really offered. Your soul doesn't do you any good while you're alive. Its value after death isn't all that clear either, except that those of us who survive you would like to think you're floating around out there somewhere. But the point is, at the time, I needed to know I was packaged with one. In case of accident.

When I first told Bill why I'd sought him out, this is what he said to me: "That is such infantile horseshit, Nora."

And he convinced me. When you see how a picture is made, with pieces of glass and celluloid and machinery and paper and chemicals, the idea that there's something spiritual going on in there is hard to nail down. It's just light and shadow duking it out.

We had just finished making love when he said that to me. Knee-deep in the first real passion I'd experienced in a long time, I blurted out my theory and he stopped everything.

Horseshit, he said.

He was suspended over me, still a reasonably well built man in those days, a man of fifty-four, a vigorous man, a man with large, long hands and appealing vision, and he stared into my eyes and said, "If there were such a thing as the soul, not even I could manage to get a picture of it."

And then we both started laughing. We were in his bed, with posts about as big around as telephone poles, and he was hovering over my face laughing. I got laughing so hard I had to bury my face in his neck and hair and scream with it, and I started to feel that I didn't need a soul per se if I could do this on a regular basis.

And I could. We did. All the time. It was the life.

I MADE BILL my Grandma Elsie's quarterly spaetzle one night in our ninth year, and he got violently ill. It was acid reflux of the gods. He was up all night belching and sick, pacing the old wooden floors, trying to will himself better.

I got out of bed and found him looking out the front window into such complete darkness that all I could see in the glass was our own ghostly reflection. I said, "Hmm. That poison's taking longer to kill you than I expected."

He shot a stream of air through his nose, making a faint whistle. "If you ever do want to kill me, do it with a quick knock on the back of my head with a fireplace tool while I sleep."

"You think I have the upper-arm strength to manage that?"

"Hit me just right and you don't need a lot. But swing it way up over your head anyway."

I patted his belly the way a husband pats his pregnant wife's, asked him if he was going to be all right. These pains were getting bad. The medicine doesn't much help, he said. It felt as if his body was moldering from the inside out.

"There's a lovely thought."

"I'm sour inside." He looked at me with dread in the eyes.

That's when he told me he wanted to go back to Pianto. He sat down in dark with his hands wedged between his knees.

"I've missed all the changes," he said. "I have it one way in my head, even though I know it's different, everyone back there is different. Forty years. And that's the thing of this new book. It's about nostalgia—which is a sickness, you know, a pathology—and how places are constant in your mind but always changing. If you weren't there you missed them, and if you were there you didn't notice the changes happening."

I lit a hurricane lamp and sat with him in its waxy light, listening to his rationale for the trip. Off the top of my head I didn't think the idea was going to be too good for him.

"People will remember my desert work when they look at these pictures of old farmhouses and churches, cowsheds, bad fences, and they'll do it subconsciously. Same metaphors. Things look inanimate, but they've been changing all along, they've been fluid and messed with and subject to weather and accident and indifference and neglect. You see what I'm getting at?"

He had a manic rhythm to the way he talked about it, like his creative juices were flowing, and truth be told I hadn't seen him that way in my entire time with him. His muses had let him alone all these years. I could tell what was really going on, though. I'd lived with him for ten years, married for nine of them. He was finding a reason other than the obvious to go home.

"This is a guilt thing, Bill," I said. "And here your hair shirt's still at the cleaner's."

His gut made a burbling sound and he looked away. "Nothing to do with it."

"You left them, hon. It happens. Men leave home." At least in my experience they do, I could have added. "And you've been punishing yourself by living like a hardheaded ram in the desert for forty years. There's nothing you can do now that would change a thing. And frankly? You'll be lucky if nobody up there takes a bead on you."

I was thinking of my own father again, of course.

"It's possible."

"It won't be anything like you think it will."

"That's what the book is about. The whole point."

After a few beats, while he was looking past me out into the empty black wash, I hit him with one more thing, hoping to discourage him for his own good. "If I were Hayes, I'd tell you which pier to jump off the end of."

He gave me a long, hard glare, but this was what he needed to understand. Hayes was his son, the gaping-mouthed toddler, who would by now have forty-odd years of bile and hard feelings built up, and let's face it, I told Bill, if you show up and act like he ought to be willing to let bygones be bygones, *he* might be the one to crack you on the head with a fireplace tool.

We sat there for a while in the dull lamplight, until Bill raised his bearish head and looked at me. His face was heavy with fatigue. I just wanted to kiss him. "I'm going up there to take some pictures. If he'll hear me, I'll say a few things to him. If he won't, he won't, and I don't plan to grow a tumor over it."

With that, he grimaced and punched at his chestbone with one fist, belched out a ball of something that smelled like mildew and bad milk.

I said, "That ain't Grandma Elsie's spaetzle."

A few days later we closed up the hacienda and packed Bill's old Jeep with a couple of weeks' worth of things. It was the orange crack of morning, when the desert is the most beautiful, to my mind, and as we pulled out I had the strongest feeling that Bill faced gigantic disappointment up there in his old cow town. I would have tried to talk him out of going if I'd thought there was any point.

WE PULL INTO Fresno after a dayful of hot driving. The Jeep is an old one and isn't air-conditioned, as if having a car with air-conditioning might ruin Bill's image as a crusty iconoclast, and I've nagged him about it. We're a comfortable old couple, we ought to have an American-made sedan with AC and power package. What the Jeep does have is a decent cassette player, and we'd been listening to Bach's greatest hits ever since we left the desert and headed up the valley. My favorite is called "Sheep May Safely Graze." It makes me feel like a little girl again, only this time someone who knows what they're doing is right in the next room.

I think we might have bucked up and made it all the way to San Francisco that day, and if we made it that far we might as well have run on up to Santa Rosa and Pianto. It struck me that Bill preferred a buffer zone of one night in a cheap motel, just to get his bearings and rethink things. There was time to change his mind.

After supper we lay on the bed with a bottle of tequila lodged between our thighs, watching the freeway traffic out the window. It was almost overstimulation compared with our normal life, which was quiet, believe me. Our house is miles from Oasis, miles from another house, miles from random disturbances. Once in a while a car will break down nearby, and the nervous driver will come to our door with his AAA card ready. Bill always startles these people by saying, "A few more miles down the pike and you're beyond walking distance. You'd have dehydrated and passed out, and then God knows what could have happened to you. Coyote food."

He sometimes liked reinforcing people's built-in fears. I've told him it borders on cruel, but when you live in such isolation, you make up little games like that.

"Is a person the person she is because of her chromosomes," I asked him in the motel bed, "or because of the way her mother treated her when she was little?"

I was a little whacked on the tequila, but I'd been reading this article in a magazine somebody left in the room. It suggested that maybe your mother treats you the way she does because of the person you already are at age two, or whatever.

"I've no goddamn idea," Bill said. His eyes were pinned on the ceiling, which had a blobby stain on it from the room above, or some ductwork up there that had leaked.

"Offer a theory, why don't you. Take a stab at it."

He looked at me and reached for the bottle, gave me a smile around the neck of it as he drank.

"I'm interested in your opinion," I told him.

"All right." He patted my thigh. "I'd say your parents go a long way toward screwing you up."

"Now see, that's what I think." And I had good reasons to. The general idea had kept me baby-free from my earliest awareness of my uterus. "But what this lady is saying is just the opposite. She says your mom and dad treat you bad because you're already a creep."

"I'll be damned," said Bill, and we both started laughing crazily and knocking heads together in bed.

"Wouldn't that be something?" I kissed him on the mouth and tasted the bite of tequila there. "I'd have to rethink Cary Lee altogether, wouldn't I."

He didn't answer me because, I'm sure, he was letting himself think back to some things his dad had done to him and wondering whether he'd done them because Bill was a creep from birth. I let him be with his thoughts for a while, until I nudged him and said, "Let's agree on something."

"What's that?"

"This isn't retroactive. It applies to future generations, not us."

"Sounds good."

"I like pissing on Cary Lee too much," I told him, and he gave me a little squeeze on the thigh because he knew the whole story.

Cary Lee's my mother.

THE NEXT DAY Bill waited until we were driving on the Golden Gate Bridge over a huge pie of fog to tell me that Pianto means "We Wept" or something like that in Italian.

"There's no reason for a place up here to be named in anything but Spanish," I said. Just playing. "Italians didn't come over here in boats and colonize. It was the Spanish. And some Russians. I'd take an Indian name over a stupid Italian word that means 'we wept.' "

"I didn't name the goddamn place," Bill said. His eyes were on the city, which was visible beyond the fogbank, all lit up in the sun. I nearly forgot that he had lived there for a while.

"You don't have to go around telling people what it means, then. It's so maudlin. 'We Wept.' "

I don't know why I got stuck on a thing like that. I think maybe I was getting a little nervous the closer we got, on Bill's behalf. He'd been fairly quiet ever since we left Fresno too, and didn't even express any interest in the Fish Museum we saw along the way. It was nowhere near any water.

We went through a couple of towns after we got off the freeway, and Bill told me to head west. From there the road wound through apple orchards and vineyards and dark old woods, the air sweet to my nose. It was nice being away from the desert heat for a change. Then we topped a ridge, and this lovely little cow valley opened up in front of us. I noticed that Bill was staring hard down there and getting a strange little twitch in the corner of his eye.

He didn't say anything. In a few minutes we could see a small collection of houses in the distance, a white church, an old school with a bell tower, nothing much else to speak of, and when I asked him if this was the place, all Bill could do was nod and touch his knuckle to his upper lip.

WEDDING DAY—1957

Cam

Their wedding day at the modest white church in Pianto. Annie, sweet thing, in her white dress, smiling painfully and kneading her hands, Bill in a white suit with a black bow tie. Annie was a beauty, there was no doubt about that, her red hair stunning in the bright day against the green eucalyptus trees and the blue sky. Her eyes were often down that day, so that when she did look up and meet yours, you would almost melt with affection for her.

Cameron Argus found it hard not to think of this girl making love with his older brother. He had difficulty keeping his eyes off her, difficulty steering his thoughts from the idea of Bill and her in the woods together, in the cellar, in the attic, in the grassy drainage ditch at the far end of the big pasture—by God, it was all he could think of, this beautiful girl rolling around naked with his big brother. Cam was sixteen. These were the kinds of mental pictures he conjured. But he also looked at Bill and wondered what kind of seductive powers this guy had been hiding, how he managed to snag a daughter of the Hayes family, and how on earth he'd persuaded Annie to give herself to him long before marriage. Now here they were in what amounted to a shotgun wedding (Annie three months along), though against cliché it would have been the groom's father forcing the issue, not the bride's. The bride's papa, Big Don Hayes, had he known what was really going on, would probably have sequestered young Annie at a convent in the Midwest to grow big in the belly, give birth, and turn the infant over to the nuns. But he didn't know any more than Cameron's father did, or the two mothers, for that matter. Nobody knew but Bill, Annie, and Cam.

Cam had nearly cried when Bill told him. They were out by the big oak tree at the back of the pasture, and Bill was starting to climb the tree. When he got to the first limb and squared himself, he was grinning, and Cam had to turn away so Bill wouldn't see his grimace. It was the worst thing that could have happened. "I've knocked her up," Bill said. There was pride in his voice.

On the way to the church door, Bill took a tumble and scarred up the knees of his white trousers. Too late to change. Cam looked down at his brother's knees and saw the yellow-green grass stains and the brown edges that made it seem as if his pants were burning away. Bill seemed unperturbed by it. He brushed at the marks with the back of his hand and came up smiling.

Cam felt like a monstrosity in his too-small suit. The slacks were high-water waders, the jacket tight in the shoulders because he'd been growing since the last time he had to wear it. His Adam's apple stuck out like a knob. His hair wouldn't sit right. Somehow his legs had grown so long he felt like he was walking around on stilts. In fact, he had begged Bill to find somebody else to be his best man because he didn't want the attention.

Bill had said, two days before the wedding, "There's nobody else who I'd *want* to be my best man, kiddo. You and me have been through it together."

As groom and best man stood at the altar, Bill nudged Cam

and said, "Look at Bad Ray—his eyes are screwed in upside down."

The brothers called their dad "Bad Ray" because there was another Ray in Pianto, and he was a decent kind of man, worked on diesel engines and farm equipment. He became "Good Ray." Sometimes Cam had a small pang of guilt over disrespecting his own father, but Bad Ray never did much to change the thought behind his name. It was the kind of thing that other people, overhearing the brothers, could nod at in confirmation.

Music began on the piano, McCloud the barber's wife playing with hams for hands. It sounded to Cam like she was trying to stick to just the white keys, but her fingers were too thick not to blunt some of the blacks too. And it wasn't "Here Comes the Bride" or some familiar thing like that; it was a piece Bill said Annie had requested, something by Bach, which was no more recognizable than a Slavic national anthem. Across the aisle stood Annie's rotund matron of honor, a figure from the Hayes family whose name Cam didn't even know. She had her hair up in a dark red bun, her dress accentuating plump rolls at her waist. As the music went on, here up the aisle came Big Don Hayes and his daughter, out of step with each other and approaching the front of the church at significantly different rates of speed, Don a good length behind. Annie, Cam figured, probably just wanted to get this over with before somebody got up and shouted out that she was having Bill's baby. Big Don wished that they'd never reach the altar.

It looked like he had overwaxed his mustache. It sprung out from his face as if it were two strands of a vine looking for a new post to latch on to. Don's eyes were narrowed and aimed at Bill, shooting a typical patriarch's threat. Cam knew, as did probably everybody else in the church, that there was no love lost between Bill and Big Don and that Big Don was against this from the beginning. He had even tried to stop it, until Bill, growing balls the size of the local Gravenstein apples, said he'd be just as happy eloping with Annie as going through this the standard way.

The night before the wedding Ray had apparently asked Big Don if he could borrow some capital to make improvements on the Argus ranch—man to man, relatives by marriage now—and Big Don had turned him down. Bad Ray had ranted about it all night long, keeping Cam's mother awake and fretting. Ray medicated himself with some Jack Daniel's he kept under the kitchen sink, making a fine blend with the beer he had indulged in at the VFW hall. The liquor seemed to nurse a seedling of resentment within him, a long-standing feeling of inadequacy that didn't need a lot of help to get going. It soon grew too big to be contained in him, and he was throwing glass things around the kitchen and shouting cusswords and oaths against the Hayes family and their precious, plentiful land. His hope, brought to the surface by Bill getting Annie Hayes to the brink of the altar, was that a new association with a good family would change things for him, forever. He had only ever really needed a leg up. Some ready cash. A chance to regroup and upgrade. From there he could be self-sufficient again, rekindle some of his pride (which, Cam thought, he wore on his sleeve anyway), become a man who could stand with Big Don Hayes and not have to grovel.

"Fucking piece of shit," Bad Ray bellowed from downstairs. Cam lay in his bed with a book, trying to block it all out. His brother was leaving the house the next day, for good, and then it would just be Cam, Ray, and Miranda. Things would be different from then on.

"Well then, Hayes," Ray said outside the church when the ceremony was over. "It's a done deal, innit. No unraveling the knot at this stage of the game."

Cam was standing near his mother, trying to keep her from hitting the ground if she were to get fainty. She'd been light-headed all morning, fluttering in and out of the bathroom to get ready, whispering (to herself, she believed) all the different things that might go wrong that day. When Cam placed his palm on her shoulder, he could feel a strong, radiant heat coming through her dress as she looked across the churchyard at Annie's mother. She wished she could stroll across confidently and say something to her.

Cam could read his mother's mind this way, always could.

Her sister, Carmen, stood a few feet away with Melvin, her husband who had flown in the Korean War. She was laughing so loudly at something he said that almost everyone had to turn to look at them. Carmen covered her teeth with one hand when she realized, then kissed Melvin on the cheek and left a bruisy lipstick stain.

What Bad Ray was up to was another matter. Obviously he wanted to make Big Don Hayes squirm a bit. And it wasn't that this was such an awful idea, in Cam's mind, but he thought his father would have shown more wisdom if he'd waited a few days. Big Don was well connected. It was possible he could get a fast-track annulment or, if the stakes were really that high, see to it that Bill got himself pulverized in a nasty car crash.

"Argus," Big Don said, "I've turned her over to you. I don't have a thing to do with it anymore."

"Turned her over to my kid, you mean."

"Is *that* how it works over here."

Ray took a couple of steps around and looked for somebody to laugh with him at the idea. "*I* didn't marry the girl," he said, loudly enough for the whole crowd to hear.

"Lucky for her!" Carmen yelled out.

"You're taking care of her when her bubble busts," said Don, the big man walking down the lawn toward his Caddie as he unwrapped a cigar.

Cam said, under his breath, "Blowhard."

"Cameron! Show some respect," Miranda said. Her blue

taffeta dress was trying to spiral around her body in the wind. "Well, anyway, his wife is a nice woman."

"Maybe she'll have lunch with you someday."

"Oh, I don't think so. I wouldn't know what to offer somebody like her."

Annie was standing beside Cam with red cheeks and a glazy look in her eye. She didn't seem to know where she was, and all Cam wanted to do was hold her face in his palms and kiss her on her sweet freckled cheeks. He tried not to let it show in the way he looked at her. Bill would beat the crap out of him if he figured that out.

"All right," Bill said. "Who's driving who to the reception?"

"Bride and groom with Big Don," Melvin said. "In the Caddie. Other than that it's every man for himself."

Cam watched as Bill and Annie traipsed down the lawn and got into the big car as if there was nothing at all wrong with the picture, except that Annie, at the last moment, threw him a sweet, kind, apologetic smile that Cam took to mean it was all out of her control. And it was.

—|—

THE RECEPTION WAS at the Hayes ranch, and Big Don had a pig roasting on his backyard spit. Tables and tables of buffet food, anything you wanted to drink, including the expensive stuff that Bad Ray couldn't afford. Cam wasn't supposed to drink, but he snuck a little of Don's finer scotch and nearly fell to his knees at the smell of it.

What Bill was good at, and Cam wasn't, was chatting up people he'd never met before. There he was, hands plunged into his pockets, his pant legs soiled, talking and laughing as if he'd known these people all his life and he was their favorite. Cam roamed around the yard looking for somebody to talk to other than his parents. He wanted to look older than he was right then. At the same time, he didn't want to come off like Bad Ray, who was struggling to wedge himself into conversations, raising his voice to be acknowledged, challenging other men with opinions that stumped everyone and rendered Bad Ray even more of an outsider. Miranda stuck to her husband like a burr, her arm wound through his.

Cam took off his jacket and hung it on the back of a folding chair. He sat down with his drink and listened to the band playing jazzy tunes on fiddle, guitar, and piano. They were good. Expensive, probably. Part of the trimmings that go with the Hayes life.

Bill had married into money. Impossible.

When Annie came to sit with him, he straightened up and tried to act like he was the happiest so-and-so on earth, but she was a perceptive one, Annie was, and she told him he looked the way she felt inside.

"What does that mean?"

"You look lousy." She angled her chair and crossed her legs under that mass of a wedding dress. Propped her head up in one hand and smiled at him. "No offense."

"I don't feel lousy," Cam said.

"Yes you do. Sure you do. I'm stealing your big brother."

"You can have him." He didn't mean it the way it came out. Actually, he was happy for Bill, but he was flattered that Annie could see that they were close. "But this is your wedding day," he said. "You're supposed to be walking on clouds or something."

There was a moment when Annie looked like she might straighten herself up and leave, but she let it pass by and then laid her hand on Cam's knee. She said, "I don't know what I'm going to do, Cam. Pop won't see me anymore when he figures it out."

She was starting to cry. Cam worried because other people were staring at them, thinking maybe that he had said something shitty to the bride, such an uncouth bastard. He patted her on the shoulder and told her everything would work out. "Things have a way of getting straight," he advised.

It struck him that she was only three years older than he was.

"You don't know my pop," she said.

"He bought you a house," Cam reminded her. It was the Hayes wedding gift to the newlyweds. A small farm not far from Pianto on the Freestone Road. As extravagant as it was, Cam thought it was the least a man like Big Don could give his only daughter, a pretty white house with twenty acres of sloped pasture and overgrown woods. It would take some work to get it cleared for a herd.

Bad Ray and Miranda had gotten them a porcelain pitcher and bowl, the best they could manage.

"It's in his name, Cam. He could kick us out if he wanted."

"Your dad wouldn't do that to you. Not with a grandkid in the house. He'd be afraid people would judge him the wrong way. And they would. I would."

Mrs. Hayes and some older Hayes women in tailored suits came and took Annie away from him. The groom was pitching horseshoes with a few of the men, a few ratty dollar bills in his hands for wagering, all bravado and bull.

Cam didn't know how to kill the time till the pig was ready to eat, so he walked around the Hayes pastures, sidestepping cow shit and puddles. Following the fence line, he walked a good half an hour until he came to the end of it, then went along the far barbed-wire edge for a while, shadowed under trees. The cows were giving him that anxious look they get when a stranger comes around. More than anything, on this property, it was clear that everything was in order. Big Don was a stickler for it, which was one reason, Cam supposed, he was all standoffish because of this marriage. Bill had thrown a wrench into his machine and screwed with Don's plans.

Cam remembered how Bill used to talk about getting out of Pianto. This was in the days of Bill's early adolescence, and it really didn't change until he met Annie. An interesting coincidence. But the idea was, the way Bill always talked about it when he and Cam would walk in the woods together, he'd join the army or merchant marine or something like that, and he'd get as far away as possible. He never liked the way of life on the ranch. The work was too hard—or maybe, more exactly, he didn't like the idea of Bad Ray bossing him around every step of the way for the rest of his life. Cam said, no matter where you go, somebody's bossing you around. A little piece of wisdom there. Logical, but Bill didn't accept it. He had this romantic idea that once he left Pianto, he'd be able to call his own shots and be an independent roamer like Kerouac or some kind of noble hobo. He'd see things that Pianto didn't want him to see, which was a concept that didn't hit Cameron at all. What does Pianto care what Bill Argus sees of the world?

They were hiking together up the ridge behind the big pasture at home, a few years before, when Bill told him he had a bag packed and was ready to go that night. Bill was fifteen at the most. "I got a bus ticket to San Francisco," he said. "From there I don't know where I might go, but it'll be south. I'll get you a postcard as soon as I can."

Cam had to be eleven or twelve. All he could say to his brother was "Why?"

"The old man is all over me," Bill said. "If I don't leave I'll have to blow his brains out while he's sleeping."

"It'd get on Mom," Cam said. "The blood and all."

"I know. So I'm taking the next-best choice. It might be a couple of years before I see you again, kiddo."

Bill was always calling him "kiddo." It had bothered Cam for a long time, but now he was used to it. Made him feel like at least he was in with his brother. Especially when Bill got over being mad about something.

They walked all the way to the top of the ridge that day and spent a little while looking out at the ocean as they stood upon the exposed rocks. Bill said, as he stared off at the blue horizon, that he thought the merchant marine sounded pretty good when he saw himself way out there on the water. Beyond where anybody could see from here.

And that night he left as planned. Cam heard him go, the front door creaking. He got out of bed and watched Bill walk quietly down the gravel drive toward their gate, where, he guessed, somebody was meeting him or he'd hitchhike. Bill didn't look back at him. There were crickets and frogs chirping in the dark of that warm night, but all Cam could think about was how he might not see Bill ever again, because his brother was too proud to admit a mistake.

Ray didn't take it too badly ("One less mouth to feed," he said), but Miranda was upset. She was on the phone to the highway patrol constantly. Asking around town if anybody had seen him. Cam told her Bill was beyond San Francisco by now, but she didn't want to believe him. And as it turned out, he had made it only as far as Santa Rosa, where a buddy had dropped him off at the bus station. At the last minute he got cold feet, decided to miss his bus, and then he cashed in his ticket and bought himself a bottle of whiskey. Had some older guy buy it for him, anyway. He slept under a bridge for three nights, getting good and drunk and dirty, then the cops picked him up and drove him back to Pianto. Cam thought the least Bill could have done was lie to him.

"Next time," Bill said, "I'm getting on that bus."

BIG DON MADE a production out of carving his pork, serving the hot pieces of meat on real china. The adults drank champagne, and so did Bill and Annie even though they weren't yet legally old enough. Everyone sat at the long, draped tables and made small talk while they ate, mainly Arguses with Arguses and Hayeses with Hayeses, and it was perfectly clear to Cam that this was not going to be a union forged in heaven. It was dusk, and the ladies began to chill a little and call for their wraps, while the men rolled down their sleeves and acted like it didn't bother them. Then Big Don got up and said he wanted to make a toast to his daughter, even though she went against his wishes and married this son of a gun from the wrong side of Pianto's tracks. Cam couldn't believe he said it, pinging his wineglass with a table knife the whole time.

"Now, goddamn it," said Ray Argus, rising from his seat. Miranda tried to hold him back, but he was strong in the thighs and scrambled away from her like a bantam rooster. A small but power-packed man, Bad Ray. He marched to Big Don's table and stuck his chest up close to the bigger man's, so close, it appeared to Cam, that Don's mustache seemed to reach out for Ray's forehead.

Mainly there were chuckles among the other guests, but none of them, perhaps, knew like Cam did how poorly Ray held his liquor, and he'd been drinking all afternoon. He'd never unbuttoned his suit coat, so it rode up and made him look like a pig in a blanket. Bill was smiling at the other end of the table, getting up slowly to go and contain their father. Miranda touched Cam on the shoulder, eyes on the developing scrimmage.

"I have just about had it with you, Hayes," said Ray. His eyes were on Big Don's Adam's apple, and possibly the most effective blow he could have delivered would have been with his head to Don's chest. That might have put him down. Big Don started laughing at the idea of Ray having the balls to be offended, looking to the crowd for approval. It all was pretty entertaining to him.

"I'm about to make a toast here, Argus, how about simmering down, how 'bout a cup of coffee to clear your goddamn head."

Bill was walking fast toward the two of them now. Cam could see what was building and knew that Bill wouldn't get there fast enough. Annie wasn't too far behind Bill, her dress flowing after her, strands of red hair falling down over her ears.

"You can make your toast after I've made mine," Ray said, and he whacked a champagne flute so hard with a knife that it shattered.

"You boneheaded idiot," Don said, and that was all Bad Ray could abide from him. He reared back with his fist and aimed a shot at Big Don's chin, which would have been an upward-flying punch if he could have managed it, but Don had enough time to pull his head out of the way and take the knock on a shoulder. Women were gasping and screaming, and Bill got close enough to Ray to snag a piece of the suit coat in one hand. In an instant, though, it was torn loose, and Cam watched helplessly as Big Don took his father by the shoulders and threw him against the wall of the brick barbecue chimney. Ray went down to the seat of his pants as Bill reached him. He fussed and batted at Bill with flat hands.

"Stay down," Bill said. By now Cam had been able to get right in there too, and he kept Annie away from the men, a palm on her waist and shoulder. It struck him as odd that the band continued to play all this time, professionally oblivious to what was happening.

Bad Ray let out a sound that was like the one a cow makes when it's getting branded. He was up in a clamber of boots and fists and clipped Bill in the eye in the process. Then he was on Big Don from behind, pounding at the father of the bride in the kidneys and ribs. All it took from Big Don was a whirling attack with one arm to get Ray off him, and then he aimed a fist the size of a cantaloupe and he put it in the spot where Ray's eyes and nose met in the center of his face.

The celebration was pretty much over after that.

CAM DROPPED THE bride and groom off at the house on Freestone Road after they all got Bad Ray home and dead to the world with a shiny red bruise growing on his head. Mrs. Hayes, Mabel, had promised to deliver all the wedding gifts the next day, without Don's approval if she had to, and Miranda fretted over whether the Hayses would ever speak to her again. Bill had a black eye himself, on top of his grass-stained wedding pants. Annie was pregnant.

"You ought to put a cold ham steak on that, Bill," Cam said. "It's closing your eye."

"It'll be fine," his brother said. "I've had worse ones."

Annie and Bill kissed Cam and asked him in, but he said no, it was their night to be alone, especially after what had happened. He left them standing on the porch and drove out to the road. Instead of leaving, though, for reasons that he couldn't really tell if you asked him, he stopped and got out of the truck by the gate and watched the light go on upstairs at Bill and Annie's house.

Up there together in that room, his brother and that beautiful girl, and a bad start already under their belts. He thought of his father in bed with his mouth open and his head swimming with drunken visions, and his mother sitting downstairs with her face in her hands and crying to herself. It felt like a strange corner was upon them all.

Cam stood there for the longest time, staring at that warm light in the window and listening to the crickets go at it.

FEAR—1946

Bill

When Bill Argus was a little boy, he and his father once went up in the local hills around Pianto to hunt for a couple of cows that had wandered away from the pastures. There was a piece of fence down at the far end of the Argus land, a space big enough for these two cows to walk through. From there all the trails led uphill into the woods, and Ray Argus had noted some tracks pointing in that direction. He packed Bill up (Cam was too young at the time) and walked him into the pine forest with a backpack, some food, some rope. They would stay out overnight if they had to, camping.

It was in the early spring, so the ground was still spongy from all the rain they'd had. Bill was about ten, and, like a lot of things that ten-year-olds think they want to do, this got pretty tiresome after the first two or three hours. The climb was tough, his shoes were hurting, it was dark under the canopy of trees, and Bad Ray wasn't saying much. Bill's feet were getting wet through the leather of his shoes. It smelled moldy in these woods, like nothing ever dried out, and shadowy shapes moved around in the treetops, birds or squirrels or bats. He kept ducking when he sensed that one of them was about to swoop down on him. It felt like things were lurking.

His father got way ahead of him, humping it up the steep trail, hot on the scent of those cows by the look of the shit patties they'd been finding. Bill didn't mind. He took the opportunity to slow down and gather up a few interesting rocks to take home with him. He climbed a tree to see if he could view the ranch from there. He could just barely make out the white frame house, and it looked the size of a brick. As he wandered his way up the trail again, he found a piece of branch that could be used as a walking stick and peeled the smaller fingers from it to make it smooth. It was almost as tall as he was and felt good in his hand.

When Bill came to a fork in the trail, he called out for his father. He had never been alone in this forest before and didn't know which path to take. There were no footprints that he could see. He called his father's name again and nobody called back. Then he began to run. It was an unfamiliar feeling of terror that made him do it, and it didn't matter whether he had picked the right trail or not—he had to run. In a few minutes he was out of breath and had to sit down, and he'd have cried if he wasn't so exhausted. It was a good thing that he didn't cry, too, because Bad Ray appeared from above along the path and said, "I got us a good campsite up here. Come on."

In those days Bad Ray was tall and still relatively thin. Later he'd fatten up, like a bull getting ready to be sold. Sometimes Bill had a hard time comprehending his father's age, which was thirty-four. To his eye the old man was just that, an old man. Hardened-looking. Dark-eyed. Hammered down like a wooden tent peg with its head flattened by the mallet. Bill felt that his father could tell he was close to the edge, close to crying, and so he tried not to look him in the eye. He hung his head as they walked still higher, finally arriving at an open clearing where there was a field of rocks and a wide view of the ocean. The two cows were not there.

Bill could not tell what was going on in Bad Ray's mind. He didn't show his cards much, a longtime complaint of Bill's mother. She was always saying "Penny for your thoughts" to him, and he'd wave her off like she was a fly. He had bigger concerns. Bill tried to understand that, even though Bad Ray remained tight-lipped about what those concerns were. He never admitted feeling overrun or at the end of his rope, Bill's mother trying to coax a little weakness out of him every now and then. It didn't work.

It started to get dark, so Bill gathered some firewood and his father got a good fire going. They ate leftover fried chicken and some macaroni. Bad Ray took his beer bottle and shook it with his thumb over the hole, then shot foam out like a firehose.

"You scared," his father asked without looking at him.

"No."

"Good. There's nothing to be scared of in the woods. Unless you're scared of bears and mountain lions and bats and snakes and dragons." There was a laugh curling up one corner of his mouth.

"I know there's no such thing as dragons," Bill said. He picked at the fire with a long stick and watched the sparks go up.

"Well good for you. Let me give you a piece of advice, though. While you're sleeping. If you wake up and a bear is licking your nose, you just want to play dead and act like it don't bother you. And if a coyote or a wolf comes by and scratches at your head like he wants to see what's inside, you go 'Bad dog!' "

Bill wanted this kind of talk to stop. He wished those cows would show up.

When it was completely dark and there was nothing to do, he tried to go to sleep on the dropcloth they'd brought. His father stayed up, tossing sticks into the fire, but a little while later, when Bill was half asleep, he said he thought he heard one of the cows.

"You stay here," he told Bill, and took the flashlight.

"Don't go."

"She's right down the hill a bit," Ray said. He was holding the light under his zombie face, but grinning, like this was supposed to be fun. Bill should have known that his dad's fun almost always wound up hurting somebody else. "You stay here and keep the fire going, and try not to be a pussy about it."

He walked into the dark, where the edge of the woods began. Bill heard his boots crunching long after he'd dropped out of sight.

Bill sat there in front of the fire. He desperately tried to keep it from burning out, but there was no way to get new wood for it without stepping deep into the darkness, and he was afraid to do that. It got colder and colder, and his father didn't come back. The night crept along, Bill growing terrified. When it began to get light out and he was shaking from a combination of the fear and the cold, he packed everything up in his backpack and left that place on the ridge without his old man. He was almost insane from the experience, his teeth clattering and his mind whirling with crazy images that had come to him in the night, of animals and killers. He hadn't slept at all. His father was probably dead.

At first light he started walking home with all the gear. Every step he took he felt might land on his old man's body, but in a couple of hours he had made his way down the hill without encountering anything or finding any signs of a mauling. He wondered if there really were mountain lions in these hills. He was glad he had that walking stick, and he held it in two hands the way you grip a baseball bat, though his hands were sweaty and shaking and every muscle in his body was tight. Hurting from the cold and the fear.

When he finally crossed the fence line and started across the pasture, he saw that the two missing cows were in a small corral near the barn. He went into the house, where his mother smothered him with hugs and kisses, all weeping and shrill, and his father, sitting at the kitchen table with a cup of coffee in his hand, grinned and said, "I told you he'd figure it out, Andie."

—|—

SOMETHING ABOUT SPENDING the night alone in the woods had made him feel strange inside. He couldn't put his finger on it. It wasn't brave, and it wasn't nervous. Possibly he felt deceived—but that was a word he didn't know—fooled and made fun of. Humiliated. It was a feeling he didn't like, and he took it out for a few days on his little brother, Cam, because he couldn't punish his father for it.

He found Cam out by the oak tree at the back of the pasture and dared him to climb it higher than he ever had before. Bill raced up the two-by-fours that were nailed into the trunk as steps, pushing Cam out of his way and climbing to the second tier of limbs. He taunted Cam to come up and try to reach him. From Bill's position in the tree, his brother looked tiny, a little rat looking up at him.

"You can't do it," Bill said. "You're afraid."

Fear was now something he thought you should be ashamed of. He'd had it all night long on the ridgetop, but he was ashamed of himself for feeling that way. He suspected from the way his father had laughed at him when he got home that his father would go around Pianto and tell the story of his little scaredy-cat son. But at least, Bill told himself, climbing still higher and feeling the power in his arms and legs, Cam is more scared than I was, and he's so scared he can't even catch up to me in the tree.

Cam began to make his way up into the limbs. He was only seven years old to Bill's ten and had short arms and legs, couldn't reach the limbs Bill could, yet he kept trying. He rested for a moment on the thicker branches near the bottom of the tree as Bill looked at him from above and thought the best thing that could happen to Cameron would be to experience fear the same way Bill had.

There was an immature sort of logic to it; he believed that he would have been prepared for the night alone on the ridgetop if he had lived through some genuine fear before, but he never had. It was an unfamiliar experience. He would do Cam the favor of scaring the hell out of him so that later Cam could get through the harder things that were really terrifying. It was similar to what Ray had done to him, he imagined, though Bill wondered why his father hadn't prepared *him* for that night by hanging him upside down from a barn rafter or something like that, conditioning him. It's possible that Bad Ray hadn't given Bill a thought when he went down the hill without him, and that was even more upsetting to the boy. Unless, of course, the night on the ridge *was* the conditioning, getting him ready for something even more terrifying than that was.

He wondered what on earth that could be.

"Climb higher," he told Cam.

Cam was sitting on a limb with his feet dangling, his hands gripping another branch so hard that his fingers were white. He was looking toward the house as if being there didn't bother him at all, chin down, mouth tight. Bill tossed bits of bark into his hair.

"Don't be a pussy about it," he said. "Get up and keep climbing. It's no good down there."

"I don't want to," Cam said. His shorts had gotten dirty as he made his way up to the limb, his knee bleeding from a scrape against the tree. Bill imagined he was pretty close to crying his stupid head off about it. "I can see everything from here."

"No you can't. You can't see Pianto. *I* can see Pianto. And I can see the ocean. And the Bodega Bay lighthouse." None of this was true, except for Pianto. He could see the few houses and stores, and the church steeple and the school bell tower. His father might be down there right now buying feed or drinking in the bar with Grandpa Harper. One of the few times Bad Ray had taken Bill into the bar with him, he nearly got into a fight with Grandpa Harper over what was the matter with Aunt Carmen. Ray said it was probably that gourd of a proboscis on her that was keeping the men away, and Grandpa cocked his fist back like he was going to pop Ray in the mouth. Even though that didn't happen, Bill liked the feel of being part of it, sitting there with his soda while they argued. Made him feel like a man. But then, that was long before the night on the ridgetop, and that night had changed everything.

"I can see Pianto fine," Cam insisted, and Bill tossed more debris down on him, bark and twigs and acorns, torn-up oak leaves.

"You cannot," he said. "I can barely see it. You can't see shit."

"Yes I can," Cam told him, smiling up. Then he pointed to the ground where there were a few flattening cow patties.

"Funny. Get your ass up here or I'll *beat* the shit out of you."

Cam was about the only person on earth who would do whatever Bill commanded.

It was clear he didn't want to, but Cam eased his way onto his feet again, holding on to any branch he could reach. Bill watched solemnly as he hauled himself up one level, then hugged the new limb as if he were a monkey, stomach against it, arms wrapped, and Bill spit. It landed right on his brother's back, dead in the middle.

"Keep coming, little brother," Bill sang in a strange, phony voice. "You can do it, boy! You know you can!"

Cameron managed to sit up on his new branch. Bill could see now that he *was* crying, though not with sounds. Just tears.

They were streaming down his dirty face and making clean white trails. This is just what he needs, Bill thought. He needs to be scared. He needs to feel like he'll never get down out of this tree. That's how it felt up on the ridge.

A change seemed to come over Cam. He looked up at Bill as he brushed the scraps out of his hair, he wiped at his knee with one hand as the other one clung to a limb. Then he pulled himself to his feet again and started higher. Bill was five or six feet above him now and didn't want his brother to catch him. He looked for a higher spot where he could be sure Cameron would not be willing to go, but the limbs were getting thinner there and might not support his weight. His tennis shoe was lodged into a tight, V-shaped joint, and there was no place he could reach from there. He started to shake the branches above him, knocking down acorns and loose twigs and sending a wave through the entire tree.

"Stop it!" Cam cried. He was only a limb or two away from Bill now.

"I'm not doing it!" Bill said. "Must be an earthquake." And he shook and shook the tree until Cameron looked up at him with a face that revealed his true terror and anger. Bill wanted to laugh.

"There goes a cargo ship heading for Japan," he said, though he couldn't see such a thing, or the ocean itself. "I think I see a hurricane on the horizon! This tree's a bad place to be in a hurricane."

Cam didn't bother to dispute him. He pulled himself to the next-highest level, reaching as high as he could, so that his fingers were now gripping the limb at Bill's feet. They were both fifteen or twenty feet up, and Bill knew that Cam was purposely not looking down, he was so scared.

"Whatever you do, don't look at the ground," Bill said. "You'll get dizzy and fall."

Cam immediately looked down, like Bill knew he would. He buried his face in his outstretched arm, so Bill began to shake the tree again. Then he got an idea to scare his brother even more, the reason he was here in the tree in the first place, and this was for Cam's own good, so it was all right.

"Don't be afraid," he said, and he bent his knees so he could reach Cam's hands clinging tightly. One by one he started peeling Cam's fingers off the branch. Cam looked up at him in pure terror, his mouth wide open and drool trickling out the corner, his eyes bugged and wobbly in their sockets. There's nothing to worry about, Bill thought, because he has a foothold and there are plenty of branches to grab. We'll see how good his reflexes are. Bill had to pry pretty hard to get the fingers of Cam's left hand off the limb, and then, without any reason at all, Cam let his feet come off the branch beneath and he was dangling by one hand.

"I'll get you, kiddo," Bill said. Meaning it. He would grab his brother by the loose hand and pull him up. He figured that the fear Cam must be feeling right about now was probably good enough to help him later, but that loose hand was flailing around just out of Bill's reach, grasping at empty air and branches that were too thin to support him. Bill called out that he should calm down and get his feet back on the limb below, but now Cameron was screaming, red-faced and frenzied, and just as Bill was able to touch the clawing free hand, Cameron let go with the other one. He fell immediately, descending through the branches and making them rustle like something that had just been shot. Bill watched, frozen, as his brother hit the ground and lay on his back, still in the dirt. Cameron's eyes were open, blank.

Bill made his way down the tree as fast as he could, and by the time he hit the ground, Cameron was trying to move. He had probably been knocked out for a minute. Bill stood over him, watched as he lay there with his limbs perfectly still and his eyes open and roving, trying to figure out where he was and what had happened. The pupils were wide. His head looked big and his body looked small to Bill, and there was no blood or bones sticking out of Cam's skin.

"Don't tell what happened," Bill said. "Okay? Be a man about it. Don't tell."

"I won't," Cameron said. His voice was quiet and breathy. He tried to lift himself up on elbows but couldn't do it.

Bill told him that their mother would find him before long, there was nothing to worry about, and even though he knew that it was probably the wrong thing to do and would not deflect the consequences if Cameron did tell what had happened, he started away from the tree and across the pasture, toward the trail that led into the safety of the woods.

NAKEDNESS—1956

Annie

One afternoon on a high ridge overlooking the ocean, Annie Hayes found herself alone after a nap. She had come up to the ridge through the woods with her lover, Bill Argus, the man she knew would be her husband one day, and he had been with her when she fell asleep after making love with him in the grass. She didn't know how long she'd been asleep, or whether Bill had been gone very long, or if, in fact, he was still close by. It was possible that he'd been modest enough to walk to the edge of the woods so he could empty his bladder, or perhaps he thought he heard someone approaching and had gone off to intercept the person so he wouldn't see Annie naked.

She had fallen asleep naked, and cradled in Bill's arms. The afternoon made it seem like the thing to do, a soft, warm, late-summer day. At the ridgetop, where they had gone many times before, it felt like the world was floating along in the ocean—blue-black sea beneath, open sky above—and everything existed for them, the lovers. It was like being in Eden before the fall, where nothing had meaning or function that did not attend the comfort of sinless Adam and Eve.

At first, when she woke up, she didn't know where she was. Even though this place was familiar, she had never been here without Bill, and with Bill gone she was disoriented and a bit frightened. She rubbed her eyes with the backs of her hands and looked around at the standing boulders glazed with seagull droppings and at the small bushes and trees that were permanently bent because the wind was often so strong here on the ridgetop. Her body became chilled suddenly, nipples tightening into goose bumps. She crossed her arms over her chest and stood up tentatively to see if she could spot Bill near the tree line, or closer to the edge of the plateau, where he sometimes liked to stand naked and look out over the ocean with his arms spread wide as if to claim it.

He was nowhere to be found. Their blanket was still with her, and their picnic basket. They had hiked up from Bill's house on a trail that began at the back of the Argus pasture and climbed up through a dense pine and eucalyptus forest. It was a trail Bill knew well because he had grown up using it, and he liked to tell the story of spending the night up here on the ridgetop one time when he was just a boy. He learned that there was nothing to be afraid of, he said when he first brought her here; it was the same place in the dark as it was in daylight, a beautiful, comforting place, and we can be alone here and nobody will ever find us. And they had become lovers for the first time here, and had done it again every time they came up, as if it were a place made for that purpose only. With the boulders and stunted trees, it had the feel of a place where rituals might have been performed once, and that's the way she liked to think of their lovemaking.

The sun was beginning to warm her again. Bill would return soon, she determined, so she sat on the blanket and then leaned back on her elbows with the sunlight pouring over her bare chest and belly, places that never got sun and were so white they appeared to glow. She closed her eyes and turned her face to the sun, enjoying the way it warmed her and made her feel a little more alive. She could feel it on her shins and hips, on her collarbones, on her hair, which Bill had taken down so it would spread out against the green grass as they made love. He liked to see her face against the background of her red hair and to kiss his way down her freckled body until he arrived at the other patch of red hair and then lay his head on her there.

Somehow she had come to believe in the fatefulness of their love. She would not have known him except for an accidental meeting a few weeks earlier. He was changing the tire on his father's old truck at the side of the road just as she happened to be walking home from church one Sunday afternoon. She offered to call someone to help him out when she got home. He didn't say anything to that but just kept looking up at her with the sun lighting him from behind her, kneeling there on the asphalt with the tire iron in his hand. She knew who he was because her father often knocked the ranching families that weren't in his elevated league—the Tuckers, the Grafs, the Arguses. Sometimes he said the name Argus like it was a cussword. Annie didn't care if this was one of the lowly Argus boys, though, and she accepted his handshake even though his hand was dirty from changing the tire. When she introduced herself, he said, "I know who you are." He was looking at her knees and hips and the ends of her fingers hanging at her thighs.

Later, after they became lovers, she said to him, "It's fate, Bill. From the minute I saw you on your knees in the road, I knew we would be like this."

She believed in it, how real lovers are meant for each other and find each other in spite of the obstacles. A mundane life could be blessed with it. People could live on love alone. It was easy to believe in a thing that was this strong.

At the same time, she had done everything she could to hide

it from her father because he was a man who didn't believe in love. Annie knew he hadn't married for it. Her mother moved through her days like a woman whose feet were weighed down in steel boots.

Bill often spoke of taking her away from Pianto, just up and running away like fugitives who'd be captured if they stayed. He had said, more than once, "We could go right now, Annie. We could run down this hill to Highway 1 and grab a ride to Mendocino and get married there, and go as far as a bus can take us on the money we have, and we could phone them from wherever we land and tell them they can do whatever they want, we're going to be happy without them." His eyes would brighten when he talked about the kinds of places they could go, places where nobody would know them and would leave them alone. He spoke as if it were a daily struggle to stay where he was, and while it was true that she didn't quite share his need to go, she could understand him and admit that wherever he was she could be happy. Every time they came up to the ridge, she would say that this place is good enough. Look around, Bill, she'd tell him. You don't have to run away to be safe. We're here in this beautiful place together.

And just today, after they had made love and were lying in each other's arms and looking into the bottomless sky, she said, "I'd be happy if this moment was eternity, Bill."

He had raised himself up and said, "There's no such thing."

Sometimes he said things to test her, and other times he truly believed what he said. She didn't think he meant this. To her that moment *could* be eternity, and maybe would be one day when she looked back on it to recover the feeling that it carried and to relive it over and over.

When she thought about that moment, still vivid to her there on the ridgetop though Bill was nowhere to be seen, Annie felt as if she had somehow stepped out of it and was looking at herself from a distance. Here she was, lying on her back in the place where she and Bill had made love an hour before, but she could almost float above it and view it like a scene in a painting. Wind made the grass tops look like waves. The ocean reflected a sharp blue sky. Her body, as she looked at it from this distant viewpoint, seemed elongated and out of proportion, her feet far away, her legs slim and stretched out. The triangle of red hair where Bill had laid his head looked like an island or the arrow marking a fork in the road. From this distance her skin took on the color of a honeysuckle flower, her nipples the pink of a primrose. In such a private place her body was nothing to be ashamed of but instead was a thing among all the other things on the ground, the rocks and ice plants and bare patches of dirt. She could have sprung from the ground like a mushroom overnight, anchored with roots and kissed by an angel who would visit her every morning and ravish her. It made her feel as if the earth under her were part of her body, the way it pressed against her and took her shape.

Thoughts like this made her feel like such a schoolgirl. Yet at eighteen now she was finally experienced in love; she loved that her life was already here and there'd be no endless searching for it. Bill had been delivered to her on the side of the road like a milk bottle.

After a while she realized that the sun was beginning to burn her skin. There had been no motion in the woods to signal Bill's return, and really no indication that he had ever been there, except that she was there with the picnic basket and blanket. She would never have come here alone. He must have been here with her. But now she was burning and looked around to find her clothes so she could dress again and go into the shade to wait for Bill. It was a hot day too, there was sweat on her forehead and chest, and she could smell herself, her armpits, between her legs where Bill's smell was lingering. Love was smelly and messy and beautifully inconvenient. It left signs of itself all over her, as if to signal to other men that she was claimed, possibly giving her father a vague sense that something was wrong, and that was why she always rushed home after being with Bill and soaked in the bathtub before her father could detect. Her mother might already know, and that was too bad. At least her mother believed in love and knew that this was what Annie had been given, even though her mother hadn't married for love either, but for money and convenience and honoring her father's wishes and, possibly, for the relief that somebody wanted to marry her. Annie often felt sorry for her.

She felt around for her clothes and couldn't find them. She turned and crawled through the grass on hands and knees, her breasts heavy and stinging from sunburn as they hung down. Her skirt and blouse and shoes were missing. Her panties and brassiere. There was nothing here to suggest that she had been clothed when she arrived, only the picnic basket and the blanket, the indentations in the grass where she and Bill had been lying, the sound of the wind in her ears. She could feel her skin tingling with sunburn now, even on the soles of her feet, which must have been exposed to the light when she was asleep. Suddenly she felt bared and defenseless. Even watched.

It struck her that the angel who had kissed her had done away with Bill and hidden her clothes so Annie would not be able to leave, a ridiculous idea that made her laugh out loud. She stood up and tried to cover her breasts and between her legs with her hands and forearms, bent at the hips and looking toward the tree line and into the shadows. She called out Bill's name, but there was no reply except the cawing of a few crows in the treetops. They waited a moment or two before they shot out of the tree and flew in a wide circle over the ridgetop, screeching the whole time.

Annie took a couple of tentative steps in the direction of the trees to see if she could make out Bill's form there. The ground was rough on the bottoms of her feet, pebbles through warm grass. There was no reason to cry about it because there was nobody to hear her crying. Crying when you're alone is only trying to fool a fool, she always told herself, and it never makes the ache go away.

"Bill!" she said again, leaning toward the woods with her feet planted on a softer place. "Bill, bring me my clothes when you come out!"

Again there was no answer, no sign that Bill was within earshot. But she didn't understand what had happened to him. Had he gathered up all their clothes just to walk off for a pee? Had someone come along and stolen the clothes, Bill in pursuit? She was beginning to worry about him, since he had never left her like this before at the ridgetop, or anywhere else for that matter, none of the many secret places they had for lovemaking.

Standing there in the open field, she suddenly felt her nakedness drift down on her like walking through a curtain of spiderwebs. It was something that rested *upon* her, it wasn't herself. Though Bill had helped her see that her nakedness was a beautiful thing, the same way she felt about his, she still had the odd feeling that her real identity was somewhere underneath it, as if her clothes were just another layer hiding this thin, shameful coating that kept her true self from view. Her real self was so far down, so interior, that it must be like a moist nut buried in deep dark soil. Through her nakedness it might be able to receive a little light, but she didn't like being naked except with Bill, and they couldn't be together very much because they were hiding it from their parents. Nobody knew about them except Bill's brother, Cam, and Cam had accidentally seen her naked one time when she was with Bill in the Argus cellar making love. She knew that her nakedness must have glowed in the dark to poor Cam, who had scrambled down there to tell them that

Bill's father was on his way down to get something. Annie preferred that Cam have a glimpse of her that way rather than Ray Argus. Cam at least would receive it properly, her disguise, and he was perceptive enough, she believed, to see her real self behind it, if he looked closely. It seemed to her that he *had* looked closely too. A long helpless stare at her body, lying beside his brother in the white light that filled the cellar through the outside door. They had just enough time to stuff themselves into a dark corner before Ray arrived, thanks to Cam.

His reward, Bill said, was that little look at you. He'll never get over it either.

Now Annie took a few more steps toward the trees, feeling that her skin would burn so badly that it might peel, and her mother and father would ask questions about it and possibly find out that she was sunburned in places that should never have seen the sun. She trotted through the taller grass, holding her breasts in place with her arm; she could feel the wind through her legs as she ran. When she got to the tree line where the trail began, she squatted low near a fallen pine and looked around for Bill. The woods were thick there, full of shadowed hiding places, full of cover for a voyeur, a ranching man who might have been walking along and spotted her after Bill left. But why did Bill leave her to be seen by a man wandering along? Why did he leave her out there alone in her nakedness, when someone might come by and take a hard, vulgar look at her?

It was getting late enough in the day that the sun was angling down toward the edge of the plateau, the wind picking up. She raised herself a little over the curve of the fallen tree, her eyes fully adjusted to the shadows, and she realized that she had a chill now that she was out of the sun. Her body tingled with it, every part of her growing grainy and tense, her jaw beginning to lock. She wished she had thought to wrap herself in the blanket before she made her run to the woods. Huddling beside the tree, she was startled by the sound of birds in a thorn thicket close by. They scrambled and scratched and flitted, but the sounds reminded her of light footsteps, someone trying to walk quietly.

I've got to go back and get the blanket, she told herself. Keep covered until Bill gets back. But just as she got to her feet again and went to the edge of the woods, she heard a tractor engine and saw the black diesel smoke coming from its chimney as it topped the ridge and came down the dirt road directly toward her. A man sat in the open seat, pulling behind his tractor a small wagon with one sheep standing in it. Annie dropped to the earth before he could have seen her.

She made her way back into the woods as the sheep farmer stopped his tractor and dismounted very close to the blanket and picnic basket. He stretched his back, took a pipe out of his pocket, and lit it.

"Bill!" Annie called in a hissed whisper. Nobody answered her.

She hid behind a stand of drying ferns, shivering and angry. The rancher stood on the ridge enjoying his pipe while the sheep bleated helplessly behind the slats of the wagon, on its way who knew where. Maybe the rancher was selling the sheep to another farmer or taking it off to be sheared or slaughtered. Whatever it was, Annie could sympathize with it, trapped in the wagon with no way out.

All her thoughts of love and fate and eternity had gradually fallen away, yielding to more urgent ones. By now she almost hoped for his own sake that something bad *had* happened to Bill. His excuse for leaving her this way had better be a good one. If he didn't return soon with his arm in a sling or with that angel caught and tied up, she could see herself thumbing her nose at fate and losing him.

Now the farmer tapped his pipe out onto the ground and put it in his pocket. He went around to the wagon and let down the back gate of it, pulled the sheep out by a rope leash and led it to the grass to graze. What was he doing? She needed to get to her blanket and cover herself. Every moment that went by made her colder and angrier, and to make matters even worse, the farmer now produced a sack and took a sandwich from it. He sat on the ground near the sheep and began eating his lunch, gazing out at the same view Bill and Annie had enjoyed, what seemed now to be hours ago. He ate, and between bites he tried to whistle a little melody that didn't come out very well because his mouth was too full. If she were to emerge from the woods and gather up her blanket and basket, he would probably choke and suffocate when he saw her nakedness there in front of him.

Now there seemed to be nothing to do but wait. She tried to make herself comfortable in the fern thicket, hoping that the position of the sun would change so that she could get enough of it to stay warm but not so much that she continued to burn. On a different level this seemed to be the problem most people had in life—not enough or too much. Not enough of what they wanted or needed, too much of what they didn't want or what they *thought* they wanted. She believed that this was her mother's basic problem. Too much Big Don Hayes. Too much responsibility. Annie didn't want to follow in her footsteps, and Bill was not Big Don, or anything like him. He was a different animal altogether, and she doubted, because of they way they loved each other, that they would ever have children of their own. The poor children would starve for love because Bill and Annie would be unable to spare it from each other.

She thought she heard something over her shoulder—a toot, a signal—and turned around abruptly to see what the farmer was up to. To her alarm, he was standing again, only this time he was looking toward the woods as if he had detected her presence there. Had she spoken out loud without knowing it? Maybe he had caught a flash of her reddening skin between the ferns, or her hair, which was still down and loose against her back and shoulders. For all she knew, in the changing light, she might stand out like a hay bale with a target pinned to it.

He put the sheep back in the wagon and locked up the gate behind. Then, with his eyes almost precisely meeting hers through the cover, he began walking toward the tree line as if there were some kind of magnetism drawing him. His pace began to quicken as he came down the grassy slope toward the woods. Perhaps by habit, he took his pipe out again as he walked and clenched it between his teeth. He was staring straight into the ferns, intently, with demanding curiosity. Annie knew there was nothing to be done but to leave the ferns and run away, because she was so far from help that he could easily rape her and not be discovered. Until this moment she had never been afraid of rape, had never thought it was possible or that she would ever be in a situation where it could happen. He was marching right at her.

She flung herself out of the ferns into the woods again. Her arms swung wildly as she ran, catching small branches and thorns, her breasts swaying. She heard the farmer cry out, "Wait a minute! Hold up!" But she wasn't about to stop for him, wasn't about to let him see her nakedness like this, frontally, unprotected, blatant. At last, bleeding here and there on her arms and thighs, she reached the trail and continued running downhill. The farmer appeared to have stopped following, and there was no way, she was sure, that he could get his tractor and wagon and sheep into the woods, because the road he was on went off to the north and switchbacked its way down the ridge.

Annie's whole body ached, and her fear and embarrassment had made her breathless. Walking now down the soft, mulchy trail, she thought of her single eternal moment lying in Bill's arms at the ridgetop, tried to recover it through her anger and humiliation, tried to relive its smells and feelings, and somehow, in spite of her agitation, she succeeded. It came back to her in a sequence of waves, like the incoming tide, until she was back in that moment, feeling the grass against her hips and Bill's arms around her, the comfortable warmth of the sun on her skin, the gentle wind.

"Took you long enough," Bill said.

She fell out of her reverie as if she had tripped on a stone. There he was, sitting on a stump beside the trail, the pile of her clothes at his feet, a long piece of grass sticking out of his wry mouth. His eyes were sparkling as he watched her walk. He could hardly contain himself, wanting to bust with laughter.

He held his arms open for her to throw herself into helplessly, but she wouldn't do it. He could hug the farmer when he finally came along looking for her.

Instead she picked a stone up off the ground and hurled it at him, and she walked straight past, taunting him in all her nakedness.

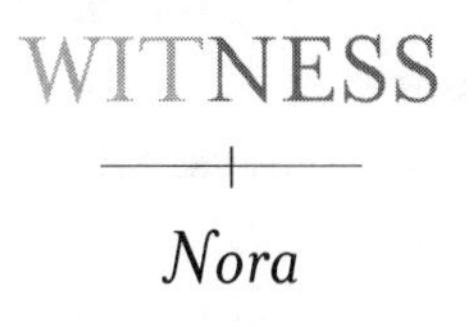

WITNESS

Nora

The way my mother told it, the night of my third birthday was the night her husband walked out on her, me in rubber training pants and a frilly plaid dress and Mother with accidental cake icing, cherry pink, on her chin. My father was drunk, it is said, or acted drunk. My tiny spiraled candles burned on down their wicks as he told her something lamebrained about why he couldn't stay, but as far as I know, that was it. He didn't come to kiss my forehead or straighten the red ribbon in what passed for my hair. He collected his keys from a ceramic dish in the front hall and he left.

To this day I do not know what he looked like.

Now, my mother may have been a normal woman up until that night—I wouldn't have any way of knowing. But she was never to be normal again. She left me at the table with my cake and candles, took herself upstairs tucking a bottle of wine under one arm, and parked herself in the bathtub to drink. After a while Grandma Elsie, her mother, arrived and pounded on the door screeching. That I can remember, believe it or not. Like the screaming of the bad water-pump belt on the decrepit Rambler that Cary Lee drove.

Grandma Elsie had a habit of arriving unsummoned. She seemed blessed with a penchant for knowing when her daughter was about to do something dumb.

Elsie figured out how to jimmy the lock, and she burst through the door with me riding on her hip. Mother was so drunk by then that she had slid all the way down in the tub, the water lapping at her nostrils and the wine bottle floating like it held a desperate message Mother wanted to get out to sea. Elsie plopped me on the toilet seat, where I swiftly (thinking I was doing what she wanted) wet my pants. I told her so too, but her attention was on Mother, getting her out of the tub and wrapped up in a towel, keeping her bowed over the basin in case she started vomiting right away.

I felt sorry for her—Elsie—even as early as that third birthday of mine, because I had the obscure feeling that she'd been doing things like this for my mother since the day my mother was born. Elsie died before she could tell me one way or the other, but that night she was working with the efficiency of someone who knew the drill.

"Cary Lee," she said, as sternly as she could manage, "you're a mother, you can't do this. They'll take your little girl away from you if you do this every time you hit a roadblock."

"Take her away from me!" my mother cried, meaning at first, I think, the way you'd say it if you didn't want it to happen. Take her *away* from me? Then she said it again: "Take her away from me. Take her away from me!"

That's an order.

Then she vomited, right on target, and Elsie wiped her face and mouth with a washcloth and put her in her pink robe while Mother continued to whine, "Take her away from me. Please, Mama, take her away from me."

All the evidence to the contrary notwithstanding, I think that was the most clearheaded moment she was to have for the next twenty years.

DADDY HAD LEFT before he could knock Mother up with a sibling for me. That might have made things a little more interesting. A sister.

Nowadays I bet Daddy goes by an assumed name. Frank Something. His real name was simple enough—Joe, that much I always knew—but I had to think he wanted to seem like a different man altogether by the time he cleared the state line. Those kinds of men are generally named Frank, it seems to me.

I remember growing up and seeing Daddy's razor in the medicine chest. Among other personal articles he left behind, it had remained in there until I was old enough to need it for my legs and armpits. It never went away. And the styptic pencil in the medicine chest for his cuts. And the slim, dimpled bottle of Skin Bracer in there, which seemed to lose about a quarter inch a year to evaporation. In his closet, shoeshine brushes and shoe stretchers and a few ties he'd been too hasty to pack. He seems to have been a well-groomed man, but like other women who've been dinged, Cary Lee wouldn't say. He was nothing but shaving gear and shoeshine supplies to me. His smell still permeated that closet, where the wool suits once hung. I whisked my bedspread clean with the horsehair shoe brush and made the stretchers into awkward puppets that were half robot and half reptile, and the legend I made up was they were on a lifelong search for shoes big enough to bury their heads in because that was the only way they could get some sleep.

You guessed it. They never found any shoes like that.

I think she kept his things because she had this idea that he might be back one of these days. Ridiculous.

It was all the worse that I didn't even have a picture of Daddy that included his face. I had one of him dipping me into the little wading pool behind our house, his handsome strong arms holding me, his belted swimming trunks like you'd see Burt Lancaster wearing in the forties. Mother must have taken the picture, and I bet she was jealous that I wasn't looking at the camera. I couldn't take my eyes off Daddy, looking up at him with a gigglepuss. Mother was no Bill Argus, though. She cut his head right out of the frame.

There's me again on my third birthday, ready to patty-cake my cake. Daddy must have been near when that was taken.

A few years later, before I was old enough to stop her, she took a razor blade to every one of his pictures that had survived that long, and shredded them into fine, glossy ribbons. If I'd had the presence of mind to save those ribbons, I would have killed a few hours trying to glue them back together one day when I was older. Out of a futile need to know what the man looked like. And whether I came from his stock or Mother's.

I never did know why he left her. Was she nuts, and that's why he went? Or did she go nuts later, ex post facto. Some things you just never get the whole story on, I guess. Not that knowing would have changed what happened.

I WAS FOURTEEN, and Grandma Elsie had been gone so long it was hard to remember what she looked like. Mother perfected a hands-off parenting technique that rendered me pretty much my own guardian, plus the victim of my own crappy judgment, and her several boyfriends had the universal habit of coming on to me after she passed out from her overindulgence in French Columbard and Tareytons. One night I stay up late watching *The Bijou Picture Show* and finishing my supper of raw hot dogs and shoestring potatoes, and right on schedule here comes the boyfriend, Dick, so appropriately named I almost have to laugh. He's in his boxers and his tee and fresh from diddling Mother's lifeless bones, saying, "You're a nice-looking girl, Nora. Anybody ever tell you that?"

"Yep."

"Your mother has a nice personality, but she's getting fat. You're going to hold on to your figure, I can tell. You have a nice shape, beautiful tits. You're gonna make some man very, very happy."

He leers the same way they all do, like the next move is mine, and I slide out on the sofa like I'm Lolita, wetly willing, dying for him, but as soon as he comes over and puts a hand on my bottom, I say, "You can go jack off in the bathroom, Dick. I'm watching TV."

"Goddamn little bitch."

"Are you going to be my stepdaddy?"

"Fuck yourself," he says. "Your mother likes being peed on, she ever tell you that?"

Oh, those were the days, when the world presented its true colors to me—fair enough—instead of making me think the sky was rosy pink and the sun was made to warm the fur on my back.

I MISSED GRANDMA Elsie. She used to have me over and would feed me Brown Cows until I got sick. We would stay up watching TV all hours, talking about the baseball game or a dreadful Movie of the Week we'd just sat through.

Elsie took the warm place my mother should have occupied, but I didn't care about that while she was alive. I preferred her company. I liked her more than I liked Cary Lee. I loved her. I asked her questions about Mother, and her answers were as generous as they could be, considering the spectacle of Mother's life. "She's had a hard time of it, hon," Elsie said. "She's suffered a lot."

Elsie always had her hands in a bowl of cake batter or cookie dough. She taught me to make that spaetzle when I was just a little thing.

—|—

WHEN I WAS seven or so, Mother accidentally set the living room on fire while I was sleeping, and I woke to find her in the frame of my bedroom door sobbing that we had to get out. It smelled funny. Mother didn't pick me up and carry me out, but simply turned and stumbled down the smoky hallway. I got out of bed and ran along behind her, dragging my Baba Looey doll by his plastic ears. Pretty soon, as always, Grandma Elsie is there with a blanket to wrap me in and Mother is sitting on the curb bawling while the firemen try to put down the flames that looked painted on our picture window.

Where is Daddy through all this, is what I wondered at the time.

We stayed with Elsie while our house was being fixed, and it was during that stay, young as I was, that I figured out my mother must be legally insane. I pieced it together, because now I had a tally of experience with her to go by. And from things Elsie told me about her too, from her own growing up. Little clues. Red-flag behavior. I figured Daddy knew this about his Cary Lee, but loved her for something she used to have before I was born. He took it as long as he could, and then he had to leave her.

The worst sin of his, the way I put it all together, was that he didn't take me with him. And the real disaster of my childhood was that nobody took me away from Mother the way she begged that night of my third birthday.

—|—

CALENDAR PAGES FLY by. I'm sitting in wet sand. My ass is damp, and the sun is in my eyes. The ocean is whispering about me in tones it means to be overheard, while Bill tries to patch things up with his brother back in the Pianto tavern that Cameron owns. I'd left him there on the curb, looking like a vagabond.

It could be that I've decided to remember things inaccurately, but I don't think so. That's where the sister I'd always longed for would have come in handy, though, and I say a sister because I imagine that a brother eventually would have picked up and left anyway. With a mother like Cary Lee, he would either have turned out magnificently gay or run off at an early age.

But no, at least my sister would be able to commiserate, and I could check my details against hers. We could have conspired. I bet we could have whipped old Cary into shape somewhere along the way, tied her up in the bathtub and made her sober, tossed her cigs and kept her the hell away from those SOBs she was always bringing home. We'd have called the shots, my sister and me.

It wasn't as if Cary Lee was nonfunctional. She held down jobs and sometimes had the wherewithal to cook me a meal. When she had a little extra money, she'd take me someplace extravagant like Disneyland and buy me these beanies and T-shirts and fill me up with fun-food, and strangely enough I'd be the one to cling to *her* hand all day long, afraid that she'd brought me there to lose me.

She also had this obnoxious way of charming the pants off people who didn't know her too well. It was a skill that Grandma Elsie had somehow managed to pass along to her, and Mother refined it in her couple of years of college before she met Daddy. The idea was, the charming girls meet the best men, which was the only reason Cary Lee had gone to college in the first place. The family wasn't well enough connected for her to land anybody halfway decent otherwise. Her charm was in a lot of different qualities, but what she could do without even trying was make people laugh—the people she *wanted* to charm, I ought to say. She could shoot out clever comments and bon mots like Dorothy Parker. In fact, I think she modeled herself after Dorothy Parker when she was young, right down to the bitterness that you could almost see under her skin. A sweet little piece of ass, though. I know that much from the surviving pics.

Anyway, the point is, I knew Mother like nobody else did, and so it burned my hide when people who didn't know her so well would say things like "Your mother is so *fun*ny and *bright* and *char*ming! Your house must be like a *car*nival!"

"A freak show," I'd say, under my breath.

She worked in a thrift shop that benefited the symphony or the opera or something like that, and she was always coming home in these clothes that the old dowagers had finally tossed out of their cedar closets, crazy outfits from the thirties and forties, weird hats with long feathers in them, tight high-waisted jackets, even stockings with seams up the calves. It was charming, all right. She'd also pick up these weird "objaze dart," she'd call them, to decorate our house with, crappy little ding-a-lings advertising tourist attractions. Carlsbad Caverns, Niagara Falls, Paul Bunyan Country. Or her African phase. She wore dashikis and wooden sticks in her hair, brought home carved masks and icons of pregnant women with their tits down to their knees and big old bellies, then, as quickly as that phase began, it ended in a flurry of Nehru wear and long white yogi blouses, brass incense burners, prayer beads and prayer rugs and prayer shawls from the Mysterious East. I never knew who was going to show up at night.

She was always using these phrases that she thought made her sound intelligent, but she got them wrong so she came off as stupid, if you asked me. Like "queer and pleasant danger." I don't know what she thought that meant. Of course, all those people who thought she was just wonderful wanted to believe she said that kind of thing on purpose, and they'd laugh and laugh. I'd be upstairs when she was having one of her parties, and down there everyone would be laughing their drunken heads off and listening to Brasil '66 or something like that, and I'd hear Cary Lee's voice rise above all the others and blurt, "Every clown has a silver lining, doll!" They'd all laugh like freaks.

The next day she'd be down with her hangover, and I'd have to clean up. The house would be a mess—plates and plates of congealed food, glasses with dregs of highballs still in them, and cigarettes tossed in to make them that much more fun to clean. There might be a stranger sleeping on the couch, or a few articles of clothing scattered around, a discarded pair of ladies' underpants, an unused condom. I mean, what went *on*? An orgy and Brasil '66 hit me as plain incompatible.

Did I really blame Cary Lee for becoming a party animal? I guess not. Here half the time she's waiting for Daddy to return, sometimes even staying up all night and sitting vigil at our picture window, and the other half of the time she's going braless in her dashiki so she can pick up some hep cat at the thrift shop. I suppose I'd drink myself into oblivion too, but then again, like I said, I don't have a kid to look after. I was wise enough not to test myself in that way.

One of these parties one time got really out of control, it sounded like, and I smelled pot smoke from down there. I had to be about ten. What made me suspicious was that things were really loud for a while, with all kinds of crazy laughing and horsing around, and then it suddenly went quiet. I had pictures in my mind of all those adults finally going nuts on LSD, strangling each other or getting naked and flopping into a big pile together. I didn't care for that idea.

It was late, and I kept thinking I heard someone outside my room, some sock-footed Dick, so I got up to check. There wasn't anybody there, but I could hear music downstairs playing low, and whispering, and when I got to the bottom of the stairs I saw that the men and women had paired off and were lying wherever they could, mostly on the floor, and making out. Even a couple of women had paired off, Mother's friends Elaine and Donna, and they were kissing and feeling each other's tits. Well, I *never.* Nobody seemed to know I was there because I was tiptoeing. I made my way over the bodies, and one of the adults finally saw me and told me to just go back to bed.

"Where's Cary Lee?" I asked her. I've always called Mother by her name. My whole life.

"I don't know, hon. She probably fell asleep somewhere. You go back to bed now."

The man she was with didn't like her getting distracted by me. He pulled her head back toward him and gave her a huge kiss that seemed to eat up the bottom half of her face. I wanted to laugh. The only man I'd have let kiss me in those days was Micky Dolenz, and it would have been a sweet one without tongues and that's it.

I went down the hall. There was an empty bottle of Mother's favorite wine on the floor by the bathroom, lying on its side. I picked it up and saw her lipstick stains around the neck of it. Out the back window I could tell that it was beginning to get light out, kind of dim and gray instead of black, and it seemed to me it was time for everybody to leave and Cary Lee to get herself to bed because she had to work that morning. I had a strong responsible streak in those days. If she got fired, I'd have to go through the want ads again and help her find a new job, and she wouldn't be able to steal things from the thrift shop anymore. There were unintended consequences to every act, I was beginning to figure out.

A little grunt came from inside the bathroom, a kind of sad whining moan. It sounded like Mother. I had a feeling that she was sick and I ought to clean her up and take her to bed, because by the time she started drinking her wine directly from the bottle, she was usually too far gone to go there on her own. I'd lay her clothes out for work and get a pot of coffee going. I'd give her an hour to sleep a little, and then I'd bring her a piece of toast to settle her stomach, or I'd hold her hair back for her if she needed to throw up. I had my assigned roles, you know.

The moaning got louder in there, and to me it seemed like time to go for her hair right away. I opened the door, and of course Cary Lee wasn't sick at all. She was back-thumped against the wall with her naked legs straddling the waist of a man named Dwight, as I recall, whose bare, pallid, hairy ass was grinding away at her like he was about to break through a stone wall to the sweet hereafter. Dwight probably wasn't aware that he had an ugly mole right above his crack. I couldn't see his face. I could only see Mother's, over his shoulder, and she gave me the kindest look I think she ever managed for me. It was like the look saints have in those Italian paintings, an expression that says, I'm in the hands of something much bigger than myself, dear. Finally, she just closed her eyes and turned her head into Dwight's neck so she couldn't see me anymore, and I backed out the door and closed it behind me.

That woman who had told me to go to bed was standing in the hallway looking at me, buttoning up her own buttons. I could tell that she wished she'd been just a little bit quicker; maybe she could have kept me from seeing that thing in there.

It wasn't your fault, I wanted to say. That guy had your face in his mouth.

Later, years later, I realized that Cary Lee was about thirty-two then, much younger than I am now. And I'm looking at forty.

I'M NOT DWELLING on her because I like to. At the time Bill and I headed up to Pianto, it had been a good twelve years since I'd even laid eyes on her, a thing that had been good for both of us, I imagine. Ever since I moved in with Bill, and then married him, Cary Lee had faded from my mind as a constant source of aggravation. It wasn't so much that I came to forgive her, really, though. It was more just "out of sight, out of mime," as she would say.

Is it fair to cut off somebody like her, who did the best she could? Well, now see, I don't accept that assumption, because I don't think she did the best she could. I think she did what she felt like doing. When you do the best you can, there's supposed to be a certain level of sacrifice. She didn't make any sacrifices at all. She drank and smoked and fucked around. She ignored me and ignored how her boyfriends wanted to fuck around with me. I was always too hostile for them in the long run (what a turnoff, I guess), and if one of them ever said anything like, "You have quite a little bitch for a daughter, Cary," she'd look at me as if I was the one who had done something wrong. She never wasted a lot of effort trying to charm *me.*

At least, thank God, her boyfriends didn't stick around. Not until Jack came into the picture anyway. That was later. I'd really have been in trouble if any of them had stuck around, because it probably would have boiled down to somebody getting hurt, me or them. I slept with a baseball bat in arm's reach, and I always envisioned some fat-assed, smelly jack-off trying to get on top of me and I haul off with this bat and knock his brains out. When Mother would bring a new one home, I'd immediately picture a target on his forehead as he leered me up and down.

I had no shape in those days, no hips and no boobs to speak of. But I was a clean slate, and young, and undemanding. Maybe Cary Lee was just too much woman for those weak men.

—|—

I DROVE UP Pianto's main drag, and there was Bill standing at the front door of the tavern, which was called The Dogleg because of the big bend in the road right there. He wasn't looking terribly unhappy. His hands were stuffed deep inside his khaki pockets.

Mister Closemouthed. He got into the Jeep and didn't say anything at first. I stared into his profile.

"So, how's your brother doing?" I singsonged.

"All right," he said. "Not half bad."

Bill wanted to be reticent, but I wouldn't let him. After all, it was the first he'd seen of Cam since their folks died. Since Cam was a gangly kid. "Did he take a kick at your balls or anything?" I asked.

"Nope."

"Hey, everything's coming up roses, Bill!"

It would be a few hours before he told me how it all went in any kind of detail, and it wasn't too pretty, really. Cameron obviously didn't recognize him right away, drew him a beer and fed him a plate of barbecued oysters before Bill couldn't keep from snickering anymore. Revealed his identity, after which Cam disappeared into a back room and didn't come out for twenty minutes.

"We're staying with him," Bill told me. "Up the road two three miles." He held out a set of keys and jingled them in front of me.

"His house? Is that a good idea?"

"Mom and Dad's house."

"They're dead, Bill. He owns it, doesn't he?"

"What's left of it."

I wasn't very encouraged by Bill's attitude, which struck me as cockier than a shamed prodigal son ought to be putting on. In short order he had already browbeaten Cam into letting us stay with him, and while I knew it was all in self-defense and meant to hide the fact that he was scared out of his mind, I didn't think he would get very far if he kept this up. I put my arm through his and squeezed hard, hoping he'd take a deep breath and try to draw a little strength from me. That's what I was there for.

We drove out the way we'd come into town, and in a few minutes Bill said to slow down, he thought the gate was coming up. It wasn't. The truth was, he couldn't remember precisely; he'd lost the picture in his head of the landmarks. Finally, we had to turn around because he was sure we'd passed it, and then, coming in the opposite way now, we stopped at a ranch gate so he could get his bearings. A gravel drive left the gate and sloped up the ridge of a small hill, and when Bill spotted a row of poplar trees back there, he said, "Jesus, those were skinny little seedlings when I left. This is it."

He got out and opened the plumbing-pipe gate, then got back into the Jeep, and we drove the quarter mile or so up the drive toward a two-story frame house, crunching gravel as we went.

The main thing I noticed was how the air was full of dust. It was like I was looking at the place through orange cellophane.

"It's because Cam doesn't irrigate the pastures anymore," Bill said. "He sold off the herd. Grows weeds and dust out there now."

The property did have the look of a place that was being left to fail. A barn that had begun to lean off plumb, scattered rusting implements. The house, though it could have been inviting if it were patched up and painted, looked like it might have been in probate for a decade or so, with nobody to love it.

"Welcome home, Bill Argus," I said.

CAM WOULDN'T BE home till late because he ran The Dogleg, open to close. The Dogleg was where we would find him if we needed him. The Dogleg, it seemed, was his real home.

I found this comforting in a way. The Argus homestead was too depressing a place to call home. And a man who lives in the home of his parents at the age of sixty would strike me as tangled in the apron strings, if you know what I mean, if he didn't have something to demand his attentions elsewhere. At least Cam had his dingy rancher bar to run, though I would have liked to see a wife beside him there.

Bill and I sat on the porch with our bottle of tequila, gazing into the far hills. Trees made the silhouette of the ridgetop way out there look like a saw blade. The sunset was nearly over with, turning the sky a buttery color and making it hard to see much beyond the fence line.

"Ah, the sweet green valley of my youth," said Bill. He was looking at his knees.

"Everything you remembered?"

"I don't remember a thing."

"Then how do you know this isn't the sweet green valley of somebody else's youth?" I leaned against him.

He laughed and said maybe it was. I was glad I could still make him laugh after ten years of desert cohabitation. You'd think people living like a couple of scorpions would grow tired of each other so far from other stimulation, but we were well suited.

"I feel like I've been in suspended animation for forty years," Bill said. "And any minute now the old man could bust out of that barn with a pair of bolt cutters and threaten to cut off my thumbs for running like I did."

Bill always got these gauzy eyes when he talked about Bad Ray.

He said Bad Ray was always sneaking up on him. Popping out from some dark place when Bill thought he was alone. Nailing him, in an eerie low voice, with an admonition or a threat. "Why aren't you out digging postholes for that new fence?" It was interesting, but sometimes difficult, to listen to Bill as he reminisced about the old man, if that's the word. Now he was leaning forward with his elbows on his knees, staring down at the overworn porch step under his feet. He was biting the inside of his mouth. I had the tequila bottle in one hand and my other hand on Bill's shoulder.

"He got his goddamn truck back," Bill said, referring to the old hay truck he'd run away in, abandoned a few miles down the highway.

"I don't think he'll be bugging you much, baby."

The way the old man died had to bother him, I guess. I wouldn't wish getting hit by a train on Cary Lee. (Would I?) No, nobody deserves that. Of course, I had to wonder, and I kept it to myself, whether Bad Ray had parked on the railroad tracks on purpose, a crazy devil like him, and with his uncomplaining wife of forty-odd years in the passenger seat too. Cameron hadn't been that specific when he informed Bill at the time, kept the details to a minimum except to assure him that their mom had died instantly, according to the highway patrol. Bill always told me he didn't take as much comfort from that as Cam probably intended.

It was fairly dark out, and Bill didn't show any signs of getting up to go in. I was tired. What we were really going to do here wasn't terribly clear to me, especially since the unspoken elements behind the trip were staying that way. A son lived somewhere near here. And an ex.

"He's still around," Bill said. "Old Ray." And he went on and told me how that would be the case as long as the Argus land didn't have condos built on it or a strip mall, because it would take that kind of monstrosity to erase Bad Ray's footprints. A tough way to think of the old man, I thought. At least I had no idea about mine, a well-groomed phantom as far as I was concerned.

"The first thing Cam told me was how Mom and Dad are buried up the road in the Pianto cemetery, under the eucalyptus trees, with a nice pink granite slab done by this outfit down the road in Cotati, and how I ought to go and have a look at it if I wanted to get a few things off my chest. I said I didn't think I'd get a hell of a lot out of yelling at a slab of pink granite, and he gave me a look like I hadn't changed a goddamn bit."

I found this silly in a way, because my Bill wasn't anything like the boy who left here. He had changed. But it was clear that his brother didn't know him if he thought Bill would waste his breath talking to the dead. The dead are gone, he'd say. Dead and gone. Hence the phrase. And to believe otherwise is naïve horseshit.

At that moment, with crickets up and at it with their hind legs, Bill began to laugh as he looked out at the pasture. I could see his face in the moonlight, his mouth pulled back like a grimace. He said he was just remembering something, a little picture came to mind, just this little moment he hadn't thought of in years. One of those ones, I guess, that prompted him to take up photography. He said he could almost see it now, playing out in front of him like a film shown on the side of the barn.

"The old man is trying to settle down this bull that was spooked over a bolt of lightning or something, and he has a lasso in his hands and approaches it with all that macho bullshit confidence he liked to think he possessed, swirling the loop, coaxing the bull in that voice of his. Cam and I are on the steps here, where we are now, watching this . . . this kabuki unfold, and Mom is standing behind us, kneading her knuckles the way she always did. Bad Ray starts trotting close to the bull, swinging his rope, clicking his tongue to distract the goddamn thing, cooing and singing and whistling as the bull picks up speed and kicks once or twice with its back legs, strong enough to take Ray's head off. Then Ray begins to sprint, launches his lasso and manages to yank it tight just as the bull gets nutty again at the next thunderbolt. He takes off, hauling Bad Ray behind him."

Bill is weeping with laughter now. He looks over at me, tears streaking down his eyes, attempts a pull at the tequila bottle but can't swallow he's laughing so hard. "And we're yelling at him from the porch, like he's a dumb-ass water-skier, 'Let go! Dad, let go of the rope!' The bull drags him like a rag doll around the pasture, and that's the whole thing of it."

He wipes his eyes and coughs and throws that grimace out at the empty fields. "That's the whole thing. He's so goddamn rigid he can't bring himself to let go of that rope." Bill shakes his head in a slow arc. "It'd mean that the bull wins."

—|—

GRANDMA ELSIE WAS still alive at the time of that first primal scene of mine, when I caught Mother in the john with Dwight. She wasn't too long for this world, but she was still around. I remember, because the next day—or rather, later that same morning—I called her up and asked her to help me get Cary Lee ready for work. I had been trying and trying, piling on the TLC, plying her with coffee and toast, apologizing for walking in on her. None of it was working. She kept herself facedown in bed, Dwight and the others long gone, the house a royal mess, and for a while that morning I liked to think she was actually ashamed of herself. As soon as Elsie showed up, though, Mother became Godzilla. You could tell her head wasn't feeling so good by the way she held it, off plumb, like her eyes were the bubbles in a carpenter's level, and when she saw Elsie, she started ranting, "Oh, you had to go and call the vice squad on me, did you? Had to bring in the sex police."

"Cary Lee," said Grandma Elsie, "this is your daughter standing here. You don't talk like that around her."

Mother was sitting up in bed at least, but she gave us a look like we might throw her in the river to see if she floated or sank. "She knows the score, Elsie, don't kid yourself. She makes eyes at my boyfriends, I'll tell you what."

Grandma Elsie, who was probably not much over sixty by then, had heart trouble and looked a little bit gray. She told me she'd get Mother dressed and ready for work, and I should go downstairs and have something to eat. It was a Saturday. She promised to spend the day with me. In the evening we'd pick Mother up at work together and keep her sober. We could watch TV in bed, all three of us, with a tray of snacks and the lights off.

It was always such a comfort to me when she would come over and take charge like that. Even though Cary Lee didn't respect her any more than she did me, somehow Elsie could get results. With me, Mother would just grumble, "You're a goddamn kid," but when it was Elsie telling her what to do, I guess these old patterns kicked in. Mainly because Cary Lee was on autopilot anyway, and it was easier to do what her mother told her.

They appeared in the kitchen doorway as I sat there at the table drawing. I smiled. Mother had her hair combed back, with a big, wide blue headband holding it down, and she was wearing a colorful dashiki and white pedal pushers. She didn't look half bad, if you liked her African phase, although her face was puffy and her pupils a little dilated. There was a good chance she'd make it through the day.

"You look nice," I told her, and she couldn't help it, she had sarcasm in her veins. She said, "*He* thought so."

Grandma Elsie thought it was a good idea to get her out of there before anything new flared up. She got Cary Lee out to the car, then came back in to tell me something. She said, "Your mother's very sorry, Nora. She told me so. She was bawling like a little baby up there."

"I know it."

She kissed me on the forehead, smelling like cake batter, and left me there. I'd have the house to myself for a while.

SHE GAVE IN TO IT—1961

Miranda

From her bedroom she could hear the three of them downstairs making sounds like the ones Ray and the two boys used to make. Only now it was just the one boy, Cameron, and it was Ray, and it was her sister, Carmen. Bill was gone and would never be let back in this house, if Ray had his will. He ran away, abandoned his wife and baby, and the vacuum that replaced his presence made her feel as if she could not breathe. It had been weeks since he'd gone, with nothing but an unintelligible postcard sent from Death Valley to hint at where he was. Miranda had hardly been able to spend more than an hour out of bed since then, paralyzed by sunlight and air, by anything other than the darkness of the bedroom.

The downstairs sounds were not comforting, the clattering of dishes, the radio. Every so often Carmen's voice would rise above the others, hollering at them, chastising them for not appreciating her—or their wife and mother, for that matter—but the men didn't react with anything but chuckles to that, it was just the way they were. They'd joke with her, or at least Ray would (Cameron had too much courtesy to make his aunt feel bad deliberately), saying, "We'd make our way somehow, Carmen. We'd eat cardboard and drink bathwater, but we'd get by without you."

"Oh, you want take a shot at it, dipstick? I'll give you a day or two on your own, and you'll see what it's like."

"Good eggs," said Cam.

"These are eggs?" his father taunted. "I thought it was shit on a shingle."

Miranda—Andie, as she was called by her family—wished she could laugh at the back-and-forth. She couldn't. There was a hole in her heart Bill had put there, a hole only as big around as a pencil, but it went clear through her body, all the way through, so that if you stood in front of her you could view the sunset behind. It was a hole through which all her joys and pleasures and her cherished innocence had drained. Everything was different now that Bill was gone.

She heard Carmen's heavy feet on the stairs and tried to ease herself up in bed slightly to make a better impression. The throb of the headache pushed her back down, and she threw her arm over her eyes because she knew her sister would toss open the blinds and flood the room with light. It would hurt.

"Up 'n' at 'em," Carmen said, busting through the door. She had a tray with breakfast on it, coffee, a glass of orange juice. The smell of the food made Andie want to retch so badly that she had to turn away and bury her face in her pillow. She heard her sister put down the tray and then stomp over to the window and throw open the blinds. She could almost *feel* the light on the skin of her arms.

"Today's the day you get out of bed and whistle a little ditty and kiss your husband and son and drag your butt into town for some groceries." Carmen tried to sound cheerful, but Andie could hear that her teeth were lightly clenched.

"I can't, hon. I just can't."

"Here. Roll over." Firm hands on her shoulders. "Once you

get some food down your throat, you'll feel up to it. Hot coffee. Little bitta toast."

The light in her eyes was sharp and searing. Carmen smiled at her and fluffed her pillows and made a fuss over the food tray, but all Andie could think about was the pain behind her eyes. And dizziness. It was as if she had become allergic to the world, and sleep was the only comfort left. Her nights were short and void, though, just a moment of dark and quiet, with Ray lying beside her and trying to console her with pats to the thigh. He wasn't a big one for soothing words.

Carmen had her hair pulled back in a tight strawlike ponytail that she had become too old to wear. Her face was puffed like a drinker's, which she was—socially anyway, highballs her main weakness—a porous and pink nose jutting out from under her eyes. Andie often felt sorry for her, the way her husband of six years had betrayed her, but now she felt sorrier for herself, and that made it difficult to keep their individual suffering on the same scale. Carmen didn't often show her disappointment and sorrow, where, here now, Andie couldn't bring herself to put her feet to the floor. Whose was worse? Carmen could still be funny and find joy here and there as she went about her business; she appeared to be capable of having fun, as far as Miranda could see. But Miranda was afflicted with this hole through the center of her body now, and it seemed to her that life would not recover its old buoyancy.

Mine must be worse, she told herself. I would get up again if I could.

"You eat, and you get your heinie out of bed today," Carmen told her. Finger pointing. A chewed nail. "That's all I have to say to you."

"I'm so dizzy," Andie said. She knew she must look awful. She hadn't combed her hair in days, hadn't bathed. She craved darkness and the stillness of the room with the window shut tight.

"You'll never get over it unless you force the issue, doll." Her sister marched around the room in those heavy shoes of hers. They sounded like army boots, and that reminded Andie of a joke, something about "Your mother wears army boots." She couldn't think of it. Who would say that? Why is it funny? "I'm serious. When you're done, you get yourself up and bring the tray down with you. That's your assignment today. You can collapse on the kitchen floor if you want, but you get that tray down there somehow."

Carmen left. The tray that remained on Andie's lap, smelling of rancid bacon and that dishwater coffee, felt as if it weighed a thousand pounds. She had to chuckle at the thought that it would cut off her circulation and cause gangrene, and she'd lose both her legs, and then they'd have nothing to say about her getting up and out of bed, would they?

IT SEEMED THAT people had been making fun of their names, Carmen and Miranda Harper, their whole lives. But the singer came along when the sisters were in their twenties already, so it was just an odd coincidence. They never heard the end of it after that, though from all Miranda could tell, Carmen didn't mind at all. In fact, she'd play to it, she'd do a little Cuban dance and snap her fingers to imaginary conga music, and she'd make people laugh.

They were the daughters of a man who had failed. An earnest enough man, one who couldn't be faulted for lack of trying. He'd tried many things, everything, yet had failed at all of it. This was why he was so persistent with the propaganda—his wife appalled by it—that his daughters must marry young and must marry the first man who asks, because there is nothing worse in life than "what might have been." He knew what he was talking about. This was his sermon, delivered almost daily while they were growing up.

Miranda loved him in spite of the appearance of a conflict of interest. Marrying the first man who came along would get her out of the house, and her older sister, and the burden on Lawrence and Trudy, her mother, would be that much lighter. The sting of failing would ease a bit. Trudy always tried to neutralize the propaganda effect by taking the girls aside and saying, "You marry whoever you want, whenever you want, and don't you let him make you feel bad if you have to turn somebody down. Better yet, you don't have to *tell* him you've turned anybody down. We'll keep that to ourselves."

The Harpers had occupied a small house near the center of Pianto, down a quiet road that followed the course of a stream. Sometimes cowmen herded their animals along that road on the way from one pasture to another, and one of the men who did it from time to time was Ray Argus, who lived on a small ranch nearby that he worked with his father. There was talk that Ray's father had turned the place over to him because he himself had arthritis so bad that he could no longer handle the work. Miranda had seen both Ray and his father on the road, and she thought Ray was not a bad specimen. "At least," Lawrence said, noticing that his daughter was eyeing the young man, "he and his pop have some land. You can't go wrong if you hold a little land. If times go rotten on you, you can sell it off piece by piece just to get by. Why don't you go say hello, Andie?"

She'd introduce herself to Ray Argus as Miranda Harper, though of course he already knew her name, Pianto was so small.

Andie had to admit that with the message having been driven into her head for years and years, it was hard not to think of this young man as a prospective husband. The pressure was on. Ray Argus was handsome on top of it, and he appeared to have the same eyes for her that she had for him. Maybe Ray was under similar pressure.

Lawrence, who was operating a junk shop at the time—the

kind of place where you bought other people's discards or things that had fallen off of trains and trucks—arranged it so that Andie and Ray might be able to spend some time alone together, walking in the woods. Ray's father approved it. He figured that Ray's marrying before he hit twenty-five would be good for the ranch, another pair of hands to help with things. So Lawrence and Miranda walked up the road to the Argus ranch, and Lawrence turned her over to the custody of Mr. Argus and Ray, and Mr. Argus turned them loose on the trail that led to the woods.

Up the trail, at the ridgetop, Ray suddenly stopped and took Andie by the shoulders, kissed her like they'd been going out for months, and gave her a long, hard look in the eyes. He was darkly handsome, especially in the shade of the woods like that, and Andie nearly toppled over from the kiss and the look he was giving her. One of her hands, on its own, went up into his hair and let it course through her fingers.

"You know why they put us out here, don't you," he said. "They want us to get married."

She bowed her head. Ray was a blunt man already. He didn't like wasting time with the dance.

"I guess we could," she said.

"I don't see why not. You're looking. I'm looking. Not getting any more beautiful. Me, I mean."

Andie was only nineteen, Carmen twenty-one. It did seem like there was a sudden urgency about it all. She tried to balance the persistent message of her father and the reassuring one of her mother before she said anything else. She wanted to believe that other men would come along and that she wouldn't look back at Ray from her forties and say, "I should have snapped him up when I had the chance." But a voice inside kept repeating her father's words, that there was nothing worse in life than what might have been, nothing like regret over lost opportunities.

Then Ray Argus told her that a thrilling idea had come to

him as they stood at the edge of the woods and looked out over the ridge at the big green ocean, the horizon like a seam opening up. And he said he didn't want to stop himself from speaking the thought out loud, because she was going to be his wife soon and it was not too early to begin treating her like one. She looked up into his eyes and smiled at the excitement in them. He had his hands on her shoulders, gripping them so she couldn't turn away even if she wanted to when he said this thing to her, and his voice was low when he said it, as low as a secret ought to be. He said, "We should get out of here and never come back. I don't want to ranch cows and get old like my dad. I want to take you someplace and live something else. I mean it, Andie."

It was a slow, dramatic moment, full of potential and limitlessness, the entire earth open to them, and the only thing he had to do was take her and go. But they kissed again, and the moment slipped by, and Andie took him by the hand and gently led him back toward the edge of the woods and home. It might have been the pivot of her entire life.

This is the way she remembered it: They came down off the hilltop holding hands, engaged.

—|—

WITH DIFFICULTY, SHE swung her legs out of the bed and planted her bare feet on the floor. It felt cold and rough. A shiver swooped up her body, tingling the top of her head, and the pounding behind her eyes increased so rapidly that she had to clench her jaw and put her head between her knees. When she finally managed to stand up, the dizziness made her wobble and swoon. The tray would be too heavy to carry, she knew it.

She made her way across the room to the window, all that light blinding her and the sounds from outdoors echoing in her ears. Yanked on the blind tassel and pulled it down so far that the wooden roll underneath was exposed. Just then, Cameron opened the door and stuck his head in.

"You're up."

"Car made me," she said. "I'm supposed to get the tray downstairs to the kitchen somehow."

"I'll take it for you," he said. "She's gone now. She'll never know."

Andie knew she ought to at least try to carry the tray, but Cameron's offer was too enticing. It made her sigh in relief. He came over and draped a sweater around her shoulders, brought her slippers to step into. Twenty-one and full of all the right gestures, she thought. My good boy.

Bill's leaving had been hard on him too, she knew, but he was under his father's management and that meant he had to buck up and be a man about it. Ray wouldn't tolerate moping. He'd take a tow chain to the boy's shins if he showed any signs of moping about his brother, and Miranda had even heard him say—her own husband and Bill's father—"If he sets foot on this property ever again, I'll have a rifle bead on him and the sheriff on the phone to listen to whatever happens."

Ray wouldn't speak Bill's name anymore. Called him any kind of awful name that came to mind, but never Bill or William, like he used to do to make his points.

"You want me to help you downstairs?" Cameron asked.

She wanted to say yes, but there was still a heavy sense of dread in her, dwelling like a tick swollen on her blood. Couldn't do it. The room was safe. Quiet. And her son's kindness made her want to fall to the floor and cry and tremble and quiet down when he put his hands on her to get her back into the bed. He stood there, so thin and lanky, uncomfortable with himself, she could tell, his collar loose around his neck, his elbows like double knots in lengths of rope. He had a hand out as if to lead her from the room and down the stairs, but all she could do was shake her head quickly and lean toward the bed like somebody in the water reaching for a lifesaver's oar handle.

"Maybe tomorrow," she said, and he dropped his hand as she let herself fall back.

Thankfully, he didn't give her a sad, parting look as he left with the tray. He said that he and Ray would be out in the pastures the rest of the day, so not to worry, but he did her the favor of keeping his back to her.

The door closed behind him, and she was safe in the dark again.

CARMEN WAS BACK that evening to cook a dinner for Ray and Cam. She brought a plate up to the room and stood there with it in her hands for the longest time, waiting, Andie was sure, for a confession. Andie wasn't about to give one. She stayed on her side with her mouth partly open.

"So you managed to get your breakfast tray down there, I saw."

"Yes." Andie turned her face away from Carmen.

"No you didn't."

There wasn't any point in fighting her. "How do you know I didn't?"

"Because I figure you'd still be down there if you had, sacked out on the couch from the strain of it. You got Cameron to do it, didn't you."

"He offered. I didn't get him to."

Carmen helped to prop her up on pillows, kissed her forehead. "He's a good kid and he's trying to help you out, but you need to get back on your feet, Andie. Your husband is making me nuts. There's no pleasing that man. He expects beef Wellington when I'm making, look here, grilled cheese. I don't know how the hell you've managed to keep from killing him in his sleep, I honestly don't."

Andie was able to laugh a little at the thought. "Don't think it hasn't occurred to me."

"Well, then," Carmen began. She set the tray on a side table and pulled up a chair to feed her sister. "Why don't you tell me how you planned to do it. What's the weapon of choice?"

"Carmen."

"Come on, I'd tell you! In fact, I'll admit I should have nailed Melvin with a baseball bat when I had the chance. I don't know why I didn't."

Carmen cut the grilled cheese sandwich into small pieces and fed one to Andie. It was rare that she spoke Melvin's name anymore.

"I'd have poisoned him, I think," Andie said with her mouth full. "A little here and there. He gobbles his food."

"I noticed. You could have gotten away with it."

Carmen gave her a sly face. "Daddy wouldn't have liked it, would he."

"I don't think so."

"But you'd never have to *tell* him you did it," said Carmen.

"That sounds like Mom talking."

"It might as well be, honey."

Andie wanted to cry. Mama and Daddy dead and buried, the little house along the stream falling down on itself, and Bill gone. What was the point in worrying about lost opportunities when all of *this* had been ahead?

She felt her sister patting her shoulder. A sweet, tender touch. "You'll take your breakfast tray down tomorrow, I bet," Carmen said.

When Carmen was gone, Andie took Bill's postcard from under her pillows, an unwise act, she knew, but one that she had performed at least once each day since it had arrived. On the picture side was a tarnished sepia view labeled DEVIL'S GOLF COURSE, DEATH VALLEY, and on the back were Bill's words in black ink. So many words that they filled the white space and crawled up along the edges of the small card, controlled block letters spelling out an abrupt new permanence. "There's empty mountains on all sides," he wrote. "Cragged, cubed, wasted, and violent. The ground under my feet is hard packed and rightly hot. Bleached bones, wide desert flats without water, salt white. Predators all around, looking for small things to kill and eat. There is no way out of here once you're in."

All of these words, but none said why he went, or when or whether he planned to come back. The postcard left more to be explained than it explained. She was dying from the obscurity of it.

She believed she'd never mend. Afraid she'd never see him again.

IT FELT VERY much like her introduction into this house nearly twenty-five years before, when she found herself away from home for the first time and in the hands of Ray and the elder Arguses. Her father had moved a few things up there for her, just personal things, a few pieces of furniture, some pictures. And there was this almost formal handing-over ceremony outside the house, Lawrence ejecting Andie from the truck and Ray taking her hand and pulling her up onto the porch that overlooked all those acres of grazing pasture. Ray's parents stood back a bit, not offering so much as a hug or a peck on the cheek for her, and then the men began hauling the things inside. They all ate pretty much in silence that night, and then later, in the same room where Andie found herself paralyzed now, she cried so hard beside her new husband that she couldn't fall asleep.

What had loomed over her all night that night was something like a premonition, a view nearly as sharp and clear as a movie, that she had just abdicated opportunities that she could never begin to understand. It wasn't a shame to admit that she didn't love Ray. There he was, lying beside her, young and lean and handsome and full of strength, but there was nothing in him that made her feel something powerful. She was still young enough to believe that such a thing existed, yet, without giving it enough thought, she had sacrificed it when she married him. He had already made love to her earlier in the night, in the dark that she insisted on because no man had ever seen her naked before, and the overwhelming feeling she got when he did that wasn't one of abiding love or passion but of responsibility.

That's how her life began in the old Argus house.

Bill was born within the first year, Cameron three years after that. Ever since, her concerns had been how to keep them fat and happy, how to keep Ray from slipping in and out of his rages when things weren't going well, how to keep from falling apart in public when somebody looked at her with a face that seemed to ask, Weren't you supposed to have a greater shake?

The blessing—and this was where she did feel sorry for Carmen—was that she loved her boys terribly. Watching them grow up and become such dark, beautiful young men was the greatest joy she ever had in life. It was a good thing she had managed to do, bringing them into the world.

Which was why, at this time in her life, sick in her bed in the dark and with Bill gone, the disappointment was more than she could bear.

IN THE MIDDLE of the night Ray was snoring openmouthed, frowning, as he had done all their lives together. This was not a new thing to endure. But with everything in a state of collapse now, Andie looked at him with annoyance and objectivity. Here was the man she had married but hadn't loved, the man who had fathered her boys, the man who wouldn't allow Bill back in the house even if he walked up the drive on his knees, the man whose touch was never lighter than the one he used on his animals. Andie pulled herself out of the bed and stood beside it.

She walked out of the room and into the hallway, looked into Cameron's room and found him sleeping soundly, lying on his stomach with his pillow clutched near his face. He didn't frown in his sleep, gentle at heart. He didn't have much anger in him yet.

Andie went barefooted down the stairs, feeling as if the darkness gave her strength. Maybe it was knowing that there was nobody else awake to look at her. The shame and disappointment couldn't be seen in the dark, the regret that she knew had to show in her eyes. It felt like an infection, something raw. Others had to be able to see it. At the bottom of the stairs she paused for a moment with her hand on the banister knob, the grit on the floor stinging her feet. The clock was ticking irregularly, it seemed to her, long moments between the knocks of the pendulum, and without any light she was unable to see the hands, only the white face of it. It didn't matter to her what time it was anyway.

She walked out onto the front porch and down the few steps to the dirty, pebbled apron beneath and looked up into the sky. The stars were clear and brilliant that night, almost spinning to her eye, in dizzying motion against the treetops and the silhouette of the barn. The cool air swept up inside her nightgown and made her skin prickle. Walking ahead, she held herself with her arms and didn't mind the sharpness of the gravel on the soles of her feet, or the cold, or the openness of the night with the sky wide and dark above her head.

What happened after tonight didn't matter to her anymore. She believed that she would live on and run her household and provide for Cam and Ray, and perhaps she would be able after this to put on a face and go into Pianto and meet people without fearing their judgment. She would not try to meet the Hayes family again, though, and she would not answer questions about Bill. She would try to be a source of strength for Annie. She would live with this pain inside her, carry on with the secret shame of it.

She went across the cold grass of the pasture, dew on her shins and the hem of her nightgown growing heavy from the moisture, until she came to the edge of a small ravine where a drainage stream ran. Sometimes the cows walked down into the stream on hot days, and they eased themselves into it and cooled their bellies in there. She had seen that happen. There weren't many ways for them to be relieved from the heat, with so little shade on the land, so they came to the stream and put themselves in it, even though there wasn't much water flowing in the summer and the effort was not much more than a little act of desperation. They did it anyway.

Andie stepped down the bank and into the cold water. It hardly came up to her ankles, but it felt good on her skin. Her body had been so raw lately, infected, inflamed, that the water was like a cure. It would restore her. She stood there on the rocks, letting it flow through her toes, praying that it might ease her fever and calm her fears and relieve her of the shame and grief and guilt and the sense of failure that had been inside her for so much longer than Bill's leaving. She couldn't begin to understand how much she had already lost in her life.

Nobody could see her from the house, where she was standing. She was invisible to the world. It was not a difficult thing, because of that, to let her knees go and to ease herself down into the water and lie back in it, facing the black sky and stars with the charge of cool, sweet water flowing over her shoulders and neck and down her chest and belly and hips as if she were nothing more than a stone obstructing it.

HAPPINESS—1958

Carmen

Carmen Harper's father was big on getting his girls married and out of the house as quickly as he could—that much all of Pianto knew—and he managed to get the younger daughter, Andie, signed up with a local rancher in short order. Sixteen years later it was the older girl, Carmen, who appeared to have developed unrealistic standards somewhere along the way, probably because her mother was always neutralizing Mr. Harper's advice with counsel of her own. In any case, with a daughter in her thirties still taking up space in the little house by the stream, eating his meat and potatoes, God love her, he was always on the lookout for a man who could step in and take Carmen off his hands, a man who at least appeared to meet the ridiculous standards she had worked up.

When Carmen heard that her father had invited a man over for dinner one evening in 1952, she threatened to spend the evening someplace else, up at Andie's maybe. She owed her nephews Bill and Cameron some attention.

"A man," she said. "You act like I'm desperate."

"No, you're not desperate," Larry told her. "*I'm* desperate."

She was starting to put on her coat to go when Larry gave her every detail he could remember about the man, who had turned up in the Pianto bar that afternoon. His name was Melvin. He was a pilot recently back from Korea, shot down over the Sea of Japan and having recuperated in Tokyo. He had medals, Larry said. Flew these new jet planes that could snap an old prop job right out of the sky and then lead a hell of a chase getting away. Melvin had been shot down through no fault of his own; the goddamn engine failed on him and gave his pursuers time to get him in their sights. He parachuted into the water and was just lucky to be picked up by Americans and not those yellow-skinned bastards he'd been shooting at.

"His term," Larry said. "Not mine."

Carmen perked up when she heard that this Melvin had fine firm hands and dazzling eyes. They were part of the array of standards that had kept her single all this time. To her own mind, a woman couldn't be expected to love a man with skinny little hands and bland eyes.

"I'll stick around," she said. "And he'd better not turn out to be a bowwow."

When Melvin arrived, Carmen nearly fainted at the sight of him. He was by far the most attractive man she had ever laid eyes on. There was nothing immediately observable about him that didn't meet her many criteria for a perfect husband. That he was a war hero didn't mean much to her, but that he was stunningly attractive and relatively down-to-earth did. She admitted to being shallow when it came to certain matters.

Her mother served a boiled corned beef and cabbage dinner, and all Carmen could think about was that she'd be farting half the night and that would put Melvin off. Larry brought out some good ale he'd been waiting to drink, but Carmen decided to abstain so she'd be of clear mind when, inevitably, Larry suggested that she and Melvin walk into town together after dinner.

"Japan is a beautiful country," Melvin said with the confidence of a man who had seen the world, "but I have a problem with those people. They're a scary bunch. Yellow sonsa bitches."

Carmen lowered her eyes. "I can imagine," she said. Not terribly proud of herself. Melvin smiled at her again, so charmingly that all she could think about was that the war was over now and he would soften as the years went by. She could help soften him.

"Why don't you two walk into town," Larry said. "Nice evening out. Get to know each other a little bit."

She didn't understand quite how she knew it, but as she and Melvin left the house and started down the narrow lane toward Pianto, it hit her that this man was going to be her husband. It was a strong, clear, undeniable glimpse of the future that had come to her. The only thing that could obliterate it was a tragic death, his or hers, and there was little chance of that. They were both young and healthy.

At thirty-seven she still considered herself young. Besides, she could pass for thirty-two, she believed, and if that was the worst of the deceptions it would take to marry this man, she was willing to deceive. Her younger sister, by God, looked five years older than Carmen. Poor Andie with her hands full up there on that ranch.

Melvin had walked her halfway into town before he stopped and turned her to face him. She looked up into his eyes—sweet, dazzling, delightful, trustworthy eyes. His hands were on her upper arms, squeezing lightly. He said, "You are a hell of a beautiful girl, Carmen Harper," and kissed her.

It was the first time in her life she recognized how lovely a springtime dusk is in the place where she grew up.

NOT MANY MONTHS later they were married in the little white Pianto church. Larry got his wish. The last girl was out of the house. It was just him and Trudy now. Melvin moved Carmen over to the other side of Santa Rosa, into a bungalow with a tidy grass yard and aluminum-framed windows and a paved asphalt driveway. Carmen was thinking of buying a garbage disposal. Melvin sold insurance and took a lot of business trips. Everyone was waiting for the news of an addition to the family.

The one thing she realized after years alone was that her happiness was a fragile thing, that it might not have come into existence at all. If her father weren't such an afternoon boozer, if Melvin hadn't been passing through Pianto on his way back from a client, if the evening hadn't been as softly warm and sweet-scented, she might not have found her way to this happiness.

Before she knew it, they had been together six years.

When Melvin was off on one of his trips, Carmen tended to spend the time with her sister. She'd drive across the valley and stop in Pianto, drag Andie into the café for a meat-loaf lunch, and then go back to Andie's house for coffee. Cameron, and sometimes Bill, would be out working with their father, hardly able to take the time to say hello to her, though Cameron was always sweet enough to come up to the house and kiss her on the cheek. Bill now had his hands full with a small ranch of his own, Annie and the new baby boy, often distracted enough when Carmen was around that he didn't even come in to say hello. He'd hardly been married a year.

Ray would finally came into the house, reeking of sweat and cow dung, and he'd offer not much more than a nod while he poured iced tea down his throat and wiped the back of his neck with one of Andie's nice dish towels. Carmen never really cared for him. He always struck her as cold and not very smart, but this was the man Andie was stuck with and it wasn't Carmen's place to make waves over him. She tried to be polite anyway.

One day she was at the house with Andie when Ray came in as usual, swabbed himself with a dish towel, poured tea down his throat, and said, "How're things over there at Happy Acres, Car?"

"Things are ducky, Ray, thanks for asking. We might be getting a new Buick. Melvin's lined up for his bonus pretty soon."

Ray had what Carmen thought of as a Depression face. It was the face of those men who stood in soup lines and slept under newspaper. The really difficult thing about him, aside from when his temper flared, was that it was so hard to tell what he was thinking. He played his hand close, known to bluff too. Carmen preferred men like Melvin, who wore his emotions on the outside, told you what he was up to. He didn't feel like he had to be a pillar of strength all the time, didn't hide his thoughts. Just last week, before he left on his trip to Chicago, he said, "I don't know what I'd have done if I hadn't met you, Carmen," and she was touched and amazed to see a tear in his eye. She flung her arms around his neck and pasted lipstick all over his cheeks.

"Funny he didn't mention a Buick," Ray said. "I just ran into him in Petaluma, and he didn't say a thing about it. You'd've thought he'd run that up the flagpole to see how I took it, me and my old trucks, eh?"

"He's in Chicago, Ray. Couldn't have been him in Petaluma."

A peculiar grin spread across Ray's face. He straddled a backward chair and leaned toward her with his elbows up like wings. "Is that what he told you, Car? He'd be in the old Windy City?"

Andie was trying to tidy up after her husband, wiping his spills and footprints on the floor. Ray twisted around to look at her. "This is getting interesting all of a sudden, Andie. Car thinks old Melvin's in Chicago, but I just caught him down in Petaluma."

"He's not due back till Friday," Carmen said. Her fingers pressed involuntarily against her lips. She could hear the blood rushing like rapids in her ears. Then Andie's calming hands were on her shoulders, and she bent down and whispered, "Don't listen to him."

"Well, God knows, I'm an uneducated piece of shit, but up till now I thought I knew my brother-in-law on sight, and considering that we talked for more than ten minutes. I mean, *Jesus,* I must be *ill.*"

It took some doing, but in a while Ray had convinced her that Melvin was not in Chicago. There was no reason Ray would want to stir up trouble where there was none, was there? He wouldn't just cook this up to get her goat. She wanted to hope, maybe, that he would, but then she recalled, the way many deceived wives remember something innocuous now loaded with meaning, that her husband had always insisted on calling *her* every night, not the other way around. He said he didn't know when he'd get back to his hotel, what with meetings and everything, so he'd call her. She had the hotel phone number back at home. It was all she could think to do, get back there and phone him right away. Proof was the only thing that would satisfy her.

"I have to go," she said, and Andie tried to stop her, saying maybe she ought to sleep on the guest bed that night. Carmen declined.

"Say hey to Melvin for me," Ray chimed as she left. Andie cracked him one on the arm.

When Carmen got back to the little bungalow and phoned the Chicago hotel, she was told that her husband was not a guest there; perhaps he had changed his plans.

"I see," she said weakly. Just like a woman would say in the movies. And she stared off into space the way that woman would too. All she could see was a wall of fog, smothering her happiness.

+

ON FRIDAY, CARMEN picked up her husband at the train station, where apparently he'd parked himself beforehand to appear as if he had just arrived on one of the trains. The moment she saw him she felt a wave of nausea and had to stop and take a deep breath. He was smiling, waving, acting as if he had in fact been on a long trip to Chicago. He wore a tie and jacket, had his suitcase and portfolio, looked in every way like a man who was coming home. He limped toward her, the old war injury aflare.

When they came together, Carmen raised herself on her toes to kiss him, and she smelled him, and loved his smell, and she told herself that she didn't want to confront him now, here in front of people. She wanted them to look like a reunited couple, a happy man and wife. She was forty-three, and the idea that her young marriage might be in trouble was too much to admit in public. He kissed her and whispered something lovely into her ear, so that she could make room in her mind for playing him a little bit longer, pretending there was a game between them.

"How was Chicago?" she asked, and he walked beside her beaming.

"Hot as hell," Melvin said, already making his way ahead of her toward the car. "They're crazy to live back there. How's things here?"

"Oh, fine."

"Hey, that's good." All jolliness and love patter. "Keep the home fires burning for me?"

A few days went by, during which Carmen tried to maintain their normal routines, but it amazed her that Melvin was such a good conniver that he didn't show any signs of it. He made up tales of Chicago and his business meetings. He must have created the people out of his imagination, given them names and faces and histories and exploits, and he described meals he had and nights of overdrinking with insurance colleagues and a couple of old war buddies he knew back there. He went to a baseball game, he said, citing the score and a couple of plays, the starting pitchers, the weather.

In a way, Carmen thought, it was quite a work of art. Yet, of course, she was devastated. The deeper Melvin's lie became, the more certain she was that her happiness had been an illusion all along and she was better off the old maid, unaware of any higher exhilaration than plain comfort.

She saw Andie from time to time in the days that followed Melvin's return. Her sister was a sweet and sensitive woman and didn't raise the issue until Carmen did. They were at the café in Pianto, having their usual lunch together, and Carmen said bluntly, "He's scaring me, Andie. I live with a man who's able to make up an entire world out of nothing but the practical need for it. I'm scared to death."

"Don't have children with him" was Andie's first advice. Carmen had the sense that her sister was voicing a little regret of her own.

"Oh, Andie!" She felt her eyes beginning to tingle, and that in turn damaged her pride because one thing that Carmen was not was a weeper. Her father had seen to that as she grew up, making the shame of crying worse than the thing that had caused her to cry in the first place.

"We'll follow him next time he leaves town," Andie said. "We'll see where he goes and who he meets." Then she paused and gave Carmen a firm but sensitive look. "If you think you're ready to find out."

It seemed a bit drastic, to lurk around and trail her husband, especially when trust is the watchword of a good marriage. "I could just ask him where he was," Carmen said. "I could say, 'I tried to call you one night, and they said you never checked in. And Ray thought he saw you in Petaluma.' "

"And he'll lie to you, sweetie."

When she wanted to, meek little Andie could nail down the truth of things.

"Of course he will," Carmen admitted. "He'll come up with something really good, from what I've seen."

"Of course he will."

—|—

THERE WAS THE most provocative photo of Melvin on their bedroom dressing table. In a stamped-tin frame her mother had given her as a wedding present, it had been taken on the Tarmac of his air base in Korea, and there he was in his jumpsuit and helmet, cords and wires and hoses dripping from him, and there were his sparkling smile and brilliant eyes, his magnificent hands dangling at his hips. To imagine that she would have one day married a man like him. It was so dreamlike as to approach one of his own fantastic deceptions.

Carmen loved the photograph, down to its small cracked corner, and now she looked at it even more often than she usually did. The man looking out at her was no longer a real man. He was something that had never lived, a creation of her imagination. In that sense, she asked herself, am I any better than he is? Didn't I do this to myself?

When he made love to her now, she couldn't bring herself to look into his eyes, as if *she* were the one with something to hide. She turned her head to the side while he moved, and when, firmly, he held her face in his hands and smiled down on her, she cast her eyes on the ceiling, acting faint.

His kisses tasted bitter now. She was falling out of love, she could feel it.

A FEW WEEKS after the Chicago trip, Melvin announced he was off to Dallas for a week. Carmen told Andie immediately, and they made plans to meet at the train station. Their plan was simply to see where Melvin went if he didn't get on that train.

Carmen drove him to the station that morning, and she found herself hoping that she was wrong. She imagined him climbing aboard the train, waving at her as it pulled away, blowing kisses to her through the window. But even this modest fantasy was destroyed almost as soon as they arrived, when Melvin said, "Looks like I got the time wrong, sweetie. Train doesn't leave for another hour. You might as well head on home, huh?"

She stood there by the car, her insides abroil. She wanted to slap him, is what she wanted to do. She wanted to say, "Why don't I just take you where you're really going, and we can get this thing over with." But she didn't. Instead she accepted his kiss, told him she had the hotel phone number in Dallas, and promised to be a good girl.

"And I'll call you every night, right?" Melvin said. He worked his big square chin back and forth. "I have no idea when I'll be back at the room, you know."

"I know."

And she watched as he walked confidently into the station with his portfolio under one arm and his suitcase hanging at his side. He looked like a man who should be easy to love.

She drove to a far corner of the parking lot, where Andie was already waiting for her. Carmen told her what Melvin had said, and all Andie could do was shake her head and cup Carmen's face with her palm. "It'll feel better when you know for sure."

"I don't think it will. I think I'll throw up, baby."

"That's all right. You go ahead and throw up if you have to."

It was only a few minutes before they saw the inevitable figure of Carmen's husband emerging from the station. An older blue sedan was waiting for him, and he threw his luggage into the trunk and got in the passenger side. Carmen couldn't make out who was driving from where they were, but there was a long pause before the car pulled away from the curb, and the implications of that were too awful to think about. A long, lingering kiss?

Andie drove because Carmen was too nervous. They stayed a few car lengths behind the sedan as it left the station and headed out the main road. After a few stoplights they were on the open road, heading south toward Petaluma. Carmen felt as if she were viewing her life on the screen at a drive-in theater, here through the windshield of Andie's truck. It was a mystery, apparently, and a tragedy (but only if somebody got killed in the process, and he might), and it was moving at a good clip, the movie of her life. Her husband was up ahead in that dark blue car, with a stranger driving, the good little wifey back home waiting for the phone call from Dallas.

"It's a woman, I know it," Carmen said. Saying it made her feel better about learning the truth. "Some goddamn slut he picked up on one of his trips I bet. A home wrecker of twenty-five, what do you want to bet?"

"I'm withholding judgment," Andie said. "I want to give him the benefit of the doubt until we know."

"God, you're so goddamn innocent!"

"I'm the one who told *you* to check up on him, Carmen."

"Then just admit it, there's a girl behind the wheel up there, and she's fucking my husband!"

"Carmen! I barely tolerate Ray talking like that."

"Drive," Carmen ordered, her heart dying on its vine.

The rest happened very quickly and in disorienting segments, Carmen's mind reeling with every turn. Entering Petaluma. Driving the pretty, tree-lined streets. Stopping down the block from a white bungalow where the sedan stopped, a house not much different from her own. Andie held her hand as they watched Melvin get out of the car and unload his luggage, and then he went around to the driver's side and stuck his head in the window, receiving, Carmen knew, another kiss. He pulled back, laughing. The door opened. A petite woman climbed out, a dark-haired woman, a woman with the features of the Japanese or the Korean or the Chinese, Carmen couldn't tell. She turned toward Melvin and kissed him right there in the driveway, and then she opened the back door and lifted a three- or four-year-old boy from the car.

"I'll be right back," Carmen whispered.

Her sister didn't try to stop her. Carmen left the truck door open and took a few steps toward them, her feet somehow hauling her along. There must have been lovely neighborhood sounds all around, but all she could hear was the refrain in her mind, What have you done to me? It was almost musical. A ditty, a chant. In no time at all she found herself standing at the foot of the driveway with her hands clenched in balls at her side, Melvin's arm around the waist of the Korean woman and the boy clinging to her opposite hand, which had a gold band on its third finger. The boy looked more like the woman than he looked like Melvin. Carmen latched on to that detail as if it would be something to relish later. The three of them walked away from her, toward the house, unaware of her presence.

"Melvin," she said, and her voice cracked. She stood there and watched as her husband and the woman turned at the same time, and their faces fell, and the boy spun and offered up a gleeful smile.

"Aw, shit," Melvin said, "all the ever-lovin' shit of it."

She almost felt bad for mortifying him like that. She almost felt bad for having to know. If only she'd had the common sense to stay home and wait for the call from Dallas. If only her father had never laid eyes on the man in that Pianto tavern, and the evening hadn't been so softly warm and sweet-scented. None of this ever would have happened.

Carmen walked away from them and got back into the truck. Andie drove away so fast that Melvin hardly had a chance to knock at the fender and cry something as they streaked by him. There he was—she couldn't help twisting around to look—trotting in the street as they flew away.

CEREMONIES—1957

Big Don

Every Saturday morning Big Don Hayes drove his Cadillac into Pianto to have his red handlebar mustache trimmed and his chin and cheeks shaved by the lone barber in town, a man miscast in the role because he hated small talk, idle conversation, barbershop chatter. His name was McCloud, and his aversion to chitchat was all right with Big Don, because Don preferred to do all the talking anyway. He had things he wanted to get off his chest—ideas, plans, rearrangements, imaginings. And since the barbershop often hosted a gathering of other whiskered men to listen to him, he liked it even more than the county meetings where he sometimes tested his rhetoric (he had run for office ten years before, after all, never lost the love of hearing himself talk). Big Don had no way of knowing that the moment he left McCloud's barbershop, the other men grumbled about what a pompous ass he was and exchanged gossip about his daughter, Annie, and the older Argus boy, who were busy finding private places around the county to screw. If Big Don figured it out, they postulated, either the girl or the Argus boy would soon be dead, or possibly both, and Big Don would wind up in San Quentin—he had that kind of temper.

This particular Saturday, though, Don Hayes was not in a rhetorical mood when he went into McCloud's shop, and there was not much of an audience anyway, only McCloud himself and another man whose name Don didn't know. He didn't know a lot of men's names, because he couldn't be bothered to learn them. Biggest landowner in the Russian River Valley, was he supposed to pay attention to these dirt farmers and small-scale cowmen who hung around Pianto's supply stores and low-life watering holes? He had more acreage and more head of cattle than most of them put together, something of a dynasty, built by his grandfather, maintained by his father, and now one hundred percent under his control.

"McCloud," he said, taking his seat in the swivel chair. McCloud already had a mug of shaving soap whipped up, and he began to strop his straight razor on the leather belt that hung from the back of the chair. Big Don exposed the white of his neck. "McCloud," he said, voice going pensive. "I just got word my old man's knocking at death's door."

"Sorry to hear that, Mr. Hayes. Your pop, though, he's getting up there in age, isn't he?"

"He's seventy-four and can't remember his own name, and I hear he shits in a diaper and can't chew his own food anymore. He's been down in that home so long I almost can't recall what it was like having him around the ranch."

"Shame," said McCloud. "Shame, a good man like that . . ."

"A good man." Big Don blew a column of hot air through his nose. You have no idea whether the son of a bitch was a good man or not, he thought. Kissed his ass every week the same way you kiss mine, and I half imagine you're not too unhappy to hear that death is in the neighborhood.

"He tipped well, anyway," the barber said. "Told a fine joke."

"Grief." Big Don tried to raise his head so he could look McCloud in the eye, but the barber was applying a subtle yet firm pressure against his head. "What do you do about the grief—"

"Well, Mr. Hayes, the grief, you just have to let the grief come, I suppose."

"That's not what I'm saying," Big Don barked. "If you'da let me finish, you'da seen my point. My point is—I'm not feeling any grief. There's none to be had in here."

The radio seemed to raise its own volume, crackling with a baseball game. Big Don felt the lather hit his neck and cheeks and then the scrape of the razor, McCloud's soft fingers on his skin. It would be preferable to forget about everything and nap under the hot towel later, but he couldn't get the thought out of his head that he ought to dig down and find some grief, even if it was mostly ceremonial.

As far as he could recall, it had been nearly two years since he'd seen the man.

—|—

BIG DON HAYES was one of those men brought up in comfortable circumstances who is used to having things his way. Maybe it's a corollary of the circumstances: When things are that comfortable, you don't know what it means *not* to have things your way. The Hayes men had been like that for a long time—Big Don, the dying Don Sr., patriarch Sam Hayes (dead a long, long time by then)—they were all accustomed to having it dropped into their laps. These men also shared the characteristic of others similar to them of not giving a rat's ass whether people liked them or not. They could convince themselves that, at the minimum, they had the respect of others. Land and money and civic clout brought that in without any extra effort. But to Big Don Hayes, whether the little men of Pianto loved his hairy bottom didn't make a bit of difference. He wasn't about to modify himself to try to get it either way. He'd run his ranch like a feudal lord, he'd call the shots in his purview, he'd chew up and swallow the smaller creatures that wandered into his path. It was the way he was raised.

"Pop's dying," he said out loud, back behind the wheel of the Caddie. "I wish I could give a flying fuck and make a big deal over it."

Troubling, it was. He'd been able to put his father out of his mind for so long that it was difficult to picture his face the way it used to be, though the last time he and Mabel had driven down to the Oakland convalescent home to see his dad, Don was shocked at the decline in the old man. His eyes had gone flat and empty, his mouth hung open as if the hinge of his jaw were in need of tightening, and his face was whiskered and gaunt. They had him dressed in a baggy hospital gown that showed too much of his scrawny chest. You could have picked him up by the scruff of the neck and tossed him down a laundry chute, he was so little. Don Sr., all dried up and empty inside.

So Big Don had put him out of his thoughts for a couple of years. Gone on about his business, which used to be his father's, and Don's dedication to it was something that Don Sr. would have understood.

From the barbershop Don drove out to the coastal highway and then north. There was some ranchland he wanted to put a bid on, high up on the ridge that overlooked the ocean. There might come a day, he imagined, when he'd want to move up there to live, a spot where you can look out in any direction and see no limits to your range, the Pacific horizon, the layers and layers of green hills fading back toward the east. He liked the old way of determining who owned what land—that everything I can see from here where I'm standing is mine, okay?

He turned off the highway and started up the narrow road into the hills. There were no trees, it was so windblown. This time of year, early spring, the grasses were brilliantly green and behaved in the wind like water.

I'll bid on the ranch up here, he told himself, and I'll win it. I'll bury the old man here. Bring up a few head and hire a Mexican to maintain the place. In a few years Mabel and I will come up to live—she'll despise it, of course—and the goddamn ocean will be our front yard. I'll build her a little Xanadu and get her a goddamn maid to dust her porcelain doodads—that'll shut her up.

He got out of the car at the ridgetop, taking a careful look at the lay of the ranchland, the fencing, the drainage—it was all a mess. But there was the ocean sprawling out before him, and it was as big a thing as he'd ever owned in his life. His father would be happy to be buried out here, with his feet aimed at China and the sun setting on his ass every night.

Big Don stood with his hands on his hips, staring out at the sharp black line where the water and sky came together, allowing the wind to buffet him and worry his mustache, and something terrible overcame him with a suddenness that made him think he might be going mad. "Papa," he said, feeling a wave of emotion flood him, his mouth pulling back in an involuntary grimace, tears spilling from his eyes. There was nobody around to hear him, but he tried to contain the sobbing that his lungs expelled from his chest. He spun around and walked in a quick, stiff-legged gait back toward the car.

"Goddamn wind," he said. "Stung my eyes."

He didn't want to admit it, because that's the kind of man he was, but he'd gotten his way again. He wanted to think he had room for some grief in his heart over the old man, and now he knew he was capable.

THE PUNK BILL Argus was at the house when he got there, little pissant who wanted into his daughter's skivvies. The only thing Big Don admired about Argus was that he didn't have an obsequious bone in him, didn't know how to bow and scrape, couldn't bring himself to say yessir and nosir if his life depended on it. But Don knew this kind of kid, and more than anything he knew the kid would never amount to much. A congenital nonachiever like his father.

Annie gave Big Don a look as if to say, Don't start, please. She and Argus were sitting together in the living room with a bridal magazine splayed open on their laps.

"Aw, Jesus," said Don, and he passed through the room without commenting. He heard the young man say, "Nice shave, Mr. Hayes. McCloud does a good job."

Annie was too pretty, smart, and rich to settle for the likes of him. Don believed this was a phase she was going through, a phase designed to confound her father more than anything. Don guessed that Bill Argus couldn't possibly be her idea of a catch, but he knew that Annie Hayes would be the best thing that had ever happened to the Argus family, down there off the Pianto–Valley Ford Road. Ray Argus would dance a fucking jig if anything came of this. He had about fifty head of anemic cows and a dusty, sparsely vegetated ranch with outbuildings that looked like dying animals. Bill, his older son, was a smart enough kid, but he couldn't compete with the range of possible mates for Annie, who was now almost nineteen, beautiful, and bound for a comfortable life. Don was working on a brokered deal with a state senator friend of his, who had an eligible son headed for law school, success written all over him. That's the kind of union that could elevate the whole family, a matter of positioning.

Mabel was in the kitchen sawing on an overcooked roast. "Don," she said, "don't get snippy, but you need to pour yourself a drink."

"It's not even twelve noon. I don't drink until sundown anymore."

"Well today you can *stop* drinking at sundown," she said. "Annie and Bill are getting married."

"Oh no they are not."

"They just told me."

"I'll make sure it don't happen," Don said. When he was under particular kinds of pressure, his grammar got all shot to hell. "I'll pull the fucking rug right out from under them, Mabe."

He did pause to take his wife's counsel, poured himself a tall scotch and downed a third of it in one swallow. A shame it wouldn't do the trick instantly. He gave Mabel a determined look and then spun on his brogan heels and pounded down the hallway back toward the living room. Mabel called for him and tried to get him to reconsider, but she should have known better than to expect results. He was going to go have his way.

"Did Mama tell you?" Annie asked. She was beaming prettily, lovely little redheaded thing. He was awfully proud of her. It was a shame she had to have her heart broken so early in life, but she was raised in this house and knew that when he said no he meant no and that he only did it for her own good. These were household laws, carved upon tablets milled from local granite.

"Yes, hon, she did tell me." Big Don had to sound eerie to the lovers. His teeth showed oddly from beneath his mustache, like Teddy Roosevelt's. Annie, maybe because she knew her father better than anyone besides Mabel, hopped up instantly and threw her arms around his neck, kissed him up and down both sides of his face.

"Say you're happy for me, Pop. I've never been happier in my life."

"Sweetheart, I need to speak with Bill here for a moment."

Annie backed away from him with her fists clutched under her chin, a look of worry starting to paint down from her forehead. Bill was looking at her for telepathic advice, but it was clear he was on his own in this situation. Big Don couldn't hear her now even if she had something constructive to say.

"Stand up, son," Don commanded. The boy's knees seemed to be locked at right angles; he couldn't quite manage. He started coughing as he rose, looking up toward Don at the same time. His eyes were big and full of anxiety, as well they should be, Don thought. When he was finally on his feet—a short lad, a skinny, shorter kid—he extended his hand toward Don for a congratulatory shake from his future father-in-law.

"I just want to tell you, Mr. Hayes," Bill began, but Big Don didn't want to hear that quivering voice speak his daughter's name. He shot one of his big hands at the kid's throat and snagged it tight between his fingers and thumb, squeezing. Immediately Bill's hands went up to try to loosen the grip but he couldn't do it, and Annie's dainty paws flew up to her mouth to muffle a scream. Bill's face went bluish right away, the signs of consciousness draining out of him like the last drips being wringed from a wet cloth. Don lifted the boy so that he was up on tiptoes.

"Tell you what," he said through gritting teeth, "I don't want you marrying my daughter. It's a bad idea. You can drop the whole thing right now, though, and I'll still be your goddamn buddy."

Annie was beating on his shoulders from behind, and in a moment his wife came into view, prying his hand off Bill's throat. She didn't scream and carry on because she knew that only patience worked with Big Don at a time like this. As she pried and Bill threw her a desperate look with his bulging eyes, she said calmly, "You let go of him now, Don. This doesn't help matters, this kind of reaction."

Big Don stood there with his hands at his sides, breathing through his nostrils like an angry bull. He felt like his face was about as red as the boy's. Annie ran to the kid, who'd landed on the sofa with his head thrown back as if waiting for his own shave.

"That's just the way I feel about it," Don announced, and he left the room and returned to the kitchen for the rest of his scotch.

IN PIANTO, DAIRYMEN milked cows by hand, and old Model A pickups could still be seen loaded with bales of hay on the Bodega Highway. It was 1957, but the valley had not changed very much in a hundred years. It had been cow country all that time, although a few radicals had thought to grow apples there too, and a couple of lunatics even put in grapes. Big Don's finned Eldo was the newest, finest piece of machinery in the region, but in all other ways his head was back in the nineteenth century, where his grandfather Sam's had been.

Bill and Annie had gone ahead and married. It was not a thing that Big Don wished to think about much, and not just because it was against his will (they'd threatened to elope) but also because Don Sr. had died a couple of weeks before, casting a lovely pall over things. By then Don had purchased the ranchland atop the ocean ridge, and he had a backhoe brought up there to dig the grave. As it turned out, though, his father had expressly demanded in his will (and he was accustomed to having *his* way too) that he be buried with the other, earlier Hayes men in the Pianto cemetery, surrounded by those old, fragrant eucalyptus trees that stood around, to Don's mind, like a bunch of old women in garish green shawls. Don found himself stuck with a useless hole in the ground up at the new ranch, a hole that overlooked the front yard, the Pacific Ocean. As a reminder of all this head- and heartache, he decided to leave the hole like it was. It would fill with water in the rainy season, waiting for its purpose to come clear.

What he'd done, as a way of expressing his sense of violation over this marriage, was to remove Annie from his will. Harsh, perhaps, but let her understand that there are consequences to our actions and that they can be substantial. Annie wasn't perturbed by it when he told her, but Mabel went livid on him, had not spoken to him in anything but monosyllables in a couple of weeks. Big Don outlined his strategy, which was as follows (and he hoped she could at least *try* to understand it): He'd set up Annie and the Argus punk in a house he owned over on the Freestone Road, a fine enough house with twenty acres of sloping land that could be used for grazing, if nothing else. The two of them would do with it whatever they could—they could plow it up and plant grapes for all he cared—but it was the only thing she'd ever get from Big Don for defying him.

Them's the breaks, he told her, and she gave him a dignified smile and kissed him on the cheek. The Argus punk was grateful too, but he had the sense to back out of the frame and let father and daughter come to some kind of understanding.

Annie said, with infuriating serenity, "You'll realize someday that I married him for love, Pop. I never cared about the will. And I love you for who you are too, not for your money."

Where did she get these piddling clichés, he wondered. I thought I brought her up to be sharper than this.

"Sweetheart," he counseled, holding her in a bear hug, "I hope you can figure out a way to live with disappointment. You picked a goddamn hard row to hoe."

She acted as if he had no idea Argus had knocked her up. Like he didn't know the way of the world.

—|—

THE REHEARSAL DINNER, thrown by that miserable excuse for a cowman, Ray Argus, was at the VFW hall in Pianto. Argus had had his wife make tubs and tubs of goulash or some such concoction, and there was a meager accordion band that played obscure polkas and limping waltzes. The host monitored the beer kegs so closely that nobody but he could drink enough to get shitfaced, and he did get shitfaced, it appeared to Don, enough to approach and request good terms on a property-improvement loan.

"I could really stand to do something about the drainage in my big pasture, Don, you see." Failing to look him in the eye, of course. "Pools up in heavy rains something awful. Needs attention. And a new truck would be a goddamn godsend, if you know what I mean. New roof on that barn too."

The smell of beer coming out of Ray's mouth made Don want to retch. He blew cigar smoke at the man to back him off a step or two.

Annie and Bill were dancing to the honking music, gazing into each other's eyes. Meanwhile, the younger Argus boy, Cameron (as Don recalled), stood off to the side with a drink and a paper plate of goulash, looking at the crowd all around as though he might flee if anyone approached him for a conversation. An introvert, but maybe it was because he knew his place and knew this was a thing that wasn't going to work. Some younger fellows are blessed with a discomforting wisdom. Lad of sixteen or so, watching his brother go in way over his head.

"Tell you what," Big Don said to Ray Argus. He looped a heavy arm around the man's shoulder, felt his suit coat bind up in the shoulders. "The day you get a penny out of me, my friend, is the day you ambush me on the way to the fucking bank and stick a blade in my chest, okeydokey?"

"I'm gon pretend I dint hear that, Donald." The father of the groom tried to get both his eyeballs on the same track.

"Good for you, Raymond." False civility tasted oddly sweet on his tongue. "And by the way, if your son ever raises a hand to my daughter, he gets butchered and sold for stew meat. You might want to fill him in on the details."

Don looked away from Ray Argus and met the eyes of Cameron from across the room. The boy was taking his measure. Or maybe he'd heard a snippet of the conversation and wanted to watch his old man get a dose of public humiliation. Don imagined it would feel pretty good to either one of the Argus boys.

Ray frowned as Big Don walked away from him. He tried to snag a bit of Don's sleeve but couldn't manage it, and Don thought, Your MO, Argus, grabbing at what you can but always coming up short. Oh, my poor little Annie.

"Word of advice," he said as he approached Cameron, whose face became as worried-looking as a jackrabbit's when you surprise one in the fields.

"Yessir?"

"You strike me as a very smart kid, a wise one. And I don't think you could do better for yourself, considering all the shit I've seen since my daughter got tied up with your family—I don't think you could do better than to get the hell out of this county and make a name for yourself as far away as you can get."

"Thank you," said Cameron. His Adam's apple moved up and down.

"Just a thought," Don replied, and walked on out of the hall with a paper cup of beer in his hand. Mabel could fend for herself in there, and for all he knew, Annie wouldn't even miss him.

IT HAPPENED TO be a clear night with a nearly full moon, so Big Don made his way up the road from the hall, pumping his legs to get the blood circulating. Aside from losing his run for

Congress, there were very few times in his life when things did not go his way. He could count them on one and a half hands, and generally speaking they'd been trivial things, things that didn't matter in the greater scheme. Hell, he hoped *he* could learn to live with disappointment. Probably could. The older he got, maybe the easier it would be. He could retreat to his new ranch up on the ridge, work the Mexican man to the fingerbone while he sat out on the veranda and contemplated his ocean.

Now, there's a thing that never disappoints. It is always vaster and more full of power and secrets than you can contain.

He didn't realize when he began walking that he was headed for the cemetery. All those gravestones in among the old ladies in their mentholated shawls. But it was only natural, he supposed, that he would want to say a couple of things to his own father, who hadn't been able to understand him those last few hours before his death. He had handpicked Mabel for Don to marry because her family had good land closer in toward the new freeway, an eye toward its future value, and Don honored him by doing as he was told. Mabel's folks were politically powerful too, a good match because Don Sr. was a doer, a mover, a stalwart man who always got his way, gently, but ended his days with dribble on a whiskered chin.

Big Don stood at the grave, able to read it in the moonlight. It didn't say anything of consequence because the elder Hayes hadn't done much of consequence, other than lose no ground. Don Sr. once told him, in a rare moment of vulnerable honesty, that his own biggest disappointment was winding up such a disappointment to *his* old man. *I'm not saying I liked seeing him go, Little Don, but I didn't lose a lot of sleep, if you know what I mean. I'd like to have earned a bit of a nod from him.*

Don Hayes kicked some eucalyptus leaves off the still-mounded plot, pounded at it with his heel. His grief sat like a cold stone in his belly.

KINDER LIES

Nora

I couldn't fault Cameron for acting like we were Huns marauding his tavern sanctuary and setting his grain and straw on fire. The way Cam had been living, there wasn't any room in his life for a long-lost brother and his wife; no room, even, for a wife of his own.

Cameron had lived a monk's life, it appeared to me. If he was still a virgin at sixty, it wouldn't have surprised me at all because he had a virgin's skittishness and a virgin's fear of directness. I wasn't a slut around him or brash or suggestive, but it always seemed to me that he was ready to flinch when I was talking. Bill wasn't much help in this area, with his sailor's vocabulary, sonsa bitches used like commas and semicolons, assholes for asterisks.

Cameron—*Cam,* he insisted—had fine manners and a certain kind of gentility that was not to be found in his brother.

I liked him from the beginning, though. I liked his inbred sweetness and his farm-boy gentility. Cam wanted to console me about being married to Bill, the kind of thing that might have made a different woman nervous, even though it's probably a refreshing quality to have in your brother-in-law. He said things that suggested Bill had more going on in his past than I'd likely have heard, at least in Cam's estimate. He'd say, "I don't know whether you've heard about Bill's temper or not, but he's got a real demon one in there, and he'll let it out when he wants to make a point. I don't know if you know."

"If he still has it, he keeps it to himself," I told him. I sent my brain back over ten years of memories and couldn't find a scary moment.

Illustrating, Cam showed me his left hand, scarred with a triangular shape the color of black cherry Jell-O. "This," he said, holding it out for me to get a good close look at, "this was his way of getting even with me for something I did that I can't even remember anymore. It's a cattle brand, Dad's old one, an A inside a triangle, I don't know if you can tell."

He seemed to have some trouble holding the hand out, so he took it away and stroked his silver goatee with it, then brought it around to scratch the back of his head. I thought he was still a fairly attractive man, but that seemed to run in the Argus family, I guess. White-haired but balding, kind-eyed behind his wire glasses. Bill was a strapping sixty-three, vigor in his veins like pepper sauce, and his face was lined in the way I always liked in older men, as if all his experiences were there to read in the same way a psychic reads palms. Cam was like that too, only gentler, with an overall sad look and that squeamishness visible in all his expressions.

We were sitting in his kitchen together while Bill slept in. How Bill could sleep so well in the house with the brother he hadn't seen in forty years right downstairs was a whole different thing to think about.

Cam fixed me some eggs and corned beef hash, poured me some coffee. He had an efficient, womanly way about the kitchen, really, like he'd become as comfortable in there as he had among the cows, and later behind his bar.

What happened with the thing on his hand, he told me, was that Bill was so peeved at him for some venial sin once when they were boys that he chased Cam all over the dirt yard and into the pastures, way out to the fence line and the sprawling oak (which is still there), and all the way back. Bill caught his little brother behind the barn and tied him in the same loops and knots he used to disable a calf, rope tangling Cam's arms and legs. He was so scared all of a sudden that he lay there in the dust without making any noise while Bill disappeared for a while. His spit was dripping down into the dirt and making a small dab of mud near his mouth; this was something he observed. He also heard a large congress of crows making fun of him from the barn roof, caught sight of their shadows as they all flew off in a black cloud. He was only about twelve, making Bill maybe fifteen, and Bill had all the strength and power and sheer will, where Cam had none of that and still, as a matter of fact, had the skinny physique of a younger boy, all rib cage and knobby joints. The rope hurt him where it was tightly tied.

He said that he lay there for quite a while, just able to catch the forms of the big white clouds as they drifted in from the ocean not too far away, looking up with only one eye because he was on his side and the other eye was against the ground. If it hadn't been for the rope and being tied up uncomfortably, he might even have enjoyed this little moment all alone, back behind the barn watching crows and clouds and listening to the lowing of his father's cows out in the fields.

Then he saw Bill's feet in the dust before his face. Bill was wearing brogans and white socks, had his jeans rolled up in cuffs flecked with mud spots. Cam said if Bill was done with his torture session, would he mind untying the knots now, but Bill didn't move at that. Instead he made his voice lower, like their dad's, and said, "You have to pay the ultimate price, kiddo."

And before Cam could see what was going to happen—he was tied so tight he couldn't crane his neck to look up at Bill—he felt one of Bill's brogans on his wrists, pinning them down, and then Bill straddled him and held him heavily to the ground. He tried to squirm around to get free but couldn't do it, and that's when the branding iron came down on the back of Cam's hand and it felt like the skin was being stripped off with a hook. He howled so loudly that he was answered by some of the cows a quarter mile away. It must have only been a second that the iron was on his hand, but it seemed like a whole, horrendous eternity, and he didn't think he'd ever be able to stop screaming like that, the pain would probably never end.

Bill was up and off of him, and he threw the branding iron a few feet away and claimed that it wasn't even that hot because he'd warmed it up with a welding torch in the barn and not a good coal fire.

You're a little pup, Cameron.

It took all the willpower Cam had at that age, which wasn't much, to say nothing about this to his parents when they asked him why he was wearing the bandage on his hand. He told them he'd burned it on the muffler of the tractor. Ray looked at him like he was disappointed. How was he going to run this ranch with a nut and a moron for sons?

Bill was frequently talked of as the nut.

"That's how that happened," Cam told me, and I'm sure my eyes were appropriately bulging by then. He took a sip of his dishwater coffee. "I didn't know if you knew."

+

I WISH I'D insisted on being in The Dogleg when Bill reintroduced himself to his brother. That would have been something to see. But Bill was private about his shames, as we all probably should be, I guess, and he had asked me to come get him later.

My first impression of Cam was when he came home from work late that first night and Bill was already in bed.

Cam said, arms crossed, "You must be the wife."

"I am the wife," I said. "You must be the brother."

He held out his hand and we shook, and then I couldn't stand it anymore—I got up off the sofa and I gave him a friendly hug around the neck and told him I was really happy to finally meet him.

"I'm sorry, I didn't catch your name when Bill was telling me." He seemed embarrassed. "I'm good with names most of the time."

"Nora," I said. "You're Cameron, right?"

"Cam." He shoved his hands into his jean pockets and rocked a little bit on the balls of his feet. Uncomfortable in his skin around me, it looked like. "People called me Cameron when they wanted to make me hop to it."

"I get that," I told him. "I'm Nora Jane for that. My mother could make me pee in my pants with it."

We laughed over the idea that we were still sniveling infants at our advanced ages. Then he coughed a couple of times and told me I was welcome to anything in the house, it was nice to have met me. He was ready to go be alone again.

—|—

A FEW DAYS went by in which Bill and I went driving around his old county and he took pictures of houses and barns and even some people that were in much better condition when he was last around here. "Perfect, perfect," he kept saying, because his theme, he reminded me, was how a place is one way in your head and another in reality, so that it's as if the one in your head never existed at all. Clear to me that he was trying to recover some of those moments he hadn't been able to hang on to.

At the end of one of these first days, Cam and I were sitting out on the front porch of his house, and he said into the neck of his beer bottle, "Let's go up and paint Bill's stomach."

Bill was already in bed, exhausted from his day of nostalgia-and-reality mismatch. Sleeping a lot lately, which had me more than a little confused. I had a feeling that shamefacedness was taking more out of him than he'd expected.

"That's not a very practical suggestion, Cam." It was a little too dark for me to make out his face, so the level of kidding I couldn't judge. "Why would you want to paint Bill's stomach?"

"To make a statement," he said. I heard the beer gurgle as he drank some. "Maybe it'll give him pause."

"This is not something Bill needs," I told him. "Pause."

"Everyone needs to take pause from time to time, Nora."

"He needs balls, is what he needs. He could use a pair of shiny brass balls."

"Oh, I think he's got those," Cam said, and I knew what he meant by that. What *I* was getting at, though, was that Bill had come up here for a particular purpose but couldn't seem to kick himself into gear. He was supposed to have a look at his son, Hayes.

However, he was unaware of some complications. Hayes happened to believe that Bill was dead, and for the simplest of reasons. Cam and Annie had told him so, years before, when he was little. And they'd made up quite a heroic history of this man too, whose name wasn't Bill in the lie, so that Hayes thought he had a sweet and noble man for a father, dead before he was born.

Hayes went by the last name Diamond. Not Argus. Diamond was Annie's mother's maiden name, which they had figured wasn't likely to come into Hayes's ears by mistake. Annie did a legal name change for herself, and the name Argus was not mentioned. Hardest, as it turned out, not on Annie or Hayes or even Cam but on Bill's mother, Miranda. She had to pretend to be somebody other than Hayes's grandma, and did it for the kid's sake.

Cam had waited three or four days before getting up the nerve to tell us that Hayes had never heard the name Bill Argus spoken, and he'd waited until this evening to tell me about Bill's heroic replacement. I was stunned at the news but decided I would keep that bit to myself for now. It was a wrinkle I thought could deflate my husband's soul, even if he didn't believe he had one.

We were both a little bit sloshy at that moment on the porch, after a couple of beers each, but it was a nice evening out and the crickets were singing, and maybe a lapse in judgment was just the thing. We went out to the barn and selected a can of red primer, because if you're going to do a job, you might as well do it right. I suggested that we spackle Bill's navel first, so that the coverage would be nice and smooth, but Cam thought he'd probably wake up when the cold putty knife hit him. Cam pried open the paint can and stirred with a wooden paddle, then picked a brush suitable for window trim, which seemed about right to me. In the weird, washed-out light of the barn, we both looked like ghosts. This was the first time I'd seen anything approaching cheer in Cam's face.

He probably remembered that Bill was a sound sleeper. That must have been it, because he didn't make much of an effort to keep quiet as we went inside and up the stairs, those old wooden risers creaking. There was enough moonlight in the bedroom to make the job easy, and Bill was doing us the favor of sleeping outside the sheets, and shirtless too. His hands were folded primly over his chest, the globe of belly rising below there and glowing kind of blue. I almost laughed out loud. It was too much. Cam held the brush up to his lips to shush me.

There's supposed to be honor among thieves, and there should be something like that among vandals too, so out of courtesy I held the can while Cam dipped. He wiped the brush on the rim carefully, then let some of the primer dribble onto Bill's stomach. Bill didn't feel it. He didn't move. He was snoring a little bit, which he always does when he's on his back, a tuneful snore that I kid him is like the kettledrum in a Beethoven symphony he's fond of.

Cam painted his brother in concentric circles, a nice, clean job. When it was done, we both stood there over the bed for a minute or two, admiring it. We exchanged moonglowing smiles.

That was just a small, happy moment between me and my long-lost brother-in-law.

+

I CAN PICTURE my father making his way across the country in a late-fifties sedan, turquoise and white, and I see him like a game piece on a colorful map of the U.S. But the funny thing is, when I picture him like this, I'm pushing his little piece along myself, down along brand new interstates, up the coast, skimming along the northern tier and sewing back and forth across the border, then south, bouncing with the ridge of the Rockies, fishtailing in the Great Salt Lake, making his way over the plains and invisible frontiers of the states, until he's farther and farther away from us, and my hand is pushing him east toward the other ocean. And then I go down deeper and I can see him—not his face, of course, since I don't know what he looked like—but his shadow, and he's weeping as he drives those byways, or is pushed unwillingly. He's crying his eyes out, running away.

When Mother talked about him, which wasn't often, she made him sound like a brilliant man who could have flown under his own power if he wished. Your father had wings on his heels, your father was always the smartest man at a party. She thought she was boosting my self-esteem maybe. If I thought I came from decent stock, maybe I'd turn out all right, because there was nothing she could actively do to help. Apparently. She was more interested in sedating herself so she wouldn't have to worry about such things. She had bagged this brilliant, beautiful man and failed to keep him, and he'd done what a brilliant strategist does when his survival is on the line—he fired up his heel wings and he flew.

There's a tiny little moment I recall, of being on my tricycle in the basement of our house, and my father picked me up, tricycle and all, and hoisted me over his head to take me outside. We went up the steps together, and I looked down and backward on the top of his head, and I remember I was pedaling, pedaling fast like I was the one powering us up the steps and outside. I never saw his face, only the curly top of his head, light-colored hair that seemed shiny and moist, and I saw his sleeves rolled up high over his elbows. My picture of this ends before he ever sets me down on the sidewalk outside. I'm perpetually pedaling and flying up the steps with him and perpetually laughing at the surprise of it.

He's been absent ever since, or nearly, yet he's responsible for one of the most joyful pictures I have in my head. How am I supposed to hate him? Sometimes I can imagine him now as an old man, a mild tremor in his fingers, a shaving nick in the folds of his jowls, liver spots, moist yellow eyes, and I wonder if that new wife of his ever thinks of me.

It was after he went away, I'm almost sure, when Mother put me on a swing at the park near our house and declared that she was about to give me an underduck. I didn't know what that was. Mother had a cigarette pinched in her mouth, I remember, and her rowdy hair was battened down with a paisley scarf tied under her chin. Long before her African phase, this was. She was wearing a banana-colored raincoat. From behind me she started the swing swinging, and I clenched the chains so hard they felt hot in my hands, and itchy, and I could smell the strange brown-penny metal of them when I twisted to look back at her as she pushed. Her face wasn't even on me, it was on the other mother at the next swing, and they were both laughing while Mother counted down the pushes. I can't remember what they were talking about, the two mothers, but her eyes weren't on me when she got to seven, six, and five and she laughed and squinted through her smoke. Her hands were on my little bottom with each push, and near the end of the countdown I was twisting and squirming in the wide, U-shaped seat, every touch of her hand making me think something bad was going to happen when we got down to one. Finally, in a voice that was supposed to be giddy with fun but made me feel like I was about to be stuffed down a garbage chute, she cried, "Here we go!" I screamed as she gave me one last great push and began to run under me, and I twisted myself in the seat so that the chains crossed and my feet were tangled up around her head. I sailed up, afraid to fly now, screaming like I'd veer right into the sun, and then I was whirling and out of the swing seat, flying backward with the chains kinking and wobbling before my eyes as Mother kept running ahead, finally turning in time to see me hit the ground on my back. My head hit the lip of the concrete behind the swings and I think I died there for a moment, with the treetops overhead waving bye-bye and the swing seat soaring back and forth, riderless.

I'm sure Daddy was gone by then. He wouldn't have let her do this to me.

Cary Lee always told that story with a laugh. She didn't know that I remembered it happening, just like I remembered Daddy flying me up the steps on my tricycle, so in her mind it probably didn't count as one of my grievances against her, and I didn't raise it the last time I saw her either.

—|—

BILL AND CAM and I drove up to a ridgetop overlooking the ocean. It was bald and barren up there, wind-drubbed, and what few low bushes there were here and there were bending over. Cows and sheep grazed among rocks and runoff tracks.

We were up there to see where Hayes lived, Cam chaperoning. He drove in order to make sure Bill didn't try to do something dumb like actually *introduce himself* to his son. The road wandered around the lay of the land, with the ocean out to our left and the fading brown hills to our right, a beautiful place even if it was unfriendly. After a while a small white stucco house with red shutters appeared (a variety of red that I'd seen before only in Chinatown), guarded by a wooden fence that seemed to want to lean in different directions. That was probably the only thing holding it up, lean and counterlean. Sheep were grazing in the pasture that aproned downhill from the house. Hayes was a sheep farmer, and he lived up here among the stones and hard-pressed shrubs with his mother.

Cam had told me in advance that he knew Hayes and Annie wouldn't be home. They were at the doctor's getting Annie looked at again to see how much worse she'd gotten, and how fast. She had a condition the doctors compared to Alzheimer's. Cam thought, everything considered, this wasn't the worst possible thing that could have happened to her, but I saw him looking at Bill very hard when he told him about it. The thing Cam didn't know, probably, was that Bill hides his feelings so well you'd think he were carved out of sandstone.

Bill got out of Cam's old yellow Scout and shaded his eyes with his hand, even though the light was dim and gray and there was a wall of fog offshore waiting to roll in. A good stiff wind had already picked up.

"Looks like nobody's home," said Cam.

"I figured." Bill stuck his hands into his pockets, looking at the house. As far as I knew, his belly was still painted red. He hadn't said a word about it.

After a few minutes all he could think to do was set up his tripod and take a few pictures. Aside from the sheep, this place was about as harsh-looking as the desert, so Bill must have felt fairly comfortable with it. The ocean was as flat and wide and boundless as any of the hot valleys where Bill took his pictures.

Anticlimax, though. I knew Hayes wasn't going to be home, yet I half expected fate to intervene and get him and his old man together here in this place. There'd have been something right about it, the two of them meeting up in a remote camp like this one, mano a mano. Looking down the road, though, I could see there was no sign of a truck coming up, and the wind was too rough for us to stand there and wait.

It had only been a week, but Cam was ready for his brother to hit the road, I do believe. Didn't want any close calls vis-à-vis Bill and Hayes, standing there with his arms crossed and his eyes down on the rocky yard.

He was all for the status quo, now that his brother had finally come home, and I wasn't sure I blamed him.

GOOD INTENT—1962

Cam

After Bill left Pianto, Cam Argus spent a lot of time with Annie and Hayes. He loved Annie like a sister, true, but he also wanted to prove something good about the Argus family: loyalty, support, sensitivity—whatever Annie wanted to take from it. Naturally, she was crying a lot, which to Cam's eyes took away much of her lovely shine and made her look like an older woman with TB, though she was still young. Her hair hung down in yarny red strands, her clothes became dingy. The boy's nose always had a green gob bubbling underneath, poo-poo pants reeking with his mama's inattention. Cam knew that if she didn't have somebody looking after her, the men she rented her pastures to would soon begin to take advantage of her.

It struck him that Bill's departure had done nearly the same thing to both the women Cam was close to in his life—Annie and his mother.

He wondered why Annie's family found it so easy to let her flounder. It was in the early spring, after a winter of more rain than usual and escalating indifference on their part. Nearly a year since Bill had gone, and they were still punishing her for her bad judgment. It wasn't Annie's fault that his brother had deserted her. There was nothing in him that she knew of that could have predicted it. Cam maybe could have told her a thing or two on the side, he supposed.

Ah hell, he said to himself. I'll go on over and have a talk with her dad.

The Hayes ranch was a vast spread along a main road to Santa Rosa, with hundreds of head of cattle. Big Don was the third or fourth generation of Hayes men to run a cow ranch there, blessed with all the benefits of being entrenched like that—a smooth operation, plenty of paid help, good outbuildings, fine-running machinery. He was raking in the money and putting a good portion of it back into his ranch. He didn't need it to live on, is what it amounted to, a situation that Bad Ray could only dream of when he indulged in an afternoon of drinking.

Cam drove his father's truck to the Hayes place and parked it on the road shoulder, preferring to walk the paved lane to the house rather than pull up to the door in that dilapidated thing. Immediately, Big Don was out on the stoop of the colonial house with something that looked to Cam like a come-along winch in his hand. It would make a nasty wound if it happened to hit someone in the head. He stood there looming over Cam, who made the decision to stay on the brick walkway rather than put a foot on Mr. Hayes's porch step. Next to the steps a flowering wisteria electric with bees helped him keep his distance.

"What in the goddamn hell do you want, *Argus*," Big Don said. He made the name sound crude.

Cam got up his nerve—he was a boy of twenty-one at the time, and just barely that—and told the elder Hayes about the state his daughter was in lately. "She's not taking good care of herself, sir. Your grandkid is looking kind of ragged around the edges." He hated the reedy and nervous sound of his voice.

The wife, Mabel, appeared behind Big Don in the doorway and gave Cam what he interpreted as a sympathetic look. She put her hand on her husband's shoulder to settle him a bit, but he shrugged her off. Then he said, "I suppose you're thinking I ought to come on in and pick up her pieces and take responsibility for her welfare."

The brash voice of an oil-rig foreman or a crane driver. He seemed accustomed to moving large things from here to there.

"I think she needs looking after," Cam said. "She's not in great shape."

"Well whose fault is that, son? That can't be *my* fault, can it? I'm not the one who promised to have and to hold and love and support and all that horseshit I thought I heard *your brother* mention."

He lambasted Cam's father too, for raising a man who would do what Bill did, and for failing to track the son of a bitch down and haul him back home for justice. When Big Don Hayes ranted, his face grew the color of a pomegranate, highly intimidating with the pinpoint eyes and wagging mustache. Mrs. Hayes tried again to settle him, but he didn't want to hear it, began swinging that come-along winch against his leg hard enough to jingle the keys in his pocket.

"Annie is bringing in the harvest of her own idiotic choices," he said. "If she survives, she'll be a smarter girl for it. If she doesn't, then the kid will fall into better hands, I imagine."

"I want to do something to make it up to you, Mr. Hayes."

At first old Don seemed impressed, as if an Argus with a conscience were a rare specimen. Then he sneezed violently and dropped the come-along with a wild clatter. "What could you possibly do to make up for that kind of bullshit, boy?"

"Paint your house? Clean out your dairy shed? Help you pull a truck out of the mud with that come-along there?"

Hayes took out a red bandanna handkerchief and blew his nose. "Get on out of here," he said. "And if you're smart, you'll let Annie fall on her goddamn ass. It won't help her to have you cushioning the bottom. She needs a big black bruise from this."

Cam did as he was told. He knew to do that when it came to the older men. You do what they say and you'll be all right. Bill never did get that.

So he did as he was told and left, but that night, under cover of darkness, he drove back over to the Hayes ranch pulling a tractor with a mower attachment and he mowed Hayes's front pasture, twenty acres of overgrowth from all the rains. The headlights of the tractor made the landscape look painted on the inside of a tin can, and when Cam approached the house for his turnarounds, he could see Mr. Hayes standing there on the porch watching the job as he smoked a pipe.

Looked like Mr. Hayes wasn't about to stop him.

BIG DON'S GRANDSON was approaching the age of four. Cam thought it was interesting that he favored Annie's line almost entirely, hardly a tint of Argus in him. Curly red hair, pale skin, gentle-looking hands, and the bantam-chestedness of a Big Don too. It was probably a comfort, or would be, that there was so little sign of Bill in him. Luckily for Annie, the kid had a sweet disposition. While his mother was lying on her sofa in a mood, Hayes would entertain himself with improvised toys like a hand mixer or a pair of Bill's suspenders that he had failed to take with him when he left.

One Sunday, not long after Cam had mowed the Hayes pasture, he went over to Annie's house and invited her to drive up to Calistoga with him to see the geyser go off. He had never seen it himself and thought maybe little Hayes would like it, if not Annie, too.

Like his mother, Annie seemed to become light-headed when she tried to get up off the couch. She was dressed in jeans and a man's white shirt, another thing of Bill's, Cam imagined. It struck Cam that there was something about Bill that had given Annie balance, and now that he was gone she was without it, sick when she stood up, queasy from the feeling that she might fly off the surface of the earth.

"Have you been drinking a little bit, Annie?"

"No. Uh-uh," she said. She rubbed her eyes and steadied herself with a hand on the arm of the sofa. The room was dark, the heavy drapes pulled closed even though it was a nice day out. Hayes came waddling into the room holding a dustpan on top of his head like it was an antenna. He said, "Uncle Tam."

"Good. That wouldn't be a good idea with Hayes in the house." He picked up his nephew and spun him around a couple of times to make him dizzy, which he always loved.

He was twenty-one and had this nephew. It sometimes made him feel a lot older than he really was. Fatherly emotions had seeped into him where the kid was concerned, unexpected and completely uncontrollable. It wasn't his job to make sure the kid was all right, but he was the one who seemed to think about it more than anybody else, including Annie. At the same time, Bad Ray was more and more on his case about working, since now, with Bill vamoosed—it was the word Ray used, "vamoosed"—Cam would inherit the ranch one of these days and be responsible for the whole thing. He had to prove he could handle it, Bad Ray insisted, as if there were anything about it that Cam didn't already understand. Everything depended on routine. If you did things according to the daily and seasonal routines, you'd be all right. Milk and beef prices would go up and down, but your routines smoothed things out. That was all you needed to know about running a cow farm as far as he could see, even though the routine had turned his father into a mean, sad, quiet man with few friends.

Bad Ray's lot in life, Cam thought, and I inherit.

"Get him dressed in something cool—it's warmer today. And you ought to put on a dress and a little makeup. Get that squirrel's nest out of your hair."

Annie walked past him and took Hayes by the hand. The two of them went upstairs together, leaving Cam to himself, and the first thing he thought to do was throw open those drapes.

When they came back down in twenty minutes, Annie looked almost human again. Her cheeks were pinkish, and she'd combed her hair into a loose ponytail. There wasn't much that she could do with the blue bags under her eyes, the drawn mouth. It was as if her aging had sped up the day Bill left, body and soul going to pot on the fast track, a crying shame.

Hayes was in a pair of overalls and a striped T-shirt, his hair combed flatter too. "You want to see the geyser shoot up into the sky?" Cam asked him.

The boy didn't know what to say to that. His eyes widened.

"He doesn't know what a geyser is," Annie said.

"The best way to find out is to see one," Cam said, and led them outside. Annie squinted at the hard sunlight.

The three of them squeezed into the bench seat of Cam's truck, and they headed out. The route he decided to take through Santa Rosa and then over the mountains brought them right past Big Don's house, a mistake, maybe; he hadn't thought about it ahead of time. Annie stiffened up as they approached it, that front pasture looking like a nice flat carpet thanks to Cam, but she couldn't help looking past him out his window to see if there was anyone on the porch as they went by. The big colonial seemed to rotate to keep an eye on them, as if the entire ranch lay on a large turntable.

"I think Big Don will come around pretty soon," Cam said. "Don't worry about him."

"Do you really think so?" Annie asked. A touch of sarcasm. "What about Bill? Have a feeling about Bill too?"

"I'd like to have Bill back as much as you would."

"Really? God, you must love him a lot." The sourness in her voice made him wince.

"He's my brother."

"He's my husband. You were at the wedding, if I remember right." She was looking straight out the windshield now, her arms folded over her chest, while the boy rolled the passenger window up and down. "He's Hayes's d-a-d," Annie said, spelling the word.

The road narrowed on the other side of Santa Rosa as it began to curl into the mountains. For a while Cam tried to imagine that he was out with his own family, Annie his wife, Hayes his boy, and it felt good to him. As long as Annie didn't say anything bitter. The *idea* of being out with his family was a good one. It made him feel paired-up and important, and he wondered if Bad Ray ever had that feeling when he and Andie were first married, when their boys came along. And whether Bill ever had it, at first.

Somehow, though, Cam found it hard to imagine finding a woman to love, busy as he was, and bogged down. If it happened, it would happen well down the line.

They peaked the ridge and started down the other side toward Calistoga, not talking the whole way. Cam was content with that. Annie was out of the house, getting some air. What she needed was air, more of it, as much as she could get.

When they arrived at the geyser, Cam parked in the dirt parking lot and helped Hayes and Annie out of the truck. He bought their tickets and led them out back to the gardenlike area where the spout would be, rimmed by poplar trees and a bamboo fence. Picnic tables were set up all around, so he put his little makeshift family at one and gave Hayes a pair of cookies he'd brought to keep him quiet.

"Nice day," he said.

"Beautiful," Annie said. "I do still notice things like that, you know."

"Good, I'm glad. I'd be worried if you didn't."

Hayes left the table to wander around a little bit, a half-eaten cookie in one hand. "You stay away from the geyser!" Annie called.

"There's a fence around it," Cam told her. In fact, the fence looked misplaced, circling a large bare spot in the grass where the hole was. The geyser was due to pop in another ten minutes. EVERY TWENTY MINUTES WITHOUT FAIL, EXCEPT WHEN IT DOESN'T, a sign near ground zero said.

In profile Annie reminded Cam of someone who didn't know her picture was being taken. Her mind was elsewhere, and the thing that her mind was on showed in every crease and shadow on her face. She sat with her head bowed, eyes on her knees, it appeared, hands folded in her lap. He noticed that she had put on a thin chain necklace, and that she still wore her wedding ring. Hopeful, he was sure, that Bill would drag his sorry ass back into Pianto one of these days and she would get to show herself to be as kind and forgiving as she always thought she was. It was her reputation. The ultimate test of it would be a chastened Bill Argus standing before her with his hat in one hand and something for the kid in the other.

"I don't know what to do," Annie said. She did not look up at him. He saw that tears were dripping down from her chin onto her chest, darkening her pale green dress there.

"What's the matter?" It felt awkward, but Cam put his arm around her shoulders. If they were husband and wife this would be expected, but they weren't, and he was afraid she would take it the wrong way. Yet she seemed to need a hand on her body. He pulled on her opposite shoulder in a couple of friendly tugs, and she let her head fall against him.

"He's asking about his daddy," she said. "He wants to know where he went."

"He remembers?" Cam looked at the boy.

"I don't know for sure. I don't see how he could. But he's asking anyway, and I don't know what to tell him."

Cam should have known this would happen eventually, but he'd never thought it through. In his mind, he saw Hayes growing up in the company of his mother and grandparents, his uncle. It didn't occur to him that the idea of a daddy would kick in so soon, and strongly. Annie said it was just about all he talked about lately, yet there were no pictures of Bill in the house, and she never mentioned him for Hayes's sake.

There were a few other people in the garden waiting for the geyser to pop. It seemed like the anticipation was building as the clock at the snack bar ticked down the minutes. Everyone else there was staring at the hole as if they could make the thing go by willing it.

"It's supposably a fifty-footer," said a man in a straw hat. "Ought to be pretty impressive."

Hayes was squatting to pick at a grasshopper at his feet, and when it hopped away from him he screeched and looked over at Cam and Annie. "Grasshopper," Annie said. "That was a grasshopper, baby."

"What are you going to do?" Cam asked.

"I don't know. I have no idea." Her eyes went to the top reaches of the poplars.

He felt her stiffening under his arm and pulled it away from her. His fingers brushed over her neck where her hair came out in faint red strands. She didn't react. He hadn't done it on purpose. "Maybe he'll just stop asking," Cam said.

"Maybe he will. I don't know. But he'll ask later, I'm sure. When he's older."

This problem seemed far beyond Cam's realm of experience. He knew a lot about how to handle cows and pasture grass, and he could repair a truck engine or a chain saw. He had ways of making his mother laugh when she was in a low frame of mind (which was more often than not these days). He could avoid his father's temper with the finesse of a bullfighter. All told, he had learned to get along in his life, but this was more than he knew what to do with.

"Maybe you could lie to him," Cam said.

"Lie to him?" Now Annie looked over, red lines in her eyes. Cam thought of her on her wedding day when she was as bright and sweet as ever, and Bill had grass stains on his pants.

"Make something up," Cam said. "A story. Maybe tell him the truth someday when he can handle it."

"I don't know," Annie said. Her eyes were fixed on the muddy hole in the ground.

He wasn't sure where the idea to lie came from. It was more or less an impulse, but it struck him now as the only way they could handle it. Telling Hayes simply that his father was gone, vamoosed, was about the cruelest thing they could do, especially when later the kid decided to have a look into it. He'd tear himself up searching for the old man. He'd never stop wondering what had made Bill go.

Hayes came back to the table and said, "Mommy's laughing again."

Annie took him in her arms and gave him a kiss. "That's what I tell him when I get this way." She wiped at her eyes with one knuckle. "I say I'm laughing at something funny I thought of."

The hole in the ground began to bubble with steaming water, and the attention of everyone around was drawn to it. There were oohs and ahs, and the man in the straw hat said, "Here we go, baby."

"Get ready for the geyser, Hayes," Annie said. "It'll shoot high up into the sky."

"How high?" the boy wanted to know.

Cam took one of his hands and squeezed it. He felt like kissing the kid on the head and hugging him. "About as high as the moon," he said. "How's that?"

All Hayes could do was stare at the bubbling hole with his

eyes wide and clear. Steam began to shoot up as more and more water boiled out of the ground, forming a small pool around the hole. Everyone was smiling.

A man in a ranger uniform came around and said, "Any minute now! Everybody ready?" He winked at Hayes, and Hayes hid his face in Annie's stomach.

"Don't look away now, sweetie! Here it goes."

The steam became heavy and loud, and soon a column of water began to rise from the pool, struggling, it seemed to Cam, to take off. It rose and receded, rose a little higher, fell back again, all the while surrounded by the hissing steam. Hayes was watching in astonishment now, pointed with a snub finger while the other hand went instinctively to his mouth.

"Thar she blows!" the ranger said, and the geyser rose again to a height of six or seven feet. Then, to the disappointment of everyone standing there, it pulled back into the ground like someone had shut off the spigot. The pool drained in behind and the steam dissipated into the clear air.

Cam and Annie looked at each other, and then, without conspiring over it, they began to clap and hoot. "Wasn't that something?" Cam said. "That was spectacular!"

"What a sight!" Annie said, and Hayes began to jump up and down and clap. His face wore an expression of pure pleasure, mouth in a wide-open smile, eyes dancing.

Cam had never before appreciated the power of a well-intentioned lie.

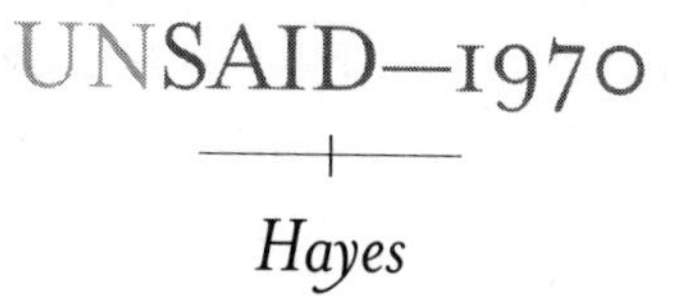

UNSAID—1970

Hayes

In his thirteenth year, in the May of it after school was out, Hayes Diamond went to live with Cameron Argus. Some things had been happening out of his view, having to do with his mother. She was not always as clearheaded as she probably ought to be, often had daylong episodes of walking away from the house in just a dress when it was too cold for that, and not coming home until after dark with dust on her clothes and pieces of moss and fallen oak leaves caught in her hair. Hayes wondered if she had just gone to nap in the woods, which didn't strike him as a very bad thing, but on the other hand he didn't know where she had been, couldn't vouch for her movements. He was old enough at the time to talk to the different ranchers who rented her land surrounding the house he had grown up in, answering their questions, taking their rent money, even, sometimes, ordering them around. A lot of the time they muttered something in Spanish as they walked away, something meant to intimidate him, but it didn't work because he didn't understand them.

Things were happening out of view though, he knew that, because he wouldn't be going to live with Cam Argus if sleeping in the woods was the worst thing his mother was up to. It bothered him to know she had secrets that she was keeping from him. They had been as close as friends for years, their isolated life contributing to that, and out of respect he had never kept a secret from her. They had always talked. Now there was something unsaid going on, his things were packed in Cam's truck, and it was time to leave his mother on her own for a while.

She was, he thought, about thirty-two, but it didn't seem right, strangely, to leave her alone.

Annie sat cross-legged on the porch as Hayes stood over her with his duffel hanging on his back. He said he was on his way.

"Don't worry," she said. "I'll be over there a lot. And you'll come back here to see me. It's all real temporary."

He was already tall, so it felt as if he loomed over his mother like a fir tree. She was craning her neck so their eyes could meet. Cam tapped on the horn of his truck to hurry them along.

"Seems like a lot of trouble for nothing," Hayes told her.

"It'll be good for you, baby. I'm sure." And she looked off the end of the porch now, into the eucalyptus in that direction, where a trail entered deeper woods. "You get going. I'll see you in a few days."

He bent down and kissed her on top of the head, found her hair coarse to the touch.

Hayes threw the duffel into the truck bed with the rest of his things and got in. Cam hauled himself sideways behind the wheel to back up for the turn down to the gate, his arm behind Hayes on the seat back. Annie was bent at the waist and rocking, as if she were having a hard cramp, but she managed to wave as they pulled out.

CAM LIVED CLOSE to Pianto, in a small bungalow not far from the cemetery. He hadn't moved out of his parents' place till he was in his late twenties, and now he was about thirty as far as Hayes knew. He still worked on his father's ranch, a few miles up the road, but he finally got out of that house a couple of years before. Probably so he could feel more like a man, Hayes reasoned. Independent. His dad tended to boss him around, the way an owner who could afford to hire Mexicans would talk to them. The money was not too shabby, Cam always said, and he'd inherit the land someday, and that's when he'd hit his stride.

Hayes liked him. Cam was an old friend of the family and treated Hayes like a blood relative much of the time, which he didn't mind at all. He was short on relatives.

That first night they sat at the little kitchen table eating as the moon started to rise in the frame of the back window. Frogs were out in the yard.

"So we'll start early tomorrow morning," Cam said. "Ray likes me there at sunup. Thinks it makes me hardier, I guess. We might as well get you going down that road too."

Hayes wanted to say that he had finally figured it out. The only reason Cam had him staying there was to work on the ranch for Ray Argus, now that school was over with. He decided not to make a fuss though.

"What's Ray planning to pay me?" he asked instead.

Cam looked at him as he drank from his beer bottle. "That's a good question. Some days he might give you a few bucks. Other days he'll say that not cutting off your thumbs was your pay. He calls the shots, I'm afraid."

"Cut off my thumbs?"

"Long story." Cam wasn't laughing. "He always had his way of getting us to do what he wanted."

Hayes wasn't sure who he meant by "us." He hadn't been around Ray Argus all that much, a few times a year, but when he was around him he got the feeling that the man was like a tree that had grown with a big iron railroad spike driven into the trunk. Like there's always this thing sticking in him, and the scar is visible and ugly. Nobody ever said what it might have been.

Hayes had been to Cam's house many times, but sleeping that night in the back sunroom of the bungalow felt strange. The moon eyed him through the window, a big white moon with a hazy yellow corona around it.

All he could think that whole night was whether his mother was sleeping in the house or out in the woods now that he wasn't there to keep tabs on her. And how there was nothing he could do about it either way.

BEFORE DAWN HE was standing in the middle of Ray's bare yard, hugging himself and dancing from foot to foot it was so cold, and too late in the season for it. Still dark out. The moon now on the other horizon and ready to drop behind the trees. Hayes could see his breath, and he was relieved when Cam invited him inside.

Miranda Argus was in the kitchen, pouring coffee into three browned cups. Hayes felt like she was staring at him at first, but then she smiled and gave him his coffee. Her free hand came around the back of his head and gave him a kind pat, a tousle of the hair, and he wasn't sure what to make of that except that it probably meant she felt a little sorry for him on a cold summer morning like this. "It's good to have you," she said. "And you've gotten so tall since Christmastime. I'm just amazed."

Hayes was no judge of what's going on inside a person's mind, but by the look on her face it seemed to him that she was about to bust out crying. He didn't know what to say to her other than, yes, he was getting tall. His mother said so all the time.

Ray Argus pounded down the hollow staircase and came into the room just as Cam was saying, "You'll have him all summer, Mom. As promised."

"That's right," Ray bellowed. "So you don't have to turn him into a pussy overnight."

Mrs. Argus, holding her robe tightly at her neck, gave Ray his coffee but didn't lean in to kiss him.

"Don't work him to bones the first day," she said. "Cam? Keep your father in line for me."

To that, Ray Argus grimaced, like his coffee tasted awful. He set the cup down so hard it hit the table with a gunshot report, then turned on a thick heel and left without saying anything else. In a moment Hayes felt Cam's arm on his shoulder guiding him out. Miranda watched them all the way through the dining room and to the front door; he could feel her eyes on him.

Once outside, Hayes detected the sound of the herd moving around in the big cowshed behind the barn. They banged up against the pipe gate and knocked into wooden rails. They shuffled against one another, kicking at straw on the ground. They seemed to want out, even though to them it must still seem like night.

Ray, bundled in a plaid coat with thermals underneath, looked at Hayes and said, "That's all you're wearing? Don't tell me you're a dumbshit like my kid here."

"No, sir."

"We both know it'll be warm in a couple hours," Cam said. "You'll be peeling off your thermals like sunburned skin."

"Well, until then you're up a fucking creek, aren't you." Ray looked at Hayes and winked.

After he let the cows out of the shed, Ray stood next to Hayes at the open gate and peered inside, pointing with a lazy hand. "First chore," he said. "You take that spade there and you get rid of all the cow shit in that shed, then you lay down new straw. That'll take some time."

Hayes looked at Cam as if to ask whether he really had to do it.

"It's not so bad after you've been at it a while," Cam said, and the two of them left Hayes with his shovel and his shit wagon.

ONE OF THE things he didn't like about the Argus family—as close as he was to Cam—was how there always seemed to be these unsaid things between them. They were always in the middle of a conversation, and they'd clam up tight as soon as some topic got hit—he never could tell what. He'd ask a few innocent questions, and they'd get thin-lipped and scatter off in three different directions. Why his mother thought this was a good idea, putting him more or less in their care over the summer, he couldn't figure out, although she would never say anything bad about them.

He could still remember the first time, he was maybe eight or nine, when the Arguses, all three of them, came to his mother's house on Christmas. It hit him as a very odd thing, since they had never come around on Christmas before and they all acted stiff and uncomfortable. They overshowered him with gifts too, incredible things he'd never have had the guts to ask for—a real .22 rifle that Ray said was for killing squirrels and raccoons and anything else he was good enough to hit—and they stayed for dinner. Normally Christmas dinner was just Hayes and Annie sitting over a couple of game hens she'd roasted.

While he worked in the cowshed, he thought about that Christmas when the Arguses first came over, and he realized that that's when Cam started coming around all the time. It was as if Annie had just chosen the Arguses randomly out of the Sonoma County phone book to come over and share a holiday, and it stuck, became a tradition. The Arguses were a little awkward, it seemed to Hayes. Uncomfortable with themselves. Cam looked at Annie a lot and touched her sometimes. They did some whispering in the hallway.

The second year, Mrs. Argus's sister, Carmen, began coming to dinner too, a loud, unmarried woman who liked to get out in the front yard with Hayes and throw the baseball around even though she had to be going on fifty. He didn't have much choice but to accept her along with the other three, and he liked them all well enough, especially Cam, but he just had to wonder what they were doing there.

Now he was here shoveling Ray's cow shit and wondering if he'd been sold into slavery because Annie couldn't pay the bills anymore. He almost had to laugh. All those Christmas dinners had been the groundwork, and the gifts were to keep him from running away.

The big handwagon was full of greenish cow patties, the floor of the shed scattered with new straw. Hayes realized he was sweating hard now that he'd been working so long, and the smell of the place no longer bothered him too much.

Ray Argus was standing in the gateway with his foot up on one of the rails. No telling how long he'd been there watching. A long piece of grass stuck out of his mouth, and Hayes noticed that he had stripped off his coat and thermals just like Cam said he would. He had on faded green pants and a sleeveless T-shirt now, his face grainy with whiskers from not shaving that day.

"Cameron had to go out and run an errand," he said. "Come on in for lunch now."

They headed toward the house without saying anything.

+

ONE NIGHT WHEN Cam was out of the house, Hayes picked up the phone and called his mother. She hadn't come over to see him yet, nearly two weeks, and it wasn't like her to renege on a promise. He missed her too. Not anything especially motherly about her, but her company more than anything. He missed—it sounded a little strange to say—the *brother*hood of her company, like she was on his level more than a parent's and they were both equally responsible. He missed the kinds of conversations they had, which were comfortable and all over the map. She was always asking how he felt about different things.

There was no answer at home. When Cam came back, Hayes decided not to tell him that he'd tried to call his mother.

On the following Sunday, Ray let Cam and Hayes have the day off. Hayes asked if he could borrow Cam's bike and ride around a little bit, stretch his legs. He said he thought he'd ride over to the beach and lie around all day, and when he took off on the bike he even went in the direction of the beach so Cam wouldn't think anything of it. Cam had packed him a lunch and a cold bottle of root beer, said it would be good for him to have some time to himself.

Instead of heading all the way down the main road to the ocean, Hayes made a turn to the north on a small road that ran along behind Pianto and cut back to the highway between Cam's house and the Argus ranch. From there he rode to the Freestone Road and home, where he found the gate closed, Annie's car parked beside the house. Everything looked fine, but when he tried the front door it was locked. He looked inside through the oval glass, tapped on it a few times. There was no answer. Then he went around to the back door that opened into the kitchen. It was also locked. No lights were on inside. He could see through the back window that there wasn't even a pot of coffee cold on the stove, his mother's habit to warm it up later in the day. Everything was put away.

He left the bike leaning against the front porch and walked toward the trail that led into the woods. After the eucalyptus grove, the forest turned into deep pine and oak cover and not much sun could get through to the trail. He had spent a lot of time in those woods growing up, knew their dark corners and tangles, knew on top of that how easy it was to get lost in there.

But he also knew that his mother was even more familiar with the pine- and oak-covered hills than he was.

The trail climbed, soft-packed powder under his feet, the treetops creaking against each other with the wind. Hayes didn't see any tracks, no sign that she had passed by this way, yet he couldn't think of any other place she might be. He kept climbing, taking the path as far as he imagined she might go, where the trail came to a high meadow full of grass and wildflowers. Once he had run away to this spot when he was briefly feeling sorry for himself over one thing or another—he could hardly remember now what it was—and he had fallen asleep in the grass and gotten sunburned so badly that Annie had to take him to the doctor. She said, "Instead of running away next time, you come and talk to me about it, okay?"

After that, once in a while he asked her what his father was like.

Annie would grow a trembling smile and tell him—nodding toward the picture on the mantelpiece—that his father was a good man. Not much more than that. "Am I like him at all?" Hayes would prod, and she'd say that, yes, a little bit, he was like his father here and there. I can see him in you, and you'll be a good man too. This was usually enough to make him feel better and stop asking questions, even though he felt like she was leaving out an awful lot.

Sometimes, confusingly, kids at school would throw out unexpected insults about his father. Coward. Drunk. Runaway. Sometimes a teacher would intervene and set them straight, other times he was left only with his own certainties. Hayes did not believe what they said, and he didn't answer them. His father was a hero pilot.

He couldn't tell from the picture his mother kept on her dresser what kind of man his father might have been beyond a hero pilot. The helmet covered up much of his face, except for the eyes squinting into the sun and a smile that looked like it had been held too long before the picture was taken. He was wearing a flight suit with all kinds of belts on it, clips and hardware, straps coming up from between his legs and over his shoulders, and an oxygen mask hanging under his chin. He had hands that looked like they wanted to grab hold of something.

In that silver frame, frozen in his pose, the man would never reveal more than what the gray, cracked picture showed.

Heading back down the trail, into the shadows, Hayes put the thought of that picture out of his mind. He didn't want to think about it while his mother was gone. He wanted to find her—for his own sake—and get her back home, then tell Cam and Ray that he'd just as soon go back and live with her again for the rest of the summer, where he belonged.

After waiting on the front porch for Annie to return, he had ridden the bicycle back into Pianto and acted like he spent the day at the beach. He decided not to tell Cam what he'd discovered. Cam would probably say that Annie's whereabouts weren't really something he should be worrying over, that she was free to roam around all she liked if she didn't need to take care of Hayes. And that was probably true.

The next morning Ray had them walking around the pasture with a cart full of posts to repair fences. He led the way while Cam and Hayes pulled the cart, which was loaded high with four-by-fours and a big spool of barbed wire. It was a hot day already too, a big turkey buzzard soaring overhead on the thermal currents that rose up from the pasture. Hayes thought he made eye contact with the thing for a minute, and it bobbed its head at him.

Ray put Hayes in charge of digging the post holes with a hole digger. He didn't mind it, liked the idea of stabbing this thing into the ground and coming up with a canister of earth. Some of the cores he pulled up had worms wriggling in them. Ray snapped at the old barbed wire with a pair of wire cutters while Cam pulled old fence posts out of the ground and threw them onto the cart in place of the new posts. Together, the three of them made decent progress along the back side of the pasture, moving post by post until they'd covered about two hundred yards. It reminded Hayes of the tenants at his mother's ranch, men in straw hats and sweaty shirts with their boys, and they're all speaking Spanish while they fork hay onto the ground or move irrigation pipe from one side of the field to another.

"That's about it for me," Cam said when it was getting close to noon. "I'll be back in a couple hours."

Hayes looked at Ray to see if this was expected, and Ray said, "I think me and Hayes'll keep at it for a while longer."

"That's fine with me," Hayes told him.

When Cam was gone, Hayes put his hole digger down and took a long drink from the canteen Ray had brought. He didn't know why he did it, but he looked at Ray straight on, eye to eye for maybe the first time in his life, and he told him that Annie was missing. Ray immediately turned away and bit at the old fence with his wire cutters.

"I went over there yesterday," Hayes said. "Her car was there, but she wasn't home."

"I wouldn't worry about her." Ray was looking at his own boots. "She's a big girl."

"She said she'd be over here to see me sometimes."

Now Ray took off his hat and swabbed his scalp with a bandanna from his pocket. He took a drink himself, tossed his wire cutters onto the cart. There was something unsaid in the air, Hayes could tell.

"Your mom's having a kind of a hard time right now," Ray told him. His normally low, gruff voice was quieter, almost cracking. "That's all I know."

"Do you know where she is?"

Hayes stood near the older man with his hands on his hips, wanting an honest answer, a simple fact for a change. He wanted somebody to tell him the truth. There was too much going on beneath the surface nowadays. Ray looked like he was ready to bite through his top lip, and he took a couple of steps toward Hayes and wrapped him up in his long, tight arms, held him close to his chest and patted his back. Hayes didn't know what to make of it, Ray Argus acting like Annie had died or something, and the very thought of that possibility made Hayes pull away so he could look at the man.

"She's not dead, is she?" He heard his own voice crackle.

"No, no. Jesus, God, no, son. She's just having a little trouble. Cam's going to see her right now."

"Where is she?"

Ray stood beside him now and looped his arm around Hayes's shoulders, the two of them staring out into the wide field dotted with black-and-white cows. The clouds seemed to hang just above the hilltop, trees scraping their hulls. Hayes let his hands dangle at his sides the way he remembered his father's in that picture.

"We put her in the hospital for a little while, that's all. She's fine. She'll come out all right. She just needed some time to recoup a little energy, I guess you could say. Everything's fine."

Hayes felt himself nodding, almost aware that he'd known something had been wrong with her lately. He might have told somebody before now, he thought. Maybe he could have saved her a little trouble. It would have been a good thing to spare her some trouble; that's a thing he could do for her the older he got.

Hayes felt Ray's grip tighten around his shoulder, that wiry arm lying on him heavily.

The work was over for a while. The two of them just stood there like that for a long time, looking out at the contour of the pasture where the fence ran down, still needing repair.

MOTHERS' VOICES—1977

Miranda, Mabel, Annie

"It was when the postcard arrived that I got ill. I was bearing up until then, I was holding my own. Ray acted like his son was dead, vanished without leaving remains, no ashes, but I for some reason kept holding out hope that Bill had gone away looking for work or settling some debts he had, ashamed to tell us what it was all about. The card arrived six weeks after he had gone missing and Ray's hay truck was found down in Olema, parked on the side of the road with the keys still in it. Ray had to have a neighbor drive him there to claim it at a police station, fit to murder Bill for that stunt, even though he wasn't sure what Bill was really doing. At that time we could still believe in the possibility that he had been taken away against his will. *I* did, I mean to say.

"But when the card arrived and Ray stood in the doorway with it in his grimy hand, I felt the blood flushing out of my head, and my hands and feet went numb as I fell. Ray said, 'I don't know him anymore, in case you ever wonder.' He stood over me and handed me the card, which said, as best I could read between the lines, that my boy was not coming back. He did not explain. All I knew from it was that he was in a kind of agony I hadn't been able to see in him before. And I feared it had come to him through me.

"I went to bed and didn't get up for weeks.

"Eventually I needed to return to purpose, because the cows were alive and full of milk, and Ray and Cameron were there, and the way for me to live was to come to the understanding, like everyone else, that Bill was dead to us. Where do they go when they die like this? Do they sit and watch us from someplace internal and see how hard we have taken it? Or do they think about us at all? Are they surprised at how quickly we go back to something close to normal? Do they imagine a homecoming one day, when they have gone full circle in whatever kind of impossible search they've been on, expecting to be kissed and adored again?

"I would have agreed to die if I thought Bill might come home hoping for that.

"Annie and I became friendlier, because we needed each other and Cameron had been helping her after the shock of it. She had received from Bill a letter in that same black handwriting not long after the postcard, which failed to tell her much more than that he would not be back. Cameron was with her on the day that she decided the letter was telling the truth, a year or so after it had come, and he watched her light it with a punk from her fireplace. It browned and curled up, and then she let it drop as the flame got near her fingers. Cam told me he had read it and was disappointed that it was little more than a 'Dear Jane,' right off the shelf, and full of hollow sorrow and regrets and faint excuses. Signed 'Bill.' It was enough to change Annie from then on. She went into a kind of mourning, drifted away from us, or would have if I hadn't kept her close. Another year later came the request for divorce.

"She and Hayes and I—ten years ago now—went up to the

redwoods together and rented a cabin for a week. For the first couple of days we had a quiet time, Annie and I talking about things and wondering out loud and drinking a little bit, I confess, while Hayes was out exploring. Annie was still a pretty girl and (when I stopped to think about it) only thirty years old. Most of the time she was a capable mother and was doing fairly well renting out her land to make a living, since the house was free and clear, thanks to her father. Sometimes, though, she gave in to this mourning of hers, which had never really subsided but only got pushed back. And when she gave in to it, she was like I had been those first weeks after Bill left, and she couldn't be talked to. One of those nights in the redwoods, I remember, I said to her as we sat on the porch and listened to the wind playing the treetops, I said, 'Don't you think it's about time to put it behind you, Ann?' And she looked at me there in the half dark and she said, 'It is behind me. There's just not much in front anymore.'

"She became tense and quiet after that, spending whole hours alone. I wished I hadn't been so blunt with her.

"It was tempting go further though, if I didn't think it would hurt her more than she was. I already knew that she had married Bill for a flavor of love that nobody could believe in but a young girl, and it would just have been cruel to go on pressing her."

—|—

"DON AND I live comparatively separate lives, which, believe me, is the way I like it. He has his concerns—the animals, the land, the workers, the price of feed and diesel—I have mine. And I don't tend to share mine with him.

"Why is it the status quo, do you think, that the husband and the wife have their own territories and there's a wood and wire fence running all along the border between them?

"I was saying to Annie, not all that long ago at one of our rare meetings, that she has been wiser than she probably realizes, keeping her independence—including from her father—because she's been able to create her own destiny. It sounds pretentious, I know, but I said that it was a thing to be cherished, independence, and most women have to battle for it if it's something they really want. I have been 'doing' feminism these last few years, so I know, and I'm lucky that Don hasn't decided to put up much of a fight.

"Annie said, though, it's only independence if you wanted it. Otherwise it's something else. Isolation comes to mind, she said. Loneliness. To which I said (because I wanted her to see that life has a way of reaching balance even if it's not an ideal state of it), 'You're not lonely. You have Hayes. You have Miranda.'

"I wish I could have added that she had me too, but that hadn't been true for a long time. I gave up the right when I stood by Don's inflexibilities.

"She looked at me with that little angle to her neck, her blue eyes narrowing just a bit as they do, and she said, 'That's not what I mean.'

"Obviously Annie has things going on in her that she doesn't want to let out into the light, and I say fair enough. She is a big girl, and casting light on these things tends to change their character anyway. In that sense I actually agree with my husband, who always said that Annie will sink or swim. It looks like she's done quite a bit of each.

"Whatever she is thinking and feeling, though, it does not come out in the things she says but instead shows in her face. Now, almost forty, she looks like a woman who has suffered through a string of unexpected mournings. Her youth is a thing of the past.

"Funny, that phrase. Her youth is a thing of the past. Everyone's is.

"It was two years ago, I think, that I took a weekend trip to San Francisco and stayed in the Huntington on Nob Hill, just a little opportunity to get away from the odors of the ranch and the general summer haze caused by all that dust. It's hell on the lungs. San Francisco is cold in the summer, and the air is moist, a comfort. I'd had a habit of taking these refresher weekends for a few years by that time, a gesture of independence on my part that Don did not object to in any way because he got to play the rye-drinking bachelor while I was gone, and I didn't care what he was up to. It was one of those compromises that old married couples like us relied on for that all-important balance.

"While I was in the city, I went to an art gallery near Union Square, hoping to find a small painting I could give Annie for her birthday. Over these years I had made it a point to search out an annual present for her. A way, I suppose, of feeling connected, close. I was looking for something with color, playful, for one of her walls in that dark house of hers. Instead, as I browsed around in there, I found a collection of photographs by Bill Argus, and I wasn't prepared for the shock of learning that this was what he had gone on to do. We hadn't heard of him or from him since the divorce, and both Don and Ray Argus ranted, when in their cups, that he wasn't welcome again in the general vicinity of Pianto. Since we didn't expect him to reappear, we all agreed to erase his memory and give Hayes a father he could be proud of. A dead one.

"That sounds so much worse than I mean it to.

"I stood there in the small white gallery and looked at the photographs. At first I hadn't seen the name of the photographer, so I immediately found them beautiful, these black-and-white desert studies, everything in them inanimate but completely alive, if that makes sense. I said to myself, This artist has a gift (always proud of my ability to know quality when I saw it). And then his name came out of the wall at me, and I had to sit for a while and justify hating the work.

"There was one shot that I kept letting my eyes go back to, of a tall, lonely palm tree gravid with dead fronds, rising out of what looked like nothing but a gray rock pile. It was surrounded by hostile mountain angles and natural debris, and it looked doomed. Whether there was anything intentional about the metaphor or not, I had no idea, but I kept staring and appending my own anxieties to it, and I came to the conclusion, by myself in that empty white room, that it was a blessing that this thing had come to exist."

—|—

"THEY ALWAYS TELL me that Hayes doesn't look like his father and that it's a good thing he doesn't, because I would be reminded all the time if he did, I wouldn't be able to stop thinking of Bill. But they don't understand that I'm reminded of him anyway. Hayes doesn't need to look like anybody to remind me. His presence is enough.

"Bill had been gone eight years when I had a little breakdown in front of Miranda. It was one of a series. I'm sorry. I've been able to hang on and keep my grip most of the time, but once in a while I just let go, the way you can hang from a tree limb and allow yourself to fall, and that's what I did to Miranda last year. We were at her house, in the kitchen, and she was telling me that she didn't understand people like me and Cameron, who refused to face facts and marry. I sat there at her table with my iced tea and my lunch. Hayes was out walking the fence alone to kill the time and probably wondering why we had this connection with the Arguses anyway, they were nobody to us as far as he knew. Miranda, that day, wouldn't stop harping about marriage, and when she said that about Cam and me, I misunderstood her. I thought she was saying that he and I should marry, so I knocked my tea glass off the table and shrieked at her, 'I've *already* had my heart torn up by *one* of your sons, Andie.'

"She looked at me as if I was going mad. I must have been screeching or wailing or something uncontrollable, because she came to me with her arms out and saying, 'Baby, it's all right, I'm sorry,' and in a moment I found myself wrapped up in her and pulling us both to the floor. We sat there on the kitchen tile and embraced, with our dresses spread out around us. I remember that her hands, wiping my hair away from my eyes, smelled like ham and onions.

"It was a good thing that Hayes didn't come in to find us like that, because at twelve he wouldn't have understood. He had no reason to think I was anything but fine and lonesome, nothing more, so this would have been a shock. It was even better that Ray Argus didn't come in. I might have gone at him with my nails if he'd said anything mean.

"That was one time, and there had been others, but at least Miranda stopped telling me to marry. She finally understood I couldn't. I would have to be able to love someone, and I didn't have the nerves for it anymore. My own mother, on the other hand, was pleased I was alone, a widow of sorts. She wasn't unhappy with all the lies we had to dream up just to protect Hayes, and she wasn't above asking people in town to keep the lies going for his sake. I don't think she minded all that much not knowing him. At least outwardly didn't show it. She's a practical woman above almost everything else.

"Cameron was the one who understood best. He thought up the lies. It was as if he was more ashamed of Bill than anybody and, like me, couldn't forget him so easily. He understood how I couldn't be in love anymore and never once said that I should find some man and marry again so Hayes would have a father. He said, 'Hayes can't do better than Captain Diamond, we'll make sure of it.'

"The strange thing—and I used to tell Cameron this—was

that I didn't think I'd ever have fallen in love with Captain Diamond, whoever he was.

"It's one of those what Mother calls ironies. That the man who was best for Hayes wasn't only dead, he never lived at all. And the man who would matter most to Hayes (if Hayes even knew about him) was so far away in the world that he might as well be dead.

" 'Women who don't marry for love are very lonely,' I told Mother one time, and she said, 'So are lots of them who do, honey.' "

+

"DURING THAT TRIP to the redwoods, Annie vanished. It was our last evening there, and I was going to cook a meal in the cabin kitchenette for us all. Hayes came in from exploring the nearby creek and told me that he had grabbed a lizard by the tail and the tail came off in his fingers. He had it to show me, a souvenir. I was feeling playful by then—like I rarely felt at home—and I said to him, 'Let's put it in the stew. Maybe it'll add an extra-special flavor.' Hayes, with his pretty blue eyes smiling, made a nasty face and said that he didn't think he'd like the taste of lizard tail. I wanted to kiss him.

"The food was ready to eat, and I went out on the porch and rang the supper triangle they had hung from the eaves. It was a lovely, pure sound, and I liked the way it carried into the trees. 'That's pretty, isn't it, Hayes?' I said, and he was sitting on the rocker peeling a stick of all its bark and studying its grain. 'Where's your mom, honey, do you know?'

" 'In the woods, probably,' he said, unconcerned.

" 'In the woods? She doesn't know these woods.'

" 'That doesn't matter to her.'

" 'She'll get lost, and it'll be dark soon.'

"Hayes just wasn't upset by how his mother was absent. He told me that she often took long walks in the woods around their house, climbed up to the ridgetop, spent whole days up there. 'She says just to think,' he said. At this tender age of ten he seemed used to it. I'd have quizzed him about how long she had been doing that and whether she ever left him alone for more than a little while, but I was worried about Annie now and asked him to take me to the trail where he thought she had probably gone.

"We left the cabins and entered the woods between two enormous redwoods that seemed to mark the open mouth of a tunnel. If it was growing dark in the clearing, it was almost pitch-black in the forest, and I let us walk just a few paces along the trail before I stopped and began calling Annie's name. My voice drifted up the hillsides and caught in the ferns. There was no echo at all. I didn't think she would be able to hear me.

"The little boy, my grandson, held my hand and told me it was all right, she sometimes came back after dark and she was always fine, even better than she was when she set out on one of her walks. They made her feel good, he told me.

"This boy, talking like he had the wisdom of a man. He didn't even know he was putting me to shame.

"Back at the cabin, Hayes and I had our stew and bread and salad on the porch and kept an eye on the edge of the woods, but soon it was clear that Annie wasn't coming back while we watched. I got him ready for bed and told him that everything was going to be fine. 'I know,' he said, looking up at me calmly from his pillow, and I was struck almost to tears at the unshakable faith he had in his fragile mother.

"It was in the middle of the night, with nothing to see by but a faint reflection from the moon, that Annie slid into bed beside me smelling of pine and soil and dried sweat. I couldn't see her face, but I could hear her breathing as she settled in, and it was regular and calm and unperturbed, and she was somehow revived."

+

"I SPENT MORE than two hours looking at his pictures in that gallery. The prints were luminous, even their oil-blacks, and the figures in them—mostly gnarled desert plants or curious stones and mountain silhouettes—spoke of loneliness and exile. There might be blasts of harsh light in one corner of the picture, but the subject cowered in shadow, vague and reluctant. The forms were geometric, angles and long straight lines, a rare curve appearing in the spiral fibers at the end of a frond or shapes under the surface of a stream. It was difficult to believe that my once son-in-law had produced these remarkable things.

"The last piece in the room was accompanied by a picture of the photographer. He was not the man I remembered—or the boy, I should say—but instead had gone gray in the temples already and had a salted beard, hard crow's-feet at the eyes. He was fourteen or fifteen years older than when I had last seen him, of course (which put him close to forty), but there was something in his face that made him appear even older than that, the look of a man who dwelled on things. I stood there looking at him for a long time and even talked to his image—under my breath—when there was nobody else in the room, asking him how he stumbled on this talent of his, where his vision seemed to come from, why he couldn't have grown into it in Pianto, with us. There was nothing in his face that answered these questions, except the obvious traits of a man in a state of perpetual regret.

"Or at least that's what I chose to see in him that day.

"I left the gallery and spent the rest of my time in San Francisco in an unsettled mood, calling the pictures back to mind as I walked downtown or as I let my head dip into the bathwater. There was nothing I had ever seen in Bill Argus that would have given me a hint that he would one day become what he now was.

To me he had been a poor rancher's son with the imagination of one, something of a charmer when he wanted to be, blessed—if anything—with the ability to talk to anybody and forget or set aside his origins (which Don never let him or his family forget). I was always a little leery of him. Like he was playing a scheme.

"I thought of all the pain and difficulty and sourness and lies that had followed his departure, all of which were still alive in Pianto in everyone from Miranda Argus to Don, in Annie, of course, and in me.

"Hayes, by design, was the only one who didn't feel any of it.

"It might not be surprising, but when I got back to Pianto I did not mention the pictures to anyone. I had to fight myself to keep yet another secret, but I couldn't think of a good thing that would come from Annie knowing about Bill. It was clear that he had reinvented himself.

"It occurred to me that the photographs would never have come to light if Bill Argus had stayed with us. The photographs, because of the suffering behind them, the trouble, the illness, the confusion and anger, contained more than their images. They contained the stunning irony that it was our pain that allowed them to exist at all.

"Oh, I was very drunk when I came up with that idea, but it did stick."

—|—

"HAYES IS A beautiful young man of twenty, and I am glad that he looks like me. Red hair, blue eyes. He reminds me that I have something good and strong inside. I drift into these moods and I let myself get dark over it, but then I came to the surface again and emerge and there he is, loving me, and I'm grateful for him.

"It has been so long, and I feel so old already, but it will always break my heart that Bill doesn't know his boy and his boy will never know of him. That's the tragic thing."

AVAILABLE LIGHT—1979

Bill

Because you carry your home port around with you, he was always telling himself, drag it behind like it's snagged on your anchor chain. You take the customs and ways with you, you take the local games, the rituals, the superstitions, the never changing annuals, the narcotic smell of the air, silhouettes of hill shoulders and saddles, tree lines, and maps of the place as seen from above. It never goes away, none of it.

Bill Argus was forty-one years old and good with a camera all of a sudden, possessed of an eye. It was as if the talent had been invested in him by a muse or a succubus who came and fucked him while he slept in his dirty little trailer, gave him the gift by mouth-to-mouth infusion. Now, in 1979, there were those in places as far away as Ohio and 'Bama, Big Sky Country—Liechtenstein, for all he knew—who'd heard of him because of the pictures. He was famous, in circles, treated well no matter where he went, but he was smart enough to stay the hell away from where he wouldn't be too welcome, Pianto, the home port he kept clamped to his ankle like an iron weight. There'd been drinking and feeling sorry for himself, there'd been half-assed suicide attempts, the slow-cooking kind, such as walking a hot longitude across the desert floor without water and hoping to pass out before the suffering began. Failed. Or challenging bigger men to dustups in some parking lot over a slight he meant only as provocation, no offense. Took a few punches, broke a nosebone that way. The pain felt worthwhile, the salt-blood in his mouth a reminder that he was one wicked dog and deserved worse. There's a point where you can't get enough of it, no punishment adequate short of some kind of Guatemalan military torture, testicular shocks, cigarette tips applied to tender parts.

But he worked his way through it and took pictures of the desert, a kind of penance. The desert was a place that reflected his interior in a way that no other setting held a torch to, a place that looked empty until you studied it, a place that seemed unquestionably hostile until you lived there. His spirit felt at home there, canned in his trailer like a thing to be kept unspoiled in a vacuum until emergency called for it. Pop the seal on that thing when the time comes.

Money arrived in unprecedented heaps. Bought himself a house near Oasis, and the irony wasn't wasted on him.

His boy would be out of high school by then. Looking like either me or Annie, he thought, or the blend of us, and making his mother crazy with his Billness. He'd have asked the key questions and gotten blunt answers, the truth, no soft-soaping from Annie or Cam or Big Don Hayes or Bad Ray. Only Bill's mother would have found a kinder thing to say, he imagined, and even then she probably said it in tears and showed what a prick her boy was that way. He'd been gone eighteen years.

It never went away, the pain of all that, the ache of his regret. It never would. He didn't want it to. It gave him reason to keep pointing his camera at things and hoping some kind of exoneration would show up in grays and blacks on the paper.

+

HIS AGENT SUMMONED him to Los Angeles for a party to celebrate the publication of his second book of photos. The book was called *Sin Nombre*, "Without a Name," because many of the shots were taken in a canyon with that label on it, not far from Oasis. The artsy-fartsy crowd liked the idea of an unnamed thing that nonetheless had a name. They made the mistake of thinking he meant the canyon in the pictures.

He drove into L.A. for the party, a suit coat draped in the back of his Jeep, cameras and gear packed on the floor of the passenger seat. It wasn't something he was looking forward to, this get-together, because he had a hard time with the vapid chitchat and the cheek kissing, the declarations of spiritual orgasm, the running bullshit. His agent, Cleo, watched him like a snake at these things, fearing that he'd run amok and get his name in the papers, along with a mug shot.

"There's good publicity and there's bad," she often said. "That would be the bad kind."

"Then make sure I have a Wild Turkey in my hand at all times and I'll keep a cool head," he'd tell her.

And of course she'd do as directed and keep him in a fine foam all evening, drive him to his hotel at the end of things, because a DUI was of the bad-publicity type.

At the Brentwood soirée he took a great helping of grappa and was discovered by the host with his shoes and socks off, soaking his feet in the koi pond. When this host tried to extract him, politely, from the water, Bill became surly and took a couple of ineffectual swings. Women gasped, and some of the men circled the two and muttered, "Now see here, pal."

Bill shook himself away from the flimsy half nelson someone was trying to put on him. He spun around the courtyard, shouting, "You assbites wouldn't know a good picture if you had it tattooed inside your eyelids."

Cleo rushed him back to her car as if he were the dauphin being secreted out of revolutionary Paris, a ladies' sweater over his head in case there were any tabloidal photographers around. And then, back at his hotel, she begged him to consult a therapist. He nearly took a swing at *her*. She stood more than arm's length away from him in her slink-dress and said that if he didn't find a way to settle down, she'd have to take a pass on representing him.

His tongue felt like gum in his mouth.

"Whatever you have on your mind, Bill, it has to be taken care of. Surgically removed, if need be."

"Fine."

"See somebody. Promise me."

"I will."

"Get your head together." She was such the doting *madre*, smoothing his jacket for him. "We're making good money. I don't want you screwing it up."

And off she went in a trail of Mercedes diesel smoke, Bill left alone in the horseshoe drive of the hotel with ocean view, dizzy from the fingers of grappa plying his mind from the inside out.

BUT THERE WAS a story behind *Sin Nombre*, and it was one he wouldn't tell anybody. A compeer from the darkroom, Bill's equal in temperament but not in talent, gave him some magic rocks that turned out to be dried peyote buttons, a thing Bill hadn't heard of before. He said, "You chew a few of these up and then go out to some canyon and see what you can see. I guarantee you your camera won't be able to do justice. You might want to turn to painting after this."

"We'll see," Bill told him. Drove off in the Jeep with his gear and his peyote buttons and some Wild Turkey to wash them down with. He hit his trail head in the late afternoon and started out with a heavy pack and a walking stick, the stick his habit ever since a childhood experience in the woods. He avoided a rattler sprawled comfortably across the trail for the sun heat. It took hardly any notice of him, his footfalls were so easy, and when it did it merely flicked its tongue to get a whiff of him. A little later he spotted a tarantula walking ahead of his shadow. All the poisonous things were out. He wondered if it boded a little bit poorly for his trip.

Barrel cacti leaned off plumb to grab the best sunlight. He stopped to catch them on film with the afternoon shadows slashing over the ground, light and dark duking it out. He set up his tripod and Leica, screwed a filter into the lens, a rubber hood to keep out some of the glare, using a wide-angle lens so the cacti loomed taller against the mountain behind, which was throwing shadow like the imminent past.

When he did this, and this was nearly all he did, he was not aware of time. He was aware of the changes in light but not the time itself; it was as if he managed to slip away from the clock when he worked, the light meter becoming his timepiece. He had managed to float through some sixteen years like this, losing himself in the work and the desert and growing older without notice, gaining specks of gray in the beard and subtle, nagging changes in his joints. Where other men might have asked, "Where'd the time go?" Bill didn't indulge. The time was not a thing he paid attention to because it only increased the damage, the disgrace, and he knew it, so he asked, "Where'd the light go?" He could keep living if there was enough light, simple as that. He slept through the dark and rose early to receive the light. It was the way he had been living for years.

It became too dark to photograph, so he packed and walked on. Dusk in the desert, the sun at his back and making his shadow forty feet long into the mouth of Cañon Sin Nombre. It made him look like a Sasquatch who got off at the wrong turnpike exit. Easy to maintain his own company out there. Nobody else around. He liked it that way, because he didn't care to get into it with other people—bullshitters, truck drivers, women at the tavern. One thing always led to the other, and he was inclined to make up a past for himself rather than get into it. Make it up as he'd go along, creating a scarecrow filled with sage straw and looking flimsy in the spine. When a woman starts to ask about his family is when she is thinking of snagging a husband, and he couldn't do that anymore, with his problem. He'd divorced, but never seeing her again was like leaving things in limbo, unstamped, unfiled. Annie back there, wondering why he'd done it. He couldn't begin to explain, couldn't put a sentence to the drive that had made him go, but it was for her own good, he knew that much, and she and the boy were better off without him. What he had in those days was an anger that smoldered in the stomach like a fire in your basement box of greasy rags, and it flared sometimes in unpredictable ways that he couldn't control. Or chose not to. It was palpable, a kind of hand-me-down anger, and familiar. Like the time he faked a problem with the truck on the way back from Bodega Bay one dirty wet day in November. Annie and Hayes in the bench seat next to him when he began making the thing pull hard to the right on the slick road, scaring up gravel showers as he wrenched back into the parallel lines. Went on like that for a couple of miles, all their mouths sewn shut from the fear, until he pulled over at last and made them get out. He said he'd drive into Pianto himself, get it checked out, then come back for them. "I want to be with you," Annie said, with the still-little Hayes looking out at the austere hills over her shoulder, and Bill answered, harshly, "I won't have all three of us going over some cliff and dying. I'll be back for you as soon as I can."

Instead of going into Pianto, he went home. He stayed a couple of hours there on his own, calming himself with whiskey as the cold rain came down. Went out again to drive, without aim, until it seemed time to look for them, but by then they were nearly home, soaked on the Freestone Road. Upon first sight of them he found himself growing furious again, at how in their wide-eyed expressions it was clear that they didn't know they'd been done in, duped for no reason other than that it had occurred to him to do it. They trusted him.

His head was full of such moments, real and maybe imagined. Things might have been on the drawing board. He remembered branding his brother's hand, knocking him out of the oak tree, and wondered if he was capable of hurting people like that anymore. He could see this anger of his getting insistent, thanks in large part to Big Don's accelerating bullshit and Bad Ray treating him like a worm, and this anger could become all-consuming, he foresaw, could take itself out on the innocents.

It was a done deal when he drank too much one night, took himself out of bed, and opened every window in the house. Freezing. He stood over Annie, who slept through almost anything, and considered burning the borrowed house down around the three of them, a way of snapping Big Don out of his ignorance and into a shot of real grief. But a wiser voice in him came to prevail, and it said, You need to leave. You just need to get out.

All of this was long ago. So this woman in the bar, she would just have to make do with his hems and haws, his innocent fibbing, and bring him home anyway. Sometimes they did, these women. When it came down to it, they didn't want the husband so much as a thing to hold on to in the night, which was a thing he could be.

He set up camp at the foot of a slot canyon, built a fire with dried mesquite wood and dead sage, soon had a little bubble of light he could be comfortable in until sleep. Cooked a pot of canned stew and ate an apple with it, washing it all down with the

Wild Turkey that would make him nod off later. The silence of the desert was a thing he had become accustomed to, an absolute silence that was interrupted only by the popping of the fire and the organic hums and gurgles of his own body. It was the same thing, the same idea, as a blank page or unexposed film, filled with the potential of everything there is, but limited, too, by his own neuro-confines. There was only so much he could think to fill it with, only so much material in his head. There were recurring themes and variations, always going back to the main thing, the past and all that, and imaginings of how it was now back there, what he might be if he had stayed, who might have died, and who might be alive only because he was gone. That's the meaning of the silence out here.

Some people might have called him a tortured soul.

After he ate, he dug in his pants pocket and found his buttons, chewed them up, swallowed them down with the whiskey. Did it without thinking much because he didn't want to talk himself out of it. Bitter as hell, and they made him want to puke. No idea what to expect from little pods full of vision, and for the longest time there seemed to be no effect at all other than the nausea and headache. He sat there in his bivouac as the desert grew black around him, except for his firelight, and the stars came out like the holes in a great colander overturned on the land and trapping everything under it. He told himself that there was nothing a little button could do for him that swigs of rye hadn't been able to accomplish, but maybe it was a matter of quantity. Tiny little beans, shots and shots of rye, all taking something away from him as they gave him his ease, which struck him as a fair deal in the end. His friend had told him the peyote would not take anything away at all, it just gave and gave and gave.

Horseshit, Bill said, and he screwed the top onto his bottle and lodged it in his empty boot. Leaned back on his elbows to rest, and was then puzzled in a while when the flames of his campfire began to extend themselves up in crystal arms. The change was subtle at first but then became almost alarming, the fire growing by the moment, trying to light the underside of the dome and expose the holes. Or, it seemed like when he looked at it another way, the starlight was coming down to invest his fire with some kind of new life, like the light focused through a magnifying glass. And colorful. It was releasing blues and greens, glassy ones, and infrareds, and ultraviolets, and all the hues in between. The heat remained modest against his feet, though, enough to keep him this side of afraid.

He began to laugh. The peyote, he said to himself. Finally kicking in. It's opened up my pupils like a full aperture on the Leica, is all. And if this is it, these things aren't worth the trouble of getting some more.

And the light was one thing, but he couldn't keep from laughing. Laughing alone was a sign of madness, maybe, he had no idea, but everything hit him as funny, the whole show. Comic. Everything leading up to here and now, a vaudeville, slapstick, a setup. He was a stooge wobbling through a plot, and now's the first time he was able to look about and see that they were laughing at him, making fun. It was funny as hell. Here all along he thought he was something else, a walking shame, when in actual fact he was nothing but a clown.

It figured.

The fire danced for him, shooting arcs and arrows into the sky. He could have watched it all night, as long as the fuel was handy, but out of the silence came the tone of an animal's hooves on trail rock, like wood mallets on broken china platters. He sat up and looked around, the streaking firelight washing out the far distance. Couldn't see a thing, but it sounded like a horse without saddle, no leather creaking or tackle rattling on him.

No sound of a rider either. Just the hooves on rock, the snort of the animal as it hauled itself up a rise.

"Who is that?" Bill called out, but there was no answer. The thing ambled closer, so close now that Bill felt it was just outside the reach of his firelight. His vision was sharpened and attenuated by the bean, but he had no depth of field.

He got up and took a couple of steps toward the darkness. The animal stopped, heaved a heavy breath. Bill understood in spite of the drug that the only weapon he had was a camera. Whoever it is, he told himself, if he wants to make a meal of me, he's getting what he came for. I might get his picture before he eats me up.

From beyond the edge of the light, a man's voice said, "Have a seat."

"Who's there?"

And it was funny to him, the bean turning everything funny.

"Just take a seat and we can have a little talk," said the rider, and Bill fell back laughing, on the ground with his knees locked up in his looped arms.

Oh, Jesus shit, he said.

Like something that appears from inside a thick fog when you're out walking pastures, the animal came into view. A bull, full-horned, black-eyed, red-coated. On its back, sitting in casual posture with one hand on the bull's reins and the other resting in his own lap, was Ray Argus. Bad Ray, awhile dead by then. Bill looked at him in bewildered silence.

He should have recognized the voice. Dark, deep, as full of intimidation as always, a mildly mocking undertone.

"I thought I'd find you here," Ray said blithely, guiding the bull fully into the firelight. The flames began to settle down. "I said to myself, Where would you expect to find your son but out in that lonesome canyon with his bottle and his camera and his head full of self-pity and regrets."

"It isn't the first time I've been here."

"I didn't say it was. I've followed you out here before. Watched you do your thing. Hey, you call those pictures? I can't believe you sell them goddamn things."

Bill said, "Why are you here, Ray." A defensive burr in his throat.

The bull shuffled a bit, head hanging like it wished to graze, but Bad Ray didn't dismount. He remained at high angle to Bill's eye, on the other side of the fire so that the light gave him full detail. He was, Bill had to guess, about forty years old, a figure Bill remembered, long-faced, deep-eyed, not so much chiseled as chipped. Ray hadn't been much older when Bill left.

"Just to catch up, son! Shoot the shit! It's been a long time, hasn't it? We probably have a lot to say to each other." Ray eyed him without affect.

"I heard you died. Cam told me. You and Mom both."

"You in touch with Cameron?"

"Once in a while." Lying to the dead. "A letter here and there."

"Uh-huh."

"I heard how it happened."

"Well now." Shaking his head. "I don't think I came all this way to talk about that."

He was becoming accustomed to the image of his father astride a massive bull. The peyote was making him inclined to accept whatever happened, but what he did find was that seeing his father again did not provoke feelings of nostalgia and loss. He felt like he was about to hear a threat, notice of impending punishment, a trampling.

"What will we talk about then?"

"What a shit you always were, how's that?" Bad Ray started to laugh dementedly, the way he always did, a high, unrestrained cackle. He scratched the corner of his nose, then tipped his overseasoned hat back on his head, the same hat he used to wear on the ranch, straw, worn black on the rim where he handled it.

"Fair enough," said Bill.

"Oh is it." Ray's laughter settling into a judgmental chuckle. "I can't stop you, let's put it that way."

Bill didn't ask first, took up his camera and began shooting all this. Bracketing his shots to get at least one keeper for each composition. His father all but posed, whipping his hat off and holding it high like a rodeo bull rider. Through the viewfinder the bull and rider took on an even ghostlier texture, the grain of the lens and mirror, but the firelight was enough to capture them by.

"You think you're pretty good with that, don't you."

"I don't think about it."

"You're a disappointment to your son."

"I imagine I am," said Bill.

"He doesn't know your name."

A sharp stroke to the head, that one was. "Why should he," Bill replied, still shooting.

"He doesn't know you."

"Same way I never knew you." Bill's jaw was locked as he stared up at the man.

He knew that the drug was keeping him from breaking into a hundred jagged pieces, flinging himself at his old man to pummel and then hug his head close. But he had a feeling this wouldn't be happening without the drug. The fire was pulsing now, cracking on dry fuel. Bill clicked away, the shutter speed down to long open seconds to catch the dark ghost in the firelight.

You don't ever know what you'll want to say to your dead father when he shows up on the back of a bull one night while you're wacky on peyote beans and Wild Turkey, do you? Unless you're smart enough to rehearse ahead of time. Bill hadn't anticipated.

"Don't start in on your whining," Ray said.

"I'm not whining. Just stating the fact."

"I'm a lot smarter now than I was back then, boy, so I'm not about to get lured into a sobfest with you. I'm here to say something."

Now Bill managed a laugh of his own. "You have some words of wisdom for me, eh?"

"A pearl, call it."

"I guess it'll have to do, since I didn't get squat in your will."

The ghost gave him a patient smile. "You didn't deserve anything, son. Not even the cow shit on the land, because you might figure out a way to sell it as fertilizer. Cam deserved it. He's doing all right. You jealous?"

"Not in the goddamn least."

"Well goody-goo for you, bud."

"I'm doing fine myself, if you haven't noticed."

"Hey, that is just ducky, kiddo. Just fucky-ducky. I'm happy for you."

On peyote, Bill didn't find it as strange as he might have that he and his dead father were conversing like a couple of four-year-olds with potty mouths. The bull gave him a pacified look and chewed on invisible cud over the multicolored fire. Bill would not have been surprised if it had spoken in baritone: "He's just jerking your chain, Bill."

"So what's this pearl you have for me. Not that I need the advice. And not that I'd take it from you anyway." Clicking and cranking away with his thumb at the film advance. Focusing underhanded, bracket the f-stop and shutter speed, aperture wide open.

Bad Ray sat impassively astride the great bull, looking down on Bill with a face of pity like the face of a saint who knew that the shit was about to hit the fan. Both his hands now folded in his lap. In the sweetest, gentlest voice Bill had ever heard from his father's lips, he said, "Life's too short."

"Life's too short?"

"Life's too short, son."

"You come back from the dead on a bull's back to tell me life's too short? I had that figured out for myself! Judas Priest, what kind of a pearl is *that.*"

"Listen, the best ones are always the simplest. Life's too short. It boils down to that, clean and straight."

Bill shook his head and let his camera down, eyes into the dark middle of the fire where the flames were boiling together in colors and swirling into knots. In many ways, to him, life seemed extraordinarily long. Unnecessarily. Repetitive and often hollow. Dark. When he looked up again, the rider was pulling up on the reins and turning his bull around.

"Hey, wait!" Bill climbed to his feet as the animal began to stalk away. The back of his father, fading into the night. "Wait a minute, Ray! Where's Mom? Get Mom out here, I want to talk to her! I want to apologize to her! Tell her that much for me, all right? Tell her I'm sorry."

With the mount and rider vanishing, he took up the camera again and shot rapidly with the shutter speed high and the field as deep as he could get it, and the fire was shooting sparks now, high-flying ones that appeared to salt the black sky. In a few moments the hallucination—that's what Bill immediately began to call it—had vanished, and all that was left was the silent wilderness.

Bill stayed awake the rest of the night expecting something else, but he did not eat another peyote bean. He hoped to be lucid for the next thing.

—|—

WHEN THE PICTURES appeared in his book a year later, they did not show the bull and rider or the striking display the fire had put on. Instead, the barrel cacti leaned in a stifled glow out of the dark and their shapes and indistinct edgings took on the eerie quality of people standing back from something too wild to trust.

Bill kept the story to himself. His father had told him he was without a name, and this was not the kind of thing he wanted to get into with people.

WHAT SEEMED TO BE HIS ASHES

Nora

My childhood wasn't the stuff of a horror movie, I know, but it wasn't that much fun either. Cary Lee on the rampage. Grandma Elsie trying to save me with her sweetness. Fights and grudges, a fair number of running-aways on my part, and always getting dragged back home, where Mother would try to make me feel welcome again. But would quickly fall back into her wicked-witch ways. She'd ply me with these meals she'd make of goose livers and shallots and other things I hated, drinking while cooking, and by the time the stuff got served she was mad at me again and inviting me to walk out the door if that's what I really wanted.

Elsie died of a heart problem, all alone in her apartment, and I thought I was going to have to run away again. Mother's boyfriends and their groping. And her way of leaving me to my own worst instincts when it came to dressing myself and deciding whether to go to school or not. I was almost fifteen. Mother had quite a mouth on her, and she'd howl at me if she found out that I'd skipped a few days or that I'd worn a miniskirt and no underpants, and she'd blare in front of her man of the hour,

"No daughter of mine is going to school dressed like a slut!"—which only mesmerized the boyfriend standing there in a shiny suit coat with one hand deep in his pocket, diddling. She wanted to prove she was a good mother, but what she was doing was making me out to be a toy for these guys. Maybe they paid her for a little something, I don't know. Maybe I was for sale and nobody told me.

White slavery on the home front. I was tallish and thin-hipped and built like a rope doll, but still those men loved me. Of course, I still loved myself back then too.

This all kept up until Jack came along. I haven't said much about Jack until now because . . . not because he slipped my mind. Because he was different and I was saving him up. He was an older man, polite and kind and, God help me, fatherly. I wanted him to stay. He wore nice suits and cologne, always had a wad of cash in what he called his billfold.

I've loved that word ever since. Billfold.

Mother was out of her league with him, even though he was just a retired policeman and nothing but a high school graduate. (Cary Lee, remember, had gone to a fancy eastern college to meet the man she would marry, taught to expect the best.) Jack had homegrown refinement, a sense of style, a chin like a hard-boiled egg. He was funny and alarmingly charming to my pubescent feel for these things.

Mother said to me one day, "How would you like it if I had Jack move in with us?"

This was possibly a trick question, I knew enough to suspect. I shrugged. I was a girl of few words a lot of the time back then.

"Because I think he might be the one, sweetie. Finally." She raised her wineglass to me and sipped from it, a smile irrepressible on the rim. The happiest I'd seen her. "At long last love, how 'bout that, bunny!"

I had reached an age, almost sixteen, where I could hold my own against Mother's boyfriends, could haul off and smack them if I felt like it, or tease them into anger so that they'd be seen by Cary Lee as men who might hit. She would not let herself be hit by a man, God love her, and some had tried. But since I felt like I could handle this Jack if he ever made a move on me (though his cologne and his style and his egg chin were awfully appealing to me in an unfamiliar way), I said it was fine with me.

"As long as I get to keep my room."

"Dear heart," Cary Lee said, her glass drained down, "he sleeps in my room. You ought to know that by now."

"You want to marry him?" I asked, and her eyes flashed at me in warning. Then she must have let herself consider the thought for the first time, poked her way through her own defenses.

"There's plenty of time to think about that," she said. "You know me. I don't rush into a bad situation, do I."

Laughed herself silly. Poured some more wine.

I wouldn't dare say those next couple of years were great. They weren't so great, but they were better. Jack was a funny man and knew how to handle Mother, and the two of us worked out ways to gang up on her and make her behave. He was my advocate and defended me when she wanted to blame me for something I had nothing to do with. He chastised her when she trashed my room for a perceived slight on her part, a little display of disrespect, and then he came to me and said, "I know it's tough sometimes, Nora, but if you don't respect your mom, she isn't too inclined to respect you."

I looked at him as if to say, What's to respect?

He said, "It ain't necessarily fair, sweetpea." A Brooklyn accent, because that's where he was from. Lapsing into "deze" and "doze" once in a while.

Jack and his creased and pleated trousers, his shirts with the fleur-de-lis patterns. His shaving nicks and his hairy hands and arms. Slapping the cologne on his cheeks, spraying the Right

Guard into his mossy armpits. He often left the bathroom door open when he showered so there'd be less steam, and I watched him through the glass door from time to time because I had never seen a man like that before. It wasn't as if he was really my father or anything.

And anyway, Mother never caught me watching.

It was good, fairly good, even after I barged into Mother's bedroom one Sunday morning and caught them fucking, and I was old enough to appreciate what they were up to. I got engrossed in the sight of it, Jack on the upswing, Mother's legs on his shoulders like she was wrestling him and nearly pinned. A glimpse of their wet pieces, and Cary Lee's tit pouring down one side like a frying egg that hasn't set.

She saw me. With her head turned to languish, I guess, and her eyes rolling down from inside her head, she saw me and I took a step back, wanting to vanish behind the door.

The strangest thing, though. Instead of screeching and hauling Jack out and off, instead of roaring my name and threatening to toss me out on the street, she gave me a look of nonchalance that said, You're old enough to get it now, hon. This is what I have to put up with to keep a man on the premises.

Jack chugging along unawares, that hairy bottom pumping and pumping. I thought of that other oh-well time I'd witnessed when I was younger.

Bowed my head and tiptoed off, Mother laughing as I backed down the hallway. Downstairs, at the easy chair where Jack smoked in the evenings, I emptied the ashes out of his pipe for him and got it all nice and clean.

IT WAS A few days after Cam took us up to the ridge to see where Bill's son lived when Aunt Carmen made her entry. Bill and I were at the house, Cam working his bar. Midmorning, and we were still a little bleary-eyed from staying up too late drinking Jim Beam after Cam got home the night before. Gradually Cam had started talking to his brother a little more openly, raising memories and impressions, asking Bill if he remembered them. He half wondered sometimes whether he had dreamed up a lot of the things in his head, he told us, with nobody reliable to confirm or deny them. Since Mom and Dad died. Since Annie lost her flair for detail. I felt sorry for the poor man. Such a kind soul he struck me as, and I liked him more and more the longer we stayed.

That morning Bill was sitting at the dining room table with a bunch of contact prints scattered out in front of him, his magnifying eyepiece strapped onto his face. In the little time we'd been in Pianto, he'd managed to locate a darkroom in Santa Rosa and had gone in to develop some of his recent shots. They were pretty good too. The falling-down outbuildings, the paintless school walls. Fences that hadn't been mended in almost as long as he'd been gone. I was starting to see the point of his book.

There was no knock on the door, just a few heavy footsteps on the porch, a brisk rattling of a key in the lock, and then the door flew open. A very old, shriveled lady in Sears khakis, a Sears blue work shirt, and Sears steel-toed boots came in and caught me lying on the couch with my legs spread wide open, since it was getting to be a hot day already.

"You can slap that mantrap shut," the woman said. "Who the hell are you, by the way."

Her face was wrinkled and tanned, like she'd been in the sun almost as much as I had in the desert, and she had what I'd call blond hair on a paler woman but metallic yellow on her.

"I'm Cameron's sister-in-law," I said, raising myself. "His brother and I came up for a visit from down south."

"See now," she barked. "That's how I know you're lying, missy."

She closed the door behind her as if to keep me from running off.

"How?"

"Because Cam's brother wouldn't dare show his sorry ass here in this house. Who are you."

Bill, in his typical way, was viewing all this from a safe, objective perch at the table. He could have popped off a roll of Tri-X Pan as we argued. At last, he got up and came through the archway and into the living room, his eyepiece still locked onto his face. He went up to her, took her hand, lifted it to his lips, and kissed it the way he'd learned to do when he was famous. "Aunt Car," he said, raising the magnifier. Smiling like a cat. "It's Bill."

It was his mother's sister. I'd heard some stories about her over the years, not many. Enough to know that she came dangerously close to being an old maid, finally married a man only to become a soured divorcée in a flash. Naturally, I could relate to her when it came to that. I thought *I'd* mated for life the first time too.

Aunt Car gave him a long stare, peeling away the years of hard aging and pushed-down guilt. I suppose it was all still in his eyes, and she studied them fiercely to see if he showed the signs of regret that ought to be there.

"Why are you here, Bill? Why couldn't you stay in your own yard?"

She was visibly angry with him. She heeled the floor with her steel boot once. I couldn't tell if she was satisfied that there was regret in Bill's eyes, but she definitely accepted that this was him.

"To see you, Aunt Car. Just to see you one more time."

He leaned close to kiss her on the cheek, and she leaned back like she was prepared to do the limbo to avoid it. Her bony, freckled hand went to his chest and pushed.

"You have not. You couldn't give a ladle of shit about me, or about your brother, or anybody else alive or buried or cremated since you left." Aunt Carmen made her mouth so small it vanished inside her wrinkles. "And you know it," she said.

"Well," he said, "Cam doesn't have a problem with it. It's good to see him again. It's good to see *you* again, for that matter. How are you."

She dismissed him with a wave of her hand. Then she looked at me and said, "You married him, huh. Was there full disclosure before you went through with it?"

"You don't look a day over seventy, Carmen."

"Oh, thanks," she said. "I'm flattered. And you look like shit on a tin shingle."

I wanted to get out of the house, but Bill had it in his mind to take some pictures around the ranch and then drive them over to Santa Rosa to the darkroom. I asked Aunt Car if she was going into Pianto. She offered to drive me to The Dogleg, where I could spend some time with her and Cam if I wanted. She promised to burst my bubble where my husband was concerned, if I'd have it.

"He's flawed," I admitted. "That I know."

"You don't know the half of it, sister."

Bill gladly let us go. I think he had mixed feelings over his reunion with Aunt Carmen, who, it was clear, wasn't about to cut him any slack.

I got in her car, an old green Impala coated in summer dust. She took off as if the place might close before we got there, driving with one hand on the wheel and a concrete foot on the gas pedal.

"What you don't know could fill a book, my love," she told me, looking my way instead of at the road. "I could begin to curl your naturally straight hair right now if I wanted to."

"Well I guess everyone has a past they don't care to put in lights, don't they? I know I do."

"Sweet thing like you? Baloney. No. Here. Once Bill branded his little brother with the hot Argus brand. Knocked him out of a tree. And you do know what Bill did to his little wife and boy, don't you?"

"Yes." I believed I had all the facts now, disturbing though they might be.

She squinted. "And you still *married* him?

"He told me after the fact."

"Then you maybe could get it annulled, sweetie. Do it when you get back to Cactusville, whatever the place is called."

"Oasis."

"Well isn't that a load," she said. We were already in Pianto, spraying gravel in the parking lot next to the bar.

Cam wasn't too happy to see me and his aunt together. I think he'd just as soon have had to break up a fight between the two ranch hands who were there playing pool and drinking beer.

Aunt Car began to give him a lecture on how he should have put Bill out the minute he showed up—no offense to me—and how nothing good was going to come of this little visit. She had promised Cam's mother that she'd have Bill's scalp if he ever showed up in Pianto again. It appeared to be a promise she relished the keeping of. I had a feeling, and Cam confirmed it up front, that his mother didn't want that. She'd have wanted Bill home no matter how long it took him. She'd have wrapped him up in her arms and sobbed, as Bad Ray loaded the shotgun.

"He's here, Car. I don't think he'll stay too much longer."

"No," I said. "He's taking some pictures for a new book. Then we'll go. Scout's honor."

Aunt Car was drinking ginger ale dressed up with maraschino cherries so it seemed more like alcohol. She said she'd been off the booze for thirty years, tricking herself with little garnishes like the cherries. "Well that's good," she went on, skeptical and leery. "That's good, because I wouldn't want to think Bill had it in his mind to mess things up around here."

She gave Cam a blatant wink.

"Nora knows all about Hayes," said Cam. "And I told Bill that Hayes is deep in the dark."

I thought back to our days in the desert when Bill's regrets were still abstract and gave him mere bellyaches. Troubles were so uncomplicated when they could be blamed on Grandma Elsie's spaetzle.

"Nora here," said Carmen, "needs to be brought up to speed on Billy's crimes."

"I don't think so," Cam told her. He had nothing but politesse in his voice. "She's fine with him. They're nice together. You leave her be."

"I wouldn't mind hearing about Hayes," I said. "And Annie. For my own sake, I mean. I know it's not a good idea for Bill to—"

Carmen looked at me, gauging my trustworthiness. A cherry stem was sticking out of her mouth, and she worked her lips around it.

"Hayes," she said. "Hayes Diamond is a gem, and his mother is the sweetest doll on the face of the earth. Everything good about both of them has nothing to do with Bill Argus."

Cam offered a shrug to that thought, but he had an apologetic grin for me too. You could tell he still wanted the best for me, even though I'd been dumb enough to marry his brother.

When Carmen tottered off to the bathroom and Cam poured drinks for a few dusty-shirted ranching types, I opened up my ears to the low talk of a pair at the pool table. Two older men in tight-around-the-gut western shirts, who used the table and cues more as props than as tools of the sport. The one says, "I heard she's here with Bill Argus." He nodded toward me. The other: "He has big-league balls coming back here, dudn't he?" And then they discussed, between sips at their bottlenecks, what could happen if Bill Argus made himself known to Hayes and undid thirty-five years of their patient storytelling.

"He could get his thumbs busted, I'd say," said the one.

The other: "I'd do it myself if he did that. Or I'd run him off the road. I'd make him wish he never took his first gulp of air. Hayes Diamond doesn't need that shit in his life at this stage of the game."

I took it all to mean they were almost as protective of Hayes and Annie as Carmen was.

"WHAT ARE THEY like?" I asked Carmen. We were driving out toward the beach because she wanted to show me where her ex-husband had proposed to her. This was almost fifty years before, and she was still rehashing it, sticking voodoo pins into the memory of old Melvin.

"What are who like?"

"Hayes and Annie."

"What are they like? Let's see, what are they like." Carmen raised her eyes to the rearview. "They are like babies. How's that? Little kids."

"I'm not sure I see that," I said.

"They're like a couple of innocent babies, both of them. Not a mean bone in their bodies. They don't know anything bad. Annie's addled, of course, sad thing that is, and Hayes is just isolated as hell. That's what a sheltered life will do."

She left that hanging as if there was the littlest doubt that it was okay. I had lived an isolated life for a long time by then, and I liked it so I wasn't put off. But after a few minutes of driving, the ocean now in view ahead of us, Carmen poked me in the arm and said, "That's a good thing, by the way. It's been his salvation."

"I thought so."

"And I'm serious, Nora. He's the nicest man on earth. He doesn't need to know anything bad, if you get me."

I did. Status quo. She didn't want Bill spoiling his son's

innocence. The "father," after all, the one made up by Annie and Cam, was a pilot, a bigger-than-life hero that God had snatched from the sky. Captain Diamond, he was known as in the family, Captain Diamond who had flown missions in Korea and was test-piloting a new plane at Edwards when something went wrong over the desert floor. Ball of flames. Glory, courage, selflessness, and all the rest, except that none of it was true.

Why they'd gone into such detail, I didn't know. It seemed to me that Hayes might one day have decided to look into it all, do a little digging. And if he had, he would have discovered pretty quickly that there was no Captain Diamond and no crash in the desert, and there was no hero. He'd have found out that his whole family, Hayeses and Arguses alike, had lied to him from the start, all because of this man who'd run away when Hayes was a little one. Like me.

"Carmen," I said, "what I don't get is how Hayes managed not to find out from other people. How'd you get Greater Pianto to keep up a story like that all these years?"

She looked at me as if the thought were outlandish, one eye pursed shut. "One," she said, matter-of-factly, "people liked Annie, people liked little Hayes. People liked my sister, and people like Cameron. I don't wish to toot my own horn, but people also like me. Two, we asked them, and nicely. We suggested it was like being adopted: The parents get to tell, not the gossip mill, if it's to be told at all. Three, Don Hayes wasn't too proud to make demands that people were smart to honor. And four, there was just nothing to be gained in bringing up your husband's name in front of our boy. No point. Bill was steam in the air. He was on the other side of the moon."

"I guess he was."

"There were some close calls," she added, characterizing them more as slips of the tongue than anything malicious, but the way Annie and Hayes lived, alone, off the main circuit, in among the eucalyptus trees, damage control was always fairly easy. A visit to the offender over coffee, a sober plea, never need for a threat or warning. "Small-town living," she said. "We know a lot about everybody!"

BUT MAYBE THERE was something to be said for a big lie. Maybe I'd have felt a lot better about things if Cary Lee and Elsie had lied too, and I thought Daddy was killed on that game-board interstate, rushing home instead of flying away.

Carmen parked on the shoulder and walked me out a sandy peninsula full of plump-fingered ice plants. There was a flock of brown seabirds all gazing at the horizon. They were waiting for a signal, it looked like. Carmen said, "Here it is. Melvin's standing where you are, I'm here. He says his thing, I say yes. That's that. Oh boy oh boy."

"Tell me about him," I said.

"Not on your life."

A little way up the road, and north of Bodega Bay, the cliffs looked like they were ready to crumble right into the tide. The highway would slide in along with the bleached holiday houses along there. Everything would go back into the water, from whence it came, or "from rinse it came," as Cary Lee might have said. Which made a weird kind of sense.

I had been along here before, and Carmen made the same turn that Cam had made the day he took us up to the sheep ranch on the ridge. In a few minutes we were parked in front of the little white house with the Chinese red shutters, only this time it was clear that somebody was home. The front door was open. I could see into the house through the screen.

"You're my niece, let's say," Carmen told me. "And there *is* no Bill Argus, got it? Never was."

"Got it."

She honked the horn, and in a moment out came a slender man in a faded green T-shirt and sack-khakis who looked a few years younger than me (even though I knew him to be my senior), trailed by an old, white-haired woman in a thick denim jumper. They were both grinning like the Prize Patrol had just come calling, Hayes redheaded and sweet-eyed with a scraggle of red and gray hair under his nose and chin, and Annie kneading her fists from anxiety. Her face had the innocent candor of a dog's. Wanting to make a good impression, I smiled and shook both their hands, when Carmen introduced me as her long-lost niece from Southern California. Hayes had a comfortable, calm touch, but Annie snatched her hand from me quickly, skittish or maybe coy. Somebody who wasn't any good with the shears had given her a lousy Dutch-boy haircut.

I could see in her eyes right away that there wasn't anyone driving anymore. Her mind lived someplace else. Her pale eyebrows were knitted as she tried to fit my presence and Carmen's into something she must have been thinking about from a long time ago.

"Well," said Carmen, "I just wanted her to meet you two before she heads back down."

Hayes was looking at me with a wry smile, as if this might be some kind of trick blind date Carmen had thought up. "You never mentioned a niece from Southern California before, Car."

"Well, babe, the Harpers are far-flung, and I've stopped trying to keep track of them. Goddamn Christmas cards. Nora here looked me up."

"Out of curiosity," I said, playing along.

"She has the habit of bringing strange girls up for me to marry," Hayes said. He had an affable lift in his eyebrows. The more I studied him, the more I saw, thank God, signals of his age and maturity. There were those telltale crow's-feet and those sun specks on his cheekbones and hands. And the way he managed himself struck me as the way someone who is happy inside would, someone who grew into himself over the years.

"I do not bring strange girls up here," Carmen grumbled. "And anyway Nora's not strange."

"You do seem eligible to me," I admitted.

"I've got bachelor's manners," Hayes said. "Hold my fork overhanded and leave the toilet lid up."

Annie said, "He does. He does do that." Looking pleased to know what he was talking about for a change.

Hayes invited us in for lunch, but Carmen turned him down and said that we were due back in Pianto. Annie couldn't keep her eyes off me. Staring so hard I felt like she could read right through my little lie.

"No, we can't stay. You look good, though, kiddo. Tanning up real well this year."

Hayes was looking at me with a tinge of embarrassment. His eyes were the blue of deep seawater. Innocent, just as Carmen said. Without the burden of facts.

Bill's son. He struck me as a man who made a living doing good works, just like you're supposed to. I looked hard at him to see what there was of Bill in there, a little downhearted to find not much. There was a flash of Bill's eyes in him, and, strangely, Hayes wore Bill's hands on the ends of his arms.

We went inside for a few minutes so Annie could show us her drawings. This was a sudden talent she had acquired, Hayes told us. Six or seven years ago. She just began drawing scenes—houses, landscapes, people he didn't know. They weren't bad either. Her sketchbook was full of charcoal drawings good enough to show.

There was one of a thin-faced, clear-eyed, smiling man who reminded me of a young Bill but couldn't be. I was told she no longer remembered him, a backhanded blessing.

I was struck by a little irony as I leafed through the sketchbook. How Bill's eye for taking pictures had descended on him all at once, how Annie could suddenly draw old visions from deep in her head. Almost, I speculated, as if Annie had kept in a loose sort of touch with Bill that way.

Carmen and I were standing in the small living room, Hayes taking care of Annie's lunch in the kitchen. Carmen took me to the mantel over the old stone fireplace and pointed to a black-and-white picture in an old tin frame, showing an air force pilot in his flight suit, hoses and belts dangling from him, big white helmet. A cocky smile, nice hands hanging at his sides. Beside the picture was a brass urn for cremation ashes, and I knew who it must be.

"Captain Diamond," I said, thinking how nice for Hayes. At least he knows what his fairy-tale father looks like. "He's handsome."

"You forget," Carmen whispered. She took the lid from the urn and put her nose to it, as if to smell what was cooking in a boiling pot. "There *is* no Captain Diamond."

"Then who's this?"

I looked again at the photograph to see if I recognized anybody. Then Carmen took me by the upper arm and pulled me outside so nobody in the house could possibly hear.

"That's old Melvin, my ex," she said. "My contribution to the effort. And in the urn are some ashes from a driftwood fire, with a little beach sand mixed in. We said it was right off the desert floor at Edwards."

I didn't appreciate right away what all this really meant.

We said our good-byes in a few minutes, Hayes waving at us as we drove away, Annie right next to him with her dirty sketcher's hands folded over the knot in her sash.

What they didn't know, as Carmen might have said, could fill a library.

—|—

WHEN I GOT back from the house on the ridgetop where Hayes and Annie lived and Captain Diamond presided over the ash-filled fireplace, I went straight up to our room and found Bill there looking out the window at the lay of his father's land. He didn't know where I'd been and I didn't tell. All I did was go to him, and I took him in the tenderest hug I could offer, cradled his head in the cup of my hand because I was so sad for him at that moment. Here he had told himself all along that they would be better off without him, but I was sure that secretly he wondered if he might still be important to someone. Instead they'd made him all but invisible, as if he'd never existed at all. His son was given a bookful of myth, while all that Annie ever had of Bill was lost for good.

My Bill. Grabbing at life with his pictures, and it was a snapshot of Aunt Car's Melvin that had displaced him in his family and all their lore. As it should have, I guess. He hadn't earned a place on the mantel (which maybe was Cary Lee's thinking too, when she ribboned Daddy's pictures to shreds).

In a perplexing way, I loved Bill even more at that moment, as the man who had no history in this place anymore, my husband, who might as well have been born the day I met him in the desert.

There were times I could keep a secret to protect someone.

DEFEAT—1946

Big Don

Back then Big Don was Little Don. His father was Don Sr. or sometimes, addressed by his Mexican employees, Señor Don. Nobody had thought to call him Big Don because he wasn't that big and his boy was Little Don, and that seemed to take care of the confusion. When somebody said simply Don in those days, the 1910s and '20s it would have been, they meant the father. If they meant the boy, who would one day grow the most intimidating handlebar mustache in Northern California, they said Little Don, even when he was well into his teens and had outgrown his father by a few inches and many pounds.

It wasn't until he ran for Congress in 1946, the same year Kennedy and Nixon got in, that someone thought to call him "Big Don" Hayes for the campaign, and it stuck for all time thereafter.

He lost.

What a season that was, though. The war was over, things looked robust across the board, and Big Don was living the charmed life at the age of thirty-three. A pretty wife, a cute little bug of a daughter. All the political trimmings and, on top of it, standing to inherit the Hayes ranch, which even in those days was worth a tankerload of money. His dad was slowing down just enough to give Big Don a glimpse of what it would be like controlling the place, but that was years off. He tried to counsel himself wisely. Years off, and besides, I'll be in goddamn Washington pulling strings and writing agriculture bills as easy as limericks.

This was the way he thought back then. Had it all mapped out.

Most young men of the county didn't have the luxury of thinking the way Big Don thought, because their families had barely made it through the Depression, or hadn't, or they themselves had become scarred or startled or spent by the war and didn't have the wherewithal. They felt lucky to be able to go back to some kind of work that would keep their households afloat, whereas Big Don's family was in fine shape and always had been. In the local valley, in fact, there was nobody else who would dare to think about running for Congress in '46. It would be easier to consider flying by flapping your arms.

It was no secret that Big Don Hayes had married Mabel Diamond for her family's political connections and landholdings. Her father had contacts in Sacramento, had a line to the speaker of the Assembly, could get things done. Señor Don thought it was a pretty good idea to get his kid set up this way, and Big Don himself didn't mind marrying for practical reasons either. Mabel was a bonny gal in those days. Slim-hipped, sculptured legs—a decent set of pins on her, as Don used to say to his friends. She fit the picture of a congressman's wife and in her own way had been groomed for the job by her father. They were made for each other, Mabel and Big Don. Through her he got himself a navy desk job in the Port of Oakland during the war and never had to stand in harm's way, except when he rolled the car over coming home late one night, a little bit drunk. Split his lip wide open, vertically down from the nose, which was why he grew the mustache. Mabel used to beg him to shave it off but gave up asking eventually. She kind of liked the scar.

One day, in the middle of the '46 campaign, which at the time Big Don felt was going well, his father was riding with him through the district and said, completely out of the blue, "You know you don't have to do this to make me proud of you, Little Don."

He said Little Don for a reason, Big Don thought.

The old man wasn't looking at him at the time. He was looking out the passenger window at the browning mountains, his bare elbow jutting into the wind. Big Don was driving, and the backseat was packed full of campaign signs, posters, and patriotic bunting.

"I know that," Big Don said, thinking that making the old man proud was one of the last reasons he was doing it and finding it almost funny that this was what was on his father's mind late in the campaign.

His father wore small wire glasses and kept his shirt collar buttoned to the top. It didn't look right with his sleeves rolled up, but that was his style. He had a pipe stuck in his pocket, and he wore his watch with the face on the underside of his wrist. At times, Don thought, he was still a handsome man, but more often than not—in his sixties—he looked tired and abused and sometimes like a man who had been deceived.

"I'd be as happy to see you take over sooner than later," his father said. "I'd step aside. Up your salary. We'd get things going the way they'll be after I'm gone."

"I don't want to get into that bullshit again," Big Don said. "You're still in charge."

"By a hair, kid."

"Besides, I'll need you to run the place when I'm in D.C. You can set up a manager if you want to. Somebody who knows his ass from a cherry pie."

This was meant to appease his father. That phrase was one Don Sr. had been using for years.

It was too hot for a suit coat that day, but Big Don had one anyway. It was the way to distinguish himself from his Democratic opponent, who thought he'd win the heart and mind of the rural common man by appearing in shirtsleeves and without a necktie. Even at his age Big Don knew there was a right way and a wrong way to win in politics, and that was the wrong way. The common man wanted to respect his representative, and a dirt farmer who goes around without a tie is nothing but a peer. People don't respect their peers. They envy them, they gossip about them, they wish they'd have an accident, but they sure as hell don't respect them.

Authority comes from standing higher than the rest of them. A milk crate will do.

The speech was staged in the Healdsburg main square before a crowd of mostly Spanish-looking men in straw hats. Big Don stood up there behind the microphone wondering if they were understanding him and where the hell was his real constituency, the men who owned a little land and didn't want the feds telling them what to do with it. The applause was scattered. Somebody kept blowing a trumpet from the back of the square, as if to put him off his rhythm, while around the perimeter other people were just going about their noontime business and taking no notice of what he was saying. He was ready to pass out from the heat. His necktie was up against his Adam's apple so tightly he couldn't look left or right without moving his shoulders as a unit, and damn if he didn't catch sight of his opponent's red panel truck going down the road with its loudspeakers blaring typical Democratic baloney, which only made the trumpet player bleat a triumphant bullfighting riff. Big Don felt like he'd lose Healdsburg, but that wasn't a tragedy. He'd pick up the slack in Cloverdale, Sebastopol, Petaluma, Santa Rosa.

The Democrat was a goddamn union man, for chrissakes. Pinko written all over him.

Big Don wanted to wrap it up. The crowd was thinning before he reached his rhetorical crescendo. Seemed like they knew what he was going to say. As they shifted on their booted feet and eased away backward so the illusion of their attentiveness was still intact, Big Don saw his father down below walking among them with a sheaf of flyers, passing out copies like it was the Word. His pipe was sticking out the side of his mouth, his hat set back on his head and exposing the recession of his hairline.

I don't entirely know, Big Don thought—even though he was still speaking his memorized lines and wagging his finger at the crowd—that I'm not doing this to make him think of me as somebody besides Little Don.

—|—

THE DAYS IMMEDIATELY after the election were the worst ones. Mabel was afraid to approach him, tied herself up with busy work and sudden commitments, taking little Annie with her so that the house was empty all day long. Big Don's mother had taken the train up to Seattle to visit a friend, leaving Don Sr. on his own. The two Dons acted like they wanted to keep their distance, each going about his business, except that Big Don no longer had any business.

A few days after the election he went out to walk the perimeter of the ranch. He put on his candidate's straw skimmer to keep the sun off his head and a pair of stout brogans like he hadn't worn in months while vying for the public affection.

His father was out supervising the operations, getting the herd moved from here to there, maintaining irrigation pumps, whatever all else he did each day, and Big Don decided to avoid him by sticking to the fence line. Oddly, his own ranch was a portion of the district he didn't know all that well. He knew the general lay of the land, the properties of this or that section, but he didn't know it yard by yard the way his father did. Now he started at the back door of the house, headed for the white-washed fence, and walked it like a lineman, stirring up crickets as he went. The grasses were brown from the summerlong absence of rain, except where the pastures had been watered for grazing. The oak trees growing along an empty creek had begun to shed their leaves, surprising him at first, until he realized that entire seasons had passed while he was busy running and that things went on with or without his attention. Imagine. He had neglected Mabel and Annie. His foresight had been so narrow, focused on D.C., that he had forgotten his real place.

The ranch was enormous. It took him nearly an hour to reach the farthest point from the house, sticking to the fence line, where the fence cornered and there was an old well housing and a rusted-out truck that Don Sr. had probably left out there when it died on him twenty years before. Big Don opened up the truck door and ducked as a couple of sparrows shot out past his head. He sat in the driver's seat and took in the smell of the decayed leather. It was similar to rotting wood or old newspapers in the basement, reminiscent of anything left unattended to disintegrate. It occurred to Big Don that he had ridden in this truck with his father many times as a boy, either in the passenger's seat or in the flatbed in back, as his father drove into town on errands or made his way from one part of the ranch to another. It was the first truck he'd ever driven on his own too, when he was twelve, perhaps, and Don Sr. had told him to go out and shut off such and such a well pump or get a cow unstuck from the berry brambles along the back fence. And here it was, sitting like a monument to some skirmish that the world had forgotten.

It wasn't the time to grow sappy, but while he was sitting in the driver's seat, hands on the old wooden wheel, Big Don thought about how much of his father was in this place and how big the place was. Each, somehow, contained the other. And somehow, in his own arrogance, Big Don had always wanted to rise above it, wanted to make it seem small in comparison to *his* accomplishments. It was an idea he could not remember being without, instilled he didn't know how, but always there. The conceit! Wanting the biggest ranch in the valley to seem paltry. Who did he think he was to have given it a moment of credit? Here Don Sr. had worked it on his own and grew it parcel by parcel all these years, and it wasn't enough for the son. The son had to have more. Don Sr.'s idea was to have his kid pick up where he left off, but the kid wanted an empire.

Couldn't even get elected in a little cow district where he spoke the native dialect and knew all the ropes. With married-into connections, no less. A forfeit.

He pushed the clutch pedal against light resistance to his sole. Then he moved the gearshift lever on the steering column from first to second, tried to double-clutch to get to third, but the thing was stuck there and wouldn't move. Big Don felt himself getting frustrated, pushed the clutch in harder, so hard he nearly put the pedal through the rusted-out floorboard, hammered the wheel with one palm, and found himself with his head on his forearm, crying in a wave of self-pity that had come on him from nowhere. All he had ever tried to do, and he was back here, a boy again, Little Don. He'd have to take the silver dollar that was the ranch and be happy with it, put it in the bank and make it turn into a buck and a half. That would be the extent of his success.

There were footsteps in the grass, and he raised his head in time to settle himself a bit before Don Sr. reached the truck. His father was walking slowly, with measured high steps through the weeds, pipe in his teeth, a straw hat on his head of the kind the Mexican men wore. Big Don tried to put on a smile, but he felt too much like a kid who'd been caught where he shouldn't be and wiped it off. Don Sr. leaned with his arms on the window ledge.

"Probably out of gas," he said. A joke so dry it was sawdust. "Wouldn't you think?"

"Shit. Didn't even think to check."

Big Don saw his father glance at the skimmer band—HAYES FOR CONGRESS!—then back down and out toward the contoured pastures. He stood there with one arm on the window, the other hand nursing the pipe as he gazed at his land.

"You know, Don," his father said, "we could tow this thing up to the barn and get it running over the winter. A little project. Something to do."

"You have your hands full," Big Don said.

"I don't know about that. I'm slowing down. Like I was telling you. Time to get you in charge."

A couple of hawks were circling the field and making flight look effortless.

He was supposed to be in D.C. that winter, with a new wardrobe of suits and a young lady receptionist, all hobnob and influence. He was meant to be able to decline his father's charity by now. Yet, here it was, the silver dollar. Heavier in his palm than he expected.

COMFORT—1982

Mabel

It was an easy decision, when Mabel Hayes's husband died of heart failure, to see that he did right by their daughter and grandson. He had hardened his heart where they were concerned, considered them strangers (even though the boy was a complete innocent), and while she had argued with him over the years and asked him to search his conscience, she always knew that he was too stubborn for that and too proud. He'd say, "My conscience has taken a hike, Mabel. I haven't got the time to go looking for it now."

Mabel had become what they call a "handsome" woman in her middle age, possessing the style and finish expected of someone from a family like hers, meaning the Diamonds. The Diamonds had been moneyed and well connected, which was what attracted Don's father in the first place, and with the money and connections came refinement and manner and a sense of propriety. She dressed in slacks and crisp navy jackets, drove a Mercedes sedan, kept herself looking respectable, even after Don died. It came naturally, but it was not lost on her that the manners and refinement and political connections had not made for a life of paramount happiness. She had loved her husband more than he loved her, if he had loved her at all. Her daughter had been more or less estranged from them, at the time of Don's passing, for more than twenty years, the little boy growing up at a distance even though he lived minutes away.

How had she allowed all this to happen? Mabel often wondered. Where were the opportunities to make a stand, which she had willingly (she insisted on blaming herself) passed up? She could review the rosary of years and identify in each bead chances to broker if not love and affection then diplomatic tolerance, getting along, appearances. Sometimes—and this was something she had seen in her own family—appearances breed familiarity and familiarity comfort. Comfort is really all that is required to approximate happiness.

She had lived in comfort for many years now, loving her husband and accepting his faint affections as if they were love too, taking this as a proxy for happiness but brokenhearted inside because it fell so far short of her hopes. She had not married for love, that was never a question, but she had given birth in love and sacrificed in love and ached in love through all these later years when there was nothing but the comfort, and only outsiders took what she possessed to be happiness. They thought the house and the properties and the livestock and the workers and the money all did the trick, even knowing the situation with Annie and Hayes.

Many times, when Don was still alive, she had driven to Annie's house on the Freestone Road and sat in the car outside the gate for a while to watch Hayes play on the front steps or run around the field. There were times when she knew that Annie had seen her but hadn't come out to ask her inside, other times when she nearly worked up the nerve to go up to the door and knock and present herself and leave it to Annie to welcome her or not, but she had always lost her resolve when the thought of Don's reaction came to mind and she couldn't decide which battle was easier to wage. The line of least resistance won out. Drive on. Leave it be. Conscience came in the middle of the night and rendered her restless, that man beside her with his low, rhythmic breathing and his unearned sleep of the just.

Mabel had invited Annie to Don's wake, of course, but she hadn't come and neither had Hayes. None of the Arguses had come. Out of Mabel's presence, before the cremation, Annie had appeared at the funeral home and signed the memorial book, using the name Annie Diamond and not identifying herself as the daughter.

Hayes's name was not in the book.

Mabel didn't know what she had expected, really.

Don had asked not to be cremated but rather buried up on his ridgetop ranch in a hole he seemed to have dug, morbidly, twenty-five years earlier. This was a property that he had not spoken of much over the years, though he'd held it for a long time and rented it out to sheep ranchers. Mabel didn't understand the significance of it until she drove up there while he was still in the hospital, and she saw that it was a splendid green balcony overlooking the ocean and that Don must have envisioned himself in repose up there with the world sprawled out at his feet. She knew him well enough. At first it was not her intent to deprive him of this wish, but she was careful not to make a promise to him. He drifted in and out of consciousness during those last days and was not in a condition to pursue it. Luckily, his desire to be buried up there was not in writing. She had discretion.

The way to compromise, the way to find some comfort in all of it, was to take his ashes up to the ridgetop and scatter them over the bluffs, which is what she did. Alone, without a ceremony. It was a calm autumn day with a deep sky and a cobalt ocean, blooming ice plants under her feet as she walked with him to the edge of the land behind the vacant whitewashed house. She was dressed in her signature white slacks and jacket, a pearl necklace, a pair of dark blue flats with gold buckles on them, and she had made herself up for this even though there was nobody around to judge her. There were a few birds overhead riding the winds up the bluff face, hawks and seagulls, and there was a sailboat bobbing a few hundred yards out on the water. The sun was almost directly over her, giving her a blunt shadow at her feet and warming her through her jacket. Up from the beach wafted the odor of drying seaweed and dead fish.

Surprisingly, she couldn't think of any words to say into the air, Don's ashes in a crude wooden box he had owned since boyhood. The thoughts that might lead to words were too complicated and mixed, pleasant ones mated with bitter, all tagged with the swallowed emotions of fifty years. Had someone been there, even Annie, she might have been able to put up appearances and hit the appropriate mourning note, but as it was, without an audience, she couldn't bring herself to do it. She took the lid off the box and let it fall to the ground, and then she looked inside and saw the shards and dust of his remains and she simply said, "Good-bye, Don," emptying him over the bluff.

The warm updraft caught him and gave his bone powder a startling ride into the air over that empty cove. Mabel watched as her husband became a sudden cloud and a seagull flew through it to see if there was anything edible in there.

—+—

HAYES WAS NOW a young man of twenty-five. Mabel had not seen him in ages, but she knew that he was raising sheep on a portion of Annie's land, making his way but not thriving. It didn't so much trouble her as make her wonder why he hadn't left home yet, a man his age. She supposed it was because he couldn't afford a place of his own, and Annie was unable to help him out. At first it didn't occur to Mabel, though later it did, that he was a kind young man in his heart and was staying home to keep his mother company. Annie had never remarried after Bill left, and in fact had become reclusive and a bit tormented, which broke Mabel's heart. Mabel knew that Hayes had even gone to live with Cam Argus for a while when he was younger, but that after a year or two of it chose to go back to Annie because he could make things easier for her that way; he wanted to be able to keep an eye on her.

Before Don died, Mabel used to assure Annie the rare times they met that she was better off, and free. If her own marriage was a model, there was as much loneliness inside one as out. Annie accused her of being cynical.

Now, with Don gone, Mabel felt that she could finally approach her daughter. There were no longer the loyalty problems, and no fear of Don's judgment or contempt. Don was a good rancher and a solemn man, a man of extremely high standards, but if there was one thing he could do better than anything it was the cold and the ice and letting you know how you'd disappointed him. He had done it to Annie, threatened Mabel with it. He'd lived his last few years in relative isolation because of it, keeping his own company and counsel, estranged from his daughter and grandson. Parcel by parcel, he sold off his cherished ranchland because he had no one to pass it to other than Mabel, so that by the time he died, there was only the big colonial house and a few acres surrounding it, along with the ridgetop property. Big Don had left her in complete security and comfort, though, and with discretion, which she now intended to use.

On a November morning in 1982, a few weeks after Don died, Mabel parked her Mercedes across the road from Annie's house and waited there until she saw Hayes drive away in his truck. She didn't know how long he would be gone, so she acted quickly, without thinking about it any more than she already had, and she drove through the open gate and up to the house. If nothing else moved her to keep going, it was that Annie probably had seen her already and would think Mabel was taunting her or had gone mad herself. She got out of the car and climbed the steps to the door, knocking lightly on the oval glass. Only a few times, early in Annie's marriage, had Mabel set foot in the house, and now she found herself picturing the interior and some of the moments she'd had in there, when her daughter and grandson were young and she was, herself, younger than Annie was now.

When the door opened and Mabel saw her daughter there, her hand instinctively went to her mouth and pressed at her lip to keep from crying. Annie didn't look healthy. Her hair was long and not cared for, red but streaked with gray, strawlike around her face. She had blue pockets under her eyes and pale skin, the rough texture that goes with aging unhappily.

"Besides Pop," Annie said, "you're the last person I expected to see at my door."

She stepped aside as if to invite Mabel in. Mabel didn't want to be flip with her, but the thought crossed her mind that maybe Bill Argus qualified as the last person Annie expected to see, not her own mother. It was a testament to Annie's misery that she wanted to throw out a barb like that, here at their first reunion.

"I'm not here to make you feel sorry for me, or guilty, or anything else," Mabel said as she entered the old house. It smelled familiar, wooden, mildly dusty. "I just wanted to tell you what I planned to do for Hayes."

Annie led her directly to the kitchen, where she poured coffee from a pot on the stove and sat down without fanfare. The kitchen was well shaded by the eucalyptus trees all around the house, almost too dark for the time of day.

"Hayes is out running errands, Mom."

"I know. I watched him leave. I don't want him to hear this from me."

It was easier to be businesslike than to let her emotions get the better of her, the sorrow she felt for her daughter at that moment as hard as a piece of rock lodged in her chest. Annie wore a faded print dress and sandals, no jewelry, no makeup. She looked like she had lived naked in the woods for years and had emerged in front of this house and imposed on the charity of whoever lived here; Hayes, that happened to be. Mabel couldn't stand to look at her face and so kept her eyes on the scuffed surface of the table as she told Annie about the ridgetop property and her plans to make a gift of it to her grandson, to do with whatever he liked, to work it or sell it or use it as a place to hide once in a while. Annie did not ask questions. Nor did she nod with Mabel's arguments and justifications. She didn't seem to grasp either that this would likely take Hayes out of the house and force her to live on her own, if Hayes chose to work the place as a ranch. She didn't ask how they would explain the gift to Hayes or what they might do if he didn't wish to accept it. Mabel raised these points herself and said that it was reasonable enough for Annie to say that she had inherited the land from one of the Diamonds—people Hayes knew as his father's distant family—and there would probably be no questions from him after that. It wouldn't be difficult.

Annie sat with her elbows on the table and her hands folded at her mouth. She appeared to be kissing her knuckles and thumbnails, trying to sort all of this out in her mind before she agreed to it. To Mabel it didn't matter whether she agreed to it or not. It was the one thing Mabel could offer, aside from impersonal money, to help Hayes and show Annie that she was sorry.

"I don't mind it," Annie said after a while. Her eyes seemed out of focus, aimed through the hallway behind Mabel's head.

And then, before Mabel had a chance to say anything more about the ranch and how good this would be for Hayes, Annie reached out and took one of her hands, wrapping it up in her own and taking it to her mouth. She kissed it softly and turned her eyes up to finally meet Mabel's.

"Did Pop have anything he wanted you to say to me at the end?"

Mabel started to weep, quietly, without sobbing, and the tears ran from her eyes and down her cheeks and off the line of her jaw. She said yes. It was not the truth, but she said yes, Annie's father had said things at the end, and he had made Mabel promise to tell her that he was miserable in his soul and always had been and he hoped she could forgive him one day. It was a lie that Mabel hoped would give Annie some peace.

Annie let go of her hand and nodded as if this was what she expected of her father. Cowardly. Too late. Feeble. It was a lie, Mabel wanted to blurt suddenly, but she managed to keep it as it was, an appearance of truth, something for Annie to have. She rose from the table and took her daughter's head against her chest and stroked it as if Annie were a child again, misunderstood and harmed by all the things she didn't comprehend.

BEING IN THAT house raised an old memory that brought Mabel a wave of sad nostalgia. It was the Christmas of 1959, when Hayes would have been two. Annie had brokered a passable truce among the different figures in her life: her husband, his father and mother, his brother, Don, Mabel. She invited all of them to the house for Christmas dinner, and all of them came, the first and only time the two families were united in anything but hard feelings.

By the time Mabel and Don arrived that day—a dark, rainy Christmas Day—the others were already there, and Annie had poured them all drinks and stacked Christmas albums on the record player and dressed up little Hayes in a red-and-green outfit with bells on the buttons. Don carried a heap of gifts through the door and went to arrange them under the tree while Mabel greeted everyone on his behalf.

"Ray, Miranda," she said. "Nice to see you again."

"You better get started on the mulled wine," Ray told her. "We're way ahead of you already."

Annie rushed to her mother and kissed her on the cheek, then kissed her father on the cheek as he turned his face as if to avoid it. That mustache of his could be a big deterrent, but Annie moved in and got him. She hugged him around the neck and let her hand linger on the side of his head. Bill, too—ordered to behave himself—came and kissed Mabel's cheek, offered his hand to Don, who took it and pumped once or twice and muttered, "Happy holidays."

The house smelled wonderful with Annie's cooking and the tree, the spices in the wine. Everything was beautiful, including the faces of the Argus men—Bill, Ray, and Cameron—glowing from their drinks and the firelight. Cam was flushed and chuckling, shooting his fist into his brother's arm from time to time.

"A tall scotch will set me up fine." Big Don plunked himself in the most comfortable chair in the room, which apparently had been saved for him.

"Coming right up, Pop," said Annie, and she was beaming and rosy in the cheeks and happy in the eyes. Mabel noticed it all.

The baby waddled from person to person, and the adults all held their cigarettes up and away from his little hands as he patted their knees. Mabel took her Brownie from her purse and started snapping pictures.

"I'm taking the whole roll," she said. "Smile, Carmen, it isn't that bad."

"I'm too pink," said Miranda's sister. "My eyes'll come out red and I'll look like a lab rat."

As it turned out, the men were clustered together in a corner of the room, all of them in the width of one frame in the Brownie lens, and Mabel summoned the girls to squeeze in and get ready for a keeper of a Christmas picture. Ray had on a Santa Claus tie, probably the only tie he owned, and Cam and Bill were in matching ski sweaters that their mother must have given them. Everyone posed around Don, grinning at Mabel, with the boy in Annie's arms (all of the men, ranchers after all, in heavy-soled work shoes), but it was her own husband who crossed his arms and sat as rigidly as a fireplug.

"We need some tinsel to hang on old Don's mustache," Ray said.

"If you want your nose broken," Don muttered, "go right ahead."

Mabel took the picture before anything could happen.

Her memories of the evening dimmed a little after that, but she remembered how Bill and Annie seemed happy, at least as far as the surface revealed. Miranda was, she had almost forgotten, a sweet-tempered woman who quietly set the table and then cleared the dishes after dinner. Carmen—poor thing, who'd lost her husband to a scandal—smoked and chatted with the men all night long, once in a while taking a moment to scramble the little boy's hair and pinch his fat cheeks.

Mabel recalled being uncontainably happy that night, especially after Don loosened up with another scotch or two and there was laughter and talk and good-spirited argument and singing. They all tried to sound like Elvis on "Blue Christmas."

She had the photograph of the men someplace, she was sure. Buried in a dresser drawer, maybe. She'd have to dig it out. It was the only time they were all together after the wedding.

Nothing was the same after that. Everything became a painful pose for the outside world.

—|—

NOT LONG AFTER she visited Annie and told her about the ridgetop land, Mabel decided to sell the big house and move someplace smaller and quieter. Don would never have approved, since the house had been in his family for generations, but Don was gone and couldn't make demands anymore. The old ranch was now a group of smaller ranches and vineyards owned, some of them, by men who once worked for Don, Mexican families. They used to call him Señor Don and bow and scrape and ingratiate themselves to him, and here now they owned part of his land and smiled at Mabel when they saw her, in a way that told her they took a kind of justice from the way things had gone.

She didn't know about that, but she sold the house and remaining acreage to a well-off San Franciscan who was planning to turn it into a winery with a tasting salon and a patio café. None of her business, that was, and she hoped to move far enough away that she wouldn't see it happening.

With Annie's blessing she signed over the ridgetop ranch and asked again that Annie lie about the gift. There was no reason to mention her name, or Don's for that matter, and no reason to impose anything on Hayes other than the freedom to do with the place what he wanted. This was a thing she was determined to give him.

"Sweetheart," Mabel said, "will you be all right if Hayes moves up there?"

Annie had come to meet her at the old house, where she had been raised, a day or two before the move. Mabel knew that the place must seem unfamiliar to her now, especially with everything in boxes and the furniture pushed aside so the floors could be washed.

"I'll be fine," Annie answered. A ball of ambiguity in her throat. "I've been fine all along."

Mabel looked at her to see if she could detect the intent to tell a lie. With Annie it was always hard to tell because she had been an earnest, open girl her whole life. She'd been weathered, though, like a house that hasn't been painted in a while, and the weathering revealed in her, Mabel thought, a little bit of doubt and delusion.

"I want you to know, Annie. If you ever want to, you can come move in with me. The new place has a little cottage out back and lots of trees and birds, and it's quiet and nice there. You could move in, and we'll be like a couple of college girls sharing digs. What do you think?"

Annie didn't answer the question. She walked through the house instead, her heels on the hardwood echoing off the walls and ceiling. She went upstairs, Mabel trailing her, and looked in each of the bedrooms and the closets, checking, perhaps, for signs that she had lived here at one time herself and that she hadn't fabricated the clutter of memories she'd been hanging on to. It had been a long time. Her hand went to the glass doorknobs and the varnished windowsills, touched the plaster of the walls. She looked up into the corners of the ceiling as if to see whether the cracks had grown since she left, or had never been there at all. Mabel felt sorry for her as she toured the rooms of her childhood and mixed in the longing to recover what she could of it with the half mourning for her father she must be feeling, and the regret that her boy would never get to know the truth of her.

"Are you all right?"

"Mama," she said, rubbing the smooth wood of the banister, "I can't figure out why I'm meant to be alone."

There was no emotion in her voice at all, just a clear, low frankness.

Mabel felt that jagged rock in her chest again. She took her daughter in her arms and held her, smoothing down her wild hair and pressing at the wrinkles of her dress. "Well, baby," she said, trying to sound comforting, "it won't always feel so bad. You're loved. You've always been loved."

Annie broke away and went back down the stairs and out onto the front porch where Don used to throne himself in a big rattan chair and view his little empire.

Mabel watched as her daughter sat on the top step with her chin in her hand, looking down the length of the driveway as if she expected someone to return to her.

IT WAS A few months later, in midwinter, when Mabel Hayes took herself out for a drive in the old valley where she had lived most of her life. She passed her daughter's house and found Annie's car there and some of the men who rented the pastures leading sheep down the hill. She was glad to know that Annie had not given up the house and moved in with Hayes at the ridgetop. Her daughter had not contacted her during all this time, had left everything unsaid that Mabel had almost hoped to hear: words of anger, resentment, and confusion. It was Annie's way to hold it all, keep it, hide it, lose it in herself.

Mabel carried the guilt, though. And she would never beg for a true reconciliation because she didn't feel she deserved it. She had let opportunities go by like wood floating along in a river, visible and close for a long while, then suddenly out of reach, and then gone.

She drove through the redwood groves along the Freestone Road and then into Occidental, where she and Don used to come for Sunday dinners once in a while at an old Italian restaurant. It was still there, the pinkish neon sign stuttering. Very little had changed, in the sense that everything *looked* the same. Yet, the thought struck her, façades don't reflect much of importance and don't reveal the fundamental differences, the losses, the harsh effects of longing for impossibilities. When things appear to be the same as they were forty years ago, you have given in to fooling yourself.

From there she took the winding road that led to the ridgetop, and in twenty minutes she stopped in front of Hayes's ranch and the place where her husband had gone into the air on his way to the hereafter. It almost made her laugh to think that there might be remnants of Big Don Hayes clotted on damp tree trunks and in among the branches of squat shrubs all along the ridge. And his grandson living right here. Mabel was delighted to see the pastures full of sheep, many more than Hayes used to manage down at Annie's house, and she noticed that the open yard was full of gear and machinery, a galvanized water trough, a tractor. She got out of the car into the light mist that was in the air, leaning there in her raincoat for a while and looking at the place that Don had saved for himself all these years. What he had in mind she couldn't begin to guess. A retreat, a hiding place? Maybe he intended to run away here, leaving her one day when the familiarity of acting like he loved her was too much to bear anymore. She would never know, but she liked Don's comeuppance—his grandson making something useful of it.

Hayes came out of the house in a long green raincoat and began hitching a wagon with big rubber tires to the tractor. He wasn't wearing a hat or a hood, so Mabel could see his red hair, which he wore a little longer than she'd have liked. But he did remind her of Don when he was that age, in the years before he ran for Congress. Hayes worked at the hitch with a big wrench and then walked the wagon over by hand, strong in the back and legs, and hooked it up. Nothing but concentration in the way he worked. Don would have admired him for that, and it had come without Don's influence.

She was about to get back into her car when Hayes straightened up and noticed her. So few people came by this way that her presence must have startled him, and he called with his hands cupped at his mouth. "Need any help, ma'am?"

Mabel acted as if she couldn't hear him and approached the gate. He came over to meet her there and asked again if she needed anything. She hadn't planned to speak with him when she came up, but here he was, her grandson, a man who looked like he was happy with himself and where fate had finally landed him.

"Someone told me there was a rancher up here who might have a breeding ewe for sale," she told him. "I was thinking of a little Dorset or a Southdown."

Hayes put his hand up to his forehead like a visor and peered into the mist across his own pastures. The ocean beyond looked like a sheet of wrinkled metal. "I'm fairly new up here myself, so I don't know if anyone else might be selling. I'm afraid I'm not."

He had some whiskers on his cheeks, living up here without a wife to make him shave every day. A kind face, long and fine-featured. And there was just a trace of his father in him, in his deep-set eyes. That's the way Mabel remembered Bill Argus, even as the forty-year-old photographer whose work she had seen in San Francisco, a man whose face revealed more than he wanted it to. Hayes revealed nothing but the appearance of contentment, and she was glad to see that. It must be lonely for him up here, she thought, but she realized she was applying her own ideas about loneliness to him.

"I'm sorry to keep you from your work," she said. "I'll drive on along here and see what I see."

"You're welcome to come in and use the phone if you want," he said.

It was a strong temptation to accept, to enter the house of her grandson, but she was afraid that she might tip her hand somehow, slip and mention his mother or his father, or learn something about him that would make her wish to know him better now, when it was impossible.

"Oh, no thank you," she said. "This was really a fool's errand, coming up here. But I appreciate the offer."

"Okay then," Hayes said, "good luck to you." And he gave her a casual two-fingered salute as he turned to get back to his work.

Mabel started the car and drove away slowly, lingering enough there along the fence line to see him pull off in the tractor with the wagon bouncing behind.

She wanted to believe that he was as happy as he appeared to be.

LIFE DRAWING—1998

Annie

She had a feeling that there was a forgotten story inside her. Often the feeling came on the same way a dream of dropped responsibility comes, with a sudden panic, a sense of failure. But the moment she put her mind to the task of recalling the story, it melted away like a chip of ice on the warm oven top. It was gone, if it had ever existed at all.

It was strange, she noticed, how it bobbed to the surface from time to time, and then dipped back down, and how she was able to grab at some of the details of it by drawing them as soon as they occurred to her. Drawing was a gift she never used to have (to the best of her recollection), although now it seemed as if she had been doing it all her life, born with the skill, so that for all practical purposes it might as well be the truth. And she used it to contemplate these details that kept coming up in her mind and then falling away, the smallest things from a life that couldn't possibly have been her own.

There was a house sitting on a gently inclining hillside, surrounded by pines and eucalyptus trees, with a wall of blackberry vines overgrowing its fence, thorny and wild. She drew it. It came to her easily, down to the pattern in the vine tangles and almost to the flavor of the warm, sweet, ripe blackberries. She could very nearly see herself wiping the berries clean of spider-webs, and then the purple stain on her fingers and thumb. And she could see herself walking up the dirt drive toward the house and observing the rocky pastures on either side, a few cows grazing near the fence line, the tops of the trees as jagged against the sky as a length of torn paper, the sun in her eyes and washing out the scene around its edges so that she could not name the man who was standing on the porch waiting for her. The house had a large oval of glass in its front door, with a frosted bevel all around, and the man was framed in the oval like the figure in an old photograph, stiff of leg and spine. She couldn't see his face or his hands, but she felt as if she were smiling as she walked toward him.

Who he might have been didn't matter very much now.

Hayes was her son, or said he was, and this she took at face value and hoped that it was true, because he was a nice young man and handsome, gentle. He appeared to know a lot about her, but she didn't think he knew the story that she had forgotten. He was kind to her, helped her dress herself each day, helped her in and out of the bathtub and didn't seem to mind her nakedness if it didn't bother her, and it didn't. She didn't know why. She was comfortable with him. If he was her son, she had done well in her time, gave the world a kind man when there were supposedly so many who weren't. She didn't know about that anymore.

And if Hayes was her son, as he reminded her every day, she imagined that there had to be a father in the story, even if he was a man she knew only long enough to make Hayes with. She remembered how it was done. It made her happy to think about it, even though she couldn't recall any particular experience of her own, a time when she was with a man and he was upon her and inside her and telling her things that made her feel like she was a gift to him. Nothing came to mind, yet Hayes said he was her son, and he didn't mean it in a symbolic way. There were pictures of him with a pretty redheaded woman who was his mother, Annie, he called her, and he said, "You were a beautiful girl, Mom."

"Thank you," she said, and studied the pictures as if she had drawn them. "I think I was. Yes." But there was something wrong in the girl's face, with her ten-year-old Hayes under one arm and pressed against her side. Something wrong that showed she was not capable of happiness. If she was the girl in the pictures, then something had happened to her that made her numb, and it was something that she could not remember. An accident? A death? Whatever it was that happened to "Annie," she had evicted it from her mind. Except for the scant details, the berry vines and spiderwebs, the glimpses of a man, all scattered in her head like the things from a house hit by a tornado.

—+—

IT WAS A day that began in fog and turned bright. Hayes told her to stay in the house because he had to round up the sheep for marking and he didn't want her stumbling into any trouble while he was busy. He put on the television for her and gave her a big plastic cup full of juice, made sure her sketch pad was at her side, and her box of charcoals in case anything came to mind that she wanted to draw. She wanted to make a joke about how he would strap her into her chair like a baby if he could, or leash her to the porch post like a dog, but she couldn't think of the right words for it and instead smiled as he kissed her on the forehead. He was so kind to her that he had to be her son. Nobody would be this kind to an old woman who couldn't remember her story if he weren't her son and felt he owed her the kindness.

Nearly as soon as he left, the television went blank. She got up and went to it and cracked it on the side the way she had seen Hayes do that. A good, flat-handed whack. Nothing happened, and she did it again, on the other side, but it was no good. She began to whine and knead her hands together, which she hated to do, but it seemed like she did it whenever she became frustrated, and it helped in a strange way, because usually it brought Hayes to her side quickly. This time he was out of earshot and didn't know she was whining. She knocked over her cup and watched the purple juice spread across the table and floor. Impassively, she saw how it crawled in irregular arms, seeping into cracks in the wooden floor.

She was not going to do well without the television, she sensed, so she picked up her sketch pad and let her hand drift over it, the charcoal barely touching the surface of the textured paper. There was no picture in her head at the moment, no details, but she knew that they always came when she opened her mind up to them, and she expected one to come now. A piece of the story that she could not imagine until it appeared, because she didn't know the story anymore. It could be anything. She lived for the surprise that came from these random visions. They hinted at a depth of memory that would be right for a woman her age, but also at dreadful experience, the kind that might harm her if she ever were able to recover it. Yet she couldn't push the pieces away when they came, they were too valuable. Puzzling and odd, dangerous, risky, but belonging to her somehow.

She sat in her chair and let her hand work. In a little while the charcoal lines hinted at the shape of a rock, a tall, rough rock that had been exposed by wind. These were all over Hayes's sheep ranch, standing up over the green grass like men. She was not surprised to find one coming from her hand. But then she began to draw the surrounding land, and it was soft with tall grasses that bent down under the wind as if someone were blowing patterns in them, and the slope of the hillside ended at a wall of dark woods. At first it appeared to be just a line on the horizon, but it quickly turned into the opening of a forest at the edge of a meadow, with ferns and downed limbs and the possibility that someone was inside there waiting for her. Then into the picture arrived a pair of bare feet, girl's feet with the toes painted, and long naked legs crossed just below the knee. She did not recognize them. They were certainly not her own feet, which had grown wide and flat and gnarled from corn and callus, discolored, misshapen, ugly, and these feet were pretty ones. The legs ended midthigh at the bottom edge of the paper, cut off as if her mental view were through a small square aperture in the black wall of her memory.

She turned to a clean sheet and began to expand the view. It wasn't as if she knew what was beyond the edges of the paper, no. It was only that she wanted to find out if her mind would be able to look wider and tell her where this was and who the girl might be, and when, and who was in the woods looking at the naked girl.

The wider view came more easily than she imagined. The girl was in fact naked, and she was lying on a blanket in the middle of a pool of grass. She drew a gently curved arrowhead where the girl's legs joined her body, the patch of light-colored hair there, the deep navel, and the breasts with their small raised nipples. The girl's ribs, her hipbones, her hands resting lazily on her belly. But she couldn't see the girl's face. It was as if the girl were seeing her own foreshortened body, viewing down from chin to chest. The grasses rose on the sides so that her view of the meadow was blocked, and all she could see was the sky and the tip of that tall rock, the black gash of woods off to her left pulling her attention like a drain pulls water.

She wanted to get the girl onto her feet and into those woods, but the next sheet of paper did not begin to fill with charcoal lines. It remained blank and inert, her hand over it and starting to tremble.

There might have been a time, she thought, when I was

there. Or someplace like it. The woods were safe, only cold. The meadow was in the sun. There were birds flying around, and I had the feeling that I had slept there.

It wasn't possible. At least it didn't seem possible. And, anyway, if it were true, then more pictures would be coming to her, and they weren't. Her mind closed at the edges of the last drawing, with the girl's naked body and the grass and sky, and the woods off to the side, with someone in there watching her.

Hayes wouldn't know that she had ever been gone, not if she left and returned before he came in from the sheep. She locked her sketch pad and box of charcoals under her arm and went out of the house, careful to follow a shallow creek to the far fence line so her son wouldn't see her.

If he was her son.

She walked briskly for what seemed like a long time, but time had become a problem for her as well as memory. It was often hard to tell whether it was still the same day she had reminded herself it was earlier, or whether an hour had passed or only a minute since she'd had her lunch. If she was wearing clothes that she had been wearing the last time she noticed, it was either the same day or another day, later, when the same outfit had come back into her closet from the wash. She was either the same age as she had been when she went to bed the night before, or much older—never younger—and this was the reason she liked to go to the mirror first thing and see what she looked like. There was a piece of paper on her dresser where she wrote down the time and day it was as she looked at herself, the only reliable way she could tell. Carefully, she always crossed the boxes off the calendar to mark that she had been there already.

Where the stream crossed under the road through a culvert, she stepped over the fence stile and began to walk toward the ridgetop. She had never been able to see what was on the other side of that ridgetop and felt like the scene she wanted to look at must be there. Beyond, maybe, but someplace over there. She sensed, as she walked, that if she could stand at the ridgetop and see farther than she could see from the house, everything would become clearer. It was possible that all her lost memories would come flooding back if she were able to get to that place, because that place seemed to reside in her like a special sort of focal point. It had come to her before, a glimpse of that spot, with its rock and its woods—never the girl before, and never anybody else—complete with a feeling that she had been there herself. There were snippets of it in her sketchbook, small jagged bits that were like a broken plate with a scene painted on it.

She made her way over the ridge and looked down into a cupped valley with its own garden of standing rocks. The little road wound down into it invitingly. She walked, careful at the cow grids in the road, tentative and timid when a rancher's truck came by and slowed as it passed her. The driver called out something to her but she ignored him, holding her sketch pad over her face so he wouldn't see the fear in her. He drove on. In case he decided to come back for her, she veered from the road and into the grass, which was as tall as her thighs and waving like a crop of blond wheat.

After walking for a few minutes, high-stepping her way through the grass, she sat in a meadow and looked around. Her hand wavered over a blank page in the sketch pad, feeling almost like a radio antenna ready to receive signals. Fingers black with the charcoal, her hand dotted with age spots, though Hayes insisted that she had always had freckles—pretty redheaded woman with freckles all over—but she wasn't sure she could believe him because her hair wasn't red at all, and never had been, in memory. It was gray. It was short and as gray as a hank of moss, and that was what it had always been in her mind.

She didn't know why Hayes would want to tell her a thing like that, yet she had seen those pictures too, and that woman was redheaded and pretty and freckled. If that was her, she was glad she didn't remember because now she didn't look anything like that girl. It would be sad to have lost her looks, and the other things that the woman in the picture might have had once.

A few strokes began to show on the paper, and then more of them, coming rapidly. Grasses, rocks, birds, motion in the air. Two bodies close together and naked. The girl from her other pictures, with a man—or a boy. The bodies were wound up so closely that it was hard to tell which limbs belonged to which body, hands appearing unexpectedly, a knee protruding between the backs of the girl's thighs—more limbs, it seemed to her, than two people ought to have. They were as close to being one body as two could be, like a wax figure of two that had melted in the sun, the spaces between them lost, their bellies melding together, their faces joined at the mouths and cheeks. They were beautiful in a way that she wished she could remember for herself, because she knew that if this image was coming out of her, she must have experienced it. He could be the man she made Hayes with, but his face was fused with the girl's and couldn't be recognized.

He was trying to assume her, or she him. It was difficult to see who was more powerful there.

When she was finished with the drawing, she looked around and saw the black line of woods that had been in her mind, a short distance down a mild grade through the grass. It was trying to get her to come into it, but she was suddenly afraid of that, fearful that there would be something in there that would not let her back out. The shadows of the woods moved, the eucalyptus trees creaking.

In there, she believed, waited the man in her drawing, but she wasn't sure she was ready to meet him again. He was elusive and playful and he might try to trick her. He might try to take her away and melt into her body the way those lovers were in the picture, and Hayes would never know what became of her.

"I know you," she called toward the woods. The blade of one hand was raised to her mouth.

Then, on a new blank sheet, she drew his face. Swiftly, without thought, she made it come to the surface, and it was a handsome young man with deep, sympathetic eyes and bare cheeks, a smile turning up in mischief.

LOST

Nora

Aunt Carmen told me that the young man's face in Annie's sketchbook *was* Bill's, in fact. She and Cam had nearly dirtied their pants when they saw it in there the first time, though Carmen had to admit on seeing Bill's image after ages of hating his guts that he was a handsome devil when he was young. I was sorry I never got to see him that way (because he had widened up by the time I met him; his face had thickened, along with his waist and his opinions).

"But Annie remembers him, deep down," Carmen said as she drove me back to Cam's house that day. "I don't know how. She's forgotten everyone else she ever knew. Rotten justice that she can still draw a picture of the one person who did the worst thing to her."

I wasn't sure that was much of a puzzle. Even though I hadn't seen her in twelve years, I could see Cary Lee in my mind as clearly as if I'd just wiped her mouth for her after a party and put her to bed.

IT WAS A few days after I met Hayes and Annie—with the summer just beginning to turn on the heat, the grass going brown as toast—that Bill and I were out driving around in the Jeep, reviewing more stomping grounds of his. It had become our daily habit, or his anyway, to drive around with his camera gear and find old haunts. His mind was a junk drawer, he said. Full of knotted strands, tangling bits and pieces.

This day he took me through the village of Freestone, out along a stretch of horse pastures. After a while the road took a hard right, and Bill stopped the Jeep there on the widened shoulder. It didn't bother me, because this was his MO, to screech to a sudden halt when he saw a thing he wanted to get some pictures of. Without saying a thing to me, he got out and snatched his tripod, set it up, screwed the Leica to it, and aimed his lens at a fine white house up top a sloping field and surrounded by eucalyptus trees. The house was fairly far from the road, so he had a zoom lens on, cranking the ring back and forth until he had a composition.

I liked the place. It looked quiet and safe, nestled in its grove of trees. There was an old fence running along the road, clogged with a wall of blackberry vines that stood nearly as tall as the Jeep, almost like a moat around this serene little home.

I don't know how, but I knew this was the house where he and Annie and Hayes had lived their more or less five years together. Talk about ghosts. I could almost feel the whispers of all three of them, hovering among the eucalyptus tops. The house all but buzzed with their history, as short as it was.

Bill snapped pictures, keeping his eye to the viewfinder and bent at the waist like one of those old dolls whose key needs cranking up.

"Look the same?" I asked him.

"Pretty much."

"The berries were always this high?"

"Not quite this high. I used to cut them back." He stopped to screw a different lens into place, biting on his bottom lip. "Maybe she didn't have the wherewithal."

"Least of her worries, I imagine. Berry vines."

He gave me half a look, as if I'd pinched him too hard. Maybe it *was* a little unkind of me, I don't know. Here lately, I thought he'd been letting himself off a little too easy. I was thinking of Daddy and all. How I'd let him have it between the eyes if he ever showed his face to me.

And then, of course, I'd probably pick him up off the ground and smother him in my arms—but not because I wanted to.

"She was stronger than people thought," Bill said. "Took care of herself. Knew how to stand up to her pop like nobody else. Everyone was afraid of what Big Don would take away from them. So was I, and I'll tell you what."

"What."

"I can't say I never thought about getting us back in his good graces. Into that will of his. I was prepared to kiss his ass."

"Well off, was he?"

"He had more than he needed, put it that way. There are people who make money every time they sneeze; well he grew his ranch ten percent every time he took a shit."

Bill, who had taken a practical vow of poverty when he left Pianto (though his bank account was always healthy after the first book), never showed me a greedy hand since I'd known him. Money wasn't the thing he was contending for. He was always after something less clear, and harder to get.

"You were young," I told him. Came up beside him and patted his back so he'd know I didn't mean to nail him like that.

"Tell me about it." He straightened up and began to dismantle his gear. "I was crazy as a soup sandwich too."

A few minutes later, under heavy redwood canopy and deep black shadows, he asked me to drive him up to Hayes's. He announced he was ready to meet his son.

—|—

ALL ROADS LEAD to Pianto, apparently.

For Bill anyway, that's true. For me it's Long Beach, where Cary Lee pitched her tent, and Elsie followed her from the Midwest to be close by, and the legion of boyfriends came calling, and stepdad Jack finally showed up. No matter how far away I get, the very distance I've put in between refers to that place in spite of myself. Cary Lee's still there too, residing, I've heard, in a mint green cement-block bungalow not far from the ocean, probably with my high school graduation pic still on her dresser top and the remnants of her thrift-shop vocation hanging in the closet.

Do I want to admit that being in Pianto with Bill as he crawls his way on hands and knees to the altar of his past has made me begin to linger on the thought of Cary?

Not yet. I might get over this. Bill might fall on his nose and ruin everyone's peace. He has it in him to manage that.

A cynical skeptic, that's me. I've seen good loaves of bread go black with mold before my eyes. I've seen a tornado tear a house apart but spare the cat box.

Take Jack, for example.

I loved Jack as if he were my own father (as if, as if), which wasn't as easy to do as it sounds. Because I had lots of cardboard father figures come and go before Jack, and I knew not to put much faith in them. It's easy to resist after a few bad turns. But Jack, like I said, proved himself to me over time. I came to love him. So much so that Cary Lee, in her dogged suspicion, began to think that Jack and I were in some kind of league against her, wanting to dismantle her raggedy little empire.

Jack and I would look at her and start laughing and exchanging google eyes, as if we could see right through her print muumuu. We'd stop talking the minute she came into the room, just to mess her up. We'd hide in my bedroom closet when she got home, listening to her mutter to herself as she went around the house searching for us, then we'd run out when she wasn't looking and plop ourselves in the living room like we'd been there all along, TV tuned to Papa Cronkite. Mother would act like nothing was wrong, joining us with a jumbo highball in one hand and her beaded cigarette case in the other.

God, I took pleasure in deviling her like that. It was the biggest act of civil disobedience I could engage in without being thrown out of the house before I turned eighteen. A legitimate fear.

Jack took me to the racetrack one day when I was seventeen and taught me how to bet on horses. We won a few bucks on a horse named Tippy, and when we got home (Jack a little flushed from the scotch or two he had in the racetrack bar) Cary Lee was livid, swooping through the house with her arms out to knock as much stuff off shelves as she could. I called her Chopper 7 when she did that, and Jack was slowly getting used to it as long as she didn't knock anything breakable that belonged to him. A photo of his then-grown kids was vulnerable, and a German beer stein he cherished, full of pennies, among a few other mementos of his former life. This time he managed to grab her from behind before she could get to them, and he kissed her neck and said, "I won some money, dollface, let's go out to eat tonight."

Calmed her right down. Even when it was clear that *I* was invited.

We went to a steak and seafood place down near the docks, where there were red candle jars on the tables and breadsticks that shattered as you bit them. The place smelled like crab boil and steam from the dishwasher. Mother began to glow in that red-jar light, Jack smiling like the man in the moon, and I swear to God, at that moment I felt like I was in a bona fide family unit, even if it was borderline schizoid. They flirted with each other across the horseshoe booth, me between in some kind of symbolic referee mode, and they were playing with each other's feet under the table. I flicked at Jack's shin with my sandaled toe even though I shouldn't have (I knew he'd think it was Cary Lee), provoking in him a sly come-hither aimed across the table, and you could just tell the springs would be squeaking that night as soon as the lights went out.

Which was fine with me. There's a little comfort in that when you've seen bread mold before your eyes. Let love run amok, I say.

A grotesque disappointment to me a few days later when Jack made Cary Lee so mad—I don't even know how—that she threw a pot full of spaghetti sauce at him across the kitchen. He was all Ragu and bad burns, breathing too fast as I worked on him in the bathroom, and I think we both saw how little it would take to make all this go boom. In a lot of ways it was even out of our control, like that bull Bill's father tried to handle but wouldn't let go of.

"I was trying to make her laugh," Jack said. He met my eyes in the bathroom mirror, brought his hand up to give mine a scratch.

"Big mistake. She hates that."

"Wish I'da known."

And we both started laughing at ourselves like we were watching a peculiar sitcom that takes place in the mirror. I liked seeing us happy together though.

—|—

IT DIDN'T SURPRISE me so much as trouble me that Bill wanted to go up and visit Hayes. At first I tried to make some excuses. I told him that Aunt Car would come and slit his throat while he slept if he tried to do it. I told him it wasn't really fair to Cam to go behind his back. I said I really didn't trust him to be a sport right now.

"It's my kid," he replied, indignant in the passenger's seat. He was looking into a choppy green pasture where two chestnut horses had their snouts in the clover.

"You can't tell him who you really are, Bill."

"No intention to."

"It wouldn't be fair."

"I can see how things are. I'm not a dumbshit." He tried an apologetic look on for size. "I *was* a dumbshit, but I'm not anymore."

"Good," I said, "because if you do anything stupid, I'll leave you here and go straight to a divorce lawyer. Aunt Carmen will be glad to recommend someone."

"Don't worry."

"I'm just saying, Bill."

And I drove him through redwoods and the town of Occidental, then up the back way toward the ridgetop where Hayes tended sheep in utter innocence, like a man in some fable with lessons weaved into it.

I CAN'T SAY I really remember a time when I was one hundred percent innocent like that, unblemished. The night Daddy left is one of my first memories, so things before that, when I had to have been clean, are all but erased. A glimpse here and there, a flash, like the tricycle on Daddy's shoulders.

What're you gonna do?

But I will say this about innocence. Innocent, you're a hair shy of naïve, when you think about it. Naïve has a stupid ring, doesn't it. The list of things that can hurt you is a hell of a lot longer than the one of things that protect. And when you're cynical, like me, there's not a lot that can cause you all that much pain anymore. You've gone soldierly, learned to grit your teeth through it. You've come to expect downside surprises.

Which is why I felt iffy about giving Bill a chance to let me down.

Infantile horseshit, I can just hear him saying.

We came out of the woods and into the top clearing where the ocean fog was racing inland. The air was cool up there, briny, wind battering the Jeep head-on.

And there, to my surprise, was Annie walking along the narrow road with her sketch pad and charcoals under one arm and her head down against the wind. She wore a light cotton print dress with high sleeves that let her arms bust out like bologna. Walking toward home, her back to us, and she didn't seem to know we were approaching until the last second, when she spun and gave us a horrified look. Almost dropped her things, and then she scrambled off the road and toward a stream cutting through the plateau.

I honked and called for her to wait up. I told Bill, without thinking, that it was Annie.

"That old lady?" His eyes inflated. "How would you know?"

Tersely, "I've already met her, Bill." And I got out of the Jeep and left the road myself. He had to be blind-baffled.

By the time I caught up with Annie, she was trying to hide herself behind a tall rock, covering her face with the flag of her dress, which left her white belly and turquoise underpants exposed to the elements.

"Remember me?" I asked, baby-voiced. "Sweetie? I'm not gonna hurt you now."

She lowered her dress and looked at me, and her face softened a bit. "'Member?" I said. "Carmen brought me up and you showed me some of your pictures. I met your son, Hayes."

"If he *is* my son," Annie replied.

"I'm pretty sure he is, honey. Listen, let us give you a ride home. It's cold out here today."

"I was drawing."

"You can show me what you drew when we get you home, okay? How's that."

As I walked with Annie, arm in arm, back to the Jeep, I could see Bill already beginning to squirm. I don't think he counted on reuniting with his ex-wife in such an accidental way. I'm not even sure he counted on a reunion with Annie at all while he was here, what little it could do for him—or her. There was no apology that would mean anything to Annie. Bill knew that.

"Bill," I said, "how about sitting in back and Annie here can have the front."

Annie was staring at Bill in a relentless wide-eyed gawk, like the look you give a baked ham that you intend to cut into. Then it softened a bit, the three of us all standing there beside the Jeep, and she suddenly began to cry, a sweet, soft, mild cry, of the kind you might have if you ever came upon your childhood self wandering alone someplace.

She threw her arms around his head and kissed his cheek, pulled back and let her hands linger on the sides of his face, and she said, "You poor thing, you got lost, didn't you. Poor little guy."

As if she were Bill's *mother*.

Bill looked at me queasily for advice until Annie stood back to regard him with a wide-angle view, knitting her hands with a vigorous rub.

There wasn't much I could tell him, was there.

WHAT DO YOU suppose it would be like to come upon your childhood self as she wandered in the woods? Would you take her in, you think? Would you tell a little lie, like "It'll all be fine now"?

ON THE WAY to the house, I don't know why, but I introduced Bill as Bill Lark, my husband. It was my maiden name, Lark. Daddy's family name, sounds happy and light, even though there were a few suicides in that branch of the family, I'd always heard from Cary Lee. I caught a look at Bill in the rearview mirror when I said it, and he threw me back a shrug—why the hell not? I said that Bill was a photographer, but Annie didn't seem to acknowledge it.

"You both make pictures," I said. "Isn't that interesting?"

What a relief that she didn't appear to recognize him, though she did keep turning around to have another look, always with that blank cat face of hers that didn't reveal much of what was going on behind it.

Annie flipped through her drawings as we drove along, then abruptly turned toward Bill again with her arm flung over the seat back, and said, "Are you mad at me, Mr. Lark?"

Caught him by surprise again, I guess. He stuttered, no, he wasn't mad. Why would he be mad?

"I don't know," she said, content now. "I just had the odd feeling that I could have helped you and didn't."

Bill was looking down at his hands, gray-faced. "That's all right," he said. "You didn't do anything wrong, ma'am."

The formality there made me wince. The girl he'd knocked up and married. *Ma'am*.

"Good. I'd hate to think I did something bad and can't remember it. I hope you'd tell me if I did."

She had her sketchbook opened to a drawing of two faceless people making love in tall grass. I wasn't about to ask her where that idea came from or who those jaybirds were.

And suddenly there's Bill standing in front of his son for the first time. And there's Annie watching keenly from one side, as if she'll be drawing this, and there's me biting my fingernail as these two shake hands and talk sheep ranching for a minute, and I'm dreading Bill's second thoughts and the possibility that he'll take Hayes around the neck and call him "son" and tell him everything that everybody here didn't want him knowing, but what happens instead is more to my liking. He keeps his composure and looks at his son the way you'd look at any man you admire on first meeting—good, solid eye contact, friendly pumping handshake (those identical hands), two fellas talking about the things they know—and the only thing troubling me now is how Bill has the wherewithal to hide his true feelings like that. It makes you want to wonder.

Grateful when Bill makes an excuse and tells his boy that we have to be moseying along, because it means this is a bit too much for him right now. He asks Hayes if he might come up in a day or two with his cameras and gear (even though it's all at hand in the Jeep now) and take a few pictures of Hayes at work for this book he's working on. Of course Hayes says it's fine, as long as Bill doesn't mind stepping in sheep shit and having Annie wandering in and out of the frame from time to time.

He thanks us for bringing his mother home. She must have sneaked out again while he was in the bottom pasture, a habit of hers these last two or three years. He takes his hat off, and there's a hat line across his brow, a nice-looking man from decent stock, it looks like to me, but still a redhead, a Hayes, like his mom and his grandpa.

I know Bill notices.

We pull away with Annie waving from the front stoop as if we're family leaving the Thanksgiving feast. Hayes has his arm around her shoulders, giving her a whispered lecture, I'm sure, and then I look over and find my husband, hardhearted and pragmatic Bill, with his hands over his face and sobbing into the palms like he wants to wash in his own brine.

—|—

WOULD IT SURPRISE you to hear that Cameron was not tickled that Bill had met his son? He went into a hard mope when he found out.

But Aunt Carmen, stopping in for supper with her nephew that night, threatened Bill with a gruesome end if he so much as struck a paternal *pose* with that boy. Bill was not in a mood to respond to threats one way or another, sitting there at his parents' old dining room table in the dim chandelier light and taking his medicine like a killer listening to the judge rant about what dirt he is. There was a lot on his mind.

"Cameron," the aunt said, "I thought you were supposed to keep an eye on him!"

"I have a bar to run."

"And you, Nora. I didn't take you up there so you could play diplomat. I wanted you to see what we're dealing with here, thanks to *him*."

You got the feeling that Aunt Carmen carried the family's torch because she was the only one left who had the enthusiasm anymore to keep hating Bill. Cam, I could see by the way he slumped at the table and continued to eat while Carmen ranted, was tired. He had his big brother at one elbow, not entirely unhappy about it, I believe. And I felt for him, too, considering the complexities, the ramifications. The regrets.

Carmen stormed around the table in her boots, picking up the dirty dishes. She did a monologue while she was at it, until I finally got up to help her and said, "He promised me, Carmen."

"Oh he did, did he?" Amber teeth emerging from the wrinkles of her lips. "I don't know where I'd put a lot of stock in one of *his* promises."

And she was out of the room and slamming around in the kitchen. Bill finally raised his head and shouted, "I'd let you beat me with a tow chain, Car, if I didn't think you'd take the chance to kill me while you were at it."

He pushed away from the table and hammered his way through the front room and out the door. I heard his boot heels on the porch steps like the heartbeat of a bull.

It was just Cam and me at the table now, sitting over a gravy bowl and empty milk glasses. Poor, tired man with his baldy and his chin hair. A good boy, deep down, always had been, and that's a big burden.

"I wonder," said Cam, as deadpan as he could be with his eyes on my wedding ring. "I just wonder if you're having any second thoughts right about now."

Around eight I went out in the dusk to see what had become of my husband. The Argus cow land draped down from the barn over a scrubby gray hill, knee high with weeds and dry grass, which I walked through imagining I must be a holiday turkey to the ticks out there. In about ten minutes I came up over a small crest and saw Bill standing at the fence below, one foot up on a crossbeam and his hands out wide, gripping the barbed-wire strand.

It was a moment, as I stood a few yards behind him, when I wasn't completely sure which team I was on, at least as far as sparing people's feelings was concerned. I liked my new in-laws a lot. Those back at the house, and those up on the ridgetop. Bill was the one carrying a loaded gun, and the others—they were innocent.

He didn't know I was there until I arranged myself on him, over his shoulders, around his back, so he wouldn't know about this inside struggle of mine.

Without taking his eyes off the dimming land out there, he said, with a sad creaminess to his voice, that he almost wished Annie had been able to recognize him. "Because," he said, "I deserve whatever she would want to dish out to me."

For reasons I didn't want to learn at that moment, he was dwelling on Annie and not Hayes. It was almost as if he had, for the time being, placed Hayes in a mental box marked TURNED OUT ALL RIGHT, a box easily left aside while he considered the contents of the other one, TURNED OUT ALL WRONG. Annie's box.

"I ruined her," he said in those low tones meant only for your shadow to hear.

"Bill, that was so long ago. And you didn't do this to her. It's a disease."

"I was mean to her, and careless," he said, craning his neck to glance at me with harder eyes than I was used to from him.

I was tempted to tell him, as a survivor of the wars, that if he was taking responsibility for Annie's illness, then he could take responsibility for Hayes being such a decent man. And that, Bill, I'd have said, you can't. Instead I told him, with all the care I could get into my voice, "That isn't going to be undone."

He looked back out toward the ridgeline, where the tail end of the sunset made the sky a faint mustard color. The frogs and crickets had begun to worry.

Bill took a deep, almost desperate breath with his mouth wide and his eyes on the horizon.

"God, I needed to get out here to breathe," he said. "I'm almost crushed being in that house. I'm just about leveled."

"I expected that, baby," I whispered, and kissed his ear.

"You know it still smells like my mother in there?" The words were in his throat like cotton gauze. "It smells like her clean smell, the smell of whatever soap or solvent she would use to make us fresh again after those days in the pastures, stamping through all that cow shit. It's almost more than I can handle, smelling my mother all around and feeling like she's here and looking down on me. And she's sad for me. She's looking at me and saying, 'This is what you left us to become, Bill?' "

I gave him some flimsy comfort, patting him here and there on his body. Feeling a tautness in his ribs and shoulders, a tremor in his breath. He didn't seem to notice my hands on him, though. Kept talking, as if to himself.

"I thought I imagined every possible picture, what it would be like coming back. Reunion. Apology. Contrition. I'd hang my head, I'd scruffle the boy's hair—the man's, I mean. I'd cry. And she'd look at me and forgive or not forgive, or she'd scream and slap, or she'd walk away. But nothing prepared me for this, what it really is. She looks at me like she trusts me. She thinks she hurt *me*, Nora."

"She doesn't remember any of it anymore," I said. "She doesn't remember you."

"I'm almost jealous of her for that. At least her pain's on the back burner."

Immediately a guilty look washed all the color out of his face, rendering him gray, and he covered his eyes with one hand and breathed hard again. "Everything's this close, and I can't get far enough back to see it right. It's all on me."

He was fighting that old fifteen-round bout with self-hate. I'd never seen it in him like this before, not even the spaetzle night he conceived the idea of his homecoming. That night he couched it all in terms of his pictures, his new book.

"Bill," I said. "Distance always makes the pain duller. Of *course* it's harder being at the scene of the crime."

A harsh thing to say. But I had that thought again, about my own daddy coming home to see me after all this time, and the truth is, I'd want him feeling something hard. For his own good.

"What was easy," Bill finally said, in a voice like parchment, "was telling myself they'd be better off without me."

I couldn't help him filter that one through the net of all he had seen since coming home. He was facing the old ranchland again, his back to me, land that Cam had rightfully sold off, and the mustard sky was going brown on us.

He wouldn't look at me. Said, "What's hardest is admitting I could have changed."

Here was Bill Argus, the famous photographer, a man who had brought the world a batch of profound images to chew on and marvel at (even if he didn't recognize them as meaningful himself), telling me he wished he'd have stayed a poor cow rancher in this dust-obscured village and guided his wife through her dementia, till death might they part, and never met me.

That hurt a little bit.

—|—

I HAD THE dream that night where I go back to Long Beach to meet up with Cary Lee, and it's always the same, I go into her mint green bungalow—where I've never been in my life—and I sit with her in the tiny living room, knee to knee in uncomfortable chairs. She's in her African phase, dashiki and clackety wooden jewelry, a bleached-blond tribeswoman with an alcoholic's nose and the pushy smile of a guilty one who doesn't want to confess just yet.

And there's no action in this dream, no words, just the two of us sitting there and looking out the window at a palm tree from different angles, our knees almost touching. It's a simple reunion dream, I think. It has to do with what you feel when you can't possibly resolve things, at least not without choking a person, so your brain puts together this nice little film for you to view, showing you there's no point in going down there to have it out with her.

It never shows the part where she falls to pieces weeping, though, begging me to forgive her, wailing about how bad and self-absorbed she was and how I bore the brunt of it, God bless me, and could I find it in my heart to forgive her now, here at the end, before she croaks?

Actually, I'm glad that I don't get to see that part. In real life or in the dream, I'm pretty sure it wouldn't pan out the way I'd like it to. Afraid I'd start bawling before she had a chance.

+

BILL AND I went into Santa Rosa the next day so he could develop contact sheets of his latest pictures, that white home on the hill. We weren't saying a lot on the way in, though his hand rested on my knee as I drove. Through the woods and apple orchards that were the eastern gate to his sweet little valley, then on through Sebastopol and across land as flat as any you can find in Nebraska. They were building beige crackerbox homes along both sides of the highway, eating up what used to be good sheep and cow land, and there was a place where you could get out your clubs and practice driving golf balls—huge, tall nets strung between untarred telephone poles to keep the balls from coming out onto the highway. Fore!

"I couldn't look him in the eye," Bill said, staring at the white line on the shoulder.

"Not surprised." It was time for him to dwell on Hayes now, apparently.

"He doesn't look like I did at forty. He looks content, doesn't he? Looks young. But like he knows himself."

"He's older than *me*," I said. "I noticed some gray in his whiskers. Some wrinkles."

"He has a built-in bullshit detector, too, I can tell."

Bill disregarded my little plea for a compliment, so I went terse. "Then you have your work cut out for you, bud. Don't you."

He looked over at me and tried to smile. "I have to drip sincerity at this late date?"

I looked over at him and gripped him behind the neck. His shoulders rose instinctively. "No," I said. "You have to bullshit better than you've ever bullshitted in your life."

I left him to his work at the darkroom and wandered around downtown Santa Rosa for a while. Left alone, I remembered some things that were not the best. Self-esteem killers. Things I should have thought twice about before doing. Things that made me feel like a whore, which I never thought of myself as at the time. I know, a fine distinction I was making, but no man ever paid to get inside me. That's where I drew the line, as if it made a bit of a difference to anybody. I let plenty of them in, don't mistake me. I just didn't charge them for the privilege.

Thinking back on those compensated oral efforts of mine, I often wondered whether I was punishing myself, punishing Cary Lee, or just pursuing what came naturally. Prostitutes are made, not born, you might say, but I'll tell you one thing I learned through it all: Men like women who will do certain things, and they will stay and bless you with their company if they think you have something luscious to offer. I liked having the power of that, at least in theory.

I remembered coming to Bill's ranch near dawn after a long night of driving ten years before, and this memory, it turned out, was still fond. I knew he lived there, in that handsome adobe hacienda out in the middle of a big, broad wash, and I knew that if I sat at his gate long enough he'd turn up. He did. He'd been out all night camping at a spot in the desert where he wanted to catch the sunrise. Home now to get the film into chemical baths and on paper. He saw me sitting there and tried to ignore me as he opened up his gate, and then he said, "If you're here to see Bill Argus, he doesn't live here anymore."

"Who's Bill Argus?" I said. I knew damn well who he was, of course, and I knew this was him. His framed pic was in my trunk. "I had a flat tire."

He looked down the road toward my car. I had let all the air out of the left front.

"Come on in," he offered. "I'll make you some coffee, and then we'll change that thing before it's too god-awful hot out."

What one little lie can accomplish is something to be cherished. I thought of Hayes living on the grace of the lie they'd all made up for him, and I started to cry as I walked along the green square in the middle of Santa Rosa. Just everything about it suddenly got to me, that's all. My husband in the dark with his pictures.

Into a drugstore, where my knack for improvising led me to the aisle where pretty women look out at you from different boxes of dye, all with different-colored hair. I bought one called "Penny Red" and tried to picture Annie the way she used to be.

FUNERAL SUIT—1978

Cam

There was a time, and Cam Argus remembered it very well, when you could walk pasture lanes all the way from the Freestone Road to the Pacific Ocean, crossing twenty different ranchers' land with open-ended permission, through apple orchards where the earth would be littered with fallen, brown-skinned, rotting apples, across open grassland full of cows, through thick pine and oak woods, and out onto bare hilltops facing the water, scrubbed by wind-driven salt, where sheep grazed among the rocks. You wouldn't own a speck of it, but you could feel like you did. This was back when he was young, tending to wander away from his work. His father wouldn't notice him missing for a while. It was easy to slip away and walk across the county and eat some lunch from a knapsack at the top of the ocean bluffs. There were plenty of corners and hidden reaches that required exploration. Back then he had the legs for it too.

Ironic that he was something of a wanderer back then. You'd have thought he would have bolted long ago.

One day, in the early months after his brother left, Cam had to go to the back of the big pasture and repair a section of fence that one of the cows had damaged trying to bust her way out. She'd cut her own skin on the barbed wire, but for some reason she must have thought that salvation lay on the other side of that barrier, where the valley looked green and soft on the feet, full of lush, tasty grass. Luckily, she stopped before she'd taken the fence down completely, but it was bowed outward and one post was cracked. He worked most of the morning getting it back into shape, and then, without giving it any thought whatsoever, dropped his tools, hopped the fence himself, and began walking.

In the back of his mind was a voice reminding him that he had other chores to get to that day—the herd had to be brought back into the cowshed for the night, watered, fed, cleaned up after. Cam heard these warnings but walked on anyway, downhill along a narrow trail that had a layer of young grass coming up through the mud of it. He liked the way the ground felt under the soles of his shoes. And now that he was off his own land, he noticed the odor of eucalyptus in the air and the screech of a hawk high up in one of the pines along the edge of the valley. It seemed, for that moment, that the ranch had never existed at all, that he was like Adam himself walking the plush trails of Eden, and for all he knew he would encounter his ready-made Eve up around the next turn.

It made him laugh to think that from a chair on the porch his father might have actually seen him go. Maybe it had even startled him enough to get him up off his ass for a change. Maybe he hauled himself up onto his wobbly legs and called for Andie to come and see what Cam had done, the goddamn idiot. He's hopped the fence and started walking to Monte Rio. And Cam thought, She'll probably know what I'm up to.

The fence was an object in his way, and he overcame it. Now the valley was in his way, and after that the hill and the woods. His feet chewed up the land, sinking into the spongy ground where rainwater collected, and his eyes were on the place where the trail entered the pine and oak forest and began to climb toward the ridgetop. Never coming back wasn't the thought that drove him along, he told himself. I don't want to leave forever like Bill. I just wanted over that fence. And now I want up top and to see the ocean. It's been months since I've even seen the ocean.

When he reached the top of the ridge, he walked another half mile to the lip of it, where it overlooked the ocean. He didn't stay up there very long. There was no point in it. The ocean was so vast out there that it seemed to mock his craving for wider horizons, a different set of chances. The wind was cold too, and there was nobody else around. It felt as if he were the only human being left on earth, his future even more limited because he would always be trapped in the small hole in the world that he inhabited at the moment. There was nobody else to open it up for him.

Gradually, as he walked down the hill on the ocean side, the trail contouring through sheep pastures and bare, open fields of rock, he shed his morbid thoughts and began to see that running away would not yield him any more happiness than he had already. The advantage of working his father's ranch was that it was familiar. The work was hard but well practiced. He knew people and could talk to them, could hold his own in barbershop debates, made people laugh every now and then with an off-the-cuff remark. Wandering beyond his own fence line, he had found a wider fence here, at the lip of the ocean, and whatever was out there beyond it was bigger than he cared to imagine.

He had a grasp, now, of his destiny, which was just to hang fire. It had all pretty much been settled with Bill's leaving.

—|—

NOBODY IN PIANTO was surprised when Cam Argus, within months of the sudden deaths of his parents sixteen years later, sold most of the Argus ranch and put the money toward the purchase of the old VFW building at the dogleg in the Bodega Highway. It wasn't much of a specimen, that building, an unassuming crate with an arched, asphalt roof and dead-to-the-world stucco the color of turned milk. But Cam was determined to make something of it, and he decided it would be a tavern and that he'd be its proprietor. Far enough from the grinding routines of ranching, a different sort of grind perhaps, but better in his mind than failing at what his father had failed at. His father had failed at a lot of things, he understood, but what most people saw was the ranch—ramshackle and shabby—and they would judge Cam on how he did with it. There was nothing to do but walk away from the family business and start in on something new, failing at which would not mark him so much the loser.

In that sense, maybe if he failed at failing, the Argus reputation could shift gears entirely. The thought made him laugh, among few other things.

The VFW building needed a great deal of work, and he got to it with the help of Hayes Diamond, who was then twenty-one and looking for pin money and things to do other than mind his mother's whereabouts. It was Hayes, in fact, who came up with the name of the tavern. The room didn't have much of a personality in its gutted state, rafters and studs like rib bones, but Hayes observed while they hung Sheetrock one day and kicked around their thoughts that it sat right at the dogleg in the road, so why not call it The Dogleg?

"You're a gentleman and a scholar," Cam told him. "That's it. I'll pay you a royalty if you can beat me at darts. Otherwise I'll just steal the idea."

"You can have it," his nephew said.

"In that case you'll never pay for a drink here. How's that."

"Fair enough. But I don't even know if I like beer yet."

"Then it's an even better deal for me, kiddo." The "kiddo" sounded entirely affectionate coming from his lips.

Hayes had turned into a good-natured young man who would let you rib him without mercy. He had this thing in his Annie-blue eyes that seemed to tell you he could take it.

The Dogleg was to be the only tavern in Pianto, since the old place across the street had closed. Traditionally there had been a tavern in Pianto ever since Italians wagoned over the hills and founded the place, full of desperate gratitude that they'd finally reached their destination and could have a drink. They were close to running out of continent, with the ocean another two miles away. Worth a stiff drink. Cam knew the story, like every Pianto schoolkid, but the town never had an Italian feel to his mind, and in fact didn't much feel like a place you'd want to stay your whole life. Yet that's what he had done. Would continue to do.

And now Bad Ray and Andie were buried up in the Pianto cemetery with eucalyptus leaves browning on their plots. Hard to believe. Bill so long gone that the idea of him had faded into a handful of childhood memories, the scar on Cam's hand—and now the unrecognizable photographer who was featured in the *San Francisco Chronicle* as the heir to Ansel Adams and the great new interpreter of the desert's metaphors.

Such horseshit. Bill didn't leave here knowing what a metaphor even was. What he knew of the desert, Cam figured, was already in him when he got there.

And Cam to be a bartender in the town of his birth. It makes you wonder where people's fates are written down, because that's something you'd want to see in writing.

Cam went to a salvage yard in Petaluma and bought a plastic Pabst Blue Ribbon sign to hang out front, commissioned Aunt Carmen to paint an artist's rendition of a dogleg on it, on both sides.

"A dogleg?" she questioned him, hands on her hips. "I don't know if I can even draw a dogleg."

"Like the hind leg, was what I was thinking."

"But where would it start on the dog? At the hip? Above the knee? Would the tail show? I don't even know what damn *breed* you want!"

Everything was more difficult with Aunt Carmen, although she had been very helpful after the accident, getting Cam settled down with his work and looking into selling the land for him. She went into action. For a long spell she lived in the house with him and made sure he ate well enough to stay viable, cooked him all the old things she used to make when Andie was bedridden.

"I don't care what breed, Car. It could be a Portygeze water dog for all I care, just so it's a recognizable leg."

"Tall order, Cameron. You're straining the bounds of my talent."

It was a picture on the sign of a country bar, he thought. God bless the perfectionists among us.

—|—

AS THE WORK went on in the place and Cam spent his days from morning to night breathing sawdust and plaster cloud, he often allowed his thoughts to wander back toward Bill and how Bill had failed to respond to the word that the folks were gone. In a fit of abandonment anxiety, Cam had written a fairly caustic letter to get the news to Bill, in care of his publisher, and it's possible that put him off. There'd been no word at all from him since he managed the divorce from Annie, always via mail; then, out of the blue, he puts out this book of pictures and gets his name in magazines, gets these invitations to parties where Hollywood people must have given him hard-ons with all that praise. It made Cam a bit sick. Show me a little justice, he thought, but then again, he didn't want Bill dead too, not at this point in time. There was a little bit of solace—a little—in knowing he was still out there, flesh and blood.

Before she died, Andie had had a long, quiet chat with Cameron as they walked through an apple orchard on their way into town together. She was over sixty by then, still energetic enough to make the walk, but her voice was tired and her body was in the process of growing physically smaller, almost to the eye, so that she seemed like a child walking beside him.

"When you get married," she began, and he knew what was on its way, for she had made a hobby of fantasizing about his future wife and how happy Cam and the girl would be, whoever she was. Andie's vision of her was clear in her mind, apparently, though Cam had no idea where she was supposed to come from, this woman. "Make me a promise that you'll marry for love."

Why she was speaking like someone who wouldn't be around when he did get married wasn't clear to him, but it turned out to be prophetic. She would be gone within a month.

"I don't know why else I *would* marry anyone," he said.

"There are more reasons than I can throw out at you."

"Name some."

He helped her across a small dry streambed and up the opposite bank of it. Her hand was tiny, full of sharp bones it felt like.

"There's convenience, there's opportunity, there's boredom, there's confusion, there's the hunger for sex."

"Mom," he said, surprised at her.

"I don't know if you have a girl who gives you that or not. It isn't worth marrying for, put it that way."

In fact, Miranda's instincts were more accurate than he could ever tell her. For several years he'd been visiting a prostitute in Monte Rio who took care of that kind of hunger for him and treated him with a bighearted kindness. Melody was her name, which was fitting because she always sent him away with a song on his lips. But aside from her physical love (he also wouldn't admit to his mother), he had never come close to finding a woman he might marry. The ranch was too demanding. It wasn't a condition he'd like to bring a woman into. Some girl out there somewhere had been spared the agony of having Bad Ray as a father-in-law, and she didn't even know it.

A faint smile on his mother's lips, and it was nice to see there. He laughed and wrapped his arm around her shoulders. "All right then, suppose you tell me why you married Dad."

They walked a long distance before she lifted her head and started to tackle that one. Almost to town, near the Mill Road, where she had grown up. The house had been razed a few years back to make way for an apple-processing plant, so there was nothing for her to look at anymore.

She said, "I married your father because it was generous to marry him."

This was not an idea that had occurred to Cam.

"Generous to who?" he asked.

"All concerned." The calmness in her voice was like that of people with religious faith.

By the time they walked out together onto the sidewalk in Pianto, he had decided not to tease her that she didn't mention love when she talked about marrying Ray.

He'd have been a hard old ram to love. Cam wondered if he ever understood that Miranda Harper was the best thing ever to happen to him.

AUNT CARMEN, when she delivered the painted dogleg sign, told him that her sister was incurably naïve and married Ray Argus because she thought she could make him love her. Cam didn't know why the subject came up at that particular time. They unloaded the Pabst sign from Carmen's station wagon, and Cam was pleased to see that the dogleg on it was not just passable but anatomically accurate, haunches and musculature and toenails. It appeared to be the hind leg of a Doberman.

"Now, why on earth do you say that?" he asked.

"Because I thought you ought to know."

"Well God bless her for thinking things get better. Even if it is misguided."

Carmen followed him as he hauled the sign up the concrete front steps. Hayes would help him hang it later.

"She'd have liked this-here," Carmen said. Her sunglasses hid the slightly bugged eyes she was sporting in older age, and her blouse looked to Cam like something a barber or a dentist would wear.

"This *what*-here."

"This establishment going in. You chucking the cows. I believe she'd have enjoyed seeing you walk away from the Argus line of work, if the truth be known."

"Ah, well," he said, and it was hard to know what to add about what Andie would have liked, now that there was no way of knowing. He did know that Ray would *not* have liked this-here. "Let's see if I can make a go of it anyway."

"You ever hear how your old man tried to get your mom to run off with him and forget about ranching cows? And on the very day they were engaged too."

He held the door open for her, and she walked by as if there wasn't this provocative statement hanging in the air. He wasn't sure he believed it. Didn't sound much like Bad Ray.

"Never heard that one."

"I used to think your mom was levelheaded, talking him out of that. Now I'm not so sure it wouldn't have been a great idea. The road not taken, eh? Remind me to tell you about it sometime." She winked and headed straight back toward the toilets before he could press her for more.

—|—

HE HAD PURCHASED a funeral suit the day after his parents' accident. Not an expensive one, but a nice-enough-looking one, just something he could show up at the church in and look like he meant respect. He couldn't recall the last time he had on a coat and tie, his life so wired to the ranch and dependent on its dirty formalities. There was no call to put on a coat and tie in that line of work, as long as nobody died and nobody got married, and that seemed to be the way it was for a long time there. Bill had some things that Annie had given back to Miranda because she didn't want them in her closet. The white pants he got married in, the jacket. Variety of ties. Not that he was a snappy dresser, but he seemed to have been called to more formal occasions than Cam ever had.

None of his things fit anyway. Cam had tried on a few of them, found his brother to have been slighter than he remembered, less meat in the shoulders. Cam's fists stuck out of the sleeves like the bone ends of a turkey leg.

The tailor in Santa Rosa used to be a Pianto man, named Paul Negri, and he remembered the Argus name, had heard about the accident. Expressed his regrets. Said it was a shame that a man needed this kind of reason to buy a new suit, he'd like to see less of it, but then he went on a bit of a fume about how the country families don't wear suits on a regular basis anyway. "They overclean the old ones," he said, "to where they get shiny and the creases fade, and the styles are so out of date that you want to put these guys on a time machine and send them back to '53, whenever."

"I wouldn't know about that."

"How 'bout your brother," said Negri. "He coming in for his too?"

The tailor worked around Cam's waist and chest as if Cam were a statue. All business, and marking up the trouser legs with chalk.

"Can't quite recall his name, your brother. When's he coming in anyway?"

"I don't have a brother," Cam said before he had thought about it. He lived as if he had no brother, was the truth. It wasn't a stretch.

"I thought you had a brother. I went to school in Pianto with an Argus, I could swear. Would've been older than you. What are you, thirty-eight,-nine?"

"Thirty-six."

"This guy's closer to my age. I was probably a couple years older."

Cam stood there and let him measure, but he did not confirm Negri's memory of an Argus boy back in school.

"The suit looks pretty good," Cam told him.

"Your basic black dress suit. You can wear it to other things besides funerals too. Classic. Keep it till you get a little heavy around the middle like me, and I'll take it out for you."

Cam wanted to say he probably only needed it just this once, knowing him. Negri would have rolled his eyes.

He left there feeling like the years between his occasions for a suit were filled with an obscure and mild sorrow, as if he never stopped mourning some older, forgotten thing but couldn't draw up a strong enough memory to hurt over it anymore. Sometimes you wake up with pain in your chest and sweat dripping down your face, and you can't recall the dream that did it to you.

—|—

THE BAR WAS stocked and ready to open, a big first-day party lined up for the weekend. Hayes had been there to help Cam paint and touch up, worked his bottom off most of the day before checking on his mother and getting back to his small herd of sheep that he kept on her land. He'd been making a decent go of it as a sheep rancher, more of a stopgap than his true calling, Cam believed. The kid had a bottomless bucket of energy, didn't mind busting his ass to help a friend, which was what Cam was to him.

And just before he'd left, Hayes looked around the place and said he was proud of Cam for pulling this off.

Here's this lanky redheaded kid with good hands, paint on his T-shirt, a heartening gleam in his eye, and he's proud of Cameron's little country bar with a dogleg on its sign. If he only knew what *he'd* pulled off, Cam thought, and wanted to hug the guy around the neck until everything Cam knew about him passed from the one to the other without being spoken. He'd never tell him, but he wished Hayes could guess, wished he'd figure things out.

"Means a lot to me, Hayes," Cam said, feeling himself choking up.

"What I think?" A spurt of laughter through his nose. "I don't see why you'd give a rat's ass what I think."

Cam had begun drinking from a fine new bottle of scotch already, celebrating. After enough of that stuff he felt the maudlin mourner rising up in him and said, "Hell, you're practically family. I got you and Carmen and Annie now. That's about the size of it."

It had been a long time since he'd gone up to Monte Rio.

Hayes held out his callused rancher's hand and shook Cameron's with a steady, calm grip, smiling tightly as if he were holding a little something back too.

—|—

ON THE DAY of the opening, Cam got up early and drank coffee while he waited for Aunt Carmen to get there. The old house seemed airless to him that morning, so he went around opening all the windows that weren't painted shut, and by the time Carmen arrived the place was swirling with crosscurrents.

"You're nervous," Carmen observed. "You're standing there in your boxers and T-shirt and you're sweating bullets."

It was true. He hadn't bothered to dress for her.

She cooked him a breakfast of fried eggs and hash browns and made him a tall Bloody Mary. He should have turned it down. It went directly to his head and made him feel like he might easily lose control of things that day.

"Try not to think about it, sweetheart," Carmen advised. "Here's the deal: People are coming to The Dogleg to get snookered and have fun. Nobody's even gonna notice if you lose a little grip."

He dressed in his black suit, wanting to look, for his new Dogleg clientele, like a man who could do himself up for a high occasion. Down at the bar, where Annie and Hayes were already waiting for him at the locked door, he did a slow, arms-out spin so they could appreciate him in his duds.

"I tried to tell him not to dress for another funeral," Carmen griped. "It's asking for trouble, my opinion."

"It's fine," Annie said kindly. "It's a special occasion, and he looks nice."

Annie and Carmen—in the absence of any hired hands yet—waited tables all day long, while Cam tended bar and Hayes worked the oyster grill outside. It was busy all day long too, with nearly everyone in town stopping by for a while and leaving enormous tips for their modest tabs: a lot of people who had known Cam since he was a boy and had known the Arguses longer than that. Pianto wanted him to succeed, it looked like. Cam kept his collar buttoned all day and his tie up tight against his Adam's apple, if just to show some respect for his friends who were dropping coin there on his behalf. He liked seeing them all in his place, and he liked the whine and yodel of Texas swing on his tape player and the clacking of the billiard balls as ranch hands tried to win on brute force. The beer flowed like runoff, and the place was full of the din of voices and laughing and the music, and Cam was surprised when Carmen approached him and said it was time to go home and get her feet up in the air before they ruptured.

"It's ten o'clock," she said. "And I'm an old lady."

"It's ten already?"

"Look out the window, goof. Dark out."

Later, after midnight, when the last of the customers had gone and he was alone in the place, Cam locked the door and poured himself a drink of his own. He shot a game of pool and fiddled with the ashtrays and salt and pepper shakers on each of the tables, his own place. It still smelled of varnish and paint and sawdust, slightly burned wood from the saw work.

Nobody had noticed, but he had obtained from a San Francisco gallery two framed Bill Argus photographs and hung them behind the bar, silvery black-and-whites showing the backbone of a desert ridge with fine, spidery thornbushes filtering the backlight. They reminded Cam of what a man might see when he first wakes up in a place he didn't know he'd gone to sleep in. He liked them, envying Bill's latter-day eye. These prints were about all he'd heard from his brother in twenty years, and the pictures spoke what a phone call or a letter couldn't have.

Goddamn things cost him a little fortune, too, thanks to Bill's reputation now. He could see the fucker laughing his head off at what Cam had paid for them.

It was a quiet night, ripe for his single-malt scotch, and he drank some more of it. He took his suit coat off and draped it on the back of a chair, finally loosening his tie. Now that he was alone, he drank a few goddamn Bills and some goddamn Rays, and goddamn the hidden truth and the truth so big and glaring you can't even see it. Led himself right to the place he didn't want to go most, the graveside that day a few months earlier with his funeral suit hanging on him like a sheet of tissue paper. Ray and Andie's coffins parked there at the top of a mild rise in the cemetery, two precisely squared holes previously dug and already filling with errant eucalyptus leaves. It was an uncharacteristically nice winter day, bright and warming, the cemetery full of wavering shadows and speckled light through the trees, occasional hands on his back and shoulders, patting. Annie was there, drained with sympathetic heartache, her son by her side, and she walked into Cameron with her arms open and held him as if it were possible to assume his grief through physical contact. He felt her hands through his suit coat, the warmth of her, something more potent than kindness coming through, because she was the one person who knew the real nature of his grief. It brought him back to her wedding day, when they had first talked soberly together, Annie miserable and Cam worse. That was when they became friends, that day, and they had stayed close even after Bill left. Through the many crises.

As he held on to her at the graveside, pushing his forehead into her neck, he recalled how at the moment he learned of his parents' death all he could dwell on was getting word to Bill and getting him up here to share in this and take some of the shit and liability. And how, almost instantly, he knew that it wasn't going to happen. How everything was tied up in what was never going to be.

Worth a stiff drink and a cry, he figured. All restlessness and capitally lonesome, as unlikely in his own skin as in this black suit.

Opening day at The Dogleg, and he wound up sleeping on the floor of the bar that night with a paint-fume headache in the morning and no firm catharsis to show for it.

STEALING LIGHT

Nora

Cam knew what we were up to, though I'm sure he wished he didn't know. He left for the bar before we could talk much about it. Wanted it to happen without his knowledge or approval, but he knew. At least Bill and I were smart enough not to tell Carmen that we were heading up to the ridgetop so Bill could take pictures of Hayes Diamond at work on his sheep ranch.

It's a miracle of a thing to trust somebody you think is capable of shitting on your trust.

By that, I think you know what I mean. I was taking Bill up there to his son's house knowing that he might tell Hayes everything but trusting that he wouldn't. I'd been Bill's wife a long time by then. We were married in a little courtroom in Palm Springs and had exchanged these vows, which, truth to tell, I couldn't recite to you now, they flew by so fast during the ceremony. Standard ones, I'm sure. Your basic love, honor, cherish, obey. Yes, I'd taken similar vows before, and knew they were written on tissue paper, very easily torn. On that flimsy foundation, though, I believed in Bill and loved him. We packed up the Jeep with his gear.

We took the back way so we wouldn't have to pass The Dogleg. To my mind it was a courtesy toward Cam, nothing to do with our feelings, though Bill might have disagreed. As it was, he kept his head down most of the way and didn't say much to me. The Artist Engrossed in His Thoughts.

As the road climbed through the trees and then out onto the open plateau, I looked over at him to see if I could tell where he was in his head. To me he seemed like a boy who was stiff-upper-lipping his way through a punishment, and maybe that was the appropriate thing. But I said to him, just so he knew, that I would be close enough all day to know what was what.

"I'm not telling him anything," he insisted.

"What are you doing, then."

"Recording him. That's it."

"Fine. That's a good boy. Proud of you."

I did know him well enough to know that he was doing more than recording his son at work. For all of his earlier philosophizing about light and shadow and the machinery of picture-taking, I think Bill had come to believe—like certain American Indians you might come across on your way through the West—that the camera pilfers a little of the subject's soul when the shutter opens, a little of his light, and that's what Bill would be doing. Stealing a little light from his son for later reflection.

Otherwise, what was he doing here?

Maybe to put me at greater ease, or maybe to take his own mind off things, Bill said, "I dreamed about this big egg last night."

"Good for you, baby."

"It was the biggest egg I ever saw in my life."

He didn't say how big. "Guess the yolk's on you," I said.

Instead of laughing, he got mesmerized by the view across the plateau, where the grass moved like a broad green flag and the rocks stood up to watch. He had speckled history all through here.

When we pulled up at Hayes's, Annie was sitting out front with her sketch pad on the desk of her knees. No telling what she was yanking from her memory now, and I didn't want to know. Enough that she had an accurate glimpse of young Bill in her head. I almost believed she could re-create her entire life if she had enough time to draw the moments in order. The details only had to be gathered, that's all. Everything pieced together.

She stood and waved at us just as Hayes came out of the small barn pushing a wheelbarrow full of feed. He saluted us, and Bill, all business, began to pitch his tripod right there in the yard. Annie approached him cautiously and said, "Are you still mad at me?"

Bill a picture of exasperation, true pain there in his eyes. He looked over at me and then assured Annie he wasn't mad at her at all.

"Okay," she said. "But I don't want to hear different later on."

Hayes shook our hands and told Bill that he thought he'd stick near the house today if that was all right. Plenty of small chores to do. The sheep were all pastured nearby, and the weather was shitty anyway. Fog and mist and a good stiff wind again.

"I don't know anything about photography," Hayes admitted. "You have enough light to work with on a day like this?"

"Not a problem."

"I'll hang around with Annie," I said. "If you don't mind, Hayes."

"No, she'll be tickled. She's been talking about you. Drew you in her book, as a matter of fact."

"Well, Annie, I'm flattered to pieces."

"I can't remember your name though." Annie clutched her notebook to her chest. Troubled eyes on mine.

"That's all right. I'll answer to just about anything."

Hayes went straight to work without formalities, and Bill stood behind his tripod getting his first shot framed and focused. I couldn't resist going up to him and laying an arm around his slumped shoulders, kissing him on the side of the head. I told him I knew this was hard, but he didn't really want to acknowledge that, twisting the lens collar underhanded between his thumb and middle finger. He was all eyes right then.

I led Annie into the house and told her I had a surprise for her. Took the box of Miss Clairol out of my purse and showed it to her.

"How would you like to recover that luxurious red shine of yours, baby? Not to mention body and manageability."

Annie tried to smile at me. At most it was a strained trembling at the corner of her flat-line mouth, but her eyes appeared to be dancing at the thought behind it.

I worked her at the bathroom sink, dressed her with a towel around her neck, and combed out her Dutch boy as well as I could, it was so tangly and strawlike. "Beautiful girl like you," I said, "you need a nice lovely head of hair for when Hayes takes you into town. Turn all the men's heads, right?"

Annie threw me that inscrutable cat face from the mirror.

Mixing up the color, I thought about Cary Lee giving me a dye job for the first time when I was a kid—a teenager, I should say—and what an exciting thing that was for me. I don't know why, but as I worked the goop into Annie's hair, I started to tell her about it. I said there's nothing like the first time, eh? Got no laugh. I said there we were, my mother and I looking into the mirror together, and she was working on me just like this, the same way I'm working on you, and I'm beaming at her and asking her was it going to turn out green like her own did one time, and how was I going to look with blond hair for God's sake, nobody would even recognize me. Cary Lee said, "That's the idea, hon. You're tired of yourself, you make a change."

"She was the kind of woman," I told Annie, "who got tired of herself all the time. She used to go through phases. Redhead, blonde, whatever. Jet-black once. And not just hair phases but clothing phases, shoe phases, mood ones. Sometimes I didn't know *who* she was."

Annie was focused on her own reflection, and I couldn't tell whether she was hearing me. Her eyes were intense but blank, if that makes sense, like she was in a trance over her own image with her hair flat and plastic-wet on her head and the paste working in. I wished I could tap the contents of her head and spread them out on a table like newspaper, read all about it. Everything she had seen, heard, and felt in her life. If she felt like she'd been punished for the so-called sins of her youth I'd set her straight, I'd tell her mine and show her how punishment isn't perpetual, and now look, I'm happy.

"But then there've been times when I didn't know who *I* was," I said, "so go figure."

Even that loaded line didn't perk her up. She was deep-staring into her own eyes and seeing things behind there that I couldn't begin to guess—her young Bill with his wiry arms around her, the baby, Mom and Pop Argus, Mom and Pop Hayes. Maybe, with her hair reddening, she was watching herself yield to Bill's body like the lovers in that picture she had drawn, melting into him like candle wax.

With my hands in plastic gloves I worked that dye into her hair and talked. It started with my third birthday and Mama in the tub saying take her away from me, and I talked, at first I think, just to keep the silence filled and to keep from thinking about what was going on outside right then, Bill recording his son at work and battling the urge to kneel and confess and beg. I didn't want to know, didn't want to think I should be out there preventing it, if that was Bill's decision, so I worked that dye and talked, and I told Annie that things were bad bad bad in our house until good ol' Jack came around, and then I finally had an ally. I told her what he looked like, and how he always smelled good and carried a billfold, how his hands looked, how he treated me. I went all the way into it, how we conspired against Cary Lee and hid from her and acted like kids together, taunting her and pretending we didn't really need her around to be happy, which was an idea I enjoyed flaunting. Grandma Elsie long gone, I needed Cary Lee like you need an unreliable car. Now that Jack was on the scene, I had another way to get around.

Annie peered into the reflection of herself, deeper and deeper.

Jack, I said, would be there forever. He was the one who would stay. I loved him and needed him and we were pals and partners and he would always be around.

I was seventeen. Seventeen and settling down, losing my chip. I was, the way the school counselors liked to put it, "making strides," at least, from time to time, trying. Me and Jack, speaking pidgin French to each other and busting our brains over the quadratic equation so I could pass a test, Cary Lee at the other end of the table saying if I'd just learn to type, I'd be okay. I remember once I slipped and called Jack "Pops," or not so much a slip as a little test to see what he'd do, and what he did was take my hand and pat it and look at me with his brown eyes, smiling, flattered, I think. Out of Cary Lee's presence I called him Pops from then on, our little secret, and he called me sweetpea or dollface, and we got along famously.

He had this old T-Bird that he had owned for years, turquoise and white, his prized possession that he took care of like a fine horse. Beautiful thing, and I loved it. We'd go out for a drive every Sunday morning, sit in it together at the beach for a while, and then bring home bagels and coffee and wait for Cary Lee to drag herself out of bed. Sitting there at the ocean with him in the T-Bird was one of my favorite things, the kind of ritual that always seemed to bring us closer together even if we didn't have much to say, though there was usually something on Jack's mind. He was a talker, unlike, I'd heard from both Elsie and Mother, my real dad. Jack couldn't keep a secret, had to vent the steam in his head, and I adored being there with him in the T-Bird and listening to him confess his little sins and give his curiosities some air. He asked me what I thought about things, his big hands hanging by the wrists off the steering wheel, the radio tuned to a jazz oldies station of tinkly piano and honking sax music from when he was young. We talked about how far away the horizon was on the ocean, the size of it, vast and hard to imagine. He'd been to Japan, he said, all over the Pacific. Way out there. He'd been places that he wished he could tell his own kids about, but they were finished with him and didn't care to hear. They didn't talk to him. "What do you think about that, sweetpea?" he'd ask, and I'd say they weren't being fair, he didn't deserve it.

His voice was the consistency of gravy. Smooth-pouring. The accent. A laugh in his cadence no matter what he was talking about, because he was amused by things, even sadder things, aided, he said, by the perspective of middle age, the great equalizer. He said, Don't worry about things, Nora, because you'll be my age someday, and you'll look back, and the pains you have now will seem like little stings. Nuttin' but nips and deze vague little aches.

One Sunday I dressed up. I put on a short sleeveless dress and bangles and beads and lipstick, and we went out on our usual drive. Jack seemed to like my outfit, cast me these playful looks and shook his head but never asked what I was up to, as Mother would have, because he didn't mind. He was in his gray linen pants and his short-sleeved cotton shirt with a gold pattern in it, his big wristwatch, his ring or two. He was freshly shaved and slick in the cheeks, smelled of the Skin Bracer Daddy used to use. His hands were big on that wheel, fingers sculpted to hold a cigar. We parked at our usual spot at the water that day, and the waves were big and loud and full of silver foam. Little beach birds ran along the sand. The sky out over the ocean was the color of a canvas tarp, so gray that you could hardly tell where the water stopped and the sky began. June Gloom, they call it. I was telling Jack that I had written a letter to my father in care of his mom, my grandmother in Nebraska, a woman I'd never even met, and that so far there wasn't any reply. To this he said I shouldn't get my hopes up.

"Why not?"

"I'm a man, sweetie, and I know how men are." He looped one arm behind the back of my seat. I was leaning into him because I was cold and thinking the little dress was a shitty idea on a day like that. Shivering. "Men grit their teeth when they've made a decision," Jack said, "and they stick with it. Even if it kills them."

I didn't think he understood. I said that things were different now than when he had gone, but Jack didn't seem to hear that. His eyes were on me in the rearview mirror, which he had adjusted so he could watch me without turning his head, and we locked looks for a second until he couldn't take it and had to look away. His hand drifted into my hair and then fluttered at the back of my neck where my beads latched.

I remember the radio playing Louis Armstrong, and I was thinking, This feels like a strange moment. Something awkward. Then Jack said, in a hesitant but sweet gravy voice, that he had been wondering if I would do something for him that my mother didn't like to do. He wasn't being cruel or pushy with me, he was just asking, and I knew what it was he wanted because I was an experienced girl by then. I wasn't even all that surprised, except, all other things about her considered, that Cary Lee didn't like going down on a man. It seemed to run against her other whorey habits. I wanted to be adult about it, and strong, and blasé, and above everything else I didn't want Jack to have a reason to leave growing in his head, even the stupid thought that he might be able to find a woman elsewhere who didn't mind giving head. He wasn't a mean man, and he wasn't selfish, and when I looked at him then, straight on, I saw his mouth in a guilty and shameful smile and I managed to hide my disappointment. Didn't want him to go. Didn't want him slipping away from me, so I put my hand on him through his nice linen pants.

I undid his belt and took him out, telling myself that it was for me I was doing it, not for him, and even if he thought it was for him, that was all right, because I loved him and wanted him to stay, and as I put my mouth on him with my eyes shut and my ears ringing from my own selfishness, I tried to listen to Louis Armstrong singing, and the waves, and not the sounds Jack was making in his chest and throat, or to feel his thick hands on either side of my head.

I don't think it was something I could have avoided, when I tell it like that. I still don't see any way around it, and isn't it just the pits that in the long run it didn't help.

Annie bent over the bathtub and let me rinse out the dye. I was telling her, I'm sure, because I knew she would not tell anyone else. She wasn't capable of it. This was a story I had not even told Bill. It was the one thing I didn't feel good about telling, so I never did, and if he had ever guessed or found out some other way, I always thought I'd have lied to him and denied it.

Later Cary Lee must have taken a shot in the dark and said something to Jack, and his face betrayed him, and she read it right. I don't know.

I do know I'll never know.

At least she never caught us in the act. We were always careful about that. Neither of us wanted to humiliate her to her face, even though, God help me, the temptation was often there.

"Anyway," I said to Annie, wiping at my face with the back of one wrist, "old Cary Lee found us out. End of story."

I took a blow dryer to her and made her look like an old

woman with a penny red wig. The look on her face, though. Like she had stumbled onto young Annie Hayes, her old friend, who had nothing but high hopes and a soul dying to fly.

I nearly broke at the sight of her in that mirror.

—|—

WHERE DOES IT say in writing that you can never forget the painful parts? I would like to see where it says that. I wish, as a reformed human being and ex–fellatio whore, I could get special dispensation and have this crap of mine vacuumed out and disposed of, like liposuction. Wouldn't that be a kick? I'd be simple Nora Argus, a happy woman, free of unsightly emotional lumps. Oh, she can't account for her whereabouts for ten or fifteen years, but she is a sweet, contented thing, isn't she? The look on her face of one of those women in a Midol commercial, whose cramps have miraculously disappeared.

I wanted the relief that comes of confession. It is a blessing to be able to speak the words and have the act itself, long time past, minimized in the telling, even if you tell someone who might not be hearing you. I remember being a little girl and going to confession with Grandma Elsie one time at an enormous Catholic church downtown, and she told me that all I had to do was go into that booth and tell the priest on the other side of the screen the different bad things I had done. In those days, before my sexual awakening (to put it politely), my sins would have been such holy misdemeanors I wouldn't waste a clergyman's time with them now. You should save your confessions for the big-ticket sins, the ones that could get you landed in hell. Of course, I hadn't been to confession in years because I would have to have booked an afternoon of one-on-one with some unsuspecting priest, and there weren't enough hours in a year to say all the rosaries he'd make me do in penance. Maybe the desire to atone is as cleansing as the actual atonement. Bill would be learning more on that front.

Anyway, Grandma Elsie takes me to this big church, and I'm in my frilly church dress that reveals my bashed-up knees and the last of my baby fat, and really, who expects a girl with baby fat to have committed any sins of consequence, I ask you? She said, "Go into the booth and say, 'Bless me father for I have sinned. This is my first confession. I said a bad word, I took candy from my mother's purse, I told a lie. Okay, sweetie? That's all there is to it, and then he'll give you some prayers to say, and you're as good as new."

It is comforting to a child, the idea of good as new. Hell, it's still a tease, only by now I know it isn't a warranty that holds up to close examination.

I waddle my way over to the confessional booth and open the folded accordion door of it. I kneel down on the kneeling platform and a dim light goes on overhead. I stand up again and the light goes off, and I decide to stay on my feet for this because I prefer the idea of confessing in the dark. I speak into the vented yellow screen and tell whoever is over there that I said a bad word, I took candy from my mother's purse, and I told a lie, even though none of those things is true. Grandma Elsie told me what to say. I thought it was the way this worked.

The priest isn't telling me any prayers to say or offering any advice at all, and it strikes me that my sins might be so bad that he doesn't know what to say about them. Or maybe he can tell these weren't my sins at all but Grandma Elsie's and I was trying to take the blame for her. Who knows what these guys can tell through that screen?

In a few minutes the accordion door opens again and there's Grandma Elsie smiling down at me, and she takes my hand and leads me out of the church. Nothing more is said about confession, except, for her own sake, she says she finds it very relieving to go in and get these things off her chest. Back at her house she's already starting on a rosary, fingering the beads and mouthing the words of the Act of Contrition as we watch TV.

It was quite a few years before Elsie let slip that there hadn't been a priest in the confessional booth I went to; that I'd picked the wrong one and nobody had noticed. Spilled my guts to an empty saddle over there.

And the thing about confessing to Annie—I believe that somehow it was received. She couldn't or wouldn't prescribe a penance, that's all.

When we were finished at the mirror, I took her by the hand and we went outside together. The fog was thinning over our heads. We both looked up and shaded our eyes with our hands. Across the nearest pasture I could see Bill and Hayes, talking now, the picture-taking over with apparently, and Bill's hand-on-hip attitude told me he had not made a confession of his own. He was pointing out toward the southeast, toward Pianto, making an arc that covered a big pie piece of territory as if he had at one time owned it all. Hayes was nodding and saying something in response, a couple of guys bullshitting each other. A fine sight to behold, to my mind.

Annie awaddle, we crossed the dewy pasture toward them, sheep quickstepping out of our way. Bill's camera was there on its tripod aimed at the two men as if it were still recording, swiping their light.

"What do you think?" I asked, and Annie and I stood there arm in arm when they looked at us and saw her penny red.

Hayes began laughing, and so did Bill. Maybe Bill caught in this dumpy old lady a glimpse of his old love light, the red-headed girl he made his own prior set of vows to, and maybe that's what made him laugh. I'd have thought he might break down into tears, seeing her like this, but then we're all cooking with different chemistry, aren't we. Annie herself began to laugh in open-mouthed hooting, stuck her hands into her hair and tossed it like an impetuous young thing. I was laughing too. You could never have guessed, looking at us, who we all were to one another. It was more than you'd ever have conceived of—father, son, ex-wife, new wife, mother, husband, repentant prodigal. It seemed like, as we all stood there laughing at Annie's new head of hair, there were many more than the four of us present.

BILL WAS QUIET all the way back down to the valley. I'd have grilled him if I hadn't gotten a sense that he was now sorry about holding his tongue. He had a cameraful of his boy's light, but his boy didn't know how close the truth had come to him that day. That's enough to make a man good and quiet, so I let him be.

Back at the house I told Cam in code. I said, "Nothing new to report," respecting his desire to stay in the dark. He nodded with what I saw as gratitude in his eyes, asked where Bill was. Bill had run straight over to the darkroom to get his Hayes pictures onto contact sheets before a calamity struck, of what kind I had no idea. Heart attack? Earthquake? Who knows. He just had a feeling something might try to prevent him from looking at those pictures.

"I hate to sound mean or anything," Cam said. We were sitting together on his porch with longneck beers, as we had just a couple of weeks earlier when we were getting acquainted. Out beyond his fence line were the acres that his family used to own, green from the new rancher's watering. Long shadows out, and the light was a beautiful ocher.

"You've been anything but mean, Cam." I patted his knee. "You've been sweet and patient."

I held my beer bottle in the hook of an index finger, sipped from it while keeping my eyes on him. He looked tired-out. Completely siphoned. He said, "I was just figuring Bill got what he came for. You'll probably be heading back soon."

The way he said it, I knew it was a request and not a question. I looked at the far tree line against the sky, where the hilltop seemed as sharp as a sawblade and the haze in the summer air gave everything a coat of yellow dust. This was a pretty place. I liked it. And I had come to love Cam like a brother.

"Another day or two, I guess. Maybe he'll round out his pictures with a few more. It's going to be a book, you know."

"That's what he says."

I thought it was only fair to ask him, and take the answer for what it was worth. I said, "Have the two of you talked enough, Cam? Did you get something out of him?"

"Oh yeah," he told me, and as he leaned back his arm pressed against me and I sensed he was comfortable with that. "We've talked a lot. He's been good about it. He'd have let me chop his hand off if that's what I wanted."

"Sounds fair."

"The only thing I wanted was to get him up to the cemetery with me. We finally went up there a couple days ago. I don't know if you knew."

I said Bill hadn't told me. Not a word from him about it, even when we were lying in the dark together, our usual time for deeper concerns to come out. It was news to me.

Cam sat looking down at the porch step with his beer bottle swinging between his hands like a pendulum. He told me that standing there under the eucalyptus trees at the pink granite gravestones of his mom and dad, Bill had broken down crying and fell onto the plot, hung an arm around Cam's legs and let it all out. Every last bit of it.

"He poured it," Cam said. "Gallons of pent-up misery. Does that sound like too strong a word?"

"No," I told him. "I don't think it does."

We sat there together until it got dark, finally went in as the mosquitoes began biting and the moon was up. Bill hadn't come back yet, which made perfect sense to me. I was just as happy upstairs with a little time alone anyway.

IN OUR ROOM, which I sometimes forgot had been the room where Andie and Bad Ray slept and planned and fought out their thirty years together, I poked around a bit while waiting for Bill to return. Something came clear to me soon enough as I pushed our things aside in the closet and looked deeper. Cam—sad, sentimental Cam—had not done much in the way of cleaning out the place after his parents died. Deep in the back of that closet were his mother's old dresses (a little dowdy, subdued, no dashikis to speak of), a man's suit of the kind I could see Ray wearing to Bill's wedding, a humble row of shoes, man's and woman's, dusty, crinkled from wear. These were more or less poor people making do with what they'd had.

It was moving to find these things. I was a mess with Annie before, and now I was a mess over finding the past so close at hand. And it wasn't even my own.

Curiosity got the better of me too, now that the moon was up, the house quiet, and me still alone. (I wasn't used to being alone, not these last ten years.) I went through the dresser, trying not to catch shaming looks at myself in the mirror mounted on it, finding utterly personal kinds of things that tell more than we care to admit. Our old stockings with mending stitches in the heels. Our favored cuff links and tie clasps. Our key chains, our unexplainable childhood mementos, our slivers of porcelain we meant to glue back in place on a cup and never did. And I found, in the bottom drawer, a small, plain, tin box that might have held candies at one time, or sewing sundries, but now held some letters and some pictures tied in ribbons. Old. I had the tingle up the back of my neck that a pyramid opener might get when the wash of ancient air comes out to bathe him.

It's possible that I should have considered the family's privacy, but the thought occurred to me that by hook, crook, or accident I was now family too. So I took the tin to the bed, and I untied the ribbons. I opened up those old letters, looked at those pictures.

Naturally, Bill was represented in them. There was a letter from July 1963 in which Bill, writing from Keeler, California, wherever the hell that is, asks his mother to take the divorce papers to Annie and to persuade her to sign them without a "skirmish" over it, was Bill's word, because he had deserted her and would not be coming back. "There's the cause," he said. "Abandonment. It's not any more complicated than that."

Distressing to see his hand urge that kind of thing.

At the end of the letter, which he signed, "With love, your son," he appended in a different-colored ink, "I will never be able to explain it all to you. I am sick with myself, and I'll be years here in the desert trying to cure what's wrong. I can't even ask you to forgive me."

This was pitiful as it was, and revealing too, since Bill had never told me in much detail about his frame of mind back then. But then I had to go and find a postcard that he must have written within weeks of leaving Pianto, dated April 1961 and showing, of all things, a faded-out scene from Death Valley. Already groping for desert metaphors! He wrote, crowdedly, on the back of it in all-cap letters, black ink, "There's empty mountains on all sides. Cragged, cubed, wasted, and violent. The ground under my feet is hard packed and rightly hot. Bleached bones, wide desert flats without water, salt white. Predators all around, looking for small things to kill and eat. There is no way out of here once you're in."

The impression this must have made on poor Andie would have knocked her flat, I imagined. I could almost feel her standing at the window and reading it, weakening in the knees, swooning.

One of the photographs was pitiful too, but in a different way. It was from a Christmas, long, long ago. You could tell by the colors and the clothes on those eight people, and the blond-wood table, and the way seven of them were posed around a central man who sat in a stuffed chair. He was a large-boned bastard in a flannel shirt and sporting a mighty handlebar mustache, red, of course. Big Don Hayes. Around and behind his right shoulder stood the Arguses, BB-eyed Ray in a seasonal tie, meek and lovely Andie, and Cam—my dear young Cam with his Adam's apple like a turkey bone caught in his throat and those kind, too-forgiving eyes—and a woman who must have been Carmen (though not recognizably except that she looked a bit like Andie), relatively free of her wrinkles, dressed in a wool skirt and girly cardigan. To Don's left shoulder was Annie, holding the little Hayes in the crook of her arm. She was pretty, no doubt about it, and earnest, plastering a kiss right then on the baby's temple. And she looked tender, and she looked sweet, and I could almost understand that Bill's fear of hurting her was so heavy on him that he had to go. There he was at her side, with one hand on his boy's neck, as if petting him, and bearing the young eyes of a boyish man who thinks, as the picture is taken, that things are likely to get better from then on. He was skinny and a bit wild-looking, his one leg cocked as if it was hard to stand still long enough for the exposure.

I figured out that Mabel Hayes must have taken the picture. There's always a left-out martyr who documents the occasion for the rest.

After a while I tucked all that stuff back into the tin, and tucked the tin back into the bottom drawer. Because all of a sudden I felt as if I had spied and eavesdropped, and I, of all people, had no business studying their shames.

—|—

I WASN'T YET eighteen, already nursing regrets. I never let Jack inside me (not that he expressed the desire), but he and I stole time for that thing Cary Lee would not do for him. I'm ashamed to say that it did not bother me, I wasn't plagued with conscience, I had no qualms or queasy second thoughts. I loved Jack and wanted him to stay. He wasn't so much Pops now as he was the model of a man I could love. Never married Cary Lee, after all. And we weren't related in any way, I always reminded myself.

Where I thought it would end I can't say—maybe with my own departure one day, I don't know—but I never thought it would end the way it did.

A morning in the summertime, with sunlight streaming in my window to tell me it was later than I thought. There were muffled voices down the hall, the sounds of a fight. Not too troubling to me, you see, because I'd heard them before, Jack and Cary Lee going at it in power struggle or mind game, whatever it was this time. I lay there in my bed with an ear on what they were saying, none of it quite clear until I heard their door fly open and bash the wall, and Cary Lee screeching something incomprehensible as Jack called after, "It's not her fault." A moment later my door kicked in, and there she was heaving in the frame of it with, of all things, a sponge mop in her hand. She wasn't looking at me, as eerie as it sounds, but instead scanning the room like a predator in that ugly yellow rayon nightgown that showed her tits and the moles that lived on them in frighteningly high relief. Her bleached hair was wild on her head, her chest heaving up and down, the blunt end of the mopstick tapping on the floor like the works of a cuckoo clock.

"What?" I said. "What? What is it?" And she didn't speak a word. She went to my hope chest—I had a hope chest in those days!—and with a swift, athletic stroke knocked all my things off of it, my trolls, my pretty glass doodads, my record stacks, my radio. Then she spun and mopped things right off the wall, framed pictures and posters, tearing, ripping, hacking. I screamed, pressed myself as far back in the bed as I could, mashed against the headboard and cringing as she went through the room mechanically and took apart everything I put some value on. She opened the closet door and mopped out all my clothes. She mopped my shoes into a pile in the middle of the floor, working like a psycho maid. Tits flopping, her big hips aswing. She said, coldly and low, "Slut."

She said, "You and him, you *fucking* slut."

She said, "He's out of here and so are you."

And I was crying and shuddering from all this, scared shitless, and Cary Lee dropped her sponge mop and left me with my marching orders.

She left the house in a little while, still in her nightgown but wrapped in a corduroy winter coat like a crazy woman. I saw her through the window climbing into the Rambler.

I wanted to go to Jack and throw myself on him and beg him to tell me what to do now, but when I went into the hallway and looked toward their bedroom, I saw him there sitting on the edge of the bed, shirtless and with his face in his hands, sobbing. It didn't seem like I was going to get a whole lot of useful advice out of him. He looked up and showed me his red, dreadful eyes, and his mouth was agape like he couldn't breathe, and all I could think was, What is he going to do?

Packed me a suitcase and left. I went up to a friend's house where they had a cot in the basement, and that's where I lived while I finished high school. Jack, it seemed, had just disappeared, but he called me once a couple of years later and told me how sorry he was for everything that had happened, it was all his fault.

It took me a long time to come around to the right response to that belated mea culpa, even though Cary Lee was certifiably nuts and unstable and unfit to raise a kid, and without a conscience of her own. I should have said to Jack on the phone that day, Yeah, Jack, it was.

BILL COMES TO bed long after I'd cut out the lights and tried to sleep myself, and he arrives with the smell of Wild Turkey on him, which—I know from experience—has always been his sedative of choice. He doesn't seem to know or care whether I'm awake. He climbs into bed shrouded in his clothes and his bar smells, and he begins talking. Much as I once talked to the nonexistent priest.

"He doesn't know me and he can't know me and this"—letting it hang for a long time on his booze breath, like the rest of it's pending—"this I accept. She doesn't remember me and can't know me either, and this. I accept this too. Everything here? The way it is now?"

He seems to be waiting for me to encourage him, but instead I give him my best nasal breathing, rhythmic and adenoidal, so he'll keep going. The best confessions occur when you don't believe anyone is listening.

"None of it can be changed. And that's all right." I feel his breath on my neck, close. "It's not great but it's all right, and I accept it. I'll feel sorry for myself and miserable about it later, and back and forth, off and on. And I might have some bad days, thinking about them, but right now I accept it. I'll take it. This is good."

There's a drunken lilt to his soliloquy, but he's not so drunk that I doubt he believes what he's saying. I think he had this in him all along and took his drink just to open up a channel for it to come out. Even if he thinks I'm asleep. I fight off the urge to roll to him and hold him.

"I've had a life of unbelievable beauty and bullshit. It hit me these last couple of days. I did more bad things and saw more beautiful things than most people can invent. Made money taking pictures of rocks and snakeskins and coyote shit. Found you.

Or, I mean, you somehow found me. And now that it's over, I'm this close to seeing how good it all is." He waits, and I can hear his breathing in the pause, taking in the smell of his mother and holding it. "I can deserve to have you at the end of it."

With that, holding my breath so I don't crack the quiet with my own blubbering, I push my body into his, my back cradled into him. "Bill," I whisper, "I'm awake."

"I know it," he says, and casts his arm over me.

VENICE—1987

Cary Lee

The question never stops ricocheting around her head: How did I get to this point, how did it happen, and where was I when we made the turns? The question is endlessly repeated and gets a different answer each time: It's hard to say, you should have paid more attention, you drink too much, you're getting fat so what difference does it make, he's gone. There's no one good answer, no reassuring one, hardly even a recurring one, no consensus at all. It's fate, it's the random chance of the frigging universe, it's your own damn fault, Cary Lee.

So that when Nora came to her after a long absence and announced she had met the man of her dreams and his name was Dennis, Cary Lee thought, Oh, here we go. Here we go with the wedded bliss and the dreaming. Didn't I bring her up better than that? Naïve baloney. Poor baby. She ought to know better. What woman can be happy with a man named Dennis anyway?

This was a couple of months earlier, in September of '87, and Nora appears out of nowhere and knocks on the door. She's all dressed up in a white scoopneck dress cut to the midthighs, and her hair is dyed black, and she looks goddamn good, goddamn it, so that all Cary Lee can do is ask, "So who is he?" before Nora even utters a word about it.

"How did you know?" her daughter says. Still underestimating.

"The rock on the third finger, dearheart. It's like déjà vu to me. I had one once, you know. A nice big rock like that."

Invited her in. It had been a hell of a long time. Couple years. Nora went through phases. Forgiving ones, and not so. Sometimes rugged terrain first where they had to duke it out over who fucked up whom the worst. Always leading to dramatic departure or a little breakdown while Cary finished her drink and said something along the lines of, You make your own bed, baby. No man's an island. Water seeks its own level. Don't come crying to me.

"Don't you want to know where I met him?" Nora asks, cigarette in hand, sitting on the couch with her legs crossed daintily like a new bride ought to. She's not even thirty yet.

"Does it matter?"

"It does if you give a shit, Mother."

"Oh." And a dramatic pause so the girl squirms a little bit. Why do I do things like that? "Then by all means. Tell me all about it, hon."

Getting up there in years now, Cary Lee was. Over fifty. No longer able to attract the studly fella here and there, had to settle for the less annoying losers who could still get it up and had a few bucks in their wallet (don't tell the kids, okay?). And here's Nora looking like a doll, only tired in the eyes and worn out already, some lines pulling her mouth down. Cary knows a tough life when she sees one. Nora conveys a lovely romantic tale of meeting this Dennis at a party, and the two hit it off talking about movies and, oh, just everything, and not only is he a handsome devil but he has a decent job to boot and likes what she likes, and they have—you'll appreciate this, Mother—fantastic sex on top of it all.

"Well, honey, my goodness. You've hit the mother lode. Many happy returns of the daze."

Nora sitting there smoking and looking at her like she is the famed talking gorilla who just quoted Goethe, no less.

"It's against my better judgment," she finally says, "but we're inviting you to the wedding."

OH, AND HOW the little dear misjudges me. Cary Lee thought, There's no letting her see the whole picture, I know that. She would run screaming. *I* would run screaming if I ever took it all in, whole.

The favor of my company.

Yes, and to make me feel guilty, I can read her like a crook. Joke's on her, though, because I don't feel guilty, never did, never will, ain't got it in me, okeydokey?

There was a time, she could still remember, when she thought she might make it, might run the gauntlet and come out a whole piece. It was long after Joe skedaddled, long after a nervous breakdown and a tiny pill problem, the liquid diet of highballs three times a day, chasing down Valium. Me-oh, my-oh, and the place nearly burned down with the little one inside! She remembered standing at her bedroom door and wanting to say something, to rush to her, but rushing was not in her, the chemicals were. Nora in bed with a T-bear, no, a Humpty Dumpty, smoke and heat swirling. What happens next? A voice in her, the one that she lets drive, saying, Who knows, who cares? A sense that this was It, capital I, and not an undramatic way to go, mother and child burned up together because Joe left 'em to their own incendiary devices. Then, unpredictably, she turns and walks out, saves herself, eases down on the bottom concrete step outside with the embers beginning to fly out the open roof, and a minute later, unaided, the tough little girl sitting next to her with the egg man in her arms and leaning into Cary's body like Cary's a safe haven.

When to start 'em on the disillusionment diet, huh?

Ah, but she knew, Nora did. This was something Cary Lee had sensed from the get-go with the baby. That the baby was judging her somehow. The way it looked at her was peculiar, and oh, goddamn it, how the little thing loved its daddy. How its eyes lit up and it kicked and giggled when he came home from work and cooed to her, bowing over the crib rail. Joe squiggled her and goo-gooed her, and the two were in cahoots, it seemed like. He changed her diapers when he was on duty, leaving Cary Lee to rest in a chaise out on the back balcony and smoke while the sun went down, but all the while the two were hatching a strategy. It seemed like. Joe wasn't any different with her, always a tad aloof, always hesitant to let his hair down, and don't think she didn't know he was drinking a wee bit himself on the side, finding a tavern on his way home from work every night—a woman, too?—and looking at her like he dared her to say a word. Kootchie, kootchie, koo, little girl. How's the sweetie pie tonight? How's my little wonderball?

She fussed all day, Joe, is how.

She gets lonesome without her papa, he says, throwing Cary a sidelong look that says it all.

But there was a time when she thought she might make it, after all that, Joe long gone, the baby safe from fire and brimstone (time being), and Elsie kind of watching over to make sure Cary Lee, Tortured Soul, didn't stumble. Ever present, actually. Always around or in close proximity, as if to prevent catastrophe and headlines that might shame the family. Still, it gave her some breathing room, and she saved some money and opened up a humble thrift store of her own and kept it open for a couple of years, until she quite unthriftily squandered the profits, dropped the ball, and screwed the pooch. Workaday after that, and parties on the weekends, and all of her energy summoned to keep doing it day after day and to not wrap her once-sweet lips around the tailpipe of the Rambler the way she never could do a boyfriend.

Have you ever been that low? Have you ever thought the world ends if you take another breath? Who needs that on her shoulders, on top of everything else.

"I love you Mommy," said the little one, and Cary nearly hauled off and whacked her for that. You don't know what love is, she wanted to say. But didn't. It would confuse her even more than she already was.

ON THE DAY of the wedding she managed to set the alarm and drag herself out of bed at a decent hour for the one o'clock ceremony. Couldn't they have scheduled for later on a Saturday? Out late last night, out of habit. These things don't die.

Picked a print call-it-a-muumuu if you want, with tropical colors and huge enormous flowers all over it, and put a blossom in her hair like Billie Holiday. In the mirror the effect was floral overkill, but she didn't care. Let the bees come and get me. A rosy fragrance too, a cloud of it sprayed and walked through. She knew that her face couldn't hold its own anymore at fifty. Her face looked older than it was, the body not keeping up with it. The puff, the bloat, the blood vessels of the nose coming through like the weave in an old Persian rug. *Ayyiyiyiyi.* Nothing short of plastic surgery would do, a head transplant, how about that?

My baby girl's finally getting married, she told herself, getting mushy all of a sudden in the car. She could feel her belly resting on her lap behind the wheel, and her tits resting atop her belly like a melting snowman. Nora's getting married and I don't know whether to be happy or not.

See, she said, the thing is, nobody knows like me how hard the wringer is on your mortal soul. Fed through those rollers, not once, not twice, but dozens of times, man, it takes a lot out of you. Something to think about for a toast, when asked. Mother, would you like to say a few words? Sure, doll. Trust me. Keep your fingers away from those rollers, baby. That thing'll pull you in and never let go.

Unless it's already too late . . .

The ceremony was at a marina where this Dennis kept a sailboat. Nora told her how he had this idea of sailing around the world with his wife, who was turning out to be her, and how she didn't have the heart to disappoint him so soon, but there was no way she was going to commit herself to a little dinghy sailboat with him for a year, cooking on a hot plate and pooping into a chemical john when she wasn't puking over the rail. That's my girl, Cary Lee thought. Ever practical. Not so blinded by love that she can't look ahead a ways.

Don't tell him, though, okay? She said she figured it would come up soon enough. What kind of goofy dream is that anyway, sailing around the world with a woman? "There's a Miller commercial where it's nothing but men on the boat, having the time of their lives and swinging back and forth in the rigging," Nora said. "You can tell the last thing they need is a woman on board. They want more beer, is what they want. Now just promise me, Mother, you won't mention this to Dennis. Promise."

Cary found the marina and had to walk a damn mile to get to the wedding canopy and the buffet spread, her feet killing her. Drops her wrapped gift off at the stacked-high gift table. Whose idea was this anyway? Probably this Dennis's. Who's paying for it too? Not the mother of the bride, I'll goddamn tell you that. I can't even afford shit for my shingle much less, and can't remember when it was anything but.

A glimpse of the bride talking to the JP at a podium standing at the head of rows of wooden folding chairs. People already filling them in too. Nora is adamant about something, using her hands, looking agitated and anxious, and behind her up comes a man in a white suit with unnaturally piled hair and a pair of black-rimmed glasses like he sells business insurance by day. He wraps his arms around her from behind, and Cary Lee sees how Nora visibly melts into calm at the touch of him. Isn't it romantic?

Oh, and now that goddamn Rogers and Hart song in her head, and she can never think of it without hearing it as sung by Elmer Fudd.

It's a beautiful day for a wedding. The harbor gulls calling and the buoy bells dinging in place of church ones. A blue sky with high swirls in it, the water slapping the hulls of boats and making the dock wood groan.

This Dennis whispering something to her daughter, and Nora casts a quick look toward Cary. Dennis moves to the podium and into the mike says, "Everyone ought to take their seats now, time to get this row on the shoad." (How can you not like a man who says a thing like that?) Then, unexpectedly, he comes down the aisle to Cary and with unabashed chivalry kneels beside her chair and says he just wants to introduce himself before the deed is done.

"Only fair you get to meet me before I marry your daughter," he says, a couple of crooked bottom teeth but otherwise a fine specimen, dandy hazel eyes.

"Pleasure," she says. "I hope you know what you're getting into."

"I think so. We've talked about everything."

"Everything?"

"So she says."

Doubts whether he knows the half of it, but he seems nice enough, a big boy who can handle it when he has to. Cary shakes his hand. "Maybe you can do something with her," she says. "But I hate to be the one to tell you. She hates boats. You'll never get her on that bucket of yours."

Smiling the smile of a cocky devil who generally gets his way. "We'll see about that."

Nora's dressed in an appropriately off-white shift, and she has her pearls and she has her ring and her sheer hose and her hair up in a French twist like a Princess Grace for Us Sinners. Nobody knows her like I do, Cary Lee tells herself. And poor thing, she thinks nobody knows me like she does, but I haven't given her a look at my iceberg's bottom, all underwater. Never had the heart. Could have blown her away, I reckon. A mama's thoughts on her daughter's wedding day.

By the time the ceremony began, the wooden chairs were filled and the people there were surely all friends of this Dennis because, Cary Lee knew, Nora didn't have many friends. She eschewed friendship for personal reasons, namely, fear of betrayal, she'd told Cary one time. What's the point? They fuck you over eventually, and that's when Cary said, Good for you, hon, don't let 'em do that to you. Lesson learned. But remember, you'll want some hangers-on to fill in those seats at your wedding.

No sign of tears yet as the JP reads from the manual and Nora looks into the eyes of her beau-friend like she's contemplating the *Pietà*. They hold hands. The gulls screech and the sunlight gives it all a burnished tint, like something silver brought down from the attic after a long time up there. The youth, the optimism, the sad state of affairs—good Lord, Cary thinks, why do we all keep making the same mistakes? I remember telling her I wasn't going to marry Jack because marriage isn't all it's cracked up to be, and besides, I want the flexibility and convenience of throwing him out one day, which came to pass. She was a wee willowy baby then, with a cedar hope chest Elsie gave her and an eye on saving herself by marrying well, girlishly. Didn't want to pop her bubble just yet but found it impossible to lie to her vis-à-vis Jack, old dashing Jack with his ridiculous accent and his big hairy hands. A smile that could hypnotize you if you weren't already drunk. If only he'd been able to keep his wiener in his worsted wools, now, maybe things could have worked and marriage might have one day been the smart thing to do, Social Security–wise, Nora her maid of honor, maybe—now, that would have made a sweet little picture for the mantelpiece. But Cary had a sixth sense when it came to the hearts of men. She had a feeling, deep down and not to be shrugged off, that even while old Jack was humping away at her with her legs wrapped around his back and his mouth all over her titties the way he used to do, his mind was elsewhere.

A red flag. She'd learned to recognize the symptoms, first observed in Joe during the months before he took off. You can always tell.

And she knew where he was and could have gone to rip him to shreds or turn Nora loose on him as a teenager, sent her to live with him and his whore wife out of revenge. It would have been an appealing piece of theater, eh? Greyhound pulling up at the station and the gangly slut girl popping out looking for Daddy, hand-lettered directions in her clammy fist. "Daddy? It's me, your wonderball!" And the wife all but shitting in her bloomers.

A fond little scenario to think about before you drift off at night. Should have called him up to threaten it once or twice.

The JP says something about man and wife, and the two of them twirl and face the crowd before kissing. And there it is, a deep, slushy kiss meant to offend the fogies, but Cary Lee finds herself lightly aroused at it. Been a long time. The rock, the embraces, the tongues, and the loving. Yep. Long time ago, and those memories gathering dust like the doilies on my mother's furniture.

As they walk past Cary's seat, Nora blows a kiss her way, her eyes not exactly happy but more of an I-told-you-so squint. She's a beauty though. A piece of work, and I'll take the credit, if you don't mind, because I was the one who stuck by her, best friends. We talked of why sex is so good, I recall, on more than one occasion, after she'd learned to take care of herself and I caught her at it one time. Men love it, I says, and it ain't so bad for the girl either, okay? But the thing is, you have the man by the balls as long as he still wants it from you, you can do anything you want. A dandy little ass in the hole, as it were, ha-ha, and we laughed our heads off.

Cary Lee tried to go lightly through the buffet, but the smoked salmon was too good to pass up, and the cornichon salad and the cold shrimp too—where did Nora get pretensions like these anyway? Must be this Dennis. A glass of champagne won't hurt either, and maybe another one after that. The bride and groom were schmoozing with handsome young men friends of the groom and the groom's parents, as far as Cary could tell, a couple of older folks with glasses cut from Squirt bottles and dressed in clothes that bespoke an inheritance ready to pass down. Nice move, Nora, honey! And this Dennis owns a boat and works for a computer outfit *and* has a house on Balboa Island, hotsy totsy, hoity-toity. My little girl. All grown up. Forgive me if I gulp down a sob or two along with this champagne.

She made her way through the crowd and planted herself within a few feet of her daughter's elbow, hoping to be introduced to the parents. We are in-laws, after all. Nora saw her and ignored her for a few seconds, but then Dennis—sweet, appropriate Dennis—sees her and guides her over by the arm. My mom and dad, he says. Earl and Pamela. He looks like Rex Harrison and she like a beefier Nancy Reagan. Pleased to meet you. You must be very proud. Yes, she's lovely. Never thought I'd see the day.

"Mother," she says, all tight-mouthed. "I hope that isn't your second glass."

"Oh, Nora, please. I wouldn't dare on your wedding day!"

Some pleasantries exchanged among the folks and Dennis saying things meant to include Cary, but nothing is more off-putting than the old standby, "Nora's told me all about you."

Recovering: "Well, she's told you all she knows, let's put it like that."

And they all laughed except Nora herself. Scared shitless that Cary's planning to ruin the day for her. I'll put her at ease.

"Honey," she says through the wisps of Nora's hair at her ears, "this is your day. I'm fine. You're beautiful. Enjoy it."

"Just don't do anything nasty. Don't embarrass me, Mother."

Nora and the groom depart to mix with other people, and Cary Lee is quickly bored by Mr. and Mrs. Dennis, moving on to the sporty friends of the groom who look like extras in a Tammy flick. Blond crew cuts and pumped bods. Sailing types. She drops a few expressions of profanity, and they're in her camp in a hurry. Soon a group of them surrounds her as she talks about this and that, leading to a story of how she nearly had a shot at marrying Mr. Robert Culp when he was basically an unknown, long before *I Spy* came along, but alas . . . It was a tragic tale of deception, as it turned out. He belonged to another woman: his wife!

And they laugh and laugh, and one of them brings her another champagne. She sees Nora seeing her. Nora doesn't approve of the levity and the mirth, poor thing. But if you can't let your hair down at your daughter's wedding, where?

The call for pictures comes over the piped jazz music. A photographer summons the bride and groom and parents of each for a few posed shots under the daisied portable trellis, and almost immediately Nora begins to complain. Seems she doesn't want her ma's image to be there when she relives the memories of the day. She pleads with this Dennis, with the photographer, and Dennis throws a look toward Cary Lee that seems both apologetic and knowing, so maybe he knows more than she thinks, but it isn't long before Mr. Dennis—the father, Earl, who must be the bankroll for it all—puts one of his paws on Nora's shoulder and says something that calms her down. At last Cary Lee is invited to stand with the party, and she does, but beside Dennis, not Nora, her arm linked through his, her smile as pure and motherly as she can make it, and she's had practice. Nora manages a smile too, she sees out of the corner of her eye as the photographer clicks away, but it is a forced one and will ruin the shots in retrospect. Then there's pairing off. A series of shots with mixed doubles, until finally the inevitable Nora and Her Mom is suggested, and this is where Nora draws the line and refuses, walks away mad.

"It's stress," Dennis pitches. "She'll come around."

"Oh, I don't know about that," Cary Lee tells him, "but that's all right. It's about time for me to run anyway. Pleasure to meet you all. We'll have to get together sometime for drinks. *Mi casa su casa,* kids."

All kinds of thoughts jam their way through the pipelines of her head as she locates her jute bag and makes her way through the crowd. Nora is not to be found, taking refuge in a bathroom somewhere. Cary's mildly embarrassed and mildly ashamed of herself, wonders why she was invited when Nora can hardly bear to look at her. If you hate me, let me go. Stop coming back to me. I'm a shit, so shit on me. Don't try to make me a better human being because I ain't got the goods, m'dear, and I'll never do anything but disappoint you. To the bitter end.

I know myself that well anyway.

She makes her way through the revelers who bob to the music with paper plates balanced on their palms, drinks and cigarettes and nice watches, fine tans. The birds are flying spirals over the buffet table, they can smell the salmon.

It's a mean, rotten, cruel thing to do, Cary knows, but she has always been an impetuous one, one who lets the air out of tires and throws eggs at your front-yard manger scene if you've offended. As she leaves the wedding, she stops at the gift table and scatters and sorts until she finds the thing that she had brought, a well-wrapped, thin-silhouetted box about the size of a picture frame, because that's what's inside of it. She takes it and stuffs it into her jute bag, thinking not so much you don't get anything from me, you spoiled little brat, but rather, you don't get this particular thing at this particular time. Maybe later. Maybe another time, when I'm not bothering you so much and you need me.

In the frame was a photograph of Joe Lark as Cary remembers him, in a nice suit and sunglasses, Venice, on their honeymoon, and he's standing there with one foot up on a bench, elbow to knee, and looking off to one side like he's been caught in a moment of dreamy nonchalance, a handsome, sexy so-and-so with his hair just right and his summer suit perfect on him, the man she fell in love with and adored and who had wings on his heels. She hadn't cut this picture up because it *was* Joe to her, and he was hers, and she'd kept it hidden in her room all these years, for herself.

It wasn't time for Nora to meet him.

OFFSHORE—1999

Joe Lark

The mapmaker was retired and more often than not idle. He stood for a while most mornings at the stern of his houseboat, looking out over the calm channel at the precise reflections of trees in the glassy water. Sometimes it was intriguing to think that he could untie his boat and run it out the channel, that little shoe-box vessel, bring her into the Gulf Stream and float all the way to Ireland. There was no point in that fantasy except as a thing to think about, a kind of flight, and in any case the boat wasn't seaworthy. It was a mere box on a floating platform, all but rudderless.

Peggy used to tell him his greatest flaw was restlessness. He'd punished her with it over the years, moving her around as he went from job to job. It wasn't a matter of being unhappy. It was the belief that a better thing lay ahead, within reach but out of sight, and if he didn't take a step to bring it into view he would miss the chance and torture himself with regret later on. She'd put up with it for nearly thirty years, hadn't she, as tolerant as she could be, until the idea of the houseboat arrived and she put her foot down. Whereas he wished to take the last step and remove himself from the land altogether (but why would a mapmaker dream of taking himself completely off the map? Peggy asked), she had a strong fear of the water and would not have been able to live there. He waited until she was a year dead, then bought his houseboat and had it towed to its mooring on the calm channel, a spot in South Carolina where he and Peggy had come to vacation several times in these later years. The fishing was good, the air perfumed with pine and maple and dogwood, and the water slapped the houseboat hulls and made it a place where the mind could find plenty of essential distractions.

The light rocking motion of the boat at night helped him sleep.

What the houseboat had done for him was unexpected. Marriage, the rigors of a profession, remorse that often bit at him like blackflies—all these had ever done was make him move. The boat anchored him.

ONE DAY, TWO or three years after Peggy had died, he emerged from the cabin with coffee cup in hand to find a stranger on the dock admiring the boat. There were three other houseboats moored at the dock, so the mapmaker thought the stranger might be a guest at one of them. He said good morning, raised his cup.

"The *Nora Jane,*" said the stranger. "A pretty name for a nice little boat like this one."

"Thanks," he replied, and moved as if to go about his business. With his back turned, he heard the stranger again.

"Must be the name of a woman you never forgot."

"Something like that," the mapmaker replied. He went back to the bow and put one foot up on the gunwale.

The stranger nodded. He was a haggard-looking man with a narrow, sharp nose and a chin spiked with whiskers, eyes that seemed mildly crossed from the mapmaker's perspective. He wore a pair of olive dungarees and an old beige polo shirt, untucked, Topsider moccasins with no socks. His hair, silvered and combed back, made him appear to be about the mapmaker's age of sixty-eight.

"I know all about the staying power of a girl's name," the stranger said. "The long echo. You'd think you'd be able to forget, but it's almost like the girl planted herself in you with that name of hers and she's been there ever since sending shoots down your arms and legs like kudzu."

The mapmaker didn't wish to follow that line of reasoning. There was something about the stranger that worried him, even though the man was clearly as old as he.

"I wouldn't know about that," he told the stranger. "But my wife died a couple years back, and it's not surprising her name is on my mind a lot."

"Ah, she'd be Nora Jane, then." The stranger nodded with his eyes closed.

"I didn't say that."

Now the man fixed his eyes directly to the mapmaker's. It felt as if he were trying to extract something, a strand, a bit of light, a confession. The mapmaker stared him back, a contest, and didn't waver until the stranger finally said, "Then I guess you're a more complicated man than I took you for at first. Or a luckier one."

With that, he wished the mapmaker good morning and went back down the dock, hands clasped behind his back.

A while later, as he went out to run his errands for the day, the mapmaker stopped at each houseboat on the dock to ask if the stranger he had talked to that morning was a guest. There wasn't a lot of neighborliness among the houseboat owners on that quiet channel, but people who live on houseboats are demons for privacy and peace, and they don't require a lot of society to find their comfort. None of these boat owners claimed the stranger as a guest. One said, "I thought he was yours."

"You saw him, then. Good." The mapmaker shook his neighbor's hand over the rail of the boat. "Let's keep our eyes peeled."

He didn't like the idea that somebody had singled him out for analysis. It was a disturbing thought, one that made him feel that the pangs of conscience he experienced from time to time were actually warning signals, impulses from the interior of his body. Often over the years he'd felt as though he were being followed, tracked. Peggy, God love her, said it was just garden-variety paranoia due to the competition of his job, and at least it accounted for his desire to pick up and move all the time. The patience in her. She loved him in spite of it, and to spare her the anxiety, he kept the worst of his fearful thoughts to himself. He didn't tell her things that she didn't need to know, just as, he imagined, she had kept certain things from him, things that she might have believed would startle him if he found out and might change the way he felt about her. Everyone has secret history, shames, and befouled laundry, though to judge by Peggy's family, she was a kind, well-adjusted, good-hearted soul who had done right by everyone she knew. He loved her dearly for her sweet spirit and ability to forgive without punishment.

Strangely, even though he never confessed to her, he felt as if she had absolved him.

At least he had always had the distraction of his career. Mapmaking—cartography—had been his haven. Detailed, intricate, obsessive. Somebody had said that the map is not the territory, but for him, maybe because he was cursed with an active mind, a map was what it depicted: place. And a map was distance. A map showed the obstacles between here and there, depicted the wrinkled skin of the earth; elevation, depression, topography. It was heartening to understand how elaborate the surface was. There was an infinite number of places in which to lose oneself, such as the tiny, calm channel where he lived.

It didn't even show up on the local county map, his channel, and there was only a dirt road leading to it. Neither the road nor the channel had a name. He kept a PO box in town too, rather than a mailbox at the head of the dirt road, so that if you were trying to find him, you would more than likely pass that road right by.

—|—

LATER, IN TOWN, he decided to visit the barbershop and have his hair cut shorter for the season. It was early summer, and the weather had gone hot and humid. A radio in the barbershop was playing old jazz standards that reminded him of when he was young, but he decided he would not ask for a different station. The barber, a clean-shaven, dark-haired man of thirty, thirty-two, liked the old music, and it was something of a trademark for his shop.

"Well hey," said the barber. "Been quite a while."

"It has. I should've come in sooner, but I don't much like leaving the boat. Know what I mean?"

The mapmaker sat and held his arms in while the barber swept a cloth around his neck and fastened it. "Right. That little closet of a boat you've got. I don't get you boys who live out there. Antisocial. It's almost like you think you're goddamn better than everyone else."

The barber was joking. That's how the mapmaker took it, because the subject had come up before. As it turns out, the barber longed to sell his own house once the kids were grown, find a quiet little spot to put a boat. The mapmaker knew him to be an avid fisherman, and the idea of fishing right out his living room window was the most appealing thing about retirement that he could think of. Never mind what his wife might want to do when that time came around.

"Not better," said the mapmaker. "Just scared."

"Scared. Good one. But what's a kind old fart like you so

scared of? You been dodging taxes for a few years? Smuggling pot?"

"Ah, just the grim reaper I guess. I figure if he can't dig up my address and take a taxi there, I'll be all right."

They both laughed at the idea, catching each other's faces in the mirror. There was more to it than that, of course, and the mapmaker knew the barber knew it.

"Grim reaper?" the barber mugged. "Oh, gosh, I'm sure sorry! He's in here the other day lookin' for you, and I give him explicit directions. Tall fella with a kind of hood and sharp, nasty sickle, right?"

"That would be him," the mapmaker said in the spirit of the joke. "Maybe he's the guy who showed up on my dock this morning. In disguise, of course."

"Yeah, I'd expect a disguise. It figures he'd try and fool you."

The mapmaker nodded as the barber ran an electric razor up the back of his neck. It felt like a cold, hard chill and gave him goose pimples. "He chatted me up, basically. That's all. Nice enough."

"Taking your measure," said the barber. "Seeing how much of a fight you're gonna give him."

"Not a much of one, my age."

The barber worked for a while without talking. Both men's minds drifted into their interiors, where there was always more unfinished business than could ever be reasonably dealt with. "Ah, well," the barber finally said, "at least you got yourself a decent haircut before he does you. You'll look like a million bucks at the wake."

IT WAS A small town, and one off the main tourist and commercial drags, which was the way he liked it. He had lived in cities as large as L.A., towns as small as this one, and dozens in between. Ironically, it was in the small ones where he felt he had the greater anonymity. They do not pry in these towns. They take you as what you say you are. A comfort. He was too old now to be explaining himself, and anyway, the older he got, the more labored the explanations would have to be to satisfy the interrogator. He had, he felt, and with Peggy's absolution, earned the right to hide what he was most ashamed of, whether it was good to do so or not. Maybe it was bad for his health to suppress it, or maybe it was ultimately worse for his soul—the raggedy remains of it—but thinking in terms of a map, which was how he thought about a lot of important things, he could see that the route he had taken to get to this point was rubbed out, flooded, blanked on the page. There was no way to retrace his steps.

After the haircut he checked his PO box and found nothing of importance, and from there he went to the grocery store. As he drove around, he saw the town laid out in his mind from above, like a map, gridded, tidy, and compact. Its streets reached out into the countryside and either dead-ended or became two-lane county highways, thin red filaments on green background. Some headed inland toward cities, where they gained lanes and grew into wider red arteries on the map, and others found their way into deeper country, like the one that led to his dirt road. The roads crossed streams and rivers, thready blue lines with unpredictable courses as they followed the contours of the land, and the streams flowed into channels like his, and the channels, in turn, opened to the featureless ocean.

Sapphire, in his mind. The color of a gem.

He sat parked in his truck with the engine running, both hands gripping the wheel. There was sweat dripping from the end of his nose and hitting the bottom rim. An older woman on the sidewalk looked at him as if he were ill and asked with her eyes if he needed any help. The mapmaker ignored her and threw the truck in gear, filling the cab with a rush of air so hot that he found his vision tunneling white. He waited with his head down and his eyes closed until the dizziness passed, and then drove home.

When he arrived, walking with his two grocery bags along the dock, he was startled and a little apprehensive to find the stranger from that morning at the end of the pier, seated in a lawn chair and dangling a fishing line into the water. The man's chair had a thermal drink holder built in to one of the arms, holding a can of beer, and there was a small green tackle box at his feet, along with an orange-and-white cooler. It was hard to tell how long he might have been there, though clearly he had not caught anything yet.

The mapmaker decided to ignore him, avoided his gaze and boarded his own houseboat without saying anything. The stranger called out, but all the mapmaker could hear was something about no nibbles. After he put his groceries away, he thought maybe he should go out and tell the stranger that this was a private dock and he would have to find another place to fish. Then again, it might be better to let the man be, let him get bored with the lack of bites and frustrated with the mosquitoes. He'd leave soon enough.

The other houseboat owners and he would have to get together and talk about security, he thought. It was one thing to live in the peace of a remote spot like this, but another to expose yourself to the whims of a demented stranger. Maybe a gate at the head of the dock, or where the dirt road joined the main road into town. On the other hand, that might just draw more attention to the place. A KEEP OUT sign might pull in more curiosity seekers than the plain old dusty gap in the pines there was now, the three battered mailboxes mounted on a four-by-four stem.

Oddly, it appeared that the stranger had singled him out, pitched his little fishing camp at his end of the dock, and apparently without objection from the other houseboat owners. The more the mapmaker thought about it, the more disturbed he became. It was possible, if not even probable, that the stranger had been hired to locate him, pin him down. Peggy would have had a good chuckle at that thought, but it wasn't unreasonable. People had their obsessions and their need for retaliation or whatever you cared to call it. Run-of-the-mill curiosity. Threats. There were adopted children out there searching for their birth parents. They wanted a look at the old man, wanted to see if they favored him, if he offered a better picture. There were unhappy people looking for explanations, positioned all over the map like strategic pushpins. He saw his own pushpin, just off the mainland, linked by thread to other ones, and the other ones moved from time to time, changing the math of the triangulation, shortening one leg or another, altering proximity, now that he was in a fixed position. It was all math and angles, geometrics, trig. Sooner or later, it was easy to believe, the lines might converge at a single point.

When he realized he couldn't keep his thoughts from running wild, he decided to go out and confront the stranger. But as he emerged from his cabin and went to the bow of the houseboat, he found the stranger already standing there with his folding chair and his gear, waiting at the base of the gangplank.

"What do you want?" the mapmaker asked, startled.

"Wondering if I could come in out of the sun. Getting a bit too hot out here. Maybe you've got a little shade to spare under your canopy."

The mapmaker hesitated for a moment, but then he decided that he'd rather have the stranger in his sight than out of it. He told the man to leave his things on the dock and come aboard, and gratefully the man trotted up the gangplank.

"Didn't expect it to get so hot today," he said. "Actually, I thought maybe there'd be a little rain in the afternoon."

"Could be," the mapmaker said. "I don't know why you'd pick this spot to fish either way. It's a private mooring, you know."

"Is it? I didn't see a sign."

The mapmaker took him around to the stern, where a striped canopy shaded the deck in the afternoons. It was already cool back there, facing east toward the mouth of the channel. Beyond the wooded bend half a mile away, the channel opened onto the ocean.

"Nice," said the stranger. "Thanks."

"You like bourbon? I'll pour some on a couple of ice cubes."

"Sounds like heaven to me," the stranger replied, gazing out at the water. He seemed exhausted now that he was at rest in the shade. There were sweat circles under his arms and a dark arrow of it pointing from his collarbone down his chest.

When the mapmaker returned with their drinks, the stranger began to talk about his travels, which had taken him to and from nearly every corner of the country and, in fact, the world. The mapmaker sat in a padded chair with his feet up on an aluminum railing, listening to what was more than likely bullshit but would at least pass the time. He wouldn't have to worry what the stranger was up to either, spying or sabotaging or fishing innocently. Surprised to see how quickly he drained his own drink, left with clacking ice cubes only a few minutes into the stranger's tale.

The gist of the tale was that the stranger could never settle down, always felt like there was another place he'd rather be. He'd pick up and go, and pretty soon the feel of the new place began to grow stale. Again he'd pick up and go, more or less choosing locations from a map, randomly, or for their names, sometimes only because they were the opposite of where he found himself at the time.

"You make me wonder," the mapmaker said, a little touched by his drink now, "what on earth you've been running away from."

"Why do you ask? Is that how you got here? Running from something?"

"Not hardly. Chasing something, more like it. I'll pour us some more bourbon."

As he rose to go in for the bottle and ice bucket, the stranger said, "There's a point where it's hard to tell the difference, don't you think."

"Between?"

"Running away and chasing something."

The mapmaker plunked new ice in their glasses and poured. The stranger was looking at him with a wry smile on, as if he had guessed a big secret. "I don't see it," the mapmaker said.

"Well, it's like this. If you're chasing something with such energy—whatever it might be—and you don't care what you have to do to get it, then there's a good chance something's on your tail. Fear? Envy? Competition? Guilt? I don't know, but otherwise you'd ease up. You'd risk setting down some roots. Maybe you'd learn to hunt instead of chase."

"A real philosopher. But I asked what *you* were running away from."

"Me? Easy. I'm dodging disappointment. And at least I admit it."

"How does picking up and going avoid disappointment? There's bound to be disappointment anyplace."

"I mean disappointment in me. If I don't know about it, it doesn't exist. See what I mean?"

In fact, the mapmaker did. It was on the edge of delusional, but nevertheless valid.

They sat there for quite a while until dusk began to fall and the crickets and frogs came out. The mapmaker was a hair away from dull-drunk, and so, for all he could tell, was the stranger. The stranger's symptom was closemouthedness though. He'd been jabbering all afternoon but now was quiet and engrossed in the changing light out over the water. It was a still evening, and music could be heard coming from the next boat, a tinny old song sung by a woman whose voice the mapmaker didn't recognize.

"I believe I've got it figured out now," the stranger finally said.

"What. The universe?"

This made the stranger chuckle. "No, sir. I mean you. I've got you pinned here, all of a sudden."

He was smirking, the mapmaker could tell that much in the yellow light from the back-porch jar lamp. The mapmaker drained the last of his last drink and allowed an ice cube into his cheek.

"Then suppose you go on and enlighten me," he said.

"Okay, here you go. You've been running from a girl, I believe. Probably chasing a clean, quiet life for a certain level of atonement, I don't know, but definitely running from that girl."

The mapmaker felt a sneer come to his lips and he began to shake his head. You have no idea, he wanted to say. Who the hell do you think you are? You don't know about me. I haven't uttered a word to make you think a thing like that, any more than I could guess what your goddamn problem is.

He was a little too impaired to frame a clear speech, though. And the stranger took advantage of the pause to say one more thing.

"Nora Jane, I'd imagine. You've been running from this Nora Jane, whoever she is."

What happened after that happened fast. The mapmaker was up and hammering on the stranger's head and shoulders, knocking him from his chair with his arms up to protect his face. The mapmaker shouted unintelligible syllables, more grunts than words, and he chased the stranger around the side of the boat all the way to the gangplank and gave him a push there so that the stranger went tumbling onto the dock.

"I don't want to see you here again!" he shouted, and the stranger picked himself up, gathered his gear, and went off into the shadows.

The mapmaker was too drunk to do anything but put himself to bed, and when he did, his mind was so active and the bourbon so potent that it felt as if the boat were turning on a sideways axis. All he could do was cling to his mattress and ride it out till morning, asleep if he could manage it.

—|—

THE MAPMAKER WAS bothered all night long with dreams. They weren't specific enough to be nightmares, full of faces rising up out of the haze and then receding again. They weren't recognizable faces, but they seemed bent on delivering a message to him until, confronted with his presence, they grew mute and then faded. He was in various places where he had once lived, only with the proportions out of whack, lopsided walls and windows, too-low ceilings. Everywhere he found himself, he was alone until one of these faces would appear, alone again when it retreated. He began to beg the figures to stay with him for a while and tell him who they were. He called out the names of people familiar to him, the names of his mother and father—dead a long time. The name of a sister he hadn't seen in many years. Peggy's name. Cary Lee's name, Nora's name, as if they were dead too. In the dream his voice sounded muffled and blunt and couldn't carry far enough for these people to hear him even if they had been close by.

None of the figures answered, but the message they had been trying to get through to him finally made its way into his consciousness as he awoke in the dim cabin. It was that he was utterly alone in life. He did not need to hide, because there was nobody in the world who wanted to find him anymore.

He got out of bed and immediately boiled some coffee and made toast. As he ate, he found the rolling motion of the boat peculiar and told himself that there must have been a storm in the middle of the night, boiling the tide. That would account for the strange dreams and the spinning feeling, a rational explanation. He remembered, too, that he'd had more to drink than usual, that stranger trying to pull out a confession of some sort, a beaded string of mea culpas. His head ached as if to remind him that he had arrived at a place, finally, where he did not owe anyone explanations. If he had not confessed to his wife of thirty years, then he wouldn't let a stranger extract it from him like some kind of roaming priest offering discount penance.

When he finished his coffee and toast, he dressed and combed his hair, located the book he had been reading, and left the cabin to sit out on the deck as he did every morning. Immediately he dropped the book to his feet, seeing now for the first time that the houseboat had drifted out of the channel in the night and was surrounded by vast, level ocean in all directions, featureless, gray, and indifferent as the inside of a cloud. The ungainly houseboat pitched and rolled with the waves, and the mapmaker could not make out the shore from where he stood.

That stranger, he thought. He untied my boat. Set me adrift to get back at me.

He had never felt such complete helplessness in his life, lost on something as enormous and unmappable as the ocean, alone. Fear radiating from his chest to the ends of his limbs, he turned circles with a compass riding on his palm until he found due west, where the shore would be, and he stood there on the blunt bow with the sun coming up behind him, his long shadow thrown back the way he had come.

TRUE PRESENT

Nora

When Bill and I got home from Pianto, we found our house full of mud. Desert mud, up to midcalf. As fine a job of concrete laying as a Caltrans journeyman could have done.

There had been a freak summer storm, and the wash had flooded, pouring what amounted to thick adobe into all the doors and windows and cracks and seams. We didn't know when this had happened. All we knew was, the adobe had hardened already and all of our things were stuck in place as if cemented. Here and there in the six-inch fill were pieces of ocotillo branches, catclaw stems, and little animal bones that had been carried in the flowing muck.

This is a hell of a thing to come home to.

Bill was too tired and distracted to indulge in a lot of histrionics, so I did that for the both of us. Then we pitched a tent in the back and had some tequila by the light of the high moon.

It's easy to say that we never should have gone up there in the first place, Pianto, sweet green valley of Bill's youth. That's just the kind of twenty-twenty hindsight that pisses people off, and the thing is, we *did* have to go, or at least Bill did, and if he went then I figured I might as well go too. I couldn't have handled being alone here in the middle of the desert knowing he was there suffering through. When it was all over with, I was glad I had gone with him.

A floor of hard mud. What a peculiar feeling, walking around in the house but six inches taller than you should be, that much closer to the ceiling beams. Especially in our house, the two-hundred-year-old hacienda, built (ironically, it turns out) by a Spanish cattleman when all of this was still Mexico. The doors and windows are small and the ceiling low. The exposed wooden beams have aged to the color of coffee, the walls have gone a sweet sienna. They built back then with an eye on endurance, thinking ahead. I guess they imagined their holdings passed down from son to son and dear old Mexico sprawling beyond them up to the Oregon Territory, but whatever their thinking was, it left Bill and me a fine old house and one that I have loved for ten years. It was good to be back in it too, our disaster notwithstanding.

I was shoveling irregular bricks of mud out the bedroom window, my back aching and my thoughts dwelling on the more recent past—screw the cattleman and his sucker bet on Mexico. Bill stuck his head in the door, sweat dribbling down into his whiskers. He said, "When I croak, you get the house."

"Good. That means I won't have to shack up with some diesel driver on the I-40."

The line of inheritance, I had thought, was understood a long time ago. Bill was just trying to sort things out in his own mind.

"I want Hayes to get my old negatives. Is that all right with you?"

"Perfect."

"And the royalties to the old books. This new one is yours."

"The old ones aren't bringing in a lot of cash, you know."

"Enough to help him out a bit."

"That's fine. Okay, Bill."

This was how our conversations had been going lately, since we drove out of Pianto. A little bit clipped, a bit formal. Bill had the eyes now of a man who can't stop shuffling the deck of his own memories and choices, trying to win a game of solitaire by finessing the deal.

"Nora," he said, still there in the doorway with his head up against the top crossbeam, neck bent.

I threw him a smile that I didn't think would give away any impatience.

"He was a good-looking kid, wasn't he."

"He was, Bill. A good-looking man."

"A helluva guy." Nodding, then biting on the inside of his cheek.

"Yep."

"I was glad to see that, anyway."

—|—

A FUNNY THING struck me after the fact. Before dawn every day in Pianto, I'd be awakened by the sound of a flagpole. You might not think flagpoles make noise of any sort, but you'd be wrong. There's a piece of hardware on the line that runs up and down the pole, two pieces, actually, the clips that hold the flag, and when there's a breeze, even a light one, those clips are set in motion with the waves up and down their line. They tap against the metal pole—*ting, ting, ting*—and that's the noise I heard every morning with Bill lying beside me in the dark of his parents' bedroom. It was a subtle noise, so that I didn't wake enough to analyze it, but I was always dimly aware that it had been going on. Then I'd fall back asleep.

It wasn't until our last morning there, when I awoke not to

the flagpole ping but to Bill's mild voice, that I realized what I was hearing.

Bill had rolled over and curled into me, a hand lying on my breast and his mouth close to my ear. He was talking about how he had faced a moment up there on the ridgetop with Hayes when he almost, the very words at the base of his tongue, revealed himself to his son. The impulse had been nearly impossible to fight, rising so fast in him that he was surprised by it, and surprised that his resolve not to say anything was falling down like a ramshackle house in a strong wind. He'd had no rational desire to tell Hayes any of it, only the irrational, and that had been easy to fight off because it would cause so much trouble. But then here comes this moment, and he finds himself stepping out from behind his camera and approaching Hayes with gradually quickening steps, as if arriving there a second too late would kill the impulse, and he lays a hand on his boy's back.

"He looks up at me," Bill whispers, "and the words are coming up in my mouth, they are right here, and maybe I even said something like *I wanted to tell you this before the chance passes me by,* but he gives me this look of perfect clearness and innocence with those eyes of his, and I stuff the words back down in me and swallow them, and maybe I'll shit them out the other end one of these days and be done with it all."

Ping, ping, ting. The pole had kicked up while he was whispering to me.

I faced him and held him close, kissed his cheeks and temples. He was crying into my body. I asked him, "What did you say then?" and he gathered himself and I could see in the gray halflight that he was rubbing at his eyes with a thumb. He said he told Hayes what a saint he was, taking care of his mother like that. And he said, as a consolation prize, "Your pop would be proud of you for it."

We lay there for a while, listening to the flagpole, though I don't know that Bill was tuned to it, trying to control his fluttery breaths. I held his hand and listened. *Ting, ting. Ping.* The flagpole was playing me its one-note bye-bye song. I hadn't even seen a flagpole on the Argus property. Bad Ray, from what I'd heard of him, wasn't a flag-flying sort. Wouldn't have mounted a flagpole where grass might grow to feed a cow.

"I know it was hard, Bill," I said. "I know how hard it was."

And for some reason, as Bill sighed through his nose at that moment, the note outside changed just enough for me to recognize that it wasn't flagpole hardware tapping in the wind, it was a birdsong. There was a bird out there someplace, playing the same odd, piercing chirp over and over like an SOS.

—|—

IT TOOK US a couple of weeks to get the house cleaned up, all the mud out. Or I should say it took *me* that long, because Bill was busy working on his book all that time out in the darkroom behind the house. He was making his prints. He had hundreds of Pianto shots to go through, shots of falling-down barns and sawtooth fences, houses with greening copper roofs, two pairs of men's feet at a small gravestone, a row of eucalyptus trees hacked off at the hips—they'd gotten too old to stand up in a hard wind off the ocean. A sad thing to behold, that one. All that was left of them were their big, wide stumps and the implied shadows of their olden heights.

There was also a moving series of Hayes-at-work pictures. Though moving, I suppose, only if you knew the story of the sheep rancher and the photographer, as I did.

The phone rang one day and I answered, and it made me feel good to hear Cam's voice on the other end, asking if we had made it back all right. (I'd painted our phone number on the barn wall in the same red paint Cam and I used on Bill's belly a few weeks before.) I could hear through the line that he must be at The Dogleg, raised ranch-hand voices and billiard balls clacking together in the background, a truck gearing down for that sharp turn in the road just outside. I could picture him there behind the bar, his pair of Bill Argus prints mounted on the wall. He probably didn't think I'd noticed them.

I said, "Thanks for having us, Cam. We were a royal pain, I know."

"God, no. Didn't even know you were here half the time. How's Bill doing?"

"Quiet," I said. "But he's all right. He's out in the darkroom right now, let me go get him for you."

"No, don't bother him. Just tell him I called."

I told him to give my love to my new family—Carmen, Hayes, Annie, people I honestly hoped to see again—and we signed off with things just like that, kind of hanging but holding up. I bet Cam didn't say all he might have said to Bill, everything that had piled up in his head over the years. There's a point where you'd just as soon let go of it all rather than speak it in words and hear it out there in the air. Like I've always felt vis-à-vis my mother, what if I said my things to her and she said something like "*That's* what's been eating your craw all this time? *Jesus,* baby, there's worse stuff out there than that." And I'd have to either turn tail and vanish or knock her out cold with a wine bottle.

So somehow Bill had managed to make a kind of peace with his brother, but there wasn't a thing he could do with Annie. I did catch him looking at her with bottomless eyes and a mouthful of sadness more than once, the most he could offer, considering.

Who knows what he might have tried if she remembered him.

—|—

BILL CAME IN from the darkroom with a heap of curling, just-dry prints. He laid them out on the dining room table and put on one of his Bach records as he sorted them. I got him a glass of scotch and put my arm around him, but he was concentrating on the compositions and gray tones and not on me at the moment. I liked the work he did up there in Pianto—it was different for him. There were a great many decrepit buildings in his vision, and a lot of overgrown trails and downed fences, as if the landscape of his memory had gone untended for forty years, but I had never seen so many human faces in Bill's work before. He had captured his family, and not just in the Hayes series but in shots of Cam and Carmen, Annie with her puzzled eyes and half smile, her newly dyed hair. There was a picture of Cam leaning in the doorway of The Dogleg, looking up the road vacantly as if expecting someone, and a shot of Aunt Carmen peering into the lens like the lens *was* Bill, her expression just a tight, hard knot of judgment. I was in there too, against my knowledge. He'd caught me at moments of internal friction, let's call it, where I was probably thinking about Cary Lee or Daddy or Elsie, or Jack with his fine linen slacks and his steamy shower door and his unfortunate self-indulgence. It's all there on my face, I'm afraid.

I *am* looking at forty, you know.

I pulled up the one print I had wanted to see right away, and I was glad Bill had not rejected it. He was thinking about it, I could tell, almost from the moment the picture was taken.

We had come down from the ridgetop the day Bill almost spilled beans to Hayes, and I suggested, in front of Cam and Carmen, that we get everyone down to Cam's house for one last photograph, an Argus family portrait, as the family had come to the present day. It was my idea, since nobody else would have raised it, considering all the unsaid things, and anyway I was the new in-law and my ignorance could be excused. I said nobody had to be the wiser. Just a record of a few of us getting together in the summertime one year, the year Cam's brother came to town, or Carmen's niece, depending. Seemed like a good reason to take a picture.

That night Cam called Hayes and invited him and Annie down for lunch and the picture sitting, and the next day they arrived in Hayes's faded blue pickup. Hayes was a little confused about why I, Aunt Carmen's long-lost niece, would be interested in getting a picture of the Argus family all together and these couple of Diamonds on the side, so I bullshitted my head off and told him I had enjoyed myself so much and I was something of a chronicler anyway, a scrapbook-maker who doesn't like to forget what people look like. To this he shrugged, but Annie, listening to my excuses, fixed her eyes on me and seemed to understand. Her red bangs were growing down over her eyebrows.

Cam suggested that we have lunch first, but I knew it was really because he wanted a beer to settle himself down. He was edgy. Feared, I guess, the same thing I feared up on the ridgetop, a last-minute confession, some fireworks he didn't have the stomach for at this point. We were due to leave the next day. He took me by the arm and led me aside as the others went in. "Nora," he said, "is this really what he's saying it is?"

"Yep. I can vouch."

Bill had already proved himself to me, after all.

"Because I can't imagine what it'll be like if he fucks us over one more time."

"I know the feeling, Cam."

"Not sure he doesn't still have it in him." He rubbed the back of his hand, where Bill had once branded him, and then his palm went up and clutched the top of his bald head in worry. I made him a promise that probably I had no business making, stepped up and kissed him on the cheek to notarize it.

We ate a hasty meal at the old dining room table, seldom used. I thought so because the old walnut chairs had a creakiness about them, the table was too well polished, and the floor was not especially scuffed where it should have been. Carmen leered, Hayes talked of the cold ridgetop weather. I kept a hand on my husband's leg the whole while.

Bill excused himself a bit prematurely to go and set up his tripod out front. The rest of us cleaned up, and by the time we went outside, Bill was standing behind his camera with his hands on his hips. He scratched his salty whiskers, scrubbed the top of his head. As he bent to look through the viewfinder, framing the shot before any of us were in place, I had to wonder whether he was seeing other people on those steps, Bad Ray, Miranda, Harpers, Arguses, and maybe even Don and Mabel Hayes. As he said when we first arrived, it felt like there were ghosts all about the place, trailing a little light behind their tails that might show up on fast film. Who knows?

"Bill," I told him, "you go and sit. I'll set up the timer."

We put Carmen and Annie and Bill on the top step, sitting, with Annie in the center. She kept looking down into her lap, and Carmen would nudge her chin up with a little tickle. Red-headed Annie in her denim jumper and her sweater on a warm day like that one. She had no idea what it was all about. Meanwhile Bill stared out beyond me and into the deep fields behind, down to the foot of the hill and the oak and pine forest, the mouth of that trail that led up to the ridgetop.

Cam and Hayes sat on the step below, and I told them to leave room for me. As soon as I set the timer I was going to fly in there and land to Hayes's left, just in front of Bill. I looked through the viewfinder and saw them all stiffly in place, posed like a group of strangers recruited from some bus stop. My, my, my, how obvious the discomfort is through the veil of a camera lens.

Bill had set the f-stop and shutter speed, focused, and screwed the tripod angle down so I couldn't knock it off line. And it was odd, but I didn't set the timer right away. I wanted to keep watching them through the lens, their movements with one another, these different people who were all somehow related but either didn't know it or didn't wish to acknowledge it. Shame, guilt, remorse, innocence, confusion, and spleen, present in their faces and eyes, in the way they folded their hands and accommodated their high-riding knees with looped arms or steadying elbows. The lens mirror made them look slightly filtered, as if I were seeing them either a moment before or a moment after true present.

"Here we go," I called, the timer dial starting to buzz, and I dashed across the baring brown lawn to get to my place in time, beside Hayes, the son of Bill Argus, and beside Cameron, his uncle, and beneath my Bill and his former wife, whose feet were shifting to some half rhythm in her head, the old soft shoe, and Aunt Carmen repeating through gritted choppers *cheese, cheese, cheese,* while the thing counted down.

There was hardly an audible click when the shutter opened and closed, and we sat there for the longest time, holding our smiles and pleasant eyes as if the picture-taking had swiped enough light to paralyze us.

It was all right though. Painless and beautiful, I thought. That long moment.

—|—

I MIGHT AS well admit that the last time I saw Cary Lee was maybe a year after I married Dennis, and Dennis and I were still together and happy—as I defined it in those days—lost in our coupled routine. Cary Lee came over for dinner, bearing a jug bottle of her French Columbard, which had a loop on the neck for easy hoisting. She was in good spirits, as far as I could tell, flirty with Dennis, playful. Raved about our house, a cottage on Balboa Island that Dennis had inherited from a grandmother. Giddy over the ferry ride. She had entered what I would call a Phyllis Diller phase of lurid floral print dresses and big jewelry, and her hair was pinned up in a way that only accentuated the bloat of her face and the lines and blotches and itty-bitty popped blood vessels. I swear I could almost hear Grandma Elsie saying in my ear, "Cut her some slack, Nora. She's had a hard time of it. Do it for me."

Dennis, God love him, was charming with her, did his best to keep her content and to listen to her stories without yawning. Her stories could go on and on. He barbecued shrimp for her, presented a beautiful salad, poured her wine until it was all gone and she was shiny in her cups.

"So I assume Nora's given you the rundown, has she," Cary Lee said. "The whole Lark family history. Course I'm not a Lark, I'm a Drewes. Nora's a Lark, a hundred percent. Her father's daughter."

"Oh, here we go," I groaned. I let my head loll over the back of my lawn chair. "Den, don't let her lead you down that alley."

Dennis, well shaved and spiffy in his polo shirt, told Mother that all I did was talk, and he was pretty sure that the whole family history had made its way out.

"That is just dandy," Mother said. Her voice had that eerie singsong tone that I'd always hated. It sometimes warned of a big bad joke to come. Creepily, the sunset was behind her so that, to my eye, her face was dark and unreadable. "I guess she's told you all about her stepdad Jack, then."

"She's mentioned Jack, yes." Dennis sounded unsurprised, glanced at me and smiled. "She loved him, from all I hear."

"Mother, how 'bout a plum to stuff in your mouth. And he wasn't my stepdad anyway. You never bothered to marry him."

"Hardy har har," she said, leaning toward Dennis's lighter with her cigarette pinched between her lips and her eyes squinting at me through the first of the smoke. And then she went into a lot more detail about me and Jack than anybody else had a right to know, including my husband. Especially him. Nobody should know that unless I tell them, and I never would have told. She spewed it all out before I could stop her.

It has occurred to me only recently that the truth is always the worst betrayal. It's bare, it's harsh, it's got your name all over it.

I left. I didn't go back for days, stayed in a motel. I made up my mind that everything that was wrong with me led back to Cary Lee and that I would not see her anymore because I wanted to be better than I was. Night after night in that motel room, I said different prayers and played different movies in my mind, of a life I might have led if she had given me up when Daddy left. She had begged her mama to let her.

I'd have been so much happier if somebody had only taken me away and lied to me. I'd have swallowed it hook, line, and stinker, as Cary herself might have said.

After that, and after Dennis left me because I had already fallen into my paid extracurricular activities (as if to prove, sickly, Cary Lee's point about me), she would call from time to time and say, "So what's up?" Like nothing had happened at all. When I was feeling generous, I'd hang up on her. Otherwise I'd just walk away from the phone and let her sit while I watched TV or kissed some man I had over. Passive aggression, delivered as only a spiteful daughter can dish it out.

A long time has passed, I see. She must be old as the rocks in her patio by now, if I'm counting right.

—|—

AMONG BILL'S PHOTOGRAPHS on the table are those taken during our last couple of days in Pianto. He had wandered around the property to cement details. Graying porch posts that hadn't been painted in decades. The scalloped dip in the steps. Barn bats up in the rafters, hanging behind a wall of dust in the air. Bill had an eye for things like these. I wouldn't have noticed that the eaves were knitted with spiderwebs wherever there were right angles, and the webs were light and silky when backlit, and cluttered with the debris of hollowed-out bug bodies. I maybe wouldn't have noticed that as Cameron leaned under the hood of his truck, he pushed his glasses back atop his head so he could peer in and see his plug wires better, but Bill had shot it so that the light bounced off the lenses just right. And out by the oak tree, where once he'd knocked his brother from a high limb, he shot an old water-well pump with a sprig of wild quince growing into its mouth and a bright vine curling up along the handle.

I have taken the time, after the fact of it, to look at the family portrait from that last day, and I've wondered—thinking of old Captain Diamond in Hayes's ridgetop cottage—what kind of generous lies might be told about it when it's displayed on mantels up there in Pianto, Carmen's, Cam's, Hayes's. There we all are, our faces earnest with geniality, as if we've just come home from a picnic. What on earth can be said about who we are to one another? Six of us connected by such tangled logic and oddball coincidence, holding our smiles too long so that we look like we might bust out laughing if the camera doesn't pop soon.

All of us but Annie, I should say. Annie, at this last moment, turns toward Bill like his presence has suddenly dawned on her and there is something about him she needs to drink in and realize, his silhouette conforming to a few more leaves of memory she has managed to pull up right then. Her eyes are on him hard, painting him, her hands are up on the flattened plate of her chest, with a finger stuck into the hollow of her collarbone, and she is studying him in a way that makes me think, impossibly, she has him pegged.